Without taking time for explanations, she pulled Jacob's face to hers and kissed him soundly on the mouth.

She ran her hands around his neck and buried her fingers in the thick hair at his nape to keep him in place.

After the briefest pause, he circled his arms around her waist and pulled her tight against him, returning her kiss.

Vic cracked her eyes just enough to watch the men enter the alley.

They strode by without a sideways glance.

A relieved sigh relaxed her and she closed her eyes. But as minutes passed, she realized that neither she nor the King's Own had broken their kiss. A tingling started in the pit of her stomach, radiating to the rest of her body in warm waves. When Jacob's hands tightened on her waist, she jerked free.

"What do you think you were doing kissing me?" she demanded, trying to disengage herself from his strong arms.

"You kissed me," Jacob reminded her, letting his arms drop back to his sides. He leaned down close and whispered in her ear, "And when you're hiding from someone in a kiss, the scene is more believable when the person you're kissing is kissing back."

Titles By Author

Fate's Hand Series
Thief's Desire
Destiny's Seduction

Bonfire Night

Fire and Tears Series
Brightarrow Burning
Darkness Singed
Dawn Ignited

Kellyn's Sacrifice
The Last Guardian

THIEF'S DESIRE

FATE'S HAND SERIES

ISABO KELLY

T&D PUBLISHING

THIEF'S DESIRE

Published 2017 by T&D Publishing

Cover Art: © Cover Art by Cora Graphics
© stock / Depositphotos.com

Interior book design © 2017 T&D Publishing

ISBN-13: 978-1-944600-04-4 (Trade Paperback edition)

This is a work of fiction. All of the characters, places, organizations, and
events portrayed are either products of the author's imagination or are used
fictitiously. Any resemblance to actual persons, living or dead, business
establishments, events, or locales is entirely coincidental.

First printing T&D Publishing edition: November 2017

For information, contact T&D Publishing www.TandDPublishing.com

AUTHOR'S NOTE

Thief's Desire is one of my earliest novels, and one I'm still very proud of. It's exciting to return the book to print and to see these beloved characters out in the world again. This edition is basically the same as the last published version, with a few typos corrected. And while I wouldn't write this same book now, I'm really pleased with how it's stood up over the years. I hope you'll enjoy Vic and Jacob's story. Thanks for picking up the book!

THIEF'S DESIRE

FATE'S HAND SERIES

ISABO KELLY

PROLOGUE

❦

"Master Caul?"

The hesitant voice of his assistant brought the old sorcerer out of his reverie. "Come in, Henry," he called quietly over his shoulder. "Close the door."

For several minutes, Caul stared at the text before him, not seeing the words on the pages. A single candle on the table next to his book sputtered and danced in the air movement from the closing door. He didn't turn to face his assistant.

"You sent for me, Master," Henry said, matching the quiet tone of the older sorcerer.

Henry was always very good at reading his mood. "Yes. You've seen the signs?" The calm resignation in his voice couldn't hide the current of worry. Or the fear. Caul hadn't thought he would be alive when this time finally came about. An old man's hopes for a quiet retirement. Some of the younger mages in the school believed the signs heralded the triumph of good over evil. Caul knew the balance was precarious at best, the battle between the two forces still to come.

"Yes, Master," Henry murmured. "I've...I've witnessed what appear to be the prophesied signs."

Caul's head bobbed gently, understanding the hesitation in the young man's voice. His former apprentice, now his assistant, wasn't a dumb or overenthusiastic youth. He had common sense and used his brain above his emotions—most of the time. "They are as they seem, Henry. The time draws near. In the north, a dark power grows. Even now, forces are converging on our city from many directions. The collision will shake the ground."

"Master Caul, are you sure? Can we be positive that the time is so close at hand? Isn't it possible the omens have been misinterpreted?"

His slow exhale was almost a chuckle. "Dear Henry. Always bound by the physical. You deny your other senses far too often for this connection to the substantial. Strange in a sorcerer of your skill." Though, Caul could forgive the young man for his disbelief in this case. He didn't want to believe the signs either, didn't want to know what he knew, or see what he saw approaching.

The old magician finally looked up from his text, but he didn't turn to face his assistant. His gaze focused on the stone wall in front of him, his thoughts traveling beyond, to the inevitable future rushing toward them. "No, Henry, the time is here. The power in the north has also seen the signs and is preparing to act now. There can be no more delay. She's been born."

CHAPTER ONE

Vic looked closely at the faces of the other gamblers.

Big Charlie scowled at the cards in his hand, as his jaw muscles clenched and unclenched the scar running from his cheek to his chin danced.

Joe Missek watched the other players from beneath thick dark eyebrows, leaving his cards facedown on the table before him. He passed a steady hand over the top of his bald head and held his face motionless.

Riyack the Lean scratched his dirty neck with one hand and held the fan of his cards in the other. A scar on the left side of his upper lip gave him a permanent snarl.

Nathan Cap smiled pleasantly, wiping his brow with a thin white cloth. His ruddy complexion glowed in the dim common room lights, a sharp and gaudy contrast to his yellow hair.

Vic's eyes narrowed. Could it be done again? The gambler grinned. "Devil's High, lads."

An angry grumble erupted from the other gamblers as they tossed their cards across the table.

Vic scooped up the pile of coins from the center of the table and deposited them in a leather drawstring purse, smiling at the large number of gold coins in the pot. A person could buy a lot with that much gold. And a draw that big would make Gip happy. But that hand had been about more than the gold on the table for Vic. A hint of triumph flashed through the gambler's gut. *I did it!*

As the grumbling at the table continued, Vic decided retreat was the best option at this point in the night. Someone might catch on otherwise. "Well, lads it's been a game, but I'm afraid I'll have to call it a night." Vic stood to leave.

Big Charlie shot out of his seat. "You cheated, you little beggar," the large man bellowed.

Vic's stomach clenched with apprehension. *Damn it! Pushed it too far.*

A quick look to the exit, almost exactly opposite the gambling table, confirmed it was too far to run just yet. Big Charlie had earned his name by being almost as round as he was tall, but his size belied his speed. The man could move like a crocodile. There was no way to reach the door with him looming so close. *Not smart, Vic Flash. Not smart at all.*

Around them, the other patrons of the Red Dawn Tavern quieted. Those sitting close to the impending fight sidled to the opposite side of the commons. Some patrons ducked out the door.

Vic took a deep breath, eyes trained on Charlie. *Scold yourself later. Right now, it's time to leave.* "Listen, Big Charlie," Vic began in a conciliatory tone, palms up and facing outward to halt the large man's steps. "I just had a lucky streak is all. Cards fall as they will." *Just need to stall him. A few steps backward...*

"No one gets three Devil's High in one night," Charlie boomed, grabbing Vic by the collar, effectively preventing any more of those few steps backward.

Vic swallowed, the movement made difficult under Charlie's grip. Okay, so maybe the third Devil's High had been a mistake. *Worry about it later, Flash!* Because calming the situation wasn't working.

Vic stared at the raging man and tried to speak around his vise grip. Charlie shook Vic, suddenly and hard, addling brains and concentration with the jolt. Whatever the young gambler had intended to say was shaken loose and lost. Dancing black spots had to be blinked away. It took several seconds for instinct to kick in.

Too long, Vic thought as the grip tightened, stealing much needed air. Way too long.

Time for the straightforward approach. Threaten back. In a move too quick for the eye to follow, Vic pulled a dagger from a concealed spot and pressed it against Charlie's neck.

Charlie looked at the dagger against his neck, and his grip eased.

"I had a lucky night, Big Charlie. Let it be." The gambler's voice was quiet, but each carefully enunciated word sounded loudly in the now silent commons.

Slowly, Charlie released the crumpled collar of Vic's tunic.

For just an instant, Vic felt relief leak past the anxiety.

Then without warning, Charlie captured Vic's knife wrist in another vise grip, his big hand encompassing half of Vic's forearm. "You threaten me with this poker, boy," Charlie hissed.

His breath stank of stale ale and bar smoke. Vic held back a gag and turned full focus on the hand caught in Charlie's grip. So much for threatening.

"Enough, Big Charlie," Riyack whispered harshly. "You'll break his wrist."

With a sadistic snarl, Charlie said, "Good," and twisted Vic's wrist just a little more.

Exactly what Vic had been hoping for. A second concealed dagger appeared in Vic's left hand, slashing a shallow line along Charlie's huge, hairy forearm.

The big man howled and let go.

It was all the young gambler needed. Dashing past tables and startled patrons, Vic fled into the darkened city streets, heart pounding loudly with a rush of adrenaline. A furious roar erupted from the door of the Red Dawn, but Vic was already lost in the shadows of a nearby alley when Big Charlie charged into the street.

The heavy purse of gambling winnings hung at the thick black belt cinched around Vic's dark brown homespun tunic. It remained safely hidden beneath a black cloak, the hood of which was now pulled up over the young gambler's head. The weight of the money purse felt reassuring. Vic touched it, just to make sure it was secure. *Not a bad night's work, if I do say so myself.*

Lip sucked in between teeth, Vic had to acknowledge that the night's work could have gone better. That last hand had been a bad move. Charlie was right. No one got three Devil's Highs in one night. The winnings were worth it, though. Gip's cut would leave him happy and singing Vic Flash's praise. And Vic had enough money now to last a few months.

Best of all, Vic Flash had done the impossible. No one could cheat at a table with Joe Missek. The man saw everything. But Vic had done it. Fooled Joe Missek's eye. Three times! Few could claim that triumph. Next time, with a little more subtlety, a little more caution, not even Charlie would be able to shout cheat.

Smiling slightly, making sure not to show teeth, Vic watched from the dark alley as Big Charlie charged down the street a few yards. He was fast, but he didn't have the stamina to catch Vic Flash in a flat-out run—especially when there was no sign which direction the gambler might have gone. As far as Charlie knew, Vic was currently pounding the cobbles toward safety. He bellowed once more, then returned to the Red Dawn, cursing loudly as he disappeared back into the pub.

A quick glance around the quiet, empty street and Vic let out a slow breath. Ah, survival. It was late, nearly three hours after midnight. Late enough to leave even this night-driven part of the city relatively still. Not a single witness to give Vic away.

Standing in the alley shadows for another few minutes confirmed that Big Charlie had given up any chase for the night. Vic inhaled deeply, feeling the excitement of the moment turning to satisfaction for the first time since Charlie shouted, "cheat". The gambler turned to head back down the alley only to be stopped by a tall, dark figure leaning one shoulder against the alley wall.

Vic's knife flew to hand. Damn it, how had he gotten there? Adrenaline surged back. Second mistake of the night. Vic was gonna get into serious trouble at this rate. Being in the middle of trouble wasn't new to the gambler. But missing a stranger just standing there… That was bad. What if he'd been one of Big Charlie's men? Vic swallowed. *I'm lucky the only knife on display is in my hand and not sticking out of my neck.*

The stranger hadn't said a word while Big Charlie bellowed up and down the street, though, so there was a good chance he wasn't one of Charlie's. And if he wasn't helping Big Charlie, then they could deal. Vic wasn't about to lose all that hard-won coin to another thief—even if this man was good enough to hide his presence in the alley without alerting Vic's street-honed senses. But they could compromise, Vic hoped. Without letting the man out of sight, the gambler scanned the alley, listening intently for movement from behind.

"Did you cheat?"

His voice was rich and deep. Not familiar. Vic looked him over as he stepped away from the wall and the dim streetlamps exposed his face. Definitely not one of Charlie's men. Too wellkept for one thing. Dark hair hung to broad shoulders and surrounded a ruggedly handsome face. The man's dark eyes reflected the lamplight, and his full mouth turned up in a half grin. He stood a foot over Vic's five foot four. The dark tunic and trousers he wore were of a rich material, and a gold-hilted sword hung at his waist. The man didn't look like a thief. In fact, he looked out of place in this part of town.

Vic's heart thudded loudly. The knife stayed firmly in hand. "You weren't playing. What do you care?"

"Just a question, boy." The man looked down at Vic with an expression between amusement and indifference.

His gaze flashed to the knife, but he didn't seem bothered by the underlying threat. He did, however, keep his distance. So he wasn't stupid.

"Dangerous to cheat with those fellows. Kind of a rough lot for someone your age, isn't it?"

Vic couldn't help grinning, professional pride bursting through a suspicious mask. That "rough lot" had put a lot of money in that last pile. "I won. I'd say it was a lot rougher on them."

A chuckle rumbled from the man's chest. "What's your name?"

"Vic." There was something about the man, something in his expression. Or maybe it was the eyes. Out of place or not, he didn't seem likely to try stealing a person's gambling winnings. If Vic were being completely honest, there was enough gold in the hilt of his sword to more than cover the coin won that night. And he wasn't getting too close, wasn't making lewd comments or suggestive gestures. In fact, Vic got the feeling he was trying to look friendly, working not to intimidate.

Those impressions—and his distance—worked in his favor. Vic relaxed. At least enough to be curious. The knife disappeared, but

Vic's senses stayed trained on the alley gap to the rear as well as the man.

"Well Vic, if I were you, I'd stay out of the Red Dawn for a few weeks. Big Charlie's slow to forget."

Vic looked him up and down, once again taking in the high quality of his clothing and weapon. "You slumming it, rich man? How do you know Big Charlie?"

With another chuckle, he said, "I know everything about this city, boy."

Vic grinned again. Everything, huh? "Well, watch your neck. Thieves are about this time of night." Edging warily past the tall stranger and up the alley, Vic stopped just before the end of the building and looked back. "By the way, rich man, Vic is short for Victoria."

With an indolent grin, she shot around the building's edge and disappeared. The stunned expression on the rich man's face kept her chuckling all the way back to the Hole.

Jacob Marin stared down the alleyway for several minutes after the young gambler had disappeared. "Victoria," he said quietly, shaking his head.

Even inside the tavern, he hadn't guessed, though he couldn't claim he'd been paying that much attention. He'd come to this part of town for a quiet, relatively anonymous drink. The last thing he wanted was to be caught in a bar brawl. So when chairs started scraping across the worn wooden floor and accusations started to fly, Jacob only took a moment to notice those involved before he ducked out the door.

And was surprised when not five minutes later, the young gambler had come flying out of the Red Dawn to take refuge in the very alleyway Jacob was using to make sure the city guards weren't needed. He had to admit to being impressed with Vic. He hadn't expected him—her—

to escape Big Charlie so quickly. The man could move like a crocodile over short distances. But there she'd been, safely crouched out of sight, while Charlie pounded ineffectually up the street.

While the thug howled threats at the "boy," Jacob had time to study the gambler a bit closer. Her curly brown hair was cut roughly and hung just below her shoulders at its longest parts. Big dark eyes were surrounded by long lashes and set in a round, high cheek-boned face.

Remembering that face now, Jacob smiled ruefully. He, of all people, should have guessed. After all, Jacob knew women. It was unheard of that he could stand that close to a woman and not notice. But the features were just as easily those of an adolescent boy as a young woman, and the bulky, poorly cut tunic had hidden any signs of a female figure. Still, it was a bit humbling to realize he could be fooled so easily. She was good, that young woman. Very, very good.

Yawning, Jacob turned back to the street in front of the Red Dawn. With only three hours 'til sunrise, it was time for the King's Own general to head back to the royal castle. A pair of large brown eyes twinkled mischievously in the back of Jacob's memory as he walked through the quiet streets of Dareelia.

"You have a good night, Vic?" Ren rolled over on his mat to look up at her.

"Yeah, go back to sleep." Vic sat on her rough straw mat and pulled off her boots.

Instead of rolling away, Ren leaned on one elbow to look at Vic as she crawled under her wool blanket. "Gambling?" he whispered.

"Yeah." She matched his quiet tone so as not to wake any of the others sleeping in the small room and turned her head to look at him. Ren was one of the youngest scoundrels in Thieves' Hole, the largest ring of gamblers, beggars, thieves, spies and con artists in Dareelia.

Early on, she'd taken it upon herself to watch out for the boy. He was a good beggar and an even better spy, but he was still young. He sometimes reminded Vic of herself a very long time ago, when she was just getting started. It made her smile. She rolled her head so she stared up at the ceiling and whispered, "I'll have to stay out of the Red Dawn for the next few weeks."

"What'd you do?"

She chuckled at the room's dark ceiling. Easy to chuckle now that she was safe. "Three Devil's Highs."

"Vic, you didn't!"

He sounded so astonished, she chuckled again.

"I hope you won a lot."

"Yeah, Ren. I won a lot. My cut's better than three of the usual hauls." It really had been worth the risk, she decided, watching the patterns of shadows above her head. She'd never been able to refuse a challenge. Just to see, just to know if she could do something that others considered impossible. When she could, she gained a kind of security that was rare in her life, a reassuring rush that she could still take care of herself. That, no matter what, Vic Flash would survive. And survive well if she had any say in the matter.

Fooling Joe Missek was a challenge not even she took lightly, though. He wasn't someone a smart con messed with. But she'd done it. Three times! Okay, she'd gotten into trouble with Charlie in the process. That wasn't how she'd wanted the night to end. But she'd still managed to cheat Joe's eye. Not everyday a girl could claim that sort of triumph.

The coin she'd won, enough to last a few months, would go a long way toward easing the winter, too. Vic loved her work, and she worked hard to be good at what she did, but winters were hard on a thief without money stashed away. Now she'd enjoy the season. "I think I'll buy myself a new pair of boots," she murmured wistfully, stifling a yawn. "Maybe even a gold chain for my cape."

Ren's toothy smile could barely be seen by the light of a single street lamp just outside the window. "You know what, Vic?" he said rolling back onto his stomach. "Sometimes you sound an awful lot like a girl."

"Shut up and go to sleep, Ren."

CHAPTER TWO

T hree Devil's Highs?" Deraun stared at the grinning thief. "With Joe Missek in the game?" Deraun Gip was the current leader of Thieves' Hole. He kept the group together, made sure they always had a place to hide, and paid all the right people to keep business from getting sticky. And sometimes, he had to deal with the excesses of his people.

"It was a huge pot," Vic said, her eyes wide, her eyebrows quirked high.

Deraun leaned back in his chair and sighed. Vic never had been able to pull off innocent when she wasn't feeling particularly repentant. Even in the gloom of his office, he could see the tick of her mouth as she tried to control a grin.

"And Missek had at least a Queen's Run," she said, "maybe even a Low Devil. I couldn't have won with less than a Devil's High."

"How do you know that?"

Vic held up a hand and ticked off her evidence one finger at a time. "Missek wasn't looking at his cards, Charlie's scar was jumping, Riyack was tapping his foot and scratching his neck, and Nathan was grinning."

13

"Missek never looks at his cards," Deraun grumbled, reluctantly accepting Vic's assessment of the other player's tells. She'd never been wrong about a hand before.

"It was the way he wasn't looking at his cards, Gip."

Deraun shook his head, something close to awe joining his frustration. He settled his elbows on his desk and propped his chin on his folded hands. "Missek can see a cockroach twitch a mile away. How'd you manage to cheat that eye?"

"Talent, Gip." She smiled and winked. "Talent."

"Cheeky imp." His expression relaxed into a reluctant half smile. "Well, you definitely earned your name, Vic Flash. You're just lucky Big Charlie was alone."

"You don't actually think I'd have pulled a third Devil's High if Big Charlie or any of the others had their men in the room, do you? I'm not some kid new to the streets, Gip. And I'm definitely not suicidal."

"Yeah, but because of that little stunt last night, my best gambler has to keep out of one of the biggest games in town next week." Deraun leveled her with a hard stare, hoping to instill some sense of guilt into the woman.

Vic frowned and dropped her gaze to the floor. "Damn. I forgot about that. Big Charlie's gonna be there?"

"Damn straight. Every gambler in town's in on that match. And quite a few from outta town." Running a hand absently through his hair, Deraun leaned back in his seat again, studying Vic over the top of his desk. She stood with her hands looped through a thick black belt, face turned down and curtained by thick curls of dark hair. She almost managed to look contrite.

Deraun Gip had been working the streets of Dareelia in the kingdom of Karasnia for most of his life. He knew a good con artist when he met one, and Vic Flash was one of the best, but the woman never knew when to call enough. She was always pushing to be better. Always taking impossible challenges most cons would never try. And too often got herself into trouble along the way. What she needed was more caution. But how to convince her of that? He sighed. "All right. We'll send Brad Ruf into the game." Her head shot up, snarling at the name. "I know you don't like him, but he's the best we've got after you. And since you're out of it…"

Her shoulders dropped, and she nodded reluctantly. "You're the boss, Gip."

He was pleased to hear she remembered it.

"What's today's work?"

A pile of coins lay on the desk at his fingers, the Hole's cut of Vic's winnings. He had to admit, it was quite a sizable pile. He shuffled through the coins and pushed five coppers and one silver kern across the desk. "Take that. You'll work the Upper Market today. Get Trium to wash and trim that hair of yours. Buy a new outfit. Something bright."

"How am I gonna stay inconspicuous in bright colors?"

"In Upper Market, if a young lady isn't dressed bright, she stands out."

"You can't mean a dress?" Her face scrunched into a grimace.

Deraun scowled, looking her over with a critical eye. "No. You need to stay mobile. But something garishly bright, gaudy even. And," he said sternly, "something that shows you're a woman. If Big Charlie's got men looking for you, he'll have them looking for a boy. For the next few weeks, you're gonna be a girl, Vic."

Vic had taken to hiding her gender early in her career. A male could more easily play unmolested at the rougher gaming tables. As she could only pass for an adolescent boy, the dangers weren't lessened by much, but enough to make the masquerade worthwhile.

To compensate for the danger, she'd simply become quick, and very good with knives. Those who knew Vic Flash the gambler knew not to take his age as a sign of weakness.

She shrugged at her boss. "As long as the Hole's paying for the transformation, I'll play along. What do you want this brightly clad girl to do in Upper Market? Begging's out."

"Today, I need eyes. Keep a watch. Something strange has been happening around the city the last few days." At her questioning look, Deraun shook his head. "I don't know what…yet. That's why I need you to keep your eyes open. I've got people spread around town, but you're the only one I've got for Upper Market."

Vic nodded.

He knew she understood his meaning. She was the only woman with enough experience and, as a woman, enough anonymity to wander Upper Market without calling attention to herself. The city guard tended to be heavy in that area, and too many of the Hole's people had crossed at least one city guard. A chance sighting by a vindictive guard would bring a quick end to staking Upper Market and cause Gip to lose valuable information. And for the Hole, information was everything. Since Vic spent most of her time as a boy, the chances of being recognized as a woman were slim.

"I suppose I'll know what I'm looking for when I see it?" she said.

"You got it, kid. Watch your back. Hide your daggers. And no random pocket picking, Vic Flash. Not today." Deraun leveled another scowl at her. He found himself giving her that look a lot.

"Whatever you say. No picking today." She grinned and left the small office.

Deraun stared at the closed door and shook his head.

Trium washed and trimmed her hair to within an inch of its life.

The older woman spent a great deal of time trying to persuade Vic to take care of her appearance. Normally, Vic would grin and disappear, keeping the raggedy look that served her so well on the streets. Today, Trium hummed triumphantly as she succumbed to her ministrations.

The treatment wasn't so bad really, though. Vic kinda liked the feel of being pampered. And Trium had a way of massaging the scalp when she washed her hair that made all Vic's muscles go limp. Before she'd realized it, the woman had finished washing and trimming her errant curls into a semblance of shape.

She watched with mild fascination as Trium styled her hair, loosely pulling back the sides and securing them with small black combs. Vic almost didn't recognize her own face. It hadn't emerged from the scruffy curtain of her hair for a long time.

"There now." Trium smiled at Vic's mirrored reflection. "You look like the young lady you are."

"Thanks, Trium," Vic said through a lopsided smile. This walking around town looking like a girl thing might not be so bad. She tossed the older woman three copper kerns and hurried back into the Lower Market streets before Trium insisted on face paints. There was only so much girl stuff she could handle in one day.

Out in the street, crowds of people pushed past, hurrying to unknown destinations. The Lower Market opened into a huge square, ringed with shops of everything from tanned leather to plaster trinkets to fresh breads and pastries. The center boasted a huge, if unadorned, fountain and the cobbles surrounding the fountain were filled with temporary stalls and stands holding a huge range of merchandise. To one side of the market, a stable was set aside for small animal trading. But if she tried real hard, Vic could mostly block out the wafting smell of manure. The braying of an irate mule carried just above the chatter of hawkers and customers.

A bright blue sky hung over the city, but autumn's biting breeze cut through Vic's tunic. Pulling her black cloak tighter around her shoulders, she pushed through the market to a clothing shop where she knew she wouldn't be cheated. A rainbow of colors assaulted her as she walked through the door.

After a moment of staring at all that color she realized her teeth hurt. With a conscious effort, she relaxed her jaw and rolled her head on her neck to release the tension in her shoulders. She didn't like dressing so bright. It seemed unnatural. Vic spent most of her time moving at night. Blacks, deep blues and browns were the comfortable, necessary and preferred colors in her line of work. This much color would make her stand out like a bonfire on a moonless night.

As she was frowning at a bolt of brilliant cobalt material, a small, dark man shuffled through the stacks of cloth and bowed deeply. His near black skin and hair contrasted handsomely with the bright orange of his long tunic and yellow of his baggy trousers. "Welcome, Pfreal, welcome," he said in heavily accented Karasnian. "How might I serve?"

"Hi, Azri. I need something bright and womanly. Gip said garish, but…" She fingered the brocade pattern on a nearby vest. "Maybe you've got something I won't feel like a jester in?"

The small man smiled and moved to the rear of his shop.

"No dresses," she called after him. "Something that won't restrict movement. I'm in the Upper Market today."

"I have just the thing, Pfreal," Azri shouted back, using the word in his native language for Flash. The merchant reappeared with a bright red tunic of soft, thick silk, and a pair of long white breeches. "Bright but not gaudy for Pfreal's tastes, yes."

She smiled and nodded, taking the tunic and trousers from Azri. Not a single outrageous pattern adorned either garment. "These look great."

"With a sash of gold, you will be bright as the sun." Azri looked down at her scuffed brown boots. "And shiny black boots I think. Perhaps a new cloak." The clothes merchant drummed his fingers against his chin as he thought.

"You keep thinking, Azri. I'll go try this stuff on." She disappeared behind a privacy screen near the rear of the shop. The white breeches fit snugly, displaying the curve of her hips instead of hiding them. The red tunic's collar cut high around the back of her neck and hung open just enough at the front to make her gender obvious. The sleeves of the tunic billowed from the shoulder then collected at her wrists with a single ribbon.

Before tightening the ribbons, she refastened a scabbard to her right forearm and secured one of her daggers. A second sheath hung just below the back of her neck, leather straps around her shoulders securing the scabbard in place. A long dagger with a serpentine blade and two scalloped edges was hidden inside her left boot, and a dart-like dagger was hidden beneath the golden sash in a small sheath that hooked to the waist of her trousers.

Azri tossed a pair of knee-high, flip top, black leather boots around the edge of the screen. When Vic had finished dressing and securing her daggers, she grinned at her reflection in the mirror on the wall. Not too bad. She almost chuckled. No one would call her a world-class beauty, but at least she looked like a woman. She turned slightly, admiring the fit of the clothing. She almost felt rich. And not a single dagger showed.

"Good job, Azri," she said, coming out of the room. "Bright and womanly without being gaudy or comical."

"I am glad you like, Pfreal. And your daggers are completely camouflaged. Yes, very good." Azri ducked behind a pile of cloth and produced a white half cape with gold embroidery around the neck and a short gold chain fastening.

Vic sucked in a sharp breath and widened her eyes. All that detailing must be worth a fortune.

Azri chuckled. "The gold is paint, Pfreal. Don't worry. But it looks good and rich, yes? You'll look like rich Bthak Lord's daughter."

"I look more like a prosperous caravan mercenary, but thanks. This should let me slide around Upper Market without calling too much attention to myself." Vic handed Azri the silver coin. "Though," she said grinning impishly, "I'd better get there quick before someone tries to relieve me of my purse."

She left the shop with a wave to the merchant and trotted up the street toward Upper Market. Dareelia, the capital city of the kingdom of Karasnia, sprawled over a large, tiered hill. Most streets circled and looped back on themselves, winding through the lower, poorer sections of town all the way to the rich homes of dignitaries, ambassadors and Karasnian nobles. At the very summit, the royal castle commanded a view of the entire city, as well as the lands for leagues around. A defensive wall circled the city's base a quarter mile from the bottom of the hill, but Dareelia had long since outgrown the limits of the wall.

Lower Market was positioned between the top of the poor sector and the bottom of the mid-sector, accommodating most Dareelians. The closer to the castle one traveled, the more expensive and luxurious became the surrounding buildings and shops. Upper Market sat comfortably in the middle of the upper third of the hill. Only the most prosperous merchants and farmers from mid-sector mixed with the richer patrons of Upper Market. City guards patrolled the area, gently divesting it of beggars and layabouts sent down to Lower Market. Some guards weren't gentle, but then some beggars were more than just beggars.

Thieves' Hole kept away from Upper Market most of the time. Only the very best and quickest thieves were allowed to infiltrate the heavily guarded market, and then only occasionally. There were enough heavy purses outside of the market to keep the Hole careful.

Vic had traveled through Upper Market more than once. She knew her way around the square, but the beauty and cleanliness never ceased to amaze her. Like Lower Market, the huge square was dominated by a central fountain. But this fountain was elaborately carved of rich marble and spewed sweet-smelling water. Late-blooming flowers decorated the stalls lining the center of the market. The shops circling the perimeter were tastefully adorned and boasted an even wider range of goods than the shops of Lower Market.

Even the noise was different. Not quieter, not by far, but the hawkers were more dignified, the animals less brassy. Strolling minstrels roamed the square, entertaining the hoards of wealthy customers who sauntered through the market at a leisurely pace. The air was heavy with the delicious scents of fresh food, flowers and the heady smell of exotic perfumes. To Vic, even the gray cobbles looked cleaner—washed to near whiteness in the glare of the autumn sun. Though how they managed to keep the streets that clean was a mystery.

Here was an atmosphere of wealth she saw in very few other places in Dareelia. The royal castle was one of the few places, she thought, that might be more grand than Upper Market. Though, she wouldn't lay money on that bet.

With a definite saunter to her walk, Vic strolled past merchant stalls as if she owned the city and succeeded in blending in perfectly. Most of the customers would carry that air of rich self-assurance. Not a hard act to pull off in her new outfit. The clothing made her feel rich. She could pretend to be a wealthy mercenary, strolling for interesting trinkets to decorate her hideaway in the upper part of Dareelia. And

Gip had been right. As a woman in bright, rich clothing, she attracted no more attention than any other patron. When a group of gray–and–green–clad city guards passed without a suspicious glance, she grinned broadly. She could get used to working as a woman.

Happy with the state of her day, she wandered toward a food stall that was issuing heavenly smells. She had one copper kern left and felt sure Gip would want her to spend it on something nice and tasty to eat. Who knew? There might be gossip to be had at the food stall. A girl could never tell where important information might turn up. Scanning the market as a matter of habit, her gaze fell on a fat, green–and–orange–clad minor noble. Her trained eye caught sight of a telltale bulge in his robe—his heavy purse tucked in a hidden fold where it was supposed to be safe from thieving hands.

She'd heard about hidden pockets like that. Impossible to get at, some claimed. Vic smiled, her stomach no longer growling as loudly. Impossible, huh? She studied the noble as he bellowed at the merchants. She didn't often have the opportunity to practice working as a woman. Could she pull it off? She knew, theoretically, what sorts of moves her plan would require. But could she do it convincingly? Gip had said no picking pockets. But she really should practice while dressed as a female. Gip would understand.

She never could resist a challenge.

The fat noble was pointing at a series of pewter goblets and demanding attention from the stall's bowing owner.

Vic sauntered up to the stall, covertly pulling the neck of her tunic open just a bit more. Distraction.

She smiled prettily at the sputtering noble and batted her long lashes to good effect. Her stomach jumped a little in excitement when the distraction worked.

The fat noble stood straighter and leered.

She leaned past him, motioning that she wished to look at a pewter jewelry box on the table just the other side of him. As she hoped, the man didn't bother to move, but purposefully allowed her to brush against him. She picked up the pewter box and straightened, making a show of examining the delicate designs on the lid in order to hide her grin.

"A beautiful box, lady." The merchant smiled. "It was hand-crafted by the best artisan in Depnie."

"It's exquisite, merchant." She set the box back on the table, holding the merchant's gaze as she covertly slipped the copper from her own purse under it. It was only fair he receive some payment for the grief he was getting from the noble. "Perhaps I can persuade my husband to purchase it for me." With another sultry smile, she moved down the row of stalls, leaving a disappointed nobleman to bark at the pewter merchant. Before her shoulders shook with laughter, she ducked into a side alley and pulled the heavy purse from her sash. Her stomach danced with triumph. She'd done it. And the fat noble was none the wiser. She hefted the purse in her hand, judging the amount of coin by the bag's weight.

"I think Lord Xank will miss his purse shortly."

The sudden voice in an otherwise empty alley spun Vic around, her wrist dagger leaping to hand. Her heart stopped for an instant then beat painfully fast. Damn it, she knew better! She looked up into the grinning face of the stranger she'd met the night before, and her stomach took a hasty trip south.

In the light of day, he was a little older than she'd originally guessed, but the few gray flecks in his brown hair and the lines around his eyes and mouth only added to his rugged handsomeness. In fact, he was probably one of the most handsome men she'd ever seen. But it wasn't his exceptional good looks that interested her at the moment. It was the uniform he wore.

He chuckled at the knife in her hand. "You're very quick, Victoria."

She gasped and almost dropped her knife. "You recognize me?" she whispered the question without thinking, too shocked to realize she'd just given herself away without even trying to con her way out of this mess. She barely recognized herself dressed like this! How the hell had he recognized her? Her fingers felt numb around the hilt of her knife.

"Of course. New clothes only work on those who don't know what they're looking for." He chuckled again. "It's no wonder they call you Vic Flash. I've never seen a more elegant heist. You didn't mention your other occupations last night."

She swallowed hard against the lump of fear in her throat and licked suddenly dry lips. "You didn't mention that you were a King's Guard." She nodded at his formal green tunic edged in gold.

"King's Own actually."

She felt the color drain from her face and had only a moment to wonder if she looked as shocked as she felt. Her gut twisted painfully against terror. She'd gone too far this time. How in the name of the Goddess was she going to get out of this?

"You gonna arrest me," she more stated than asked. A sudden vision of a dark, damp dungeon with rats and binding chains flittered through her mind. People disappeared in dungeons. She swallowed hard and clenched her fists to hide the tremors.

The King's Own smiled—a crooked, amused grin. "Not my job. I protect the king. City guards are supposed to deal with thieves."

It took a full minute before the meaning of his words sank into her shocked mind. He wasn't going to arrest her. He was smiling. And he wasn't going to arrest her. Yet. The rush of relief almost overwhelmed her. Her shoulders began to relax slightly and the nearly forgotten dagger in her hand disappeared back up her sleeve.

"How'd you know they called me Flash?" She tried to fall back on cocky self-assurance, a mask she used a lot on the streets, but the shock of being caught by a King's Own still tightened her muscles. Her heart was just beginning to slow, her chest rose and fell a bit too much with her labored breathing. She knew she didn't look as recovered as she wanted, but she also knew she was recovering her composure faster than he expected. She could see it in his eyes. Eyes a very deep shade of brown that held a lot more cunning than his casual air let on.

"I told you last night. I know everything about this city."

Her guarded expression broke into a shaky grin. "Not everything, rich man." Her self-assurance began to return. He wasn't going to have her arrested, and he didn't seem the least bit interested in Xank's purse, which she'd already hidden away. Crossing her arms beneath her breasts so he wouldn't see her hands tremble, she looked him up and down. Curiosity won now that she wasn't worried about dungeons. "What's your name?"

"Jacob Marin."

Her gaze jumped to his, startled once more. "General Jacob Marin? Hmmm. Well, now I'm impressed." His quiet laugh started her stomach dancing in a funny way that had nothing to do with her previous fear. Her gaze narrowed. "How'd you see that?" She nodded toward the market and the pewter stall.

"I've got a good eye. I figured anyone who could pull three Devil's Highs with Joe Missek at the table must have a pretty quick hand."

She smiled, flushing slightly at the complimentary assessment of her skills.

"I liked the leaning over trick," he continued. "Xank's always been a sucker for a pretty young woman."

"Pretty, huh?" Vic arched an eyebrow. To compliment her skills was one thing, but no one had ever really complimented her looks before. Her stomach danced with pleasure. "What can I say, General? I'm very good at what I do." Out of habit, her gaze turned to scan the market. Her smile suddenly fell away as a figure in the crowd caught her attention. "Damn."

Three large men strolled purposefully through the crowd toward the alley. All were dressed in various styles of purple and black clothing. The center man's tunic included the silver detailing that marked his senior rank.

Vic cursed under her breath again, more colorfully this time. She scanned the alley and the buildings overhead, looking for an escape route. The three men would reach the alley before she could get to the opposite side. And there wasn't a single convenient balcony along either of the bracketing buildings. Then her gaze fell on the King's Own. Abruptly, she turned her back to the wall and pulled Jacob in front of her. A quick glance at the crowd confirmed that the three men were intent on entering this particular alley.

Without taking time for explanations, she pulled Jacob's face to hers and kissed him soundly on the mouth. She ran her hands around his neck and buried her fingers in the thick hair at his nape to keep him in place.

After the briefest pause, he circled his arms around her waist and pulled her tight against him, returning her kiss.

Vic cracked her eyes just enough to watch the men enter the alley.

They strode by without a sideways glance.

A relieved sigh relaxed her and she closed her eyes. But as minutes passed, she realized that neither she nor the King's Own had broken their kiss. A tingling started in the pit of her stomach, radiating to the rest of her body in warm waves. When Jacob's hands tightened on her waist, she jerked free.

Shock at the strange warmth flooding her system erupted into anger and she scowled up at the guard's roguish grin. "What do you think you were doing kissing me?" she demanded, trying to disengage herself from his strong arms.

"You kissed me," Jacob reminded her, letting his arms drop back to his sides. He leaned down close and whispered in her ear, "And when you're hiding from someone in a kiss, the scene is more believable when the person you're kissing is kissing back." He straightened, still grinning.

Vic frowned and looked at the ground. She couldn't believe it but her face felt hot. If she didn't know better, she'd swear she was blushing. "Well," she mumbled reluctantly after a silent moment, "thanks."

"Who were they?"

"Tracker's guards."

"The smuggler? What did you do to him?"

Her grin returned. "Some time ago, he thought little Vic Flash would be a fun pet. I convinced him otherwise."

Jacob arched one eyebrow.

"Just before I relieved him of his personal money pouch," she finished.

Jacob chuckled and shook his head. "You have a talent for trouble, Victoria Flash. Tracker knows you're not a boy?"

"Actually, he didn't at first. Boy, girl—it's all the same to Tracker. But that's not why I'm ducking his guard." She pursed her lips and flicked a gaze out to the bustling market.

"What?"

She blinked and looked back at the King's Own. "Tracker's men shouldn't be here."

"In Upper Market?"

"No, in Karasnia. They winter in Southern Depnie. They should have left here last month. They pass through Upper Depnie most of the time to avoid Breeke, and the trek through Barren Pass is a hard one if you're caught too late in the year."

The creases at the corners of Jacob's eyes deepened. "What are you saying, little thief?"

She shook her head, momentarily missing the epithet. "I don't know what it means." Then she scowled. "What do you mean 'little' thief?"

He chuckled and made a show of looking down at her.

She snorted and looked back to the market crowd. Little, ha!

"Dodging smuggler's guards, hiding from Big Charlie, avoiding the Red Dawn like the plague, lifting purses from minor nobles in broad daylight." Jacob shook his head and tsked her.

The touch of admiration in his voice made her insides feel very warm. Too warm for comfort. She met his gaze, smiled the flirty grin she'd used on the fat noble and batted her lashes playfully. "A girl's gotta find some way of occupying the day." With a wink, she pushed away from the alley and vanished into the Upper Market crowd.

The rest of the day passed uneventfully. No more unusual sightings. Nothing out of the ordinary for Upper Market. In fact, the afternoon was downright boring. And Vic had too much time to think. As she scanned the crowd while pretending to study a piece of embroidered silk, her mind turned yet again to the tall King's Own general.

Jacob Marin had quite a reputation among the women of Dareelia and from the rumors, his reputation extended to the rest of the kingdom, as well. Now she understood those whispered giggles whenever his name came up in conversation.

He was a hero of the realm, having uncovered the illegal study of blood magic by the late Prince Erick, then aiding in the defense of

King John when the Prince had boldly walked into the reception hall two years ago to assassinate the monarch. His strength and skill as a soldier sent tremors through enemies of the Karasnian Crown. But it was his sly smile and roguish manner that sent quivers through the country's women.

Vic had never considered herself fanciful when it came to men. Oh, she liked men for the most part, but they were generally more trouble than they were worth. And in her line of work, a girl had to be very careful about the kinds of men with whom she became involved. Between that and spending most of her adult life dressed as a boy, she'd just never bother getting tangled with a man. Not in a romantic sense anyway. She'd never considered that she might be missing anything. In fact, she'd always figured it showed a remarkable degree of common sense to avoid emotional entanglements.

Then she'd kissed a King's Own.

A flash of the remembered kiss sent her stomach fluttering and heat raced across her skin. With a barely suppressed groan, she moved back into the crowds. Kissing Jacob Marin had not been one of her better ideas. In fact, she'd definitely rank it as one of her worst. Not for the least because she'd be thinking about that kiss for the next month!

He probably hadn't even been trying. He'd admitted he'd been aware of her ruse, and he'd acted his part of the scene perfectly. Too perfectly as far as Vic was concerned. He could have at least had the decency not to kiss her so well! Not that she was a great judge of kisses, but the man had known what to do with his mouth. And the remembered feel of his large hands wrapped around her waist made her insides melt.

No, kissing the King's Own would definitely have to go on her list of things not to do again.

Unfortunately.

She stopped short. Then to cover her odd motion, she made a show of looking at the contents in a nearby stall. She didn't bother to notice what she was looking at. What did she mean by unfortunately? Exactly what she was afraid she meant. She wouldn't mind having the chance to kiss that particular King's Own again. Just one more time. Just to see if it had really been as nice a kiss as her memory was telling her it was. She could almost smell the leather and musk of him, feel the warmth of his breath as he moved in close…

Shaking her head roughly, she moved away from the stall. Jacob Marin was a King's Own and a general and had seduced—if rumors were to be believed—nearly half the women in the country. Vic was a con artist, a spy, a thief and a gambler. Add in her less-than-highborn appearance and Jacob Marin became a nice, dangerous dream but a decided impossibility. For once, she told herself, she wasn't going to take on the challenge of something that was supposed to be impossible.

As the evening air continued to chill and the stalls began to close for the night, Vic wandered back toward Lower Market, chuckling softly at her fanciful thinking. Ren would never let her live it down.

Chapter Three

Goblins in Karasnian Forest?" Jacob frowned at the guard before him.

"That's the word, General Marin," Captain Adams said. "They've been seen in small groups—no more than two or three at a time—coming down through the high reaches of Georna for the last few months. But they haven't been bothering travelers or the mountain folk. Then last week, a hunter spotted two sneaking through the middle of the Karasnian Forest, not more than a league from the crossroads."

Jacob's frown deepened. "Have you told the king?"

"General Thack is with him now, sir. He sent me to inform you of the situation and to ask if you'd come to the king's study as soon as possible."

"Thank you, Captain." Jacob strode down the castle's marble floored halls, deep in thought. Goblins hadn't come down from the Bthak Mountains north of Georna Barony and into lower Karasnia for almost three hundred years. The news wasn't welcome.

When he reached the king's study, Jacob nodded to the two King's Own standing outside the door. "Garath. Tekan."

They saluted, a sharp right hand over left shoulder movement, and one of the men opened the door.

"Jacob. Good, you're here," King John said, motioning the general of his personal guard into the room as the door was closed behind him.

King John was a tall, broad man, whose aging showed only in the gray infiltrating his sandy blond hair, and the deep-set wrinkles in his forehead. His features were sharp and weathered but handsome. He was well loved by his people, commanding great respect both as a man and a king. Under less foreboding circumstances, his brown eyes would have danced merrily. Now they were dark with the knowledge of a potential threat to his country.

Beside the king, a man only a few inches shorter than Jacob but several inches wider ran a hand down his red beard and stared at the map spread across the king's desk. He acknowledged Jacob with a distracted grunt.

"Captain Adams has filled you in?" the king asked, motioning Jacob over to the desk.

"Yes, Majesty. Goblins in Karasnia Forest."

General Thack twisted the end of his beard and pursed his lips. "We'll have to patrol the road, Majesty. An army garrison?"

"I'd recommend king's soldiers," Jacob added. "If word spreads, we'll have considerable panic on our hands. The King's Guard are more likely to be discreet."

"I agree," King John said. "General Thack, hand-pick the men to go. I want the travelers on that road protected all the way to the Bthak border. If anyone asks, there's been a run of bandits and we're just being cautious."

"Yes, Your Majesty." General Thack bowed his head and left the room.

"Well, Jacob," King John said, sitting heavily into his seat. "What do you suppose all this means? Goblins for the first time in three hundred years."

Jacob studied his king. Worry showed heavily in his eyes and the creases deepening his brow. Goblins could be as unpredictable as they were strong, and as cunning as they were deadly. Jacob could well understand his sovereign's fear. "I don't know, Majesty. Have you sent a dispatch to Baroness Georna?"

"He left just a few minutes ago. She sent word of goblin movement last month, but she gave no indication that it was this bad. I'd assumed it was just the usual movement—early winter storms pushing them down into upper Georna."

Jacob ran a hand through his hair. It was nothing new for goblins to be pushed by storms into Karasnia. But they usually kept to themselves in the high reaches of Georna Barony and moved back to Bthak with the spring. They were territorial creatures. It would take a great deal of motivation for them to move this far outside of their territory. "Sire, I think it best to assume something is driving them down from the north. Something besides early winter storms. Unless Baroness Georna says otherwise, I don't think we should try to force them back just yet. If they've been driven this far for the first time in three centuries, they're likely to fight rather than turn around and go back. And a goblin war..." He let the sentence drop.

They both knew the outcome of the last goblin war.

Deraun Gip stared at the wall over Vic's shoulder for long minutes. The news of Tracker's men in town was unusual enough to warrant added thought. "You saw only the three?" he asked, still staring past her shoulder.

"Yeah. Only the three. But one was that bastard, Malkiney."

"Tracker's right hand still in Karasnia. I'd heard word of their leaving two months ago. Tracker supposedly had a run up north and was going straight down to Depnie from there."

Vic shifted her feet. "Any other news, Gip?"

"Brad Ruf heard rumors of goblins in the forest. Kritta says there's a big hush over at the Magic Guild. And there's rumors that the Browan ambassador's been called back to Browan immediately. Nothing else out of the ordinary." Deraun took a deep breath and met Vic's gaze. "Something's happening, Vic. I can't nail it down, but…something's happening."

Vic bit the inside of her lower lip. Deraun didn't look nervous often, but at that moment a shadow behind his eyes looked scared. If Deraun was scared, bad things were about to happen in Dareelia. "I'll keep nosing around, Gip. As I can't play my game for the next few weeks, I might as well make use of this being a woman thing." Her grin brought a reluctant half smile to Deraun's thin lips.

"You just stay away from Big Charlie. He's still fuming over that last hand. Seems he lost almost as much to you last night as Xank lost today."

Vic's eyebrows arched, her attempt to look innocent fell flat. "Thanks for the warning, Gip."

Deraun nodded at the sentence's double meaning.

Vic fled his office. Night had fallen over the city. A cold breeze hinted at the approach of winter. It was coming fast this year, another sign that didn't sit well with Vic. She pulled her cloak over her shoulders, suppressing a shiver that had nothing to do with cold. After only a brief pause, she turned and followed the streetlamps to her favorite pub. The need to appear around town as a woman, while not being noticed by any of Big Charlie's men, limited her options. The last thing she needed was trouble with some drunk in a crowded commons to draw attention to herself. So she had to go somewhere safe, a place where she had friends to back her up.

She was still in her new tunic and breeches, as they were the only clothing she had that didn't make her look like a boy, but she'd replaced the white cloak with her long, hooded black cape. If she had to be bright, she could at least dim the colors under the cape's heavy folds. The glow of the bright white breeches in the lamplights made her cringe. Tomorrow, she promised, she'd find something dark. Just because she had to look like a girl didn't mean she had to make herself a walking target at night.

She turned down a small street, keeping as close to the shadows of the buildings as the streetlamps would allow. Going to one of her favorite haunts was a bit risky, but she'd practically been raised at the Screeching Hawk. Before her dad disappeared, they'd lived in a room above the tavern with the lady owner. Even after her dad's disappearance, Peggy had let her stay at the Hawk for a few more years. It was in the dark corners of the smoky pub where Victoria had learned how to be Vic Flash. She'd be as safe there as anywhere in Dareelia. She had friends, she had options, and, best of all, she had credit.

As she stepped through the door, the familiar smells of spilled ale, smoke and greasy pub food made her smile. *Home*. A glance around the room confirmed the absence of Charlie's men. So far, so good. With luck, he wouldn't have anyone stationed here until later that night. By that time, she'd be safely tucked in a bed with a full belly.

She was feeling quite relaxed and secure as she walked to the bar when a strong hand shot out from one of the tables to grab her arm and she nearly screeched. Ready for a fight, she spun, only to find Jacob Marin smiling up at her.

"What are you doing here?" she said harshly, the moment of surprise making her heart pound. She hadn't meant to snap at him, but the last place she'd expected to see him was in her sanctuary. In fact,

Vic hadn't expected to see the King's Own again at all, except maybe in a parade.

"Drinking," he answered easily. "Sit."

"Why?"

"Have a drink with me."

"You buying?"

"I know how much Xank carries in his purse."

Vic raised her hand in surrender. "All right, but for that little reminder, you're getting the slop ale, Marin." Vic motioned over a barmaid as she took a seat across from him, unfastened her cape and let it drop over the chair back. "One gold, and one bright, Mar."

"Right with ya, Vic," she answered brightly. "You got any money or is this on Peggy?"

Jacob chuckled.

With a scowl, Vic told the barmaid she had money.

Mar nodded, shot a suggestive glance at the King's Own and moved back toward the bar.

"I take it you frequent this place?" Jacob asked.

His smile made Vic's stomach clench. She sat back in her chair and propped her legs up on the table, defiantly casual. The last thing she wanted this rake to know was that he made her pulse quicken. "Yeah. The Hawk's like a second home. So I know you don't come here much. Slumming again?"

Jacob no longer wore the dark green and gold tunic of his office, but his cream shirt was of a heavy silk and his snug brown trousers were soft, supple leather. His dark brown boots bunched down around his well-muscled calves, drawing her attention to powerful legs she was trying not to notice.

"Something like that," he answered.

Damn the man anyway, she thought sourly. All he had to do was sit there and talk with that deep quiet voice and her body started to tingle in new and disturbing ways.

Mar returned with their ales.

"The gold's mine, Mar," Vic said through a cat's grin, locking eyes with Jacob. *Remind me of getting caught with Xank's purse will you, General?*

Mar raised a mildly amused brow, but placed the bright ale down in front of Jacob.

Jacob stared back into Vic's eyes until Mar had finished setting the drinks down, then with a sexy half smile looked up at the barmaid. "Thanks, Mar," he murmured.

Mar's mouth opened slightly as her gaze roved over him. "Anything else I can do for you?" Her implication was obvious. In the tradition of truly great barmaids, Mar was a full-figured, flirtatious young woman with an attractive if not beautiful face. She also had a healthy appetite for male flesh and was never at a loss for someone to help appease that hunger.

Jacob returned her stare easily, without so much as a twitch. "I'll let you know."

Vic crossed her arms over her stomach and watched in disgust as the barmaid edged from the table. When Jacob looked back, she was shaking her head. "I've heard about you, Jacob Marin, but I'd never have believed half the rumors if I hadn't just witnessed that little scene."

He chuckled. "It's a gift. Thanks for the drink." With two gulps, the King's Own swallowed half the jug.

"Uck," Vic said, before taking a healthy swig of her own ale. "How can you drink that slop like that?" She curled her lip at the idea.

"Easier to swallow if you can't taste it." He laughed. Sitting back in his chair, he said, "So what have you heard about me, Victoria?"

"I've heard that the flower merchants drool every time you walk toward their shops. As for the rest, I think I'll let ya guess."

Along with his notorious reputation for seduction, Jacob Marin was also known for sending each of his former lovers a single flower on their birthday. Word on the street was that the flower merchants had standing orders that filled each day of the year and then some. Vic had always suspected that bit was exaggerated. She wasn't so sure anymore.

"How old are you, Victoria?"

"How old are you?" she challenged.

"Older than you."

"Then I guess that would put me somewhere between birth and your age."

"That sounds about right."

His steady gaze was starting to make her fidgety. "So why are you really here, General? There's lots of pubs closer to the castle."

"You can call me Jacob. And I like the pubs farther away from the castle. Better atmosphere."

She narrowed her eyes. "You're hunting for information."

"Something like that." He swallowed the last of his ale and motioned Mar to the table again. "Make that two golds this time, please. This round's mine."

Vic smiled and downed the rest of her jug. When he raised an appreciative eyebrow, she said, "Can't let a free ale just sit in front of me, can I?"

Mar returned quickly with the two drinks. Smiling down at Jacob, she hovered over the table until Vic pointedly cleared her throat. When Mar reluctantly turned back to her other customers, Vic snapped, "Am I getting in the way of your night, General? I don't have to stay."

"I invited you to sit for a reason, Victoria. And no, you're not in the way of any plans."

"What reason?"

He leaned forward, resting his forearms on the table and studied her face closely. "Why were you hiding from Tracker's men today? You said the trouble between you and he was some time ago."

She shrugged. "The man in the center with the silver detailing on his tunic? His name's Malkiney. He's one of the few people in town who knows me on sight no matter how I'm dressed."

"That doesn't explain why you didn't want him to see you."

"I'm in hiding from Big Charlie, remember? Can't have a lot of people knowing I'm about like this." She glanced down at her attire. The gesture sent Jacob's gaze wandering over her outfit, too, and it was all she could do not to squirm. "And Malkiney and I don't get on so well," she said, trying to get his gaze back to her face and away from her legs. The look in his eyes made her uncomfortably aware of being a woman. And, damn it all, she liked the feeling. Dangerous. Very dangerous. "He'd sell the information to Charlie just to spite me."

His gaze was firmly on her face now. Studying. "You're not telling me the whole truth, are you, Victoria?"

"Why do you keep calling me Victoria? No one's used that name in years."

"You're changing the subject." He grinned and relaxed against his chair back again, ale in hand. "I like the name Victoria. It suits you."

She snorted into her mug. "You don't know me very well."

"I've got time."

Her eyes narrowed. "Listen, Marin, I don't know what you're after here, but—"

"Why you were ducking Tracker's men," he interrupted.

"I already told you as much as you need to know."

"I need to know what Tracker's men are doing here. I think you can tell me."

"You want information about Tracker? Tell me about the Browan ambassador's sudden call home."

"You'll have to ask the Browan ambassador."

"You'll have to talk to Tracker."

Jacob chuckled and shook his head. "Gamblers. All right, you little thief. You're going to insist on an information trade?"

"Well, you aren't gonna get it for free. And a gold ale is too cheap for payment."

"How do I know you know any more than I do?"

"You don't. I may not know any more than I've told you." She took a long swig of ale then met his gaze. "But I have ways of finding out."

"What's the going rate for borrowing one of the Hole's street spies?"

Vic dropped her feet off the table. "What do you mean?"

"You must not think highly of me if you think I couldn't figure out who you worked for."

Her adrenaline shot up, making her pulse race. "If you're trying to find the Hole through me, Marin, it won't work." There were few things in this world that held her allegiance, but she was unerringly loyal to those who had it. Thieves' Hole had given her a place to belong. She would defend its secrets with her life.

"I told you already, Victoria, I guard the king. It's the city guard's job to fight street crime. I've no interest in ferreting out the Thieves' Hole."

She licked suddenly dry lips and studied the man sitting across from her. He was dangerous in more than one way. She should cut her loses and leave. But Gip might want the connection. Working for a King's Own could be useful to the Hole. "I'll have to talk to my boss.

He may not be keen on helping a King's Own."

"Tell him I'll pay well. There's something happening in Karasnia. The king needs to be ready for it."

She exhaled slowly, nodding her head. "My boss thinks something's building too. Not knowing what it is makes him nervous. And whatever else, he's loyal to the king. I'll see what I can do."

"Thank you, Victoria."

Jacob smiled one of those heart-stopping smiles, and she found herself grinning back.

"When will you know if your boss will trade?"

"I'll let you know tomorrow night. That's not saying I'll have information, just whether we can deal or not."

"That's all I ask. Do you know the Winnow Tree Inn?"

She nodded.

"I keep a room there. Meet me tomorrow night an hour after midnight."

Vic narrowed her eyes. "You want me to meet you in a private inn room? You better not be getting any funny ideas, Marin." *Because*, she added silently, *I've enough for the both of us.*

"So suspicious, Victoria. Now, I'm curious about the rumors you've heard about me."

A quick retort died on her lips as Mar shuffled back to the table.

"Can I get you another, sir?"

She couldn't miss the way the barmaid ignored her to focus the full force of her adoring eyes on Jacob.

"Another round, Victoria?"

"If you're buying."

Jacob smiled and ordered two more gold ales. Vic had forgotten to order food before she started drinking, and as she gulped the rest of her second ale, the alcohol rushed to her head and started her lips tingling. When Mar returned with the drinks, she ordered a bowl of stew and a chunk of bread.

"You hungry?" she asked Jacob. "Peggy makes a pretty good beef stew. Her meat pies are a little greasy, but still tasty."

"I've eaten already. Thanks."

She leaned forward, resting her elbows on the table and settling her chin on laced fingers. "So, Jacob Marin…" The alcohol was also starting to relax her professional detachment. Curiosity once again got the best of her when it came to this particular King's Own. "How'd you know where to find me?"

"I asked around."

She raised a brow.

"You don't think I have spies around town?"

"Yeah, I guess you would, wouldn't you? Probably have half the women in Dareelia spying for you."

"Not quite. Is that one of the things you've heard rumored about me?"

"Hey, it's none of my business, Marin." She waved a hand expansively and missed knocking over her ale by inches. "By Mar's reaction, I can see you can't help it. You just sort of draw them, don't you? Until they're slobbering around your feet."

"You don't have any problem with that, Victoria."

"Yeah, well, I'm not an oversexed barmaid or a silly merchant's daughter."

"How long have you been on the streets?"

"Never been off the streets, so to speak." She cupped her hand around her mug.

"There's a story under that tough, cocky exterior, isn't there?"

"Everyone's got a story, Marin. Some are just better than others." She finished off her third ale in three large gulps, averting her gaze.

When Mar appeared with her stew, she ordered another round of drinks. The beef stew was chunked with mushrooms, potatoes and carrots, and its heat warmed her stomach even as it dampened the effects of the ale.

Jacob quietly watched her eat, leaning forward on the table, resting his chin in one hand.

"I got a question for you," Vic said, as she finished the last of her stew. "If you've got spies enough to find me, why do you need me for information on Tracker's men?"

He looked silently at her for several heartbeats. Just when she began to fidget, he answered, "You know what you're looking for already."

She nodded skeptically, but let his answer suffice. Working as a spy for a King's Own was bound to pay big, so she wasn't about to argue with his choice. Mar brought the fourth round and Vic gulped at hers greedily after the salty stew. Setting the clay mug back on the table with a thud, she opened her mouth to ask another question when movement at the door caught her eye.

In one lightning quick move, she skirted the table to sit in a chair at Jacob's elbow, all the while keeping her back to the door. "Sorry to do this to you twice in one day," she whispered, leaning close to Jacob's face and resting her hands on his broad shoulders.

"Another one of Tracker's men?" he asked quietly, toying with her hair while he covertly looked at the man standing in the doorway.

"No. This one's Big Charlie's. They don't know I'm a woman, but I'm not taking any chances. What's he doing?"

"Scanning the room."

Jacob leaned so close, she could feel his warm breath against her cheek, and the pleasant scent of musk mixing with strong ale played havoc with her senses.

"Is he coming in?" she spoke in his ear, whispering, but her heart sounded so loudly in her temples she felt sure he wouldn't be able to hear over its thudding. His hand, already twisted in her hair, tightened when she spoke. Vic closed her eyes and fought back a sudden surge of desire. This was no time to let Jacob Marin muddle her thinking.

"He's moving across the room," Jacob said, moving his mouth around to her other ear in order to keep the man in sight. "Looks like he's settling in for awhile."

"Damn." Vic looked over Jacob's shoulder to the bar and caught Mar's attention. With her eyes, she pointed in the general direction of the new patron, and Mar nodded imperceptibly.

"Mar's gonna distract him so we can leave. Play drunk and lean on me a lot but don't get loud." A quick flick of her wrist pulled her black cape off the chair she'd been sitting in. "Throw this over your shoulders when we leave."

Jacob moved away from her cheek and set his mouth close to hers. His gaze was still turned toward Big Charlie's man, so he didn't notice when Vic's lip began to tremble. She bit the inside of her lower lip irritably and held her breath.

"Okay," Jacob whispered against her mouth. "Mar's got his attention."

Vic sensed his crooked smile.

Flipping the cape across his shoulders, Jacob stood and pulled Vic roughly to her feet. He circled her shoulders with one arm and leaned heavily on her, tripping over her chair as they walked to the door.

She wrapped her arm around his waist and placed her free hand on his chest, as if supporting him. An extra swing in her hips finished the illusion, and they stumbled out into the street.

"Where to now?" Jacob said, still leaning on her.

They played their respective roles until Vic led them into a black, narrow alley several blocks from the Screeching Hawk.

Pressing her back against the alley wall, she whispered, "Were we followed?"

He scanned the dimly lit street, the black cape thrown over his shoulders blocking her from casual view. While he watched the street, she scanned the alley, making sure she didn't miss anything this time.

"Doesn't look like it." Jacob turned and faced her. "I don't think your man even noticed. Mar's good at distraction."

Vic rolled her eyes. Jacob's quiet chuckle reminded her that they were quite alone in a dark alley. Her heart thumped faster as his fingers lightly caressed her cheek.

"You're pretty good at distraction, too, Victoria."

She took a step away. "Sorry about using you like that twice."

"It wasn't a problem."

"I'd better get into hiding," she said, hastily taking a second step away.

"Want an escort?"

"What, are you kidding? Wouldn't be much of a hiding spot if I led anybody to it."

Jacob's laugh was tinged with irony.

"You're a very practical young woman, Victoria." He looked her over slowly before saying, "You'll be all right?"

Not if I stay here much longer. To hide her discomfort, she smiled and said, "I still have all my knives. I'll be fine."

His brow arched.

"You want an escort back to the castle, General? Streets can be kind of tough this late at night."

"You offering your services as bodyguard?"

"No. I know a guy who'll guarantee you safe passage through the streets."

With another chuckle, Jacob shook his head. "If I can't have you,

I think I'll take my chances alone." He closed the distance and swung the cloak to cover her shoulders.

"You came out without a cape?" She scowled as a chilling breeze rippled his shirt.

"I'm used to the cold. Why, Victoria Flash? You worried about me?"

"You're not the kind of man that needs to be worried about," she said, tilting her head up to meet his gaze.

"But you are worried. You're worried about being this close to me."

He cupped her cheeks in his hands, and she forgot to breathe.

"Such a young face to have such old eyes." He leaned down and brushed her parted lips with a gentle kiss. "Sleep well, little thief," he said against her mouth, then moved past her up the alley, disappearing into the inky shadows.

She leaned heavily against the wall, her breath coming out in a whoosh. She tilted her head to look at the black sky. "What are you doing, Victoria?" she said to the sliver of night visible past the buildings. "If you're not careful, you're gonna end up another one of Jacob Marin's flowers."

Jacob flopped onto his back and stared at his bedroom ceiling. Despite his well-rumored reputation, he hadn't been involved with a woman for over two years. Mostly, he chose to ignore the reason behind his unusual celibacy.

Jacob loved women. He loved to listen to them talk. He loved the way they could comfort a child and yell at a merchant in one breath. He loved their inner strength and their unending well of compassion. He adored their variety. With very few exceptions, he found something beautiful and unique in every woman he met.

And women loved him.

A fact he was acutely aware of, and one that had gotten him in trouble on more than one occasion. For most of his life, he hadn't lacked for eager female attention. The last two years were no exception.

But despite the willing, hopeful women vying for his regard, he couldn't bring himself to make any of them more than a friend. Rolling to his side, he laughed at his own foolishness. The sound echoed harshly off his bedroom walls. He'd finally decided there probably wouldn't be a new love in his life.

Then he'd met the little thief. And in one day, her big brown eyes were banishing the blue eyes that frequently haunted his dreams. Victoria was the antithesis of the woman to whom those blue eyes belonged. Yet, here he was, restlessly tossing across his bed, remembering every detail of her mischievous face, every smile, every laugh, every curve of the alluring figure she'd kept hidden for so long. She touched something in him he'd thought long lost to a woman beyond his reach.

When she'd kissed him that morning, it had sent a lightning shock of lust through him so potent it burned his blood. He hadn't felt lust like that in some time. The intrigue of that feeling had pushed him to seek her this evening. His excuse was valid. He did think she could help him discover what was happening in the city. But it hadn't been his primary reason in finding her.

Just being in her company had made him feel alive again. It had taken all of his willpower not to deepen the gentle goodnight kiss he'd given her. A restraint he was now vaguely regretting as the thought of her tightened his muscles. But Victoria wasn't an "oversexed barmaid" as she'd so eloquently pointed out. She was a hard-edged, street-smart young woman, too cautious to trip on flattery into his arms. She needed straight talk and honesty, things obviously not common in her line of work. He'd have to earn her trust, or she'd disappear back into the Dareelian night.

Quite suddenly, Jacob realized that he was contemplating a seduction for the first time in two years. The thought left him feeling an odd mixture of relief and anxiety. Maybe this time…

With a sigh somewhere between a chuckle and a groan, he threw himself out of bed and wandered into his sitting room for a drink.

CHAPTER FOUR

T hanks, Azri." Vic tossed the clothes merchant a handful of copper kerns and left the shop. Still forced to wander as a woman, she'd returned to the clothes shop for new outfits. Gip wanted her to stick to Upper Market for a few more days, so she was once more forced into buying something bright and totally unsuitable for moving about at night.

Today, she favored a bright teal tunic and tight breeches with a wraparound woolen shawl of light purple. A large silver and amethyst brooch held the shawl at her left shoulder. Azri had insisted on a pair of white suede calf-high boots, declaring they brightened the already bright teal. If Azri had his way, eventually she'd be garbed in orange and yellow with fuchsia accents. He was enjoying this way too much. Two other new outfits stayed with the merchant until she could pick them up at the end of the day. And, as she'd promised herself, one was specifically designed for night wandering, much to Azri's despair.

Lower Market bustled past as Vic stood outside Azri's shop letting the weak sun warm her face. She would have been happy if not for the sudden appearance of Brad Ruf.

"I hear you've been consorting with King's Own," he said, sidling up to her.

His black hair hung in a tangled, greasy mass around his pockmarked white face. Little brown eyes peered from above a crooked, pointed nose. He stood a few inches taller and insisted on hovering, emphasizing their height difference.

Vic snarled at him and turned toward Upper Market. To her dismay, he fell in beside her. "What do you want, Ruf? I got things to do today." She wrinkled her nose at the smell wafting off him, unwilling to guess at its origins.

"Wanna know what you're doing hanging with King's Own, Vic."

"Why do you care if I have a few drinks with a King's Own?" She lengthened her stride, but he kept pace easily.

"Just curious. Doesn't look good, one of our best consorting with a guard."

"It's business. And if Gip hasn't seen fit to fill you in, then I guess it's none of yours." She switched tactics and slowed to an annoyingly lazy stroll.

He slowed to stay next to her. "So the great Vic Flash has finally traded in her hand for a softer line. Does the King's Own carry enough secrets to make the sacrifice of your legendary virtue worthwhile?"

Her lip curled. "You know damn well I don't whore, Ruf. Not even for the Hole."

He snorted. "Because you don't like men, huh, Flash?"

She turned to face her pock-faced nemesis, flashing him a sweet, sarcastic smile. "Just because I don't want your greasy hands all over me, Ruf? Ha! I like men just fine. I don't like slugs." Turning her back on his vicious snarl, she sauntered up the street.

She truly hated Brad Ruf, and she didn't *hate* many people. When she'd turned away his lewd advances several years back, he'd thought to force himself on her. For his trouble, she'd left a permanent scar across his bony white chest. Tension between them had been high ever since.

***

Vic strolled through Upper Market with little to show for her day. Late in the afternoon, she stepped into a side street to watch the crowded market center. Casually leaning against a building corner, she breathed a heavy sigh.

Not an unusual anything all day.

After her little sleight of hand with Lord Xank the day before, even the challenge of picking a few pockets was denied her by the necessity of staying inconspicuous. The few times city guards had passed, she'd hidden her face, in case Xank had realized who'd liberated his money. Other than that little game, Vic found nothing in Upper Market to focus her attention.

As the sun dipped low in the sky and the air began to chill, she gave up. She could be as patient as the next person, especially when acting as a spy, but this was frustrating. Okay, maybe she couldn't be as patient as the next person. Still. An itch in the back of her mind hinted that something wasn't right. Somewhere out there the bit of information she needed waited to be uncovered, the detail that would prove all was not well in Dareelia. Her nerves were starting to rub as raw as Gip's because, for the life of her, she couldn't catch sight of the elusive clue.

She pushed away from the building and made her way toward the lower end of Upper Market. Passing a large alley separating a prosperous glass shop from a Depnie rug shop, she threw a quick glance up the quiet corridor. Then stopped short. The flicker of black and purple moved behind the rug shop before she managed to get a good look.

Torn between keeping her cover and curiosity, Vic turned up the alley, a rush of anticipation humming in her blood. She pulled her shawl over her head and cast a covert glance around her. The two other people in the alley were moving toward the market. Near the corner, she pressed her back to the wall of the rug shop and hazarded a glance around the edge of the building.

Nothing.

The narrow street running along the backside of the building was thinly populated, but not a single black and purple anything was in sight. Whatever she'd seen had slipped away.

Cursing under her breath, she moved back to the market.

Jacob answered the door of his room at the Winnow Tree Inn at her first quiet knock. He looked her over slowly, a sly smile touching his lips.

"Making sure no one confuses you for a boy, aren't you, little thief?"

Vic grinned and moved past him into the room. Against Azri's urgings, she'd added to her purchases that morning with a pair of form-fitting black breeches and a black shirt to help her move at night. To accent her figure and ensure she wasn't taken for a boy, she'd added a deep green bustier-style vest. The effect was flattering to her figure and practical for hiding in shadows.

"It's new," she said, as he closed the door and turned. "You like?"

"Yeah, Victoria, I like."

Her grin broadened even as her stomach jumped. She didn't know how he did it, but Jacob Marin made her feel attractive and womanly. A strange feeling.

He motioned to a wooden chair at one side of the sparsely furnished room. "You want something to drink?"

"No thanks. This is business."

He pulled a second chair in front of her and straddled it. "So, is Thieves' Hole willing to loan me a spy?"

"Boss says yes. But in our time. You get information when we're ready to give it. We'll take half the fee up-front. For expenses. The rest, after I deliver. And if I'm gonna risk my neck hunting Tracker's men, I want a little information as well."

His eyes narrowed. "What kind of information?"

She leaned back in her seat and bit her bottom lip. "I want to know what's happening when you know."

"I'm not sure I can do that, Victoria. Not if the information could endanger the Kingdom."

"Listen, Marin, I already know about the goblins coming down into Karasnian Forest, and I know about the tension at the Magic Guild. If there's gonna be a war, I want to know before it starts."

Jacob ran his fingers through his dark hair, his expression thoughtful.

She held his gaze, willing him to agree to her bargain.

"I can't make any promises," he said, finally. "Will that cost me your help?"

With a resigned sigh, she shook her head. "No. The boss wants the money. I wanted the information. I don't know what it is, Marin, but the air feels wrong. Like there's a shadow covering the city, but when you look, you can't see what's causing it. It's making me damned nervous."

"Maybe when we find out what Tracker's still doing here, we'll know what's happening."

She shrugged, unconvinced. Jacob smiled, and her mood improved immediately.

"What's the fee, little thief?"

"A thousand gold kern."

He choked visibly. "A thousand?"

"You said you pay good." She shrugged and tried not to grin at his shocked expression. "This is what the boss considers good."

"You better bring me something interesting, Victoria."

She chuckled. "Don't worry, Marin. I'm very good at what I do."

"Yeah, I'll just bet you are."

Smiling, she stood to leave.

"Stay and talk awhile," he said, half rising from his chair. "We'll order a good wine. You can drink now, right? Business is over."

A warning buzzed in her blood. "Why?"

"Why not?"

"In here?"

"Worried?"

"No."

"Yes, you are."

She scowled at his confident response.

He laughed and stood. "You think I go around luring young women to my room, get them drunk, then take advantage of them?"

She snorted at the image. "No. I know you don't need to go to all that trouble." She'd seen the man at work.

"I want to hear your story, Victoria."

"There's not much to tell."

"Then we'll only have one glass of wine."

"I thought I was a con artist." She sighed and hoped it sounded more resigned than wistful. "All right, General. One drink. But downstairs."

He agreed with a triumphant smile.

Sweeping his arm toward the door, he said, "After you, lady thief."

"Don't let the outfit fool you, Marin. I still have all my knives." His quiet chuckle sent a pleasant shiver down her spine.

"I think tonight, I'd also like to hear some of those rumors you've heard about me. I don't think they reflect kindly on me."

She turned at the door and pointedly looked him up and down. "Oh, I wouldn't say that." She was halfway down the hall before he followed.

They sat in a dimly lit corner of the Winnow Tree's common room. The inn was set near the bottom of mid-sector, so the patrons weren't quite as dirty and dangerous as Vic was used to, but a keen eye told her that most of the occupants weren't harmless either. Jacob ordered a bottle of red wine from the Inn's proprietor, a well-rounded elderly man with a perpetual smile.

"Lot of mercs in here," she commented as Jacob settled back in his seat.

"Winnow's known for that. Merchants and traders looking for honest mercenaries come here. Bob keeps an open eye and warns the traders off the less-than-reputable mercs. The highest paying jobs come through here because of that. So any fighter looking for good work pays a little extra for the privilege of sitting in the Winnow's commons."

"And that works?"

"Bob's been doing it for over forty years now."

"Good scam."

"Smart business."

"He must have a good eye for con men."

"That's how he's stayed in business so long."

She studied the proprietor as he chatted with a couple of men at a nearby table. "I bet I could fool him," she said after some consideration.

Jacob's grin said otherwise.

"How'd you end up in your line of work, Victoria?"

"Survival."

"Where are your parents?"

"I never knew my mother. She died when I was born. My da was around for a while, but…" She shrugged.

"But?"

"He disappeared one day. I don't know what happened."

"How old were you?"

"Five. He'd already taught me how to survive, so it wasn't a big deal. I stayed with Peggy, his mistress, until I was seven. Then I joined Thieves' Hole."

Jacob frowned. "Did you ever find out what happened to your father?"

"Peggy thought he was press-ganged into some foreign army. Others say he's dead. But it's the same difference." She waved away the details with a practiced, careless hand gesture.

"Rough way for a little girl to grow up."

The honest compassion in his gaze surprised her. It also made her uncomfortable. "There are worse ways. I've known a few with tougher starts."

Jacob nodded as Bob returned to the table with a bottle of deep red wine and two pewter, silver-lined goblets. Watching him pour their drinks, Vic chuckled. At Jacob's questioning glance, she said, "Didn't even take one drink to tell my story."

"Can I get you anything else, General?" Bob asked, still smiling.

"Not now, thanks." When Bob had moved away, Jacob said, "I think you left out some things in that story."

Vic shrugged and took a sip of her wine. Its rich, bold flavor ran smoothly down her throat. "I told you my story was short. This is good," she said, lifting the goblet slightly.

"It's always been one of my favorites."

She studied Jacob over her cup for several minutes. "I don't understand you, Marin."

"What's got you confused, Victoria?"

"This. You sitting here, talking with me like this. Why?"

"I'm curious."

"You're a King's Own. And I'm not what you might call an honest citizen. You're getting the information you want. Why do you need to know about my life?"

"I don't need to know. I want to. Why is that so hard to believe?"

She shrugged, frowning at her own reaction. "No one's ever wanted to know about me before. No one in the Hole talks about his past. I'm good at what I do and that's all they care about."

"I'm not in the Thieves' Hole."

"Is this your usual line, Marin?"

"What do you mean?"

"I mean, do you do this a lot? Sit over drinks and dig into a person's past?"

"Only people I'm interested in."

She snorted. "Like every woman you meet?"

"Can I help it if I like the company of women?"

"Speaking of which, won't your latest be getting worried about now?" Vic shifted in her seat and took another sip of her wine. This conversation was almost as disconcerting as his scent, a scent even the greasy, ale-tinged air couldn't cover.

"If you're asking if I have other plans for the evening, Victoria, I don't." He raised a brow. "Don't look so surprised."

"Sorry. I just thought…well, anyway." She shrugged.

"I don't know what you've heard about me, little thief, but remember most rumors are exaggerations."

"Sure." She didn't bother to hide her sarcastic tone.

He chuckled and slouched in his seat, crossing his arms over his chest. He fixed her with a look that made her pulse jump. How did he do that?

"Have you ever been in love, Victoria?"

"What's that?"

"I'm truly sorry to hear you say that."

"Hey, you can't miss something you've never had."

"I'm still sorry. Every woman should fall in love at least once."

"Why? I've seen what happens when someone like me falls in love. All it does is complicate an already complicated existence. And you end up the worst for it." She looked down at her goblet, not wanting to see the sympathy in his eyes. She didn't need or want anyone's pity. Especially over something as stupid as love. In one steady gulp, she finished her wine then stood. "I need to get going."

"I'll walk with you a-ways," Jacob said, getting to his feet.

"You don't need to. Finish your wine."

"I'm going back to the castle tonight anyway." Without another word, he tossed a few coins on the table and took her arm, escorting her from the inn. His touch made her nervous and excited all at once. She wasn't used to men taking her arm except to twist it. A burning warmth flowed across her skin from where his fingertips touched her elbow. The warmth seeped through her body like strong whiskey and pooled low in her belly. They walked for a few blocks, Jacob still holding her arm, before she pulled away.

"I'm okay from here," she whispered, not wanting to disturb the quiet night air. Her breath came out in a puff of smoke. Winter was coming fast that year.

"When will I see you again?" he said in a low voice.

"I'll let you know when I come up with something."

"When you need to, you can get a message to me through Bob."

"Tomorrow, leave the five hundred with Mar at the Hawk. She'll know how to get it to me. Orders are, if the money doesn't show tomorrow, the deal's off."

"It'll be there." Jacob stared down into her eyes for a long moment.

She felt trapped in that look, held by the steady intensity in his dark eyes. She didn't want to move, wanted to melt into the heat his eyes promised. He was like the headiest temptation, the most exciting risk. But she was afraid of what that risk would do to her soul.

Finally, she forced herself to turn toward the side street that would take her back to the Hole. But, before she moved beyond his reach, he took her arm and pulled her close.

"Not all love turns bad, Victoria," he whispered.

Before she could speak, he covered her mouth with a kiss that was at once gentle and hard. His arms wrapped tightly around her waist, trapping her close to his chest.

Against all common sense, she pressed herself against his muscled torso and returned his kiss. Her hands moved around his waist, pulling him closer still. The taste of him, the feel of his hard body against her, the flickering dance of his tongue as it slid past her lips, his heady, musky scent, all shot a jolt of heat through her body unlike anything she'd experienced before. It licked her nerves and set her on fire. She could lose herself in his kiss.

Never in her life had Vic felt the way she felt in Jacob's embrace. Secure. Protected. Excited. Vulnerable. Frightened.

A slight shift of her hand caused the strap of her wrist sheath to dig sharply into her arm, and she suddenly remembered who she was. With a rough push to free herself, she fled down the street.

Jacob was half a heartbeat from chasing her. He stopped with the last tenuous grasp on his self-control. Clenching his jaw, he drew in a long, slow breath and commanded his heartbeat to slow. He hadn't expected that reaction from himself or from her. But those huge, dark eyes had drawn him closer even as her smile had heated his blood.

And she'd responded! Kissing him back with that straightforward self-confidence he found so irresistible. Her passion had sent a ripple of lust through him so strong it had almost knocked him over.

Knowing a woman like Victoria wanted him was intoxicating. And she did want him, even if she refused to admit it.

Blowing out a breath he reined in his frustration. He could still feel her warm, agile body in his arms. With a sign, he acknowledged he wasn't going to sleep well tonight. Straightening his shoulders, Jacob turned back toward the castle. Next time, he promised himself. Next time, he'd help her forget her fears.

Chapter Five

Vic hugged the tiled roof, silently watching the building across the street. It had taken her two days to uncover Tracker's lair near Upper Market where she'd expected it to be. Tracker's men could travel in only a few parts of the city without being recognized—Upper Market was one of them.

The building she watched was a nondescript, flat-roofed, four-story brick box. At one time, the building had been an inn, then one of the more discerning entertainment houses. But for the last six months the building had remained empty. To the casual eye, it still looked empty.

A narrow gap between the inn and the trader's building to its right allowed enough room for a man to walk with an inch or two to spare at his shoulders. Midway up the gap, a side door opened into the old inn. Moving mainly at night, Tracker's men were able to enter and exit the building virtually unnoticed.

For two days Vic had watched that gap. Tracker himself never made an appearance. This was her third night's vigil, and she was growing impatient for a clue to what these men were doing in Karasnia. Briefly, she flirted with the idea of breaking into the old inn for a closer look, but for once in her life caution overrode impulse.

Years of practice kept her motionless on the rooftop, her eyes trained for movement, but her mind kept wandering. Occasionally, she bemoaned the loss of the big card game, a game that would have won her enough to last the winter without having to work at all. The game started in two nights and Brad Ruf had spent the week tormenting her with the fact that she wouldn't be present.

She was annoyed with herself for blowing the opportunity to take part in that game, just to see if she could fool Joe Missek's sharp eye. Little good that knowledge did her now. If she'd stuck to two Devil's Highs, maybe Charlie wouldn't have become suspicious. She'd still know she was good enough, and she'd still have a chance at the big game. Nothing she could do about it now, though. She'd just have to live with the mistake. At least this spying job paid enough to make up for the lost gambling winnings.

But berating herself wasn't the only thing preoccupying her. More often than not, her thoughts leapt back to the tall King's Own for whom she was spying. Jacob Marin was more of a trial than she ever expected. And a temptation a lot harder to resist. The way he combined compassion, confidence and indolence into one charming, sexy frame made her forget about being cautious. More heady kisses and she'd fall willingly into bed with the man, though she'd managed to avoid that particular life complication for all of her twenty-one years.

But it wasn't the sex that worried her so much. A girl had to try it sometime in her life, and Jacob Marin was reputed to know what he was doing. What worried Vic was her inability to separate sex and emotions. Other women managed to do it. Prostitutes depended on the separation. But she couldn't seem to manage it. One of the main reasons she'd learned to gamble and con was to avoid becoming a prostitute. Unfortunately, emotions were just as dangerous to a con as they were to a whore. She'd seen too many people ruin perfectly good careers by losing their heads to emotion.

So Jacob Marin presented a problem. She knew if she gave the King's Own her body, her heart would follow close behind. And losing her heart to a man notorious for his transient affairs could only spell trouble.

A sudden glint interrupted and focused her mind on the street below. At a few minutes after midnight, not many moved along the dimly lit cobblestones. The four that had caught her attention moved carefully, avoiding the pools of light from the street lamps. Three wore various combinations of black and purple, one was covered from head to foot in a black robe. Only the silver edging on Malkiney's tunic distinguished the small group from the shadows.

Vic watched as they neared the mouth of the gap. Dressed in black with a black scarf wrapped around her head so only her eyes peered out, she was part of the night. Her breath moved with the breeze, her eyes narrowed to slits to prevent light reflection.

One of the uniformed men slipped into the gap followed immediately by Malkiney. The robed figure and the third guard waited.

Suddenly and without warning, the robed one turned and looked up—right into Vic's eyes. She stopped breathing and her mind went blank.

Beneath the heavy folds of his cowl, the man had the whitest hair and bluest eyes she'd ever seen. He was of indeterminate age, his white face almost without lines, but his eyes held a terrible, ancient knowledge. And though she didn't move, Vic knew with an unmistakable certainty that those frightening blue eyes saw her.

Then the remaining guard motioned the robed man down the gap. A knowing smile raised his almost colorless lips before he disappeared into the darkness with the other man following close behind.

The smile touched a cold horror in Vic's blood. The small hairs on the back of her neck rose. Only when her chest began to burn, did she remember to breathe. In a movement worthy of her nickname, she soundlessly slipped to the opposite side of the building and shimmied down a drainage pipe to the street below. She took off at a loping run almost before her feet touched the ground.

***

"Are you sure?" Deraun sat behind his desk, steepling his fingers before his face.

"Positive," Vic said. She paced across the small, dim office, unable to sit while adrenaline still beat through her blood. "I only saw the one, but who knows how many were in there. And that wasn't a kind and caring Guild sorcerer. I've never been so afraid of a magician in my life. He looked right at me." She stopped and shuddered. "*He saw me.* With all the other people in those buildings, he shouldn't have been able to pick me out." She went back to pacing.

"But in three nights, you've still only seen the one?"

"Yeah." She stopped and looked Deraun in the eyes, holding his gaze for the first time since entering the dim office. "But sometimes one is all it takes."

He nodded and slipped a hand beneath his desk. An instant later the door opened, admitting the overlarge form of one of the Hole's leg-breakers. "Get me Kritta," Deraun ordered. The man closed the door wordlessly. Deraun resteepled his hands, and Vic resumed her pacing.

Five minutes later, the door opened again. In walked the tiniest, prettiest woman Vic had ever known. Her long blonde curls bounced playfully about a round face. Green almond-shaped eyes glistened above a pert upturned nose and red, heart-shaped lips. If not for the obvious curves of her figure, Kritta could have passed for a little girl of ten. She was, in fact, a year older than Vic.

"Kritta," Deraun said, as the woman took a seat, "What news from the Guild?"

"There's still a hush over there," Kritta answered.

Her voice sounded remarkably mature coming from such a girlish face.

"Henry hinted at trouble," Kritta continued, "but he's not talking. I caught him mumbling in his sleep about a prophecy or something, but I couldn't make it out."

The tiny woman had insinuated herself into the life and bed of the assistant magician to one of the leading sorcerers in the Magic Guild. When her generally effective persuasion failed, she could often glean bits of information from Henry's sleep talking. Those bits had proved both beneficial and profitable for the Hole on more than one occasion. Vic had always considered her one of the Hole's best assets.

Kritta's almond eyes narrowed as she looked from Vic to Deraun. "Something's happened."

"Maybe," Deraun said, letting his hands fall to his desktop. "Vic saw Tracker's men with a sorcerer tonight. She thinks maybe they're smuggling more into the city."

"You thinking blood mages, Gip?"

"Don't know yet. But why smuggle a sorcerer into the city otherwise? I want you to play hard with Henry. Get whatever you can about this prophecy and find out if the Guild knows about this mysterious sorcerer."

"On it." Kritta left the room with a passing nod to Vic.

"Vic, find that King's Own. He paid for the information. And he's dealt with blood magic before. But don't mention Kritta and the prophecy until we know more."

"What about the building?"

He tapped the top of his desk. His sharp, hawk nose dipped close to his hooked chin.

Vic clenched her hands together behind her back as she waited, trying not to fidget. In the always-dark office, its heavy drapes pulled closed against spying eyes, Deraun's dark eyes looked black as he studied her.

"Until we can buy something to mask you from magic," he finally said, "I want you to avoid that building and Tracker's men."

She nodded reluctantly. She'd been afraid of that decision.

"I mean it, Flash. Check your curiosity until I order otherwise."

"All right, Gip." She turned to the door.

"Vic."

She stopped with her hand on the latch.

"You didn't see any sign of Tracker himself?"

"Not a hint. Just Malkiney."

Deraun frowned and ran a hand over his black hair.

Vic quietly left her boss deep in thought. She traveled dark, back streets on her way to the Winnow Tree Inn. The fear sparked by the sorcerer kept her muscles tensed, ready for action. In her short life, she'd experienced tension, anticipation, anxiety, even fear. But only one other time had she been this truly terrified. That had been on the day her father disappeared.

Her every nerve was so alert that when a man stepped around a building to block her path, she felt him before she could see him.

"Now where would you be off to so late, Vic Flash?"

The man's guttural voice was unfamiliar. "Who?" Vic said, bluffing for time. "I think you've got the wrong person, mister. My name's Anne." Her gaze darted around, looking for other threats.

The stranger stepped forward, but light from the street lamp at his back kept his face shadowed. "Oh, I got the right person, Vic Flash. You think Big Charlie don't know how the Hole's keeping you hidden?"

"Actually," she said with a resigned sigh, "no, I didn't think Charlie would figure it out."

"He said you was a smart one," the man snarled. "But he's got people you ain't even imagined, thief. Hole might be the biggest, but it ain't got all the best. Now, Big Charlie wants to see ya about some money you owes him."

"Mm-hum." Vic had already let her wrist knife slide into her fingers and was judging what it would take to get around this threat.

"Now, he warned me about that, too, thief. You can't fool old Bagger with that knife trick. I know how they be used."

She caught the sudden flicker of light on metal in her assailant's hand. A cold knot pitted in her stomach even as numb logic seized her mind, preparing her for the fight to come. In the dark and with the light in her face, she was at a disadvantage, but the fear in her blood had heightened her other senses. When the big man leapt, stabbing at her left arm, she was already moving away. She darted around, putting the street lamp at her back.

And saw her assailant's face for the first time. She had to swallow a shocked gasp. His features were monstrously deformed, a mask of twisted flesh from a nightmare. Then the flick of his blade near her ear forced out all other thoughts beyond the fight. With an off-balance swerve, she moved away from his knife only to get her legs tangled in the edge of her cape. She cursed under her breath. In one move, she regained her balance, dropped her cloak, and dove away from a new attack.

On balance again, Vic switched tactics. Flipping her knife so the blade stretched along her forearm, she stalked her assailant. The man followed suit. The first thrusts were tentative, a clicking of metal to test the other's reflexes. Then they were slashing and blocking, arms windmilling to find an opening in the other's guard. Vic's arms, moving with the speed of her nickname, slipped behind her assailant's blade to rip a gash across his chest.

He bellowed in rage and charged forward, forcing her to retreat. The man was a head taller than her and his strength far superior. She had to use her movements and his own momentum against him. A slip turn around his side, and she slashed another long wound in his waist.

He turned and was on her again, faster than she would have guessed. The moment of overconfidence cost her a shallow slash along her unguarded left forearm. Biting off the pain and another curse, she pressed forward, the whirl of her blade arm so quick, he couldn't keep up. She left several superficial slices across his arms and drove him back under the onslaught. In moments, however, she realized that he was falling back intentionally.

Behind him, Vic saw faint movement in a dark warehouse doorway, a doorway to which her assailant was retreating. *Ambush.* Without slowing her forward momentum, she watched the space where the second attacker hid. Then suddenly, she dropped to one knee, and using her left hand, sent the dart knife at her waist flying. Before her blade cleared the darkened doorway, she was rolling past the ugly man's legs. Coming up behind him, she slashed the back of his thigh.

He screamed in pain and collapsed to the ground.

She didn't wait around to discover if any more attackers lurked. On her feet, she was moving before the monstrous man hit the cobbles. Grabbing her cloak on the run, she raced through the shadows toward the Winnow Tree.

Chapter Six

Outside the Winnow Tree, Vic watched the area for a quarter of an hour from the shelter of a nearby building. She'd replaced her black cloak and kept to the deepest shadows, the hood pulled low over her head. When she felt sure no one was watching, she silently passed into the Inn, holding her wounded arm tight against her stomach to staunch the flow of blood.

At the bar, Bob smiled happily as she approached. Her gaze darted around the room as she spoke to the Winnow's proprietor. "Is General Marin in his room?" she asked, her voice low and urgent.

"No, miss. He's not here now."

Her eyes flicked to the door, then back. "Would you tell him I'm in his room?" She didn't bother to use her name. Bob knew who she was already. With a final glance around the room, she started for the stairs at the rear of the commons.

"But miss," Bob said hesitantly. "I'm not expecting him tonight."

"I'll wait." Vic trotted up the stairs before he could reply.

Unless being used, Jacob's room remained unlocked. No one entered the inn without Bob knowing, especially with a commons full of mercenaries. Once inside, Vic closed and locked the door behind her. She didn't bother to light the lamp or start a fire, but went directly to the heavily curtained window to study the street below.

Still nothing.

Finally, she allowed herself the luxury of relaxing enough to look at her arm. In the dim streetlight coming in through the window, she peeled back the torn fragments of her shirtsleeve, gritting her teeth against a rush of nausea. The gash wasn't serious, but blood caked her arm and dripped into her hand. The cool air stung sharply.

With a hissing intake of breath, she pulled the remains of her sleeve up over her elbow. A look to the small wash table in one corner of the room confirmed that fresh water and towels hadn't been placed out. She considered calling for water and bandages, but that would attract attention.

Sitting on the squeaky double bed, she pulled the knife from the scabbard between her shoulder blades and cut a strip from the side of her cape. She wrapped her arm with a grimace. Pain shot through her arm every time she touched her damaged skin. The nausea in her stomach choked her throat and the pressure thickening in her head blocked sound for a minute.

At last, when the wound was wrapped securely, if temporarily, to prevent further bleeding, Vic moved to one of the two wooden chairs in the room. Her hearing was back to normal, but the ache in her arm kept her still queasy stomach roiling. She felt weak and lightheaded now that the adrenaline was wearing off. Staring at the cold fireplace, she wrapped her cloak tight around her shoulders to stay warm.

A flickering realization that she should start a fire moved through her tired mind, but she was too weary and dizzy to rise again. She also knew that she was probably in shock and had to stay awake.

Time passed. She didn't think. She didn't move. She stared into the fire pit and waited.

Suddenly, someone was shaking her shoulders and quietly calling her name. She blinked at the light from a crackling fire. And started to bolt out of her chair.

Gentle hands forced her back down. She looked to her side and relief made her smile. "Hi, General. What are you doing here?"

"Bob saw the blood on your hand." Jacob knelt beside her chair. "He sent word to me. The healer will be here in a few minutes."

She grimaced. "Thanks. Guess I couldn't fool him after all."

"I'm glad you couldn't, given the circumstances. What happened?"

"I was on my way here to give you news when this big ugly thing stopped me on one of the darker streets." Jacob's brow wrinkled, so Vic clarified. "One of Charlie's leg breakers."

"Goddess! Victoria, you're lucky you weren't hurt more seriously."

She smiled crookedly at the concern in his voice. "You should see the others."

"Others?"

"Well, I only know of two. The ugly guy and one hidden in a doorway. The ugly guy was good with a knife." She raised her arm slightly, wincing. "I let him get under my guard. Shouldn't have done that. But it motivated me to move faster." She shrugged then frowned. "I think I might have killed the other one. I didn't even see him. Just a glimpse. But the knife I tossed hit something solid. Lost a good knife, too."

"What about the ugly one?"

"Cut his hamstring. Made running away easier."

Jacob breathed what was almost a chuckle and shook his head. "How did they find you? I thought Big Charlie didn't know you were a woman."

"He didn't. He does now. I don't know how he found out. I think he sent them mainly to scare me. Maybe to bring me in. That would explain the second man." She frowned and bit her bottom lip. "I think maybe Big Charlie is gonna be even more mad at Vic Flash now."

Jacob rose to his feet. "Well, you're safe for the time being."

"I just wish I knew how Charlie learned I'm a woman. That part's been bothering me since the attack."

"We'll worry about it in the morning."

A knock at the door stopped Vic's question. *We'll worry?*

A large, older woman with straight black hair and wizened green eyes pushed purposefully past Jacob to Vic's side. She set down her bag, frowned at Vic's arm, removed the cloak strip, and frowned deeper. "Get her onto the bed," she ordered.

Without questioning, Jacob helped Vic to her feet and led her to the bed. The pain, no longer biting, had become a dull ache along the entirety of her left arm. She swallowed the bile in her throat and blinked back a wash of dizziness that blackened her vision, then sank to the edge of the bed.

As the healer cleaned her wound, Vic ground her teeth together and clenched the bed quilt with her right hand.

Jacob stood behind the healer until she started to apply a poultice, then he moved to Vic's side and held her good hand.

When the woman finished bandaging the cut, she stood back and smiled for the first time since entering the room. "That should hold you through tomorrow. I'll leave some fresh bandages. Leave that on 'til midday tomorrow, then wash and dress it again. Change the bandages every day until the wound has sealed itself, to prevent infection." She set a small packet of herbs on the washstand. "Drink these in boiled water tonight for the pain." To Jacob, she said, "Keep her warm and make sure she rests. She lost a bit of blood, but otherwise, she'll be fine." With a friendly nod, the healer left the room.

Jacob looked down into Vic's upturned face. "You heard the healer, little thief. Under the covers."

"Here?"

"Where else? I can keep an eye on you here. And you'll be out of Big Charlie's way." He flipped back the blue quilt.

"I have news for you, though."

"It'll wait until you've slept. I can't have my best street spy getting sick from an infection, now can I? Into bed." He returned to the fire and hung a kettle of water across the spit.

She pulled off her boots, deftly removing and hiding her calf dagger, and climbed beneath the bedcovers. She didn't bother to remove her two remaining knives. She was used to sleeping with them on.

When Jacob pulled a chair closer to the fire and sat with his back to her, she asked, "You're staying?"

"Healer's orders. I'm to make sure you rest and stay warm."

"Thanks, Jacob," she whispered.

He grinned and nodded. When the water boiled, he mixed it with the herbs in a large clay mug. He put the mug to her lips and held it while she drank.

With her good hand, she pushed away the mug, almost choking on the last gulp of bitter liquid. "That stuff tastes awful."

"Most remedies taste bad. I think the healers do that on purpose so people have reason to stay healthy."

She smiled. His gentle brown eyes and caring smile started her heart dancing. The drink had an almost immediate effect, numbing the ache that had throbbed along her arm. Lack of pain left room for a warm anticipation.

As Jacob set aside the mug, she said, "At least it works. My arm doesn't hurt anymore."

"Good." He sat on the bed beside her. "Now, sleep."

"First, while I'm feeling okay, I need to tell you what I found." When he opened his mouth, she stopped him with a hand on his arm.

His muscles bunched beneath her touch. "No. You should know this now. I found Tracker's lair. It's near Upper Market. I watched for two nights and nothing. Then tonight I saw Malkiney sneaking someone into the building.

"He was a sorcerer, but not like any I've ever seen. He had the white hair and blue eyes like so many of them, but his face was colorless. And his eyes…Jacob, I was dressed like this…" She pointed at her black attire. "Lying on a building roof behind him, and he looked right at me. And he saw me, Jacob. He smiled."

She paused, taking a long, steadying breath. "My boss thinks maybe Tracker's smuggled in a blood magician. We don't know why… Hell, we don't know if he *is* a blood magician…" She bit her bottom lip and let out a frustrated breath through her nose.

He took her hand in his but his thoughtful frown belied the comforting gesture. "That's worse than I thought," he said.

"I haven't seen Tracker either. Just Malkiney."

"Tracker hasn't shown?" Jacob shook his head then softened his grave expression. "Okay, enough business for tonight, Victoria. You need rest, and I'll have to think on this before I decide what to do."

"As soon as my boss can buy something to hide me from a magician's sight, I'll be able to snoop some more. Until then, he's ordered me away from the building."

"Good," Jacob said seriously. "Now, little thief, it's time for you to sleep."

He pushed her gently back onto the bed and pulled the quilt around her shoulders. For a long moment, he stared into her eyes. Almost unconsciously, his hand moved to caress her cheek.

"I'm glad you weren't hurt badly tonight. I want you to stay here for the next few days. Big Charlie won't be able to find you. Bob will see to that."

"I have to get back to the Hole tomorrow," she breathed, the feel of his hand on her cheek a delicate torment.

"Victoria, what if someone in the Hole told Big Charlie you're a woman? For a few days, stay here."

She looked at Jacob's chin, unable to meet his intense gaze. She hadn't considered a traitor in the Hole. "I've got to see Peggy at least. Word will be on the streets about the fight. She can get a message to my boss. And don't look at me like that. The boss wouldn't turn me over to Charlie. I trust him."

"All right, but don't tell anyone where you're hiding."

"No one would believe me anyway," she grinned. "Who'd ever think a King's Own would go to the trouble of helping a street con?"

"You're more than just a street con, Victoria. And I'm not just a King's Own." He leaned down and kissed her softly on the lips as the hand stroking her cheek moved into her hair.

For the first time that night, Vic forgot about the sorcerer and Big Charlie and the gash in her arm. All she felt was the tender touch of Jacob's lips. When he pulled back, the movement felt reluctant, a reluctance that echoed in her.

"Sleep, little thief. You've had a long night."

As he stood, she caught his hand. "Jacob," she whispered. "Thank you again. For everything."

He smiled crookedly and squeezed her hand before returning to his chair in front of the fire.

She rolled onto her side and squeezed her eyes shut, knowing she wouldn't sleep for some time.

Within a few minutes, Jacob sat listening to the slow, steady breathing of the thief.

When Vic awoke the next day, the room was empty. On a small table next to the bed, a tray of food and coffee waited. Stretching, she sat up in bed, setting her back against the brass headboard.

To her surprise, spread across the foot of the bed was a new black shirt and cloak. She found herself grinning stupidly as she pulled the new shirt up to her chest. She stroked the smooth material, a heavy, sturdy flannel, perfect for the coming winter nights.

This was too much. She pulled the heavy woolen cloak up for inspection. Jacob Marin was entirely too much. With remarkable speed, she was forgetting exactly why she should be cautious around him. *Other women haven't minded his reputation. Who am I to argue with the women of Karasnia?*

A quiet, cautious voice in the back of her mind warned her of the folly of emotional entanglements. But she'd never been good at avoiding risk. In fact, more often than was entirely healthy, she went out of her way to take risks. Jacob Marin, however, was a very different kind of risk.

She crawled out of bed slowly. The ache in her arm had started again, but it was minimal compared to the sting of last night. A quick look out the window told her the morning was half gone. She removed her tattered shirt and inspected the poultice pack on her arm. The washbasin had been filled with fresh water and clean bandages lay beside it on the washstand. She washed and bandaged the wound then put on the new shirt.

Picking up a piece of nut bread and pouring herself a cup of coffee, Vic moved to sit in one of the wooden chairs. The coffee was still warm, heating her stomach and cheeks as she gulped it down. A low fire still burned in the fireplace. *I wonder when he left?*

After her quick breakfast, she threw her new cloak around her shoulders, ran her fingers through her hair, and left the Inn. Bob waved a friendly farewell as she passed through the commons. Did he ever sleep? she wondered as she stepped into the streets.

Outside, the city had begun preparing for Autumn's End, a festival celebrating the end of harvest, the coming of winter, and the beginning of a new year. Citywide feasting and merriment, gaming and entertainment lasted for a week. On the final night, bonfires would light the streets, children would run around in costumes "banishing evil spirits", and adults, in ghoulish masks, would gather into the streets to sing and dance in the new year.

Shopkeepers had begun decorating the fronts of their stores. Banners and ribbons hung from windows and balconies. Over every door, a harvest bundle of wheat, oats, and corncobs wrapped in raffia ensured a prosperous new year. The king would hold the official opening ceremony the following afternoon, and Autumn's End would begin.

As she made her way to the Screeching Hawk, Vic watched with growing anticipation as trains of people filed into the city. Nearing Lower Market, she was forced to stop as several richly adorned carriages passed her on the street. Nobles from the surrounding provinces would be staying as guests of the king and queen during the festival. Vic's fingers twitched at the thought of so many heavy purses flowing into her city.

Mar accosted Vic the minute she walked through the door of the Hawk. "What have you done to him?" she demanded.

"To who?" Vic took a step back, surprised by the woman's venom.

"General Marin," Mar hissed. "That's who. What have you done?"

"I don't know what you're talking about." Vic guided the puffing barmaid back to the bar where Peggy stood grinning. Peggy was nearing her sixty-fifth year, making her a sort of matriarch to the patrons. She might move a bit slower than she once did, but age hadn't dampened her wit or her wicked sense of humor.

"How can you say that?" Mar continued. "Marin's been in here every night for the last week. And I'm giving him every opportunity for a little fun, but does he take it? Not so much as a pat on the butt. In fact, he's not looked crooked at any of the girls. And that's not like General Marin."

Mar had apparently heard all the same rumors as Vic. "What makes you think that has anything to do with me?"

"Because when I can get him to talk beyond a few pleasantries, he's always trying to find out about you."

"Really?" Vic couldn't hide her surprised grin.

"Yes, really. So what's going on?"

"Nothing, Mar. We've a business arrangement. Hole business."

"That's a lovely cloak," Peggy said. "New, isn't it?"

Vic wrinkled her nose and nodded.

"There," Mar declared, pointing at Vic but looking back at Peggy. "I told you there was something between the two of 'em."

"How do you know the cloak is a gift, Mar?" Peggy said reasonably. "Maybe Vic bought it herself."

"Yeah. Right." Mar moved away from the two women in disgust as an early customer whistled for attention.

Peggy's laugh turned suddenly serious when she looked at Vic. "Word's on the street already. About last night."

Vic nodded. "I thought it might be."

"You all right?"

"Little cut on my arm. Other than that, I'm fine."

"You killed the one. And Bagger will be laid up for months. Charlie's demanded the Hole turn you over. He's threatening a war."

Vic dropped her head into her hands. "All this over a bloody gambling pot."

"It was a big pot," Peggy said matter-of-factly.

Vic groaned. She had to acknowledge, if only to herself, that it wasn't the size of the pot that had gotten her into all this trouble, it was the size of her ego. She just had to get that third Devil's High past Joe, didn't she? Couldn't have let well enough be. She sighed and looked at Peggy. What a mess.

"I think he's more angry because you killed one of his men."

"Well, what did he expect me to do? Let his thugs take me to who knows where and beat the life out of me? Did he really think I'd just let myself get ambushed?"

"Honey, I've not a single idea about what Big Charlie thinks. All I know is what he does. And right now, what he's doing is threatening an all-out war with Thieves' Hole."

"Damn. Have you heard from Gip?"

"Matter of fact, he figured you'd show up here eventually, and he hoped you'd land here before the Hole. He says to stay in deep hiding for the next couple of weeks. Don't come back to the Hole. He's gonna tell Charlie he doesn't know where you are, that he can't find you. So you need to stay good and hidden. He also says to avoid every Hole member but Ren."

"Why?"

"He knows Charlie found out you're a woman and that's how he tracked you down last night. He thinks maybe someone in the Hole is playing both sides."

"Damn," she breathed again. "Jacob said something like that last night, but I didn't want to believe it was possible."

Peggy raised a gray brow. "Jacob, is it?"

She grinned and her gaze danced away from Peggy's knowing smile. "Hey, I was on my way to see him for business reasons. Just happened to be good hiding place after my fight."

"Um hum."

"Listen," Vic quickly changed the subject, "I'd better get out of here so I don't bring Charlie down on this place. He's probably gonna have someone posted here for the next few weeks."

"Oh, he's already got someone here." Peggy nodded to an unconscious lump in the far corner of the room.

Vic's mouth dropped open. She snapped it closed and swallowed. "He's not…"

"No. He's alive. Just drugged. He won't even remember. We're gonna fix him up real nice in a room with one of the girls, so he won't care that he can't remember."

"Peggy, you're my hero."

The older woman smiled pleasantly. "One last thing, honey. Gip says no spy work until this thing with Charlie's handled. Jacob," Peggy emphasized the name, "will either have to wait or find himself a new spy."

"But he's already paid half the fee."

"Gip figures whatever you've got should cover what you found last night. Don't frown at me, girl. I'm just giving you the message. You're not to do a thing but hide until Gip tells you to come out. When he can, he'll relay messages through Ren so you'll know they're clean. This place will be too hot for me to help you. He said you'd know where to meet Ren."

"Yeah. We've got a spot." With a deep breath that was almost a sigh, Vic said, "All right, Peggy. I guess I'll see ya when the air clears. Stay good."

"You, too, honey. Stay standing."

As she started toward the door, Peggy called, "And if you see him, give our regards to the general."

Out in the streets in the middle of the day, Vic suddenly felt exposed. She knew the city well, better even than others in the Hole.

But Charlie had found her once. And now he knew she was a woman.

A train of white-and-gold carriages passed across the road two blocks from where she skulked in a doorway, and an idea turned up her grin. She sprinted through a labyrinth of side streets to Upper Market, only stopping long enough to pick up a few pouches of stashed money.

In a richly appointed Upper Market dress shop, she set down a small pile of gold kern for a new, hand-tailored gown. "I'll need a hairdresser as well," she told the head dressmaker, who, after seeing the easy way she laid down her gold kern, hurried to do her bidding.

The young apprentice fitting her for undergarments stared openly at Vic's knives and her bandaged forearm, but said nothing. For all they knew, she was a high paid mercenary or bodyguard. And anyone with that much money and that many knives was best left alone.

While two ladies worked on fitting the dress she'd chosen, the thief decided to add a few new knives to her battery. She'd lost a good throwing dart last night, and with Charlie hunting her, it never hurt to have a few extras at hand. As the final stitching was completed, she sauntered out into the market to find a weapons dealer. She returned to the dress shop with a second ankle dagger and two new throwing darts.

The requested hairdresser made a fuss over her thick curls and fawned over the length of her lashes. She pulled Vic's hair up into a bun, leaving curling tendrils framing her face and neck. Then she proclaimed in loud terms that there wasn't a more beautiful woman in all of Karasnia.

Vic listened with the air of someone used to being told such things, to maintain the illusion of wealth and power. People asked fewer questions if they thought you had wealth and power. Considering her weaponry and the wound on her arm, the fewer questions she was asked, the better.

Then she tried on her new dress and looked into the mirror. The dress was made of wine-colored velvet, pulled in snugly at her waist then opened down the front of a long, full skirt to reveal a silky cream underskirt. The sleeves loosely hugged her arms to below the elbow then more cream silk belled to hang just below her wrist, where it collected in a loose ruffle. The silk perfectly disguised her wrist dagger, but she'd have to practice drawing it with that ruffle in the way. The neckline was cut high at the back and low in the front, showing her curves to good effect. A disguised strip of extra material down the back helped hide the bulge of her neck dagger and covered the laces that crossed her back. The head seamstress was so eager to please, she'd even procured a pair of calf-high burgundy suede boots with just enough room for Vic to hide her calf daggers.

"It's beautiful," she said to the anxious dressmaker. "You've done a splendid job in so short a period of time. I may have to return for another." The lady, a bigger woman than Vic by about three inches and forty pounds, bowed graciously. Bundling her old attire, Vic decided this had been worth the expense. Even knowing she was a woman, Charlie's people would have a hard time recognizing her in this outfit. The gown was also the perfect disguise for something else she had to do. She gave the seamstress an additional gold kern for her hard work and strolled into Upper Market looking remarkably like a visiting noblewoman.

CHAPTER SEVEN

Jacob grinned at the young couple walking toward him. "Well, it's about time you two got here," he said. "Tiya, you look as remarkable as ever." He took the young woman's hand and kissed it gently.

He was, as ever, struck by her ethereal beauty. In the time since they'd first met, her hair had turned from golden blonde to near white, and her blue eyes had cleared to the color of the sky. But her smile remained the same. A smile that still had the power to speed his heartbeat.

Glancing sideways at the giant of a man with her, Jacob said, "You don't look bad either, boy."

"Thanks, old man." Kevin smiled and slapped Jacob on the shoulder.

The acting Baron of Fordin, a former King's Own himself, was ten years Jacob's junior and one of the few men taller than Jacob. He was also one of the best friends Jacob had ever had.

"What do you mean 'it's about time we got here'?" Kevin asked through a half frown, his green eyes narrowing. "Autumn's End doesn't officially start until tomorrow."

"Can you blame me for being anxious to see this lovely woman?" When Kevin's scowl deepened, both Jacob and Tiya laughed. "Okay, so I was looking forward to seeing you, too, boy. How's the barony?"

"Holding together nicely, thank you."

The three stood talking in the middle of the King's Own wing of the palace. Jacob had been on his way to meet Baron and Baroness Fordin after receiving word that they'd arrived. The couple had managed to find him first. "Tiya." Jacob grinned at the young woman whose hand he still held. "How's Merig?"

"The same," she said. "Deeply involved in an old text from before the Ducal rebellion. He sends his best."

Jacob looked back and forth between the two, trying not to grin. "And how's the little one?"

Tiya beamed. "She's wonderful. She's sleeping in our suite now. You'll come by later to meet her?"

"Of course. And she's as lovely as her mother I've no doubt."

"As a matter of fact," Kevin said, "she has her mother's hair and eyes, but she has my nose." He grinned proudly.

"Well, that shouldn't hurt her too much," Jacob said with mock seriousness. Tiya coughed to hide her chuckle, but Kevin simply shook his head and smiled crookedly. Jacob let his suppressed grin out again. "Is her power under control?"

Tiya nodded. "One of the first things Merig taught me after she was born was how to shield her."

"But," Kevin added, "the instant she's old enough, she's learning how to control herself. Old man, you should have seen the damage she did to the nursery the first time she got hungry and we weren't right there."

"Babies are like that," Jacob said diplomatically. "How does Aaron like his new cousin?"

"He thinks she's too small to be very useful," Tiya said. "But after she wrecked the nursery, he decided he might like having her around."

"And Lady Badgen?"

"She's doing very well. She misses you, however."

Jacob raised his brows and tried to look innocent. "Me?"

Kevin snorted. Tiya nodded and said, "I believe her exact words were, 'Please send that lovely Jacob Marin my regards.' You were so kind to her after Edward…I think you've earned her admiration."

Jacob was about to answer when a soft voice brought his attention around.

"Yes?"

He dropped Tiya's hand and stared, open-mouthed. "Victoria? What are you... You're wearing a dress."

Vic grinned. "It's new. You like?"

"Yeah, I like. How did you get in here?" He couldn't look away from the startling beauty of his little thief.

"What? Are you kidding?" She snorted in a less-than-ladylike way. "With all these nobles moving in and out of this place? I just walked through the front door."

"No one stopped you?"

"Oh, one rather handsome young guard stopped me. I looked at him with panic-stricken doe eyes and said, 'My lady has requested I fetch this to her right away. And I've been away too long already. My lady gets very angry if I'm late.'" She fluttered her lashes and spoke in a higher, softer voice, her hands clutched around a small rose-colored vial.

"And that worked? He didn't even ask who your lady was?" Jacob was caught between admiration for the thief and annoyance at his guard.

"He sent me along with a pat on my arm and a compassionate smile. So I guess it worked."

He narrowed his eyes. "Did you get his name?"

"I don't want him to get into trouble. It wasn't his fault. I *am* very good at what I do."

Her unblinking confidence almost made him smile. "How did you know where to find me?"

"I wandered a few corridors then asked the first guard I found. I said my lady had a message for General Marin and asked where I might find you." She shrugged. "The guard found this an ordinary enough request."

Jacob scowled back at Kevin when the young giant started to laugh loudly.

Tiya smiled, visibly struggling against her own chuckle.

"I'll have to put more female guards in the front of the palace during these festivals," Jacob mumbled.

"Oh, the guard that gave me directions was a woman," Vic answered pleasantly.

"All right, little thief, I give. But I will talk to my guards after this. Now, did you break into the royal palace just to prove the vulnerability of the King's Own or did you have a specific reason?"

She turned serious in an eye's blink, and concern clenched his gut.

"Specific reason. Business," she said, flicking a glance at the couple still watching their scene.

Jacob considered his friends a moment then decided against including them in the discussion. But at a raised brow from Tiya, he realized he hadn't introduced the newcomer. "I'm sorry. Lady Tiya, Lord Kevin, may I introduce Victoria Flash. Victoria, Baron and Baroness Fordin."

Vic's eyes widened and her mouth dropped open. She dropped into a deep and remarkably graceful curtsey. "My Lord Fordin, Lady Sorceress," she said to their feet. "I'm honored."

Kevin smiled and took her hand, raising her to her feet. She had to crane her neck to look into his face. He was nearly a foot and a half taller. "The pleasure is ours, Victoria," he said.

Tiya took the young thief's hand next, and when Vic would have bowed her head, Tiya took her chin, meeting her gaze. "It's an honor to meet anyone who can cause Jacob so much trouble," she said with a conspiratorial grin.

Vic swallowed visibly but smiled back.

"If you two wouldn't mind," Jacob said, taking her arm. "I do have to talk with Victoria in private. But I'll call on you later?"

"Of course," Tiya said. Her gaze flashed from the young woman to Jacob, then back again. "Good day, Victoria. I hope we'll meet again soon." Kevin took his wife's arm, and they walked back toward the guest wing. Tiya glanced back once and smiled before continuing on.

Jacob watched them walk away then turned to look down at Vic. She was still staring wide-eyed after the retreating couple.

"I didn't realize who you were talking to," she breathed. "I wouldn't have bothered you if I'd known."

"They'll be here for the rest of festival so we'll have plenty of time to talk. What business?" Jacob said, leading her by the arm down the hall toward his rooms. The brush of velvet beneath his fingers made keeping his mind on business increasingly difficult.

"Has to do with last night," she said, nearly whispering.

Jacob nodded, but didn't question her further until they were in his sitting room. He offered her a seat on a settee by the window and sat next to her. "What's happened?"

"Seems Big Charlie's more upset about me killing one of his guys than I would have thought. He's threatening an all-out war with the Hole unless they turn me over."

A sudden surge of fear tightened Jacob's throat. He took hold of her hands where they lay clenched around the rose vial in her lap. "The Hole's not…" He couldn't bring himself to say the words.

"They're not turning me over. But I've got to stay deep under for a while."

She bit her bottom lip—a habit he found incredibly sexy—and looked down to where his hands covered hers.

"I won't be able to…to work for you anymore. At least for a few weeks."

"Of course." He was surprised by the unease in her voice. "I'll find someone else."

She looked up, her eyes wide. "You're not mad?"

"Why would I be mad, Victoria?"

"The money."

"The money doesn't matter. As far as I'm concerned, the information you brought me already was worth the fee. I don't want to see you hurt."

Her answering smile was tremulous, not filled with the usual cocky glint.

"Are you all right? Is your arm hurting?"

"No. I'm all right. Thanks again for last night." With a crooked grin, she added, "And thanks for the new shirt and cloak. I'll repay you—"

"You will not. Those were a gift."

"Well…thanks."

He ran a hand over her cheek and tugged gently at one of the loose tendrils. "Have I mentioned yet that you look very beautiful in that dress?"

"No."

"Well, you do. Absolutely stunning."

"You don't have to say that."

"I mean it."

"It was convenient, that's all. I needed to tell you what was going on."

"Nonetheless, you look devastating. You should find convenient reasons to wear dresses more often." He grinned. "But I can't help wondering where you hide your daggers in that."

"Wouldn't you like to know?"

She answered playfully, some of her usual cocky self-assurance returning.

"Well, now that you mention it…" he said, raising his eyebrows suggestively. When she bit her bottom lip again, his muscles tensed as a fresh wave of desire pounded through his blood and tightened his groin. He leaned in close, wanting to feel her in his arms again, to taste her lips.

Abruptly, she pulled away. "So, the Baron and Baroness Fordin are here for the entire festival?" she asked.

He frowned, desire still clenching his gut, but he answered, "Yes. Queen Sara requested their company. She wanted to see her granddaughter."

"Have you known them long… Lord and Lady Fordin?"

"I've known Kevin for years. Since he first joined the King's Own. Tiya, I met a little over two years ago when I was visiting Fordin with Kevin."

"Does the Lady get one of your flowers?"

The comment startled him. "What makes you say that?"

"I saw the way you looked at her."

"Tiya and I have always been just friends."

"Yeah, well, she may think that," she said, her gaze roving restlessly around the room.

"Victoria, Tiya was in love with Kevin long before I met either of them, and he was in love with her."

When Vic met his gaze, she looked into Jacob's soul. "Doesn't mean you didn't fall in love with her, too."

This time, he was forced to drop his gaze, knowing she saw more than he wanted anyone to see. "That was a long time ago, Victoria. She married my best friend. And I've wanted nothing but the best for them both."

"You don't have to explain it, Marin. Nothing to do with me."

Her tone was casual, detached, and it made something inside Jacob hurt. "So it's Marin again. Last night, you were calling me Jacob."

"I was bleeding." She shrugged.

He laughed against his will. "You're really something, little thief."

"Goes with the job." She grinned crookedly. "I'd better go now. I need to find a very deep hole to disappear into for a little while."

"You're not going to stay at the Winnow?"

She shook her head. "The boss echoed your feeling that maybe someone in the Hole gave me away to Big Charlie. If that's true, it won't be long before they know about our dealings and pay the Winnow a visit."

"At least for tonight, stay there. It'll take them days to track down that room." Jacob's hands clenched hers more tightly, suddenly afraid that he'd never see her again—a completely unacceptable situation.

"I've got other places to go, Marin. Why do you want me at the Winnow?"

"I know you'll be safe there."

"Thanks, but no thanks. Besides, you might need that room this week."

"What's that supposed to mean?" he snapped, more harshly than he'd intended. Her innuendo hit an open wound.

Vic stood, jerking her hands from his. "Nothing. Forget it. See ya around, General."

"Victoria." Jacob stood, but she was already out the door. With a groan, he dropped back on the settee and buried his face in his hands. *You fool. You handled that brilliantly.*

Jacob had spent the last two years trying to deny his feelings for Tiya. The fact that Victoria saw through him so quickly left him feeling defensive and raw. With absolute certainty, however, he also knew that what he felt for Victoria was more than just a passing fancy. The little thief was quickly overshadowing Tiya in his heart, a fact with which he was quite happy.

And then, in a matter of minutes, he'd managed to send her running away.

"You all right, old man?"

He looked up to see Kevin leaning on the doorframe, looking somewhere between amused and concerned. "Yeah," Jacob said, motioning his friend into the room. "Just…"

"You and Victoria have a fight?" Kevin sat next to him.

"What makes you say that?"

"I bumped into her on my way back here. Literally. She looked upset. And you look like a horse that's just lost its apple. So, did you argue?"

"Not exactly. I just stuck my foot in my mouth." Jacob snorted and shook his head. "I don't know what's the matter with me."

"Maybe it's the fact that, for the first time in your life, a woman hasn't fallen at your feet the minute you've shown her the slightest interest."

Jacob looked closely at Kevin for several heartbeats before saying, "Second time."

Kevin stared back for a long moment then nodded. It was a topic they never discussed, but both understood.

Jacob straightened and took a deep breath. "Anyway, why did you come looking for me, boy?" He needed to change the subject.

"I wanted to ask about the guard along the road through Karasnian Forest."

"Between us?"

"Just us."

"Goblins have been seen throughout the forest for the last few weeks. They haven't made any aggressive moves, but we aren't taking chances."

Kevin frowned. "I was going to discuss this with the king later today. We've had goblin sightings in Fordin Forest, as well. There's been nothing in the Hidden Forest, though. And they haven't come near the villages. All of the sightings were accidents."

"Very strange. We've been waiting for a message from Baroness Georna, but I suspect something may be driving them down out of Bthak."

"That would explain why we haven't seen aggression."

Jacob looked thoughtfully at his friend. "Maybe. Maybe not. Come on." He stood. "Let's go talk to King John."

***

"Pfreal?"

Vic stepped out of the shadows at the sound of Ren's voice using the Depnie word for flash. "Hey, Ren." She smiled at the boy and removed the black scarf wrapped around her head and face, tying it snugly around her waist. They met behind the Goddess's shrine, a large stone pyramid near the top of Dareelia.

"Hey, Pfreal." Ren grinned. "Good to see you standing."

"Always, little man. What's the word?"

"Big Charlie's still steaming. But, so far, Gip's been able to put him off a war."

"Does he know who may have sold me out?" Vic leaned against the stone walls of the shrine, her black attire leaving all but her face invisible. A cold wind sang through the air, but the walls provided shelter from most of its sting.

Ren pushed his sandy blond hair behind his ears. "He's not saying if he knows."

"Yeah, well, I can pretty much guess," she snarled.

"You honestly think Brad Ruf would risk a war between the Hole and Big Charlie just to spite you?"

He looked around anxiously then moved into the shadows next to her. He was also dressed from neck to toe in black, but his hair practically glowed in the faint light from the nearby monastery.

"I don't think Ruf counted on me getting away from Charlie's men. Knowing Brad, he probably figured they'd take me to Charlie, who'd either beat the light out of me or turn me into a toy, and he'd get away with a healthy bribe. Killing one of Charlie's men is what's pushed this whole stupid mess this far."

Ren looked closely at her, the worry plain on his young face. The boy wasn't quite thirteen, but already she had to look up to meet his eyes.

"You don't think Charlie will really go through with it, do you?"

His voice suddenly sounded very young. "War? Doubt it. He may be a lot of things, but he's not stupid. Fact is, the Hole is bigger, and the people are better. He'd lose. He's just beating smoke trying to get his way." She patted the boy's shoulder, hoping her words were enough to reassure him. "Any other news?"

"Seems the Ambassador's return to Browan has something to do with internal stuff at one of the temples. Nothing serious, apparently."

"They wouldn't have called him back if it wasn't serious. Anything else?"

"Kritta says the Guild doesn't know about this sorcerer. At least, no one's talking about it. She hasn't found out about the prophecy thing either. And…"

At his hesitation, Vic raised a brow, urging him on.

"Well… Gip didn't tell me to tell you this, but I think you should know…"

"What?"

"Goblins have been seen in the city."

"What?!"

"Yeah. Only they're wearing human clothing and hiding behind heavy cowls. But Barnabas saw them just yesterday afternoon, during the opening ceremony for Autumn's End. Said they were right at the back of the crowd. Three of them.

"He said they looked different from the descriptions. They were taller than he thought they were supposed to be, but he said there was no disguising those faces if anyone had bothered to look. As soon as the king and queen went back into the palace, they all moved away. He tried following, but they disappeared."

"Disappeared?"

"He says they were there and then they weren't."

"That's not good, Ren." Vic frowned and nibbled at her bottom lip. "Any word about Tracker and Malkiney? Anyone been able to get near that building?"

"We haven't been able to get a block yet. And no one's seen Malkiney or the others for the last three days."

"Damn," Vic breathed. "They're connected, Ren. I can feel it. The goblins and this smuggled sorcerer. Someone needs to get into that building to find out what they're up to."

"Don't even think it, Pfreal. You need to stay out of sight. And sneaking into the middle of Tracker's lair without a ward against detection would be suicide. Let Gip take care of it."

She smiled reluctantly at the panic in Ren's hazel eyes. "Not to worry, Ren. I may like a challenge, but I'm not suicidal." *I'll wait 'til I have a ward.* "Thanks for the word, little man. I'd better move."

"See ya soon, Pfreal. Stay standing."

Vic smiled and winked at the boy as she vanished into the dark.

CHAPTER EIGHT

The palace was alight with lamps and candles as the Autumn's End feasting reached a frenzied pitch. Nobles and dignitaries shuffled drunkenly in and out of the banquet hall and reception rooms. Along the city streets, the festivities mirrored the palace. Winter was close at hand. The harvest had been good. The time had come to celebrate.

Vic slipped along the dark castle walls, avoiding the pooled light from the balconies above her head. She'd left her cape behind to allow easier movement and the cold air bit cruelly at her face and uncovered hands. When she'd gone in to see Jacob two days before, she'd memorized as much of the castle's layout as she could. Now, she skulked back to his rooms from the outside.

The balcony to his bedroom was only one story above her head. She blew on her fingertips to warm up her hands. Then, with a skill born of much practice, she scaled the stone walls and slipped soundlessly over the balcony railing. The sitting room looked completely dark, but through a crack in the curtains of his bedroom, she saw the faint flickering of a fire.

Doubt froze her to the balcony. What if he was in there with someone? After seeing him with Lady Tiya two days before, Vic had bundled her fantasies of Jacob Marin and buried them deep inside. Realizing that his heart was already taken by a stunningly beautiful sorceress hurt more than she'd thought possible. Obviously, Vic was nothing more than a way to work off physical needs. And she couldn't accept that from him, from any man. She was nobody's whore. But it came as a shock to realize just how carried away her hopes had been, how much she'd wanted to be more to him.

When they'd talked in his sitting room, she'd tried to hide her hurt feelings behind her street mask of cockiness, but she knew she couldn't keep the hurt out of her gaze. Until she'd heard about the goblins from Ren, she'd resolutely decided not to see Jacob again, an easier option than facing him and keeping her feelings hidden. But the news of goblins disappearing from under Barnabas's nose disturbed her. A lot. Barnabas was the best tracker in Thieves' Hole. For the goblins to have evaded him, they had to have used magic. And that brought Malkiney's smuggled sorcerer to mind.

Fear for her home overrode her own turbulent emotions. Jacob was the only person she knew in a position to do something about the strange happenings. He had to be told.

Taking a deep breath, she braced herself for the worst, determined to take whatever she found with at least an outward show of grace. She edged to the balcony doors and twisted the handle. Locked, of course. Pulling out her thinnest dagger, she silently slid it into the narrow space between the double doors. With a faint click, the handle turned and she slipped into Jacob's bedroom.

He sat slouched in an oversized chair, staring into a low burning fire. On the table beside him, a half empty decanter of wine went unnoticed.

Vic couldn't help grinning. Though she tried to convince herself she was grateful to avoid the embarrassment of finding him in bed with someone, she knew that wasn't the real reason she was glad to find him alone.

Standing silently, she took in her surroundings. Against the wall to her right sat a large four-poster oak bed. Beside the bed, a small table held a single unlit night candle. Other than the two large chairs before the fire to her left, the room's only other piece of furniture was a huge oak wardrobe set against the wall opposite the balcony. Two doors exited the room. One, near the fireplace, led into the sitting room. She couldn't tell where the second, near the wardrobe, went.

Her gaze moved back to Jacob. She was just considering how to attract his attention without startling him when he turned to face her.

"I didn't think I'd see you again," he said, his voice low.

She was so startled by his reaction, she didn't answer for several moments. At last, she mumbled, "I have some news. Something you should know."

He rose and crossed the room to stand in front of her. "First, I want to apologize for snapping the other day. It was uncalled-for. I'm sorry."

She was still too stunned to react as blithely as she wanted to. "Apology accepted."

Looking over her shoulder at the door, he grinned. "You came through that lock rather easily. I think I'll have to talk to the locksmith."

The comment helped Vic regain her composure, and she was grateful. "Wouldn't do you any good, General."

"Hmmm. You make a mockery of my castle security, little thief. I should hire you to train my guard to deal with people like you."

She grinned. "Now, that would take all the fun out of it." His chuckle made her stomach dance, and all at once, Vic was irritated.

Too damned sexy for his own damned good, she thought miserably.

"Would you like a drink, Victoria? The wine is the same we had at the Winnow."

"No, thanks. Listen, I can't stay long—"

"Why not? Charlie won't find you here."

She bit the inside of her lip and stalked around him to the fire. He was making this a lot more difficult than it had to be. Just being in the same room with him made her edgy and uncomfortable. Couldn't he see that? "This is serious, Marin. I just got word tonight that one of the Hole's best trackers spotted three goblins in the city yesterday. At the festival's opening ceremony."

"Goblins inside the city?" All his friendly banter fell away.

"Yeah. And when our tracker tried to follow them, they disappeared. This man is our best. Best tracker in the city not working for the king. And they vanished right out from under him. Now, I don't know what that means to you, but it smells like magic to me, and that brings to mind a certain smuggler's goods."

Jacob began pacing the room, his brow furrowed.

Vic watched in silence. The contained power in his strides started her body trembling despite the heat from the fire. She turned her gaze to the orange flames, annoyed by her inability to be around him without getting goose bumps.

After several more minutes of pacing, Jacob went to the door in his sitting room. Vic listened from the bedroom as he talked quietly with someone in the hall. When he returned, he still looked worried.

"I've doubled the castle guard and sent an alert to the city guard," he said, stepping close. "We may know more by tomorrow morning."

He raised her chin with the side of his hand, forcing her to look into his eyes. "Thank you for bringing me this, Victoria," he whispered.

"You don't need to thank me," she said, stepping back so he was forced to drop his hand. "I don't like the idea of goblins running around the city unchecked."

He didn't allow her to get more than a few feet away before he closed the distance again and pulled her close, holding her near with one hand against the small of her back. Even as her heart thundered blood through her veins and heat raced across her body, her mind whined at being turned into little more than a prostitute.

Defensively, she shoved at his chest and tried not to notice how solidly muscled he felt through his shirt. "What do you think you're doing, Marin?"

"I'm thanking you, Victoria. And I'm apologizing for the other day."

"You did both already." She pushed harder, but he held her tight. "Let go, Marin. I don't want to have to hurt you."

His chuckle rumbled against her hands. When he brought his mouth close to hers, Vic felt her willpower waning. The last thing her body wanted was free of Jacob's embrace. His kiss was so soft compared to the strength in the single arm that held her against his torso, Vic almost forgot to breathe.

As his kiss deepened, Vic's mind suddenly produced an image of Mar parading in front of the Hawk's patrons, then her thoughts leapt to the faces of the whores she knew. Each face held that same emotional distance, the cold, determined separation of body and heart. A separation she knew she couldn't manage.

Roughly, she pushed away from Jacob, retreating to put distance between their bodies. "Listen, Marin," she ground out between clenched teeth. "I'm not here to be your evening's entertainment. Or to help you forget your real love for a few hours. I'm not one of your faithful trollops, at your disposal for the price of a flower every time you need to get laid.

"I came here—against my boss's orders—to give you information I thought important to the realm. If you're not going to take me seriously, you can find out about the damned goblins and magicians yourself!" She spun back toward the balcony doors.

"Enough!"

His bellow ricocheted off the walls. He stopped her just short of the balcony doors, lifted her off the ground and unceremoniously dropped her onto his bed.

She gasped at his rough handling.

"Now, little thief, you're going to sit there and listen very closely while I explain a few things."

She started to launch up, but he leaned against the bed, his hands on the mattress, caging her in. His closeness forced her to lean backward.

"First of all, despite the rumors you may have heard, I do not jump into bed with every woman I meet." He leaned closer. "Second, also contrary to popular opinion, I have never, ever taken any of my affairs lightly or with the casual disregard you seem to think me so readily capable of."

Again, he leaned closer, forcing her back onto her elbows.

"Third, for reasons of which I'm sure we're both quite aware, I've not even attempted an involvement with a woman for over two years—until now. That, plus the fact that I know where you carry at least three of your knives, ensures that I take you very, very seriously."

She stared up into his hard, dark eyes, the set line of his mouth, the slight crease between his brows. And suddenly, she began to giggle. She couldn't help herself. "Which three?" she asked through a grin.

His expression softened, a crooked, sexy smile replacing his serious frown. That look made her heart start to hammer. Hooking one finger into the neck of her shirt, he stood and pulled her into a sitting position at the edge of the bed. They locked gazes as Jacob's hand slid down her right arm. He lifted her elbow and broke eye contact only long enough to slip his free hand under the cuff of her shirt.

"One," he said, pulling her wrist knife from its scabbard. He didn't bother to look when he casually tossed the knife onto the bedside table.

He knelt in front of her between her legs and ran a hand slowly down the outside of her left leg and into the top of her boot.

Vic bit her bottom lip to keep it from trembling as he inched her boot knife up along her calf.

"Two," he whispered.

Her gaze flashed to were the second knife clattered against the first on the table, then snapped back to his face when his hands began moving up her thighs and over her hips. His caress sent a shiver through her entire body. One hand stopped when it reached the small of her back, but the other continued along her spine, easing her forward with gentle but persistent pressure, until her face was no more than an inch from his.

Her skin tingled everywhere his fingers touched, and her stomach clenched. His breath was hot against her mouth. She darted her tongue out to moisten suddenly dry lips, and his eyes darkened as he watched the movement. While his fingers traced fire along her back, the hand at her waist slipped beneath her sash.

"Three."

She didn't look away this time when her knife clattered onto the night table.

"Impressed?" he whispered.

His voice was a husky temptation. She could feel the movement of his lips, a tantalizing brush against her mouth. Her gaze dropped to his full, inviting mouth, then moved slowly back to meet his brown eyes. Grinning mischievously, she said, "You've only found half of them."

"Is that a challenge, Victoria?"

She let him wait for a heartbeat. "Yes."

With a throaty chuckle, Jacob captured her mouth. She threaded her fingers behind his neck, returning his kiss eagerly. Even when he stood to move her farther onto the bed, she wouldn't release her hold on his mouth. She wanted to taste him, feel him, and she was too far gone to care about the consequences. He did things to her body that made it impossible to use her brain. Crawling beside her, his urgent kisses pressed her against the mattress. She felt the beginnings of her descent to a place where only his touch mattered, where only the feel of his body existed, where fear no longer had a place.

Propped on one elbow, he ran his hand over her stomach until his fingers played with the loop holding her sash in place. A gentle tug pulled the sash loose, revealing a fourth knife.

"That one was easy," she said, as he pulled the knife from its sheath at her waistband.

"So the last two are more difficult to find?" He twisted the dagger around until he held the blade's point.

"Um hum."

A wicked glint sparkled in his eyes, as he said, "Good," and tossed the knife over her head.

She turned her head to see the dirk stuck firmly into the wardrobe, hilt quivering from the impact. "You're good at that," she said, astonished.

"That's not the only thing I'm good at."

She met his devouring kiss with a shocked gasp.

Working her fingers into the mass of his thick, dark hair, she urged his mouth closer, reveling in the taste of his kiss, the feel of his tongue dancing against hers, the not unpleasant rub of beard stubble against her skin. Her trembling insides turned to a quivering tension, echoing the dart's hilt. Anticipation pulsed heat across her thighs and clenched at the virgin area between her legs.

His fingers traced a path down her neck and across her chest to hook the top button of her shirt. She gasped against his mouth as he deftly popped open the shirt's first two buttons and ran his fingers across the soft area between her breasts. Pulling back slightly, he looked at her, his eyes wide.

"I would have bet money one of those last two blades was here," he said, drawing patterns on the inner curves of her breasts.

"You forget," she whispered, "I spent most of my time dressed as a boy. Boys don't use breast daggers."

"Of course. But you're not really a boy."

He firmly squeezed her breast to emphasize his point, forcing a low moan past her lips.

He took his time, kissing and teasing her until her nipples were tight pebbles beneath his experienced touch. She'd never realized her breasts could be so sensitive. The flick of his tongue against her skin made her moan. He kept his gaze on her face, the desire in his expression intensifying her pleasure. She wasn't sure how much more of his teasing she could take, but she knew she didn't want him to stop.

Brushing his lips playfully against hers, he breathed, "Where shall we look next?"

As his mouth descended once more to suck and kiss her aching breasts, he popped open the remaining buttons on her shirt, and slid his hand across her bare abdomen to the waistband of her breeches. She gasped as fire laced between her legs. "There aren't any knives there," she panted.

Jacob jerked open the laces holding her breeches closed and said, "I know."

"I thought you were supposed to be hunting for the last two

daggers." Her voice came out in a quiet moan as his hand moved beneath the confines of her breeches.

"Oh, I'll find them. Eventually."

"Wait, Jacob," she choked, taking hold of his questing hand. "I… you should know…I mean…this is my…"

He placed one finger across her lips. "Shh, little thief. I already know. This is your first time."

"You can tell?"

With an embarrassed grimace, he said, "Well, not all of those rumors were complete exaggerations."

Vic bit her bottom lip as she studied his handsome face, then grinned impishly. "Good."

A rumbling groan preceded his hungry kiss. But as his hand moved back down her stomach, she stopped him again. "Find the others first," she challenged.

"Hmmm."

His gaze traveled the length of her body, his expression thoughtful. He stood, still staring at her, and removed his own shirt to reveal the deep cut muscles of his torso. She studied every line of his chest in hungry anticipation, anxious to explore those taut muscles and taste his suntanned skin. She wondered if the rest of him tasted as good as his lips.

Where her feet hung over the edge of the bed, he pulled off her boots. "Five," he said triumphantly, as her second calf dagger was revealed. He removed the knife and tossed it carelessly onto his night table. Then, with exquisitely slow movements, he removed both scabbards.

"One left," she breathed as he crawled back onto the bed, this time laying his body atop hers. Her fingers sought the smooth, hard muscles of his chest and shoulders as he covered her face and neck with hot kisses.

In a single fluid movement, Jacob rolled to his back, pulling her on top of him. His hands wandered up her spine under the loose material of her shirt. Vic pressed her bare breasts against him, no longer interested in waiting for him to discover the sixth knife. The feel of his strong male body, hot and close to her naked skin, left her restless and needy. She rubbed against him like a cat, savoring each new, tantalizing sensation.

She was so lost in the feel of his skin against hers, in the heat shooting through her body, that she didn't notice when his hands pulled her shirt down over her shoulders.

With a conquering shout, he growled, "Six!"

He slid the neck dagger out of its guard and tossed it back over his head. Vic lifted her head. The second dagger had hit the wardrobe within inches of the first. Her eyes widened as she looked back down at him. "Wow."

His chuckle sped the already throbbing pulse of her blood. In seconds, he removed her shirt, the shoulder harness of her last knife, and the scabbard fastened to her wrist. She felt a renewed urgency as he rolled her onto her back again. His caressing hands touched off ripples of pleasure she didn't know possible.

When he removed their last remaining garments and lay atop her, she was nearly mad from desire. A longing unlike any she'd ever felt coursed through her core. The feel of his erection pressed hard against her thigh only heightened her body's cry.

Again she was amazed at the contained strength in his powerful limbs. The same desperate need that filled her also coursed beneath his smooth skin. She could feel it in the flexing bunch of his muscles as her hands scored him and the heat pulsing from his body into hers. Yet his touch was gentle, careful. He didn't rush to fill her, but continued to tease and taunt her body pushing her beyond the realm of thought.

Just when she knew she could take no more, he moved between her thighs to fill her. The ripping of her virgin skin passed with only a flickering of realization, the briefest sting of pain. A last remaining coherent thought reminded her that it should have hurt more, but she was far past caring. Only the press of Jacob's body, the steadily increasing rhythm of their lovemaking found room in her mind. She held him tight, digging her fingers into his shoulders and panting his name.

He brought them both to a pinnacle of urgency, then pressure exploded into shards of exquisite pleasure very close to pain. Through the blinding force of her climax, she heard him call her name, and the last fear she'd hidden behind her desire fled before her happiness. He wasn't thinking of Lady Tiya. His passions were for Victoria.

Long minutes passed before her breathing returned to normal. Jacob continued to kiss and pet her, matching the slowing rhythm of his breathing to hers. When she shivered, he rolled off of her and tugged up the rumpled quilt to cover their cooling bodies. Hugging her into the comfortable curve of his arm, he held her close. She nestled her head on the swell of his chest, tracing her fingertips along his smoothly muscled skin.

"How do you feel?" he whispered into her hair.

"Like a fat cat lying in the sun next to a big bowl of cream," she sighed. His chuckle vibrated across her cheek. She looked up to meet his twinkling gaze. "Why didn't that hurt more?"

"Because, Victoria, I'm also very good at what I do."

She giggled and settled her cheek back on his chest, feeling safe and wholly sated. Her drowsy contentment sent her mind wandering over the events that had brought her to Jacob Marin's bed. When she thought back to her most recent conversation with Ren, she began to giggle again.

"What's so funny, little thief?"

"I was just remembering something a friend said to me tonight. He told me to stay standing." She looked up, grinning at the slight frown between his brows. "I'm not standing now, am I?"

"No," he said, "but we can try that next if you like."

"Jacob," she said in mock offense. Then quite seriously she asked, "Can you do that?"

His hands tightened around her back as he grinned. "I can do lots of things, Victoria."

He kissed away her shocked gasp.

"What does that mean? 'Stay standing'."

"Basically, it means stay alive. Don't let anyone lay you down permanently."

"Good phrase. Very good advice."

A wholly inappropriate rush of pleasure tickled her stomach at the serious, intent look he gave her. This time, she kissed away his worry.

"Say," he pulled back an inch, "what happened to that velvet dress?"

"It's in a safe spot. Why?"

"I really like that dress on you, Victoria. I don't suppose I could talk you into wearing it here again?"

"Mmmm. Maybe with a little persuasion."

His answering kiss began the process of persuasion.

Chapter Nine

That night, Vic slept deeper than she had in years. When her eyes fluttered open, light flooded the room through the balcony doors. And she remembered where she was.

Her body felt the aftereffects of her night of lovemaking as a dull, yet pleasant throbbing. Her lips felt swollen, her nipples sore, and the area between her legs tender. All things considered, she thought with a lazy yawn, she could get used to waking up like this.

The bed was empty. For several minutes, she simply cuddled beneath the quilt and watched the sun pour across the wooden floor. Then she turned over and sat up. Glancing around the room, she noticed the obvious absence of her clothes. When Jacob walked in, she was sitting at the head of the bed frowning at the floor.

"I'm pretty sure I was dressed when I came here last night," she said to his cat's grin.

"You were." He nodded, sauntering to the bed.

"I'm also pretty sure I didn't bother putting them away last night."

"No. You didn't." He sat beside her and kissed her swollen lips.

"Why do you look so guilty?" she asked, eyes narrowing.

"Do I?"

"Yes, you do. What did you do with my clothing, Jacob?"

"I want you to stay here today," he said, changing the subject. "You'll be safe from Charlie's men." He played with a tendril of her hair, not quite meeting her gaze.

"I can't stay here all day."

"Why not?"

"You have to work." She nodded to the gold-edged, green tunic and brown leather pants he wore, the uniform of a King's Own.

"So?"

"So…you won't be here. I'll starve. I can't very well walk down to the royal kitchens for a snack. Especially if you don't produce my clothes."

"Are you hungry?" He stood and disappeared into the sitting room.

"Jacob…"

He strolled back with a tray of breakfast breads, fruit, a steaming pot of coffee and two cups. "Breakfast," he announced, setting the tray on his nightstand.

That was when she noticed her knives were also missing. "Where are my daggers?"

"Safe. Coffee?"

"Jacob, what are you doing?"

"Pouring you coffee."

Her impatience turned into a giggle. "You're a rotten man, Jacob Marin."

"That's not what you said last night." He cast her a knowing look.

"I was delirious. If I'd been in my right mind, I would never have…"

"Never have what?"

She looked into his roguish smile and gave in. "Never mind. I would have anyway. Now, where are my clothes?"

"Safe. Hidden."

"Why did you hide my clothes? I'm going to get cold when I climb out from under this blanket."

"So stay in bed."

"All day?" Her voice rose to an unusually high squeak. Was he crazy?

"There are worse ways to spend the day."

"Jacob!" She flashed him her most pleading expression.

He smiled. "Okay. I didn't want you running off into the city. Not today. To make sure you stayed, I hid your clothes. But don't worry." He leaned in to kiss her. "You can wear one of my shirts to stay warm."

She returned his kiss with feigned reluctance. Actually, she couldn't imagine a more pleasant way to spend her day now that she thought about it. At least, not a more pleasant way to spend the day alone. "You shaved," she said, rubbing the smooth line of his jaw.

"I tend to do that in the morning. Would you like me to grow a beard?"

"No. The stubble was rough enough on my poor mouth. Besides I want to see your face."

"Good, because I don't look very good with a beard."

"I find it hard to imagine you ever not looking good."

"Why, Victoria, you're going to make me blush."

She snorted and kissed him roughly. "I doubt you've done that since you were three." Her playful kiss turned more serious, and soon Jacob was wrapping her in his arms.

He pulled away slowly, his arms still cradling her. "I have to go."

She nodded, disappointed, and bit her bottom lip. To her surprise, he growled and pulled her tight, capturing her mouth in a hungry kiss. Feeling a bit vengeful after his morning of teasing, she pushed back and said, "You'll be late."

He didn't let her get away so easily. As his mouth moved down over her neck and across her shoulders, she tried again. "Won't the king mind?"

"Yes, he will." But Jacob didn't stop kissing her. When his mouth moved to her ear, he whispered, "And if you continue to bite your bottom lip like that, the king will probably end up quite angry with me."

"I'm sorry," she said, honestly concerned that she'd done something wrong.

"Don't be sorry," he breathed against her neck then looked into her eyes. "Remember it. I've just given you a hint as to how to manipulate me."

"Really? But if you know that I know, will it still have any effect?" Without realizing it, she bit her bottom lip again and looked up with raised brows as she thought about this comment.

He groaned low in his throat. "Yes, you little minx, the trick will still have the same effect."

To prove his point, he crushed her against him, his kiss hard and overwhelming. She forgot about teasing him or reminding him that he had to leave. She didn't want him to leave. She melted into his embrace, meeting his kisses with hungry longing.

Before she realized what he was doing, Jacob had thrown aside the covers and was pushing her back onto the bed. He continued to ravage her mouth and neck with unrelenting lips while he pushed aside just enough of his own clothing to free his erection. Vic, overwhelmed by the yearning he touched in her so quickly, arched her back to meet his hot mouth as he plundered the sensitized skin of her breasts.

When he slipped inside her, the feeling was so intense, she moaned loudly. His contained power, only hinted at the night before, cracked through his self-imposed restraints, and she marveled at the raw energy beneath her groping hands, filling her deepest void, knowing she saw only a glimpse of his strength. To be touched by that energy was to be singed by lightning.

Her climax came furious and fast. She could do no more than hold tight to Jacob, the only solid object in her realm of senses. A cry ripped from her throat as he gave her body release. His own ragged groan followed close behind, and she felt him shudder with the intensity of his own orgasm.

In the aftermath, still panting to get her breath back, all she could think or say was, "Wow."

The feel of his cheek rising in a smile forced her to grin. After a few minutes, he rolled off of her and rearranged his uniform. He sat on the edge of the bed, staring at her for a long moment.

"Will you get in trouble?" she asked. Out of habit, she almost bit her lip again, but stopped herself.

Jacob smiled, touching her bottom lip with the tip of one finger. "Worried?"

"No." With a crooked frown she said, "I'm hungry actually."

He leaned in close and kissed her cheek. "Enjoy your breakfast, Victoria." He stood, still holding her hand.

His reluctance to leave touched her heart.

"I'll have one of the servants draw you a bath in a little while. The washroom is through the door." He pointed to the door near the wardrobe.

"You have a private washroom? I thought they saved that for dignitaries and high-ranking nobility."

"One of the benefits of being a general. Feel free to rummage through my wardrobe for a shirt. But don't you dare try to sneak away. I want you waiting when I return this afternoon."

"Well…okay." She didn't turn to the waiting breakfast tray until she'd heard the suite's door close.

* * *

"General Marin," King John greeted as Jacob walked into the king's study that afternoon. When the door closed behind, King John broke into a huge grin. "You have a good night, Jacob?"

"Sire?" He sat in a chair across the desk from his king.

John leaned forward in his own seat, resting his elbows on the documents and correspondence strewn across his desk. "Yesterday, you spent the entire day looking forlorn beneath your business mask. Today, you look…pleased."

Jacob could only stare. He had no idea how to respond to His Highness's shockingly accurate insight.

"Don't look so surprised, Jacob. I'm not so busy being king that I don't take the time to notice what goes on around me." With a slight smile, he asked, "Is she pretty?"

"Yes, Majesty," Jacob admitted with a crooked grin. "She's… special."

"Good. It's about time."

Once again, he was shocked speechless by his king's remark. He raised his brows in question, but the king waved away the topic.

"Now for business." he said more seriously. "The city guards had no sign of goblins either last night or today."

"My source is a reliable one, Majesty."

"I've no doubt of that, Jacob. I also have no doubt there's magic involved. Queen Sara sent word to the Magic Guild, requesting any information they might have. She's also studying her own texts. Right now, I can't imagine a reason for goblins to enter a human city in human clothing and without attacking anyone! What are the reports from the guard along the Karasnian Forest road?"

"They've reported seeing individual goblins or groups of twos and threes, very like the ones Baron Fordin described around Fordin

Forest, but they haven't attempted to come near any of the travelers. We've also had no complaints from the citizens living in the forest."

"Very strange, indeed. Goblins. No aggression toward human populations. Yet they wander in my city. And disappear without a trace. We need to get to the bottom of this, Jacob. There's something very serious going on under my nose. I don't like it."

"Yes, Majesty."

"Have we any word on that smuggled sorcerer? I believe you're right to assume the appearance of this magician and the goblins are connected."

"A situation has arisen, Majesty, that prevents my spy from getting close to the building."

"If it's a matter of a magic block, you've my permission to use royal funds to purchase one yourself. My Lady Queen mentioned they're quite costly and hard to find."

"Her Majesty is correct, Sire. However, I have a source. It's just that…" Jacob hesitated. How could he tell his king that he was placing the safety of Victoria above the safety of the realm?

"I see," John said, settling back in his chair. "You're worried about your spy. She must be very special, indeed."

Jacob shook his head ruefully. "Majesty, your insight never ceases to amaze me. I do believe your queen has given you her secret for reading minds."

"We can arrange for another spy, Jacob. There are others of that profession in Dareelia. But I need to know more about this sorcerer. The Magic Guild can give me little more than hesitant maybes. I need facts. If we have a blood magician in Dareelia and that magician is somehow working with or using goblin strength, it's imperative that I know of it."

"Yes, Majesty." Jacob rose to his feet, standing at attention. "May I have the rest of the day before deciding? I'd like to discuss the situation with my spy. Whether I like it or not, I do believe she's best qualified for this particular job. I'll also need time to procure the magic block."

"Of course."

King John fell silent and studied Jacob for several minutes.

Jacob remained at attention, keeping his inner struggle out of his expression.

"I'll expect an answer by tomorrow morning," the king said finally. "If your spy is unable to perform this task, we'll select a new one and I'll require you to inform that person of the entire situation."

"Yes, Majesty."

The king dismissed Jacob with a nod and a slight smile.

All the way back to his rooms, Jacob argued with himself. He had no doubt that Victoria was good enough to get into Tracker's building. But he'd seen the things a blood magician could do. And he wasn't entirely sure Victoria was safe on the streets, period. Yet, with a situation this crucial, could he trust someone less familiar with the streets and Tracker?

As he neared his door, he decided that if he could arrange the world to his bidding, Victoria would stay safe and sound in his room while another took the risks. He also realized that, in the end, the choice was entirely hers.

When he entered the sitting room, he found her at the desk set against the wall near his bedroom door, shuffling a deck of cards. His cream silk shirt, the only clothing she wore, covered her body to mid-thigh but left the rest of her lean legs exposed. Her hair was carelessly tossed across her shoulders and, before she noticed him, her face was set in a slight frown as she studied the cards.

The image sent an immediate shock of lust through him, tightening his groin and drying his mouth. Never in his life had a woman set off such an intense physical reaction. Always before, he'd experienced a slow building of his desire. But with Victoria, his passion flared with the speed of an angry forest fire.

He was still staring, breathless, when she turned her head and noticed him. Her welcoming grin was almost more than he could stand.

"You're early," she said.

"I… if you dare bite your lip right now, I'll not be held responsible."

With a heavy sigh, she rose from the chair. "Close the door," she said, as she sauntered toward him.

He couldn't take his gaze away as he shut the door.

"How was your day?"

She stopped before him, so close the scent of the soap she'd used for her bath lapped around him, teasing his senses. "All right. What scent is that?"

"Honeysuckle. You like?"

"Yeah, I like."

Her fingers traced the front of his tunic and stopped at his scabbard belt. With a speed that startled him, she unfastened it and set the sword gently aside. "Thank you for sending lunch," she murmured.

"You're welcome." His breath quickened as her fingertips drew patterns along his chest. "You look remarkable in my shirt."

"Thank you. It's very comfortable. However…" She dropped her head back to meet his gaze. "It's suddenly become just a little too hot in here."

His self-control shattered. He scooped her into his arms, kissing her hard as he carried her to the waiting bed. Setting her on the edge of the bed, he stripped off his tunic in one fluid movement while she worked on the lacings of his breeches. "They're knotted," she said with a frustrated moan.

He growled, ripped the laces open and stepped out of the breeches.

Vic looked up, wide-eyed, as he lowered them both onto the mattress. "Jacob," she breathed.

He tore aside the borrowed shirt she wore, too intent on baring flesh to bother with delicacy.

"You just ripped leather ties with your bare hands."

"I have more," he said against her neck. When he felt her trembling, he stopped nuzzling her throat and pushed back to look into her face, suddenly worried that he'd frightened her. Looking into her eyes, though, he didn't see fear. Her passions burned as hot as his own. She captured his mouth roughly, and he set aside further worry.

Despite his urgency, Jacob found himself delaying their joining to explore her body in the daylight that flooded the room. He kissed and petted, nipped and sucked every sensitive area of her body until she writhed beneath him. And he marveled at her uninhibited eagerness. She gave herself to him completely and took with abandon the pleasures he gave, returning the delights as willingly.

When she began to moan for release and his own need could no longer be delayed, he plunged into her, gasping at the tight feel of her smooth skin wrapped intimately around him. With an almost inhuman self-control, he held his own release at bay until he felt her body convulse, heard her ardent cries. Only then did he abandon himself to his climax, clutching her tight and panting her name.

For long moments after, he held her close, not wanting to separate their bodies. He continued to kiss her honeysuckle-scented skin until her breathing slowed.

"I think I could get use to this, Jacob Marin," she whispered against his mouth.

"You just may have to, Victoria Flash."

"Good." She took hold of one of his hands and studied his palm.

"Not even a mark. How is that possible? You shouldn't just be able to rip leather without so much as a mark to show for it."

"You bring out the beast in me."

"Well…I guess I could get use to that, too." She grinned and bit at his chin. "So, did you return early just to make me exceedingly happy or was there a particular reason?"

"'Exceedingly happy'? I like the way that sounds. Unfortunately, this is only one of the reasons I'm back early, but I don't want to discuss the second reason yet. How was your day?"

"Fine. I rummaged through everything you own. Which is surprisingly little considering you're not a poor man."

"I'm used to traveling light."

"And I sat through sly grins from the servants."

He frowned. "I'm sorry—"

"Don't be," she cut off his apology. "I've never been waited on before, at least not without first laying down a stack of kern, so I suppose it was a fair exchange. Although, I'd like something more than a shirt to wear next time."

"Oh, but Victoria, you look so good in my shirt."

"Yes, and you see where that got us."

Her impudent grin made him laugh.

"Besides, I think you've turned that shirt into a rag. If we keep this up, you won't have any shirts left."

When he raised his eyebrows at the possibility, she shook her head.

"I'm *not* walking around this place naked, Jacob Marin."

He sighed dramatically. "Very well. If you insist." With a grin, he rolled onto his back.

Vic shifted up onto one elbow and draped one leg across his thigh. She ran her fingers in a caress along his jaw and over his neck.

As her fingers passed his lips, he captured them and kissed each tip gently. "Where did you find the cards?" he asked, remembering how he'd found her.

"They were buried behind some stuff in your wardrobe. Do you want to play a game?"

"With you, little thief? I'm not sure that would be healthy for my money purse."

"We don't have to play for money."

"What did you have in mind?"

"Hmm. Well, if I win, I get my daggers back."

"And if I win?"

"Your choice."

"Anything?"

"Anything. Equivalent to the worth of my knives."

He tapped her fingers against his lips as he thought. "The possibilities… Okay, if I win, we go get that velvet dress tonight—"

"Deal."

"And… I buy you another dress."

Her eyes widened and her mouth gaped. "Another? But why?"

"I already told you, I like the way you look in dresses. And if you do have to move around during the day, Big Charlie's men will be less likely to spot you if you're dressed in finery." He grinned at the shock in her expression.

"Jacob, I can't let you do that."

"You're not 'letting' me do anything. You're going to play me for it. I could lose."

"That hardly seems like a fair bet. If you win, you buy me something."

"Since when have you been concerned with fair, little thief?"

"All right, General. If you want to risk throwing away your money, that's your choice. But you're gonna have to win first." She leaned on his chest and shot him a cocky grin. "And I really want my knives back."

Jacob rose and went to the sitting room for the deck of cards. When he walked back into the bedroom, Vic had propped herself up on a pile of pillows against the headboard, her chin resting on raised knees, her gaze wandering over his naked body with undisguised pleasure. Under her brazen look, Jacob's lust flared anew. He sat facing her and kissed her roughly before saying, "You're not allowed to distract me, little thief. No lip biting, no accidental brushing against me."

"If you insist," she sighed.

But the look in her eyes was enough to distract Jacob.

"Would you like to deal?"

He groaned, but shuffled the cards. She kept her gaze locked with his as he dealt, one side of her mouth turned up in an expression he found almost as enticing as when she bit her lip. This time, however, he kept his lust under control. Jacob wanted to win this game. His answering grin held all the seduction at his disposal. He wasn't without talent in that arena.

Vic didn't break eye contact until after she'd raised her cards in front of her face. Jacob glanced at his hand then looked back into her eyes.

"Two," she said huskily, laying two discards facedown on the bed between them.

He dealt her two new cards from the top of the deck then laid down a single card from his own hand. She watched his hands closely as he took a new card.

Her expression never altered.

Neither did his.

She studied his face for a long moment then splayed her cards face up on the bed. "Queen's Run," she said, a note of triumph in her voice.

Only two other hands could beat her.

He glanced down at his hand then met her gaze again, never dropping his seductive half smile. "Devil's High," he answered.

Her eyes flared wide and her chin dropped. "How?" she demanded. "That's impossible. You cheated!"

He chuckled contentedly as he collected the cards. "You were watching my hands, little thief. When did I cheat?"

"You must have cheated. There's no way you just happened to draw a Devil's High."

"I seem to remember someone pulling three in one night."

"Yes, but I was cheating!"

The outrage painting her features started Jacob laughing.

"What's so funny, you cheat? I notice you failed to mention being good at this game before we started to play."

"You never asked, little thief."

She crossed her arms under her breasts and stuck out her bottom lip.

He tossed the cards onto the floor and tugged her close. "Now, what color dress would you like?" he asked.

"Purple," she said, still pouting.

He grinned and captured her mouth with his, kissing away her pout and answering the fiery hunger her open stare ignited. After again giving his body a temporary peace from her seductive presence, he cuddled her in his arms, lazily drawing circles on her back.

She ran one hand over his thigh, tracing the line of a long jagged scar. "How did you get this?" she asked, her voice quiet and sleepy.

"A boar. During a hunt. My horse…tripped, and I was thrown into the path of the beast."

"Goddess! Jacob, you're lucky you weren't killed."

"Kevin happened to be nearby at the time. He took care of the boar for me."

"Baron Fordin?"

"Um hum. It happened during a visit to the barony."

"When?"

"Just over two years ago."

"Wasn't that around the time Prince Erick tried to kill the king?"

"Just before, actually."

Vic moved closer, nestling her cheek against his chest. "I'm glad you weren't hurt worse," she whispered.

Touched by the feeling in her voice, he kissed the top of her head and squeezed her tight. "You know," he said into the tangled curls of her hair, "you're the first person besides the healer to see that scar."

Her head shot around to look him in the eyes. "Really?"

He nodded, watching her face as the reality of what he said sank in. "Did you think I was lying last night when I said that I hadn't been involved with another woman in two years?"

"I…I thought you meant a serious relationship. I didn't think you meant…"

She stared at him, mouth slightly open. Jacob felt her heart pounding against his side. Then she moved forward and kissed him, conveying emotions she couldn't utter. He hugged her tight, his own kiss willing her to understand the way she affected him, to understand how much she meant to him already.

For a long time, he simply held her, not wanting anything to alter their mood. As quickly as she'd been able to move Tiya from his thoughts, she was becoming an imperative part of his life, a part he could no longer imagine living without. The two days that had passed when he wasn't sure if he'd ever see her again had been a torment he didn't want to repeat. That made bringing up the king's request a physically painful act.

"Victoria," he whispered when he could no longer excuse further delay, "I have something I need to discuss with you."

"The second reason you came back early?"

"Yes. The king needs someone to get into Tracker's building, to find out what the magician is up to. I have access to someone who can provide a magic block, but...."

She levered up on one elbow and forced him to look into her eyes.

"When can you get me the block?"

Chapter Ten

Victoria, you don't have to do this," Jacob said, squeezing her shoulders. "It isn't an order from the king. Even the Hole doesn't want you near that building. And, to tell you the truth, I hate the idea of sending you in there alone. All you have to do is say no and we'll find someone else." He knew he sounded desperate, but he couldn't seem to keep his voice even.

"Someone who knows Tracker's men, the building, the magician's face, the city streets?" She smiled gently. "I'm your best chance of getting in, getting the information and getting out unnoticed, Jacob."

He ran a hand into her hair, mentally hunting for an excuse to keep her away from danger. It didn't matter that danger had always been a part of her life. This was different. He didn't stop to analyze exactly why. "What about Big Charlie?"

"I can avoid Big Charlie for two nights."

"Two?"

"One to watch. One to enter. I know it's unusual for me, but I don't want to take any chances."

Jacob frowned, knowing she was right, and not liking it one bit. "I don't want you to do it," he said sullenly.

A smile played at her lips. "Good. But I'll do it anyway. When do we go for the block?"

"Tonight. After it gets dark. If we're going to go wandering around town, I want you well hidden in shadows."

"Whatever you say, General. Does that mean I get my clothes and daggers back?"

"Yes, you little thief," he said, slapping her lightly on the bottom. "And, since I won our card game, we'll also be stopping to pick up that dress."

"Of course." She grinned. "I never back out on my bets."

They stayed to the shadows until they reached the brothel. Vic wore one of Jacob's short cloaks over her own black attire, pulling up the hood to hide her face. Strangely, she felt safe with Jacob at her side. Even out of uniform, he was an intimidating figure. Most people they passed on the streets kept their distance.

The Flaming Rose was one of the more prosperous brothels in Dareelia with a flamboyant façade. Across the glowing red and orange roses decorating the front of the building, red-tented lamps burned brightly. Sparkling gold-colored paint flashed between the lamps, glittering in the light. Each window boasted myriad colored gauzy curtains, giving passersby tantalizing silhouettes and hints of the pleasures to be had inside. Vic had never met any of the Flaming Rose's girls, but their reputation had spread far and wide.

From one of the curtained upper windows, a scantily clad red-haired woman hung over a banister, chatting with prospective clients. When the woman saw Jacob walking toward the building, she whistled out a greeting. "Well and well, stranger. And how are you this fine chilly evening?"

"I'm doing great, Fanda," Jacob called up. "How's your night?"

"Slow, General. How 'bout coming to my room and speeding it up for me?"

"Fanda, you're a tease."

"Ha! You're the only man in this town as would say so. What brings you 'round after so long?"

"Business."

"Ah, so you will be helping one of us through the evening?"

"Sorry, Fanda. Not that kind of business." Jacob ushered Vic through the beaded curtain leading to the Rose's common room.

From behind, Vic heard Fanda tsking above the street, "Waste of a perfectly good customer."

She looked up at Jacob as she passed beneath the beads. "So you come here often?" She couldn't quite manage to hide the jealous edge in her voice.

He shrugged and smiled.

She glanced around the common room, still frowning. Couches and cushions of every color and size lay scattered about the floor. Bright gold and silver tassels and stars accented the furnishings, most of which were of rich silk or satin. From the ceiling hung three huge chandeliers, their layers of cut crystals reflecting rainbows of dusky light onto the room. The air was heavy with the scent of smoke and alcohol overlaid by a strong layer of rich perfume. Barely clad women lounged about the room, waiting for their next customer. Even as Vic watched, two moved to the back staircase with men draped around them.

She didn't have but a moment to study her surroundings before they were accosted by a large, gaudily clad, older woman with dyed black hair and garish paint decorating her white features.

She squealed loudly and pulled Jacob into an air-stealing embrace. "If it isn't the generous and lovely Jacob Marin," she exclaimed in a sultry, accented voice. "What's kept you away so long, honey? The girls have missed you something fierce."

"Good evening, Xanthia." Jacob smiled. "I'm afraid this is a business trip."

"Well, it's about time. Who's the lucky girl?"

"Wrong business, Xanth."

"What a shame. The girls are gonna be mighty disappointed. Again. Well now, and who's this you have with you?"

The woman's eyes widened as Vic dropped the cloak's hood.

"Xanthia, this is a very special friend of mine, Victoria Flash. Victoria, this is Madam Xanthia, the foremost madam in Dareelia."

"Jacob, you are a flatterer." Xanthia's gaze flicked back to Vic and her brow furrowed. "Flash. You have a brother, girl? A gambler?"

She grinned and shook her head. "No. I'm the gambler. Everyone but Jacob calls me Vic."

"Well, now," the woman breathed. "Jacob, you've brought us a celebrity. Many's the night some poor sot's come to our humble house to find comfort in the arms of one of my girls after losing most of his purse to a young gambler by the name of Vic Flash. My girl, you're the nemesis of every player who frequents this place."

She ducked her head and shrugged, unreasonably pleased to know her reputation had spread. "What can I say? I'm very good at what I do."

"Aren't we all, girl?" Xanthia gave her a knowing, conspiratorial grin before returning her attention to Jacob. "And how did you two meet? Did she take all your money, too? Or did you come to her rescue?"

Jacob's brow furrowed. "Actually, neither."

"Vic." Xanthia turned back to the gambler, enthusiasm making her heavy bosom bounce with the movement. "Did you know that Jacob here is one of the greatest heroes of our time? He came to our rescue one evening when several of our gentlemen callers insisted on service without paying. Well, of course, I can't have that now, can I? But the situation was becoming violent, and Regina was already dealing with trouble we'd had earlier in the evening. Then in walks this hunky figure of a man. He took care of all five of those boys in a matter of minutes." Xanthia smiled fondly at the King's Own. "He's been a favorite here ever since. The girls adore him. Unfortunately, we can't get him to partake of the eager gratitude we'd so like to show him. He wouldn't even have to pay."

Vic hid her chuckle behind a cough. Jacob smiled sheepishly and shrugged. The twinge of jealousy that had been pestering Vic since walking into the Flaming Rose dimmed and a trickling of relief, which she refused to think about, washed through her.

"Oh, but enough reminiscing." Xanthia sighed. "You're here on business. Follow me."

She led them through a series of doors to a back office. The room was surprisingly plain compared to the lush decorations of the common room. Unadorned paneled walls, a thick maroon rug over a clean wooden floor, a simple set of mirror-backed sconces on the wall behind a simple mahogany desk. The scents of alcohol and smoke were faint in the office, all but gone. Perfume still coated the air, but it was subtle and exotic, tantalizing instead of overpowering.

Xanthia indicated two large leather chairs before taking a seat behind the desk. "Now, what can I do for you, General?"

"I need a magic block," Jacob said. "One that will block a spy from any kind of magic detection."

Xanthia shook her head and pursed her lips. "We have a few on hand, Jacob, but they won't do more than block a magician's sight. They won't protect your spy from magic if discovered by other means."

"I won't be discovered by other means," Vic said.

Xanthia looked at her, then back to Jacob, a strange questioning gaze that Vic couldn't begin to answer.

At last, the madam said, "Very well, then." She pulled a long velvet cord at the side of her desk. A moment later, a powerfully built young woman walked in. Two swords crossed her back and brown leather clung tightly to her muscular shape. "Regina, could you get Cecily, please? And have her bring her little black bag if you would."

Regina nodded, her face an unresponsive mask, and left the room.

"Now." Xanthia turned back to Jacob and Vic. "Cecily should have what you're looking for."

"Thank you, Xanth," Jacob said. "How much will it cost?"

"Well, I can think of all kinds of ways for you to repay me." She pointedly perused him, then looked back into his eyes. "But, as I suspect you're bent on financial recompense, I'll have six hundred gold kern."

Vic gasped. "Six hundred?"

"Magic blocks are expensive." Jacob shrugged. "And the good ones are hard to come by. Six hundred it is, Xanth. I suspect I'm getting a discount."

"Don't let that get around or every young gallant in the city will think they can win a discount with a sexy smile."

Jacob grinned at the woman, then looked at Vic. He took her hand and squeezed gently, his gaze downcast to where their hands locked together.

She returned his gesture, trying to reassure him. She knew he was still worried about her, could see it in the tight lines around his eyes and mouth, and it made her heart beat a little faster. Having someone worrying about her was enticing. But unusual.

From the corner of her eye, she noticed Xanthia silently studying her and Jacob. She turned a questioning look back to the madam, but the older woman merely smiled as if she knew something Vic didn't. Frowning, she loosened her hold on Jacob's hand but didn't drop his grip.

When Regina returned, she was accompanied by a woman very close to Vic's age. Her auburn hair piled atop her head in an intricate pattern before tumbling halfway down her back. White gauze and silk covered her entire body, but somehow gave the impression she was unclothed. Compared to Regina, Cecily was a tiny waif.

The guard closed the door as she left, leaving Cecily digging in her black bag while the other three watched. "What do you need, Madam Xanthia?" she asked, pulling her face from the contents of her bag.

She had a pleasant, singsong voice that reminded Vic of wind chimes.

"Magic block," Xanthia said. "Something convenient for a spy."

"Block from magic detection or from spells?"

"Do you have one to protect from spells?" Jacob asked, leaning forward in his chair.

"Nope. Sorry, General. Had to sell the last one I had about two months ago and haven't been able to get my hands on another one since. But I do still have a few to block from detection. If your spy is any good, it'll be all he needs."

"It will be all I need," Vic said.

Cecily raised a brow, her eyes widening, then shrugged and dug back into her bag.

"Here we are." She produced a small, round black onyx hung on a black painted wire on a black leather thong. "This should do just fine. It'll block your presence from even the most powerful sorcerer's detection spells, and the black leather should keep it from making noise or catching light."

She handed the stone to Vic. "Wear it around your neck; the stone needs to be near your throat to work properly. And remember, it won't work if you're detected by more mundane methods. All it does is blind a sorcerer's magic to your presence." She grinned as she watched Vic study the charm. "That's a good stone there," she said. "Be careful with it. It's one of the few blocks you can get that doesn't leave a hole in a magician's senses. Might as well not have a block for all the good those kind will do you, leaving this big old black hole. Might as well stand and shout, 'Here I am.'"

"Thank you, Cecily," Jacob said quietly.

"Anything for you, General." She nodded to all three and left the room.

"Well now," Xanthia said, "you've got yourselves the best magic ward on the market." She stood and crossed to the other side of the desk. Jacob and Vic both stood, preparing to leave, when Xanthia placed a hand on Vic's elbow. "Jacob, would you mind if I had a quiet talk with your young spy here?"

Jacob's brow furrowed, but he said, "No. I'll be outside when you're through. Thanks again, Xanth. The kern will be here by tomorrow night."

"I know you're good for it, honey, so don't you worry your beautiful head. Now, you go and keep my girls company, and I'll send Flash along in just a minute."

When Jacob closed the door, Xanthia turned to Vic.

The speculative look in the woman's blue eyes made Vic stiffen, her own gaze narrowing. Her fingers twitched toward one of her knifes.

"Now, honey," Xanthia started, a hesitant note in her voice, "I know this may be none of my business, but woman to woman, are you and the general on intimate terms?"

For a full minute, Vic stared at the madam and couldn't think of one thing to say. She hadn't been expecting anything like that kind of question. Heat flooded her cheeks, leaving her suddenly shy, though she couldn't explain why she felt so awkward. She was talking to a madam, for Goddess sake! Too disconcerted to answer any other way, she blurted the truth, "I suppose you could say that."

Why was she embarrassed? It was her life after all and none of this woman's business if she was sleeping with Jacob or not! Other women had lovers. And she sure as hell wasn't the first lover Jacob had ever had. Maybe it was the other woman's knowledge of Jacob's reputation that embarrassed her. Did Xanthia think she was another one of his conquests? Did she care what the other woman thought?

Was she just another one of his conquests?

She pushed that fear aside. It didn't matter. She'd gone to Jacob's bed of her own free will and fully knowing his past. She accepted that what they had was probably temporary. But that didn't mean she should be embarrassed about enjoying their affair now. So what if Xanthia knew she and Jacob were intimate.

For some reason, though, she still felt like fidgeting under Xanthia's steady gaze.

"Again," Xanthia continued after a quiet pause, "I don't mean to pry, but you're so young and, though I've no idea of your experience, I suspect that, seeing as how you've spent a goodly number of years masquerading as a boy, that the general is one of your first lovers. Am I right?"

"How could you possibly guess that?" Vic's discomfort over the conversation grew right along with the knot in her stomach. She had to work hard to keep from shuffling her feet.

"Honey, I've seen more young women in the throes of their first passion than you could possibly imagine. There's a look to it if you know what to look for."

Vic frowned and the woman smiled and patted her arm.

"Don't worry. There's not very many of us that do know what to look for. And not a one of us would ever give your secret away. Now, the reason I bring this up is to ask if you're trying to get pregnant or if, at this time, that would be something you'd like to avoid."

"Actually, I hadn't much thought about it." The possibility hadn't even entered into her thinking when she'd fallen into bed with Jacob the night before. Panic started trickling into her bloodstream. "I don't think it would be a good idea for me to get pregnant, though." Now that Xanthia mentioned it, she was absolutely terrified by the idea. The last thing she needed in her life was a baby. She didn't know the first thing about them. She hadn't exactly had a maternal figure to show her the way of things. Vic's mouth dried at the possibility that she might already have gotten herself pregnant. The implications of that kind of mistake made her palms sweat. Goddess, what had she done?

"Honey, this isn't a problem at all."

Xanthia squeezed her shoulders, forcing Vic to look her in the eyes. At the compassion she saw in Xanthia's expression, her panic subsided, leaving room for thought again. She took a deep breath and, after a moment, nodded her head.

The madam smiled. "There are certain things a woman can do to prevent the unexpected." Xanthia crossed around to her desk and produced a small wooden box. "Here now. Take one of these little pills every day and you'll have no trouble. When and if you do decide you'd like to have a child, simply stop taking the pills."

At her quizzical stare, the woman smiled again. "Now what kind of a business would I have if my girls kept getting pregnant on me? There's a powder that most of us use. You mix it with water. It has the same effect, but the drink tastes a bit chalky. I can't get my girls to swallow it regularly. The pills, though much harder to come by and a lot more expensive, are much easier on the palate."

Vic's surge of panic evaporated, leaving her lightheaded with what she could only consider a near escape. "Thank you," she said, sighing heavily, her discomfort dissolving into gratitude. "How much do I owe you?"

"This first batch is on the house, honey."

"Why?"

"Well, let's just say I have a soft spot for anyone who can swindle more men than me. And I'm fond of the general. I can see he cares for you a great deal. So, despite my jealousy, I want to smooth the way for you both."

Vic felt something strange twisting in her stomach, an emotion she couldn't quite put a name to. "Thank you very much, Madame Xanthia. This was…unexpected, but very much appreciated."

"Think nothing of it. Just be good to the general. And be careful with this spying business."

As Vic walked toward the office door, Xanthia stopped her with one last comment.

"When you need more of those little pills, you just come by and see me. I've got a good supply and I'll give you a discount." She winked and waved goodbye.

In the dim hallway, Vic stuck the little box inside her shirt and tied the magic charm around her neck, marveling at the madam's generosity. Jacob had the strangest effect on people. She turned toward the common room. She wasn't used to strangers being generous and knew that generosity sprang from her association with the King's Own. The thought left her mildly uncomfortable, but she couldn't say why.

She entered the gaudy commons, still sorting through the myriad emotions churning in her gut, to see Jacob sitting on a couch, surrounded by all of the women in the room without customers. He was talking pleasantly with them, a friend among friends. The women, on the other hand, were raptly listening to his every word, giggling and commenting in all the appropriate places, each vying for his attention. She stood in the hallway, watching in stupefied awe. Her initial resurgence of jealousy was quickly quelled, replaced by mild amusement, when she noticed how oblivious he was to their fawning.

When he looked up and noticed her, he disentangled himself from the disappointed mass of femininity to join her. "I didn't mean to pull you away from your admirers," she said through a crooked smile.

"I'm sure they wanted to get back to work anyway. What did you and Madam Xanthia have to discuss?"

She hesitated. She wasn't comfortable enough with her own feelings on the matter to discuss the conversation with Jacob. She didn't want to know what his reaction might be, either to her getting pregnant or to the madam's preventative aid. She shrugged and forced her face into a mysterious smile. "Women things," she said and headed for the front door. Jacob followed, taking her arm as they walked out into the street. She pulled up the cowl to cover her face as they turned toward the castle.

"Well, woman," Jacob leaned down to whisper in her ear. "What do you say we go find that velvet dress?"

The heat of his breath against her ear sent a delicious shiver along the length of her spine. She pulled him into a side alley, glancing around quickly to confirm they were alone. Then she kissed him hard, loving the taste of his lips. If she understood nothing else, she understood the way he made her pulse speed, the way his mouth pressed against hers made her feel warm all over, the way the feel of him beneath her hands made her hungry for more. She understood passion. For the moment, she told herself as she reluctantly pulled away from his kiss, she could be very happy with passion. "I'll meet you back at the castle," she murmured, starting toward the opposite end of the alley.

"Wait." He took hold of her arm. "We'll go together. I don't want you running around the streets alone."

She smiled and patted his hand. "I've been running around the streets alone my entire life. I won't be long."

"Victoria…"

"Jacob, I told you already, my hiding places would be less than useless if I revealed where they were to just anyone."

"But I'm not 'just anyone.'"

"I'll be back before you have time to miss me."

"I'll miss you the second I can't see you anymore."

"I like the way that sounds," she said, grinning as she melted into his kiss. Then, true to her name, she slipped out of his grasp before he could tempt her further and disappeared into the shadows, knowing he wouldn't dare shout after her.

The hiding spot of her dress and cape was actually close to the Flaming Rose, in the basement of an abandoned housing building where she'd found a warm place to stay out of sight. No one, not even Ren, knew the location, making it her safest refuge.

She'd recovered the dress and was starting back toward the castle when a shifting of shadows caught her curious gaze. Ducking into a doorway, she watched as three shapes emerged from an alley into the dimly lit backstreet near her abandoned nest. Two of the shapes were covered by heavy, black, hooded cloaks, but the purple flashes of clothing beneath their capes gave ample evidence of their identities.

The third figure stopped her breath. He faced her briefly and a shock of long white hair and blazing blue eyes stood out against the black cowl of his robe. Unlike the first sorcerer she'd seen, this one had skin the color of charcoal, making the white of his hair and eyebrows a disarming contrast. His head swiveled within the cowl as he scanned the road for observers.

Instinctively, she froze in place. She barely breathed. Her cloak, already pulled tightly around her body, remained motionless. Not even a muscle in her face twitched. Her head remained down, shadowing the pale glow of her skin.

The sorcerer didn't stop for long. His scan complete, he moved down the street, away from Vic and her hideout, Tracker's two men following close behind.

Unconsciously, Vic touched the stone at her neck then closed her eyes and thanked the Goddess that the necklace had worked. For the briefest of moments, she debated whether to follow or not. A deep breath made up her mind. She pulled the sash from her waist and wrapped it around her face. Then, keeping the burgundy velvet of her dress hidden beneath the folds of her cloak and a hand pressed to the box inside her shirt, she started down the street after the three men.

Silent feet and a quick pace kept her close behind them, completely unnoticed. Once, the sorcerer turned to scan the street again. Vic became a shadow and waited. When they resumed their trek, she followed.

At first, she assumed they'd go to the old inn where the other sorcerer hid. But they didn't. Instead, they moved in the opposite direction, toward the city's eastern gate. Several blocks away from the gate, near the base of the hill, the three men stopped before a small, nondescript house.

As one of the guards knocked a pattern on the front door, the sorcerer again turned to scan his surroundings. Vic melted into the darkness of a building. Again, he failed to sense her.

Within seconds, the door opened and all three disappeared inside. She watched the house for another few minutes before slipping back down the street. She didn't turn toward the castle until she was well away from the house.

Chapter Eleven

৯৵৵

Vic stood in the doorway separating Jacob's sitting room from his bedroom. She leaned casually against the frame, watching him pace before a cold fireplace. After a few moments, she said, "Waiting for someone?"

He turned, his handsome features passing from shock to relief as he crossed the room to engulf her in a rough embrace.

"Miss me?" she asked, enjoying the comfort and safety of his arms.

"Why didn't you come in through the front entrance?" he asked without loosening his hold. "They have orders to let you pass."

"This is more fun."

"What took you so long?"

"You'd better sit."

He pulled back to look into her eyes. "What happened?"

"Accidentally tripped over more of Tracker's men with another one of those pesky sorcerers. By the way, Madam Xanthia deserves every kern she charged." She fingered the onyx where it lay against her throat.

Jacob led her into the sitting room and sat with her on the settee near the window, keeping his arm around her shoulders.

"I'm lucky I had this thing on," she continued. "They just popped out of the shadows when I was on my way back here. When the sorcerer's first scan didn't detect me, I decided to follow—"

"You what?"

"I followed. They went to a house near the eastern gate."

"They didn't go to the original building?"

"Nope."

"What did the house look like?"

"Plain. White walls, red-tiled roof, blue door. Typical house for that part of town. But I can show it to you. I made sure I knew the exact one before I left. This was a different sorcerer, Jacob. I saw his face, too." With a crooked smile, she added, "And despite scanning three different times, he didn't hesitate once in my general vicinity. I really like this necklace."

He almost smiled, his lips twitched as if he wanted to, but the expression quickly turned into a deep frown. "What did you think you were doing following them?" he asked harshly.

"My job, General."

A muscle along his jaw jumped as he ground his teeth together.

She sucked in a breath and raised a brow, waiting for the explosion.

"I was worried," he said finally and his frown softened. "I suppose I should know better than to worry about a thief carrying six knives and a magic ward."

She released her breath on a short laugh. "That's okay, General. I kind of like that you were worried. That's new to me." She relaxed against his side and nestled her head beneath his chin.

"I don't know if I can do this, Victoria. It goes against my instincts to let you take the risks while I wait here. I'd rather take the risks myself."

"That makes two of us. I'm almost too eager to take chances. At least, that's what my boss keeps telling me. But I shudder at letting others take those same chances if I can help."

His chuckle ruffled through her hair.

"We're quite a pair, aren't we, little thief?"

She bit her lip, keeping her face hidden as she did. A pair? She'd never been part of a pair before. Somehow, it made every risk she took seem more significant. Now, she actually had something to lose. She chose not to think about the fact that she'd probably lose this someday, anyway. *Enjoy it while you can, Flash. Enjoy being part of a pair.*

"What are you thinking about, Victoria?"

"I'm thinking that I need to use your washroom." She stood. "I'll be right back."

In the washroom, she shed her black clothing, removed each of her knives and donned the velvet dress. Using one of Jacob's combs, she brushed out her hair, leaving it down. Glancing into his small mirror, she deemed herself presentable. After a brief hesitation, she swallowed one of the pills Xanthia had given her, then set the box on top of the folded bundle of her clothes.

Jacob was lighting a fire when she sauntered back into the room. She cleared her throat to gain his attention.

"Goddess," he breathed, "Victoria, you look beautiful in that dress." He walked toward her slowly, his gaze traveling the length of her body.

Her heart started to thump harder. As he took her into his arms, she smiled up at him. "Thank you," she whispered, blood already surging through her veins. All he had to do was look at her, and she was lost. She breathed in his musky scent and held his gaze.

"I'm surprised you were able to collect it. After—"

She placed a finger over his lips. "I never back out on a bet."

His hands caressed the whole of her back, and for a long time, he simply stared at her. She never looked away from his face as she moved her hands over his chest and across his shoulders. The feel of his silk shirt tantalized her sensitive fingertips.

"Tonight," she whispered, lacing her fingers behind his neck, "we won't worry about risks or danger." *I won't worry about consequences or the future.* "Tonight, we'll concentrate only on making each other happy."

He answered with a knee-melting kiss.

Vic awoke the next morning still circled in his arms. He was studying her fingers when she opened her eyes. "Good morning," she mumbled, through a yawn.

"Good morning, love. Did you sleep well?"

"Um hum, wonderful, thank you. And you?"

"Very happily."

"What's so interesting?" She wriggled the fingers of the hand he was inspecting.

"I'm just marveling that these delicate little fingers can do so many different things." He kissed one fingertip. "They can cheat veteran gamblers. They can pull a knife out of thin air. They can scale walls. They can lift money pouches. And they can set every nerve in my body on fire."

She smiled and pressed her face against his chest. "Jacob Marin, you are a rogue. What will you do today?"

"I have to meet with the king this morning about that second sorcerer. And I promised to visit with Tiya, Kevin and Arlana sometime today."

"Lady Tiya, hmm?"

"You're not still concerned over my feelings for her, are you, little thief?"

"I suppose not." She was, but she wasn't about to admit it. Two years of being in love with someone could hardly be forgotten in a few days.

He tilted her chin and kissed her. "You don't need to worry, Victoria."

"I'll try to remember that." She scurried for a new topic quickly. "Who's Arlana?"

"Their daughter."

"Pretty name. You'll be busy all day then?"

"Yes. Why?" A wicked glint lit his eyes. "What'd you have in mind?"

"Wipe that smirk off your face, General. I'll have to get into the streets early, and I wanted to know if you'd be around before I left. But you won't, so…"

"Why do you have to go into the city?"

"I still have work to do, remember?" She reluctantly sat up.

He kept his arm around her waist and wouldn't let go of her hand. "Tonight?"

"Yes."

"Will you come here when you've finished?"

"Not tonight. I have to keep a watch on that building through the night and tomorrow during the day. I'll go in tomorrow night. Unless something happens."

"What could happen?"

"You never know with this sort of a game."

"I don't want to let you go," he mumbled, staring at her hand.

She leaned down and kissed his forehead. "I'll be fine. You worry about those goblins still running the city streets." She kissed his cheek, then allowed herself to be bundled once more into his warm embrace. After a long and languorous kiss, she sighed, broke away and got out of bed.

"You're leaving now?"

"Well, I thought I'd get dressed first."

"Stay and have breakfast."

"You have things to do."

"We both need to eat. You could come see Arlana with me."

She stopped at the door to his washroom. "Why?"

"Tiya is curious about you. So is Kevin."

Through narrowed eyes, she asked, "What have you told them?"

"Nothing. Really."

He grinned crookedly, and she snorted.

From the washroom, she yelled back, "Thanks, but no thanks, Jacob. I wouldn't have anything to talk about anyway." She reemerged wearing the velvet dress, the bundle of her black clothing tucked under one arm. "Besides, I'm not accustomed to holding casual morning visits with nobility."

"Tiya is a bookbinder's daughter. She's only ranked as Lady Tiya because of the sorcery. I never tire of seeing you in that dress."

"Thank you. But I still think I'll pass on a friendly visit with Lord and Lady Fordin. Tiya may be new to the nobility, but Lord Fordin is the queen's son."

"I imagine, by now, Queen Sara will be interested in meeting you, too. Come here."

"No. I have to go before you rope me into dinner with the entire royal family."

Jacob rose and strode toward her.

Vic unconsciously bit her lip, the sight of his powerful, naked body igniting tiny explosions of heat from her belly to between her thighs.

"We'd have to wait for Lord Deacon to return from Breeke before we could arrange for the 'entire' royal family. And you're biting your lip."

Before she could stop him, he pulled her into his arms and covered her mouth in a possessive, hungry kiss. She felt her resolve waning under his demands. She could kiss that delicious mouth all day long. Unfortunately, she didn't have all day. She wiggled out of his arms and, with her free hand, slapped his firm buttocks playfully. "Get dressed before I forget why I have to leave," she commanded.

"But I want you to forget."

Before he could kiss her again, Vic ducked under his reach and circled behind him. "Go tell the king about the second sorcerer. I'll see you soon."

As she headed for the sitting room, Jacob called out. "Stay standing, little thief."

"Always, General."

***

The city moved fast and noisy in the throes of Autumn's End. Everywhere she looked people were chattering and singing. Even the normally stoic farmers were grinning and celebrating. The harvest had been very good.

Cold bit her face and hands when Vic stayed in the shade of buildings, but when she walked out into the sun, its waning heat warmed her skin. She spent the day wandering near Tracker's building. As night descended, she changed into her blacks and scaled the building she'd used on previous nights' vigils.

Despite Gip's order that she should avoid this building until Charlie had cooled, her curiosity made accepting this particular job easy. She wanted to know what the sorcerers were doing in her city. She hated the idea of abandoning the job to someone else after being the one to spot the sorcerers in the first place. A bit of professional pride mixed with her curiosity, she supposed. Being perfectly honest with herself, she had to admit she didn't trust anyone else with the job. She needed to solve this puzzle, for her own peace of mind. Not knowing what was going on in her city made her… uncomfortable.

When she'd seen no sign of Charlie's men throughout the day, she began to relax, able to focus her mind on the job at hand. Charlie might not even be looking for her anymore, but she doubted that. At the least, however, he was looking in the wrong spots. If she kept wearing the velvet dress and looking like nobility, or more realistically like a noble lady's maid, maybe she could move in more areas of the city without having to worry about Charlie. The thought appealed.

As she watched the gap between the old inn and its neighboring building, she decided to check the house where the other sorcerer lay in hiding. Maybe after she'd gotten into the inn. There was no telling what kind of information a trip to that house could produce. And information was their weapon against the sorcerers. Besides, she might as well get Jacob's money's worth from the magic ward.

Tracker still hadn't made an appearance that day. But knowing there was more than one sorcerer meant that Tracker could easily be with the other. None of his men moved during the day, making it all the more likely that she wouldn't see Tracker or Malkiney until after sunset. In the hour just before sunset, though, Vic did spy one of the purple and black clad guards disappear through the center of Upper Market. He hadn't returned by the time she took her post across from their lair. Several of the guards came and went in the hours following sunset, but there was no sign of the sorcerer, Malkiney or Tracker.

She fingered the necklace at her throat as she studied the building, wondering if the white-faced sorcerer was still inside. As each guard moved in and out, she noted their faces and kept a mental count. By midnight, she'd counted only twenty different individuals and did a quick calculation.

Last she heard, Tracker'd had around two hundred men working for him—a small army for a smuggler. Including the men she'd seen with the other sorcerer, however, she hadn't counted more than fifty in town. That meant that either there were more of these hiding holes throughout the city, or a large number of Tracker's guards were still outside the city walls. Either didn't sound good.

But something seemed—wrong. No one else in the Hole had seen any of Tracker's men as far as she knew. Granted, neither of the hiding holes Tracker had chosen were in areas where Thief's Hole normally traveled. If they had more burrows in the city, chances were they'd be in similar locations—places where Tracker's people were least likely to be spotted. But it still seemed wrong that no one had seen more of the smuggler's men. Not if there were two hundred of them scurrying around town. So either the smugglers had gotten very good at moving quietly, or they simply weren't inside the city.

So why keep them outside? Especially if you're smuggling something as dangerous as blood sorcerers? Maybe that was the reason. Except that Tracker never shied away from a profit, no matter the risks. The fact that no one had seen Tracker himself was what really worried her.

Her thoughts were interrupted by the appearance of the guard that had left before sunset. With him, a second man stiffly lumbered toward the gap. Vic stared closely at the second man. His movements weren't quite right. Too stilted and jerky, as if something else moved his limbs for him, a grotesque parody of a marionette. As they neared the gap, Vic sucked in a gasp. The second man was Nathan Cap, one of the men she'd been gambling with when her troubles with Big Charlie started.

Even as the two men disappeared into the narrow alley, Vic shot across the rooftop. She was down on the street and in the shadows near the old inn by the time the door closed behind them.

During the day, she'd hunted the best way to get into the old inn, discovering a broken window near the upper floor, which saved her from having to pick a lock, but to get to it, she had to climb to the top of the trader's building, then leap across the gap to the inn's roof. From there, she could lower herself to the window. The danger came in leaping across the gap. If one of Tracker's men came out and looked up at just the wrong time, she'd be in for a run across the rooftops to escape.

As she climbed to the top of the trader's building, she silently thanked the Goddess for a moonless night. Taking a deep breath, she sailed lightly across the gap then looked back over the roof's edge. Nothing. Her heart danced in her chest.

She allowed a second deep breath, calming her pulse, before carefully lowering her legs to the broken window's thin sill. With one hand still on the roof's lip, she reached through the broken glass, flipped the latch and pushed open the windows in slow, careful increments to avoid a squeak. Her hands and legs trembled with the need to hold herself perfectly balanced and immobile on the thin ledge. When the window opened enough to slide through, she dropped silently to the floor inside, remaining crouched low as she listened for any sign that her entrance had been detected.

Only silence.

The musty smell of a room long unused washed over her. A layer of dust beneath her fingers and feet would give evidence of her entrance, but it couldn't be helped. With any luck, she'd only have to do this once.

In the days and nights of watching the building, Vic had never seen lights through any of the boarded windows. She'd assumed that either they'd stayed in rooms with tightly sealed drapery or they'd moved into the basement. Now, she quietly searched for the staircase, keeping her ears trained for the slightest hint of noise. Her body tingled in anticipation of any sound.

Step by careful step, she worked her way down the old inn. She stopped at every floor to listen but was met by silence each time. Her fingers began to twitch expectantly as she neared the lowest floor. At the bottom of the stairs, the first sounds reached her. She followed the noise until she came to a locked door. Pressing her ear to the wood, she heard the muffled sounds of a conversation.

"The others have arrived, Master."

"They've been placed as instructed?"

"Yes. The dark one is near the eastern gate. The woman's in the northern district."

"Very good."

The soft thud of footsteps alerted Vic to the approach of the two inside the room. She scurried away, taking cover in a dark nook. From the room, Malkiney emerged with the white-faced sorcerer.

Vic held her breath.

They passed and disappeared through a door leading to a stairway to the basement. She continued to breathe silent and slow even as her heartbeat raced. Torn between following and searching the room the two men had just come from, Vic decided to test the room first.

Malkiney had locked the door again, but an ear to the door confirmed that the room was now empty. She picked the lock and entered, closing the door carefully behind her. The room's darkness was broken only by the faint afterglow on the wick of an oil lamp. Vic crossed to the lamp. It sat on the top of a large table across which maps of Karasnia and Dareelia were spread.

The single window was heavily curtained, but through a break in the boards over the window, a faint light snuck past. It didn't give her enough light to study the room well, but it did allow her to move without bumping into anything when the afterglow of the wick finally died.

In the quiet, Vic could hear a murmuring from the basement. Though she searched the room thoroughly, she could find no reason for Malkiney to smuggle a sorcerer into Karasnia. The murmuring beneath her turned to a chant. Then she heard the movement of footsteps past the door. She pressed herself to the wall behind the door and waited, swallowing the loud throb of her pulse. No one entered.

The chanting grew louder, making the hair on her arms and the back of her neck stand.

She waited, despite an irrational urge to run away. When no more footsteps passed the room, she carefully slipped back into the hall, locking the door behind her. She froze when she realized the corridor wasn't empty. Near the door leading to the basement stairs, two guards waited, eyes forward. From her place against the wall, she was hidden by the dark shadows filling the hall, but any movement might call their attention.

She watched, her breathing slow and consciously deep, waiting for a moment when she could scurry to better cover. They never moved, never scanned the hall, never took their gazes off the torch on the wall across from their post. Her eyes narrowed as she sensed something in the way they stood, something that hinted at the same sort of wrongness she'd felt watching Nathan Cap lurching along the street with Tracker's guard. It was unnatural, the absolute stillness of them. How could you guard a door without looking around?

The chanting grew louder, reverberating through the floorboards. She had to see what was going on in that basement. Sliding along the wall, she kept her gaze on the guards, her hearing on the corridor behind her. Only the single flickering torch on the wall opposite the guards cast any light. It helped keep her camouflaged, but her nerves jumped with the threat of being caught at any moment. Her ears almost hurt with the effort of trying to sense movement behind her over the sound of the chanting. Her body felt taut and strained as she measured each slow, soundless step closer to the guards. Her lungs burned with the effort to control her breathing so the sound wouldn't give her away.

She was within arm's length of the two men when she realized what was wrong with them.

They weren't conscious. Their open eyes stared at the torch without any sign of seeing it. Vic almost looked at the torch then thought better. She didn't know a lot about magic, but she wasn't going to take any chances. If looking at the torchlight was what affected them, she didn't want to fall prey also. Being immobilized in the middle of a building filled with Tracker's men and a potentially dangerous sorcerer seemed like a bad idea.

She inhaled a long slow breath, refilling her strained lungs. When her heartbeat and breathing felt normal again, she slipped between the two comatose men, wondering why anyone would bother to set useless guards. Maybe Malkiney hadn't counted on someone getting close enough to notice they were comatose. Either way, it made her entrance to the basement easier. She moved down the stairs, careful to test for creaking before putting her full weight on each step. Lights flickering below forced her to stop on the first landing. She hugged the rail and looked down. From where she stood, very little of the room was visible, but descending further would place her in the pool of light from below.

Gnawing at her bottom lip, she studied the parts of the room she could see. And a slow grin lifted her cheeks. The basement's rafters were just beyond an easy arm's length from her place on the stairs, but the thick boards were easily strong enough to hold her slight frame and wide enough to hide her from the room below. With a cat's grace, she stepped onto the stair railing and leapt to the nearest rafter, swinging her legs onto the board in a single move.

Lying motionless, she listened. When she heard nothing that would indicate an alert to her presence, she poked her head over the side of the beam. She still couldn't see into the room very well, but she hadn't attracted any attention, thank the Goddess. The dust from the rafters teased her nose, forcing her to lie still until she was sure she wouldn't sneeze. The tempo of the chanting continued to increase. When she was confident a sneeze wouldn't betray her presence and her body was sufficiently hidden by the thick wooden beam, she shimmied across the rafters until she had a complete view of the room.

A large circle, marked by long red candles, filled the entire center of the room. Outside the circle, the walls of the room were lined with Tracker's men. Malkiney stood prominently near the wall furthest from the stairs. Inside the circle, a triangle was chalked onto the basement's stone floor. At each of the triangle's points, tall candelabra bisected the angles. Three long, thin, red candles filled each candelabrum.

And in the center of the triangle, on top of a stone altar draped in black cloth, lay Nathan Cap. His eyes were wide, conscious and frantic, like the eyes of a trapped animal. But his body didn't even twitch, despite the lack of any confining ties. At his feet and sides, three large bowls sat atop metal braziers.

The white-faced sorcerer stood at the head of the altar. His eyes were closed, his hands raised above his head. The chanting Vic had heard came from his lips, but it sounded distant, hollow, as if there were still a wall between herself and the sound. The tone was harsh and rumbled through her nerve endings. It reminded her of the sound of gravel covering a grave.

Every hair on her body stood on end.

She watched in silent shock as the chanting quickened. Along the walls, Tracker's men stood motionless, their eyes unblinking, and she suspected they were under the same spell affecting the guards in the hall. All but Malkiney stared straight ahead, seeing nothing. Malkiney's dark eyes glowed madly in the candlelight, his face a rapt mask of adoration.

Vic swallowed hard and looked back to the altar. The sorcerer's chanting had reached impossible speeds. A shifting of his hands and light flickered over the surface of a silver dagger held just over his head. Then suddenly his voice fell silent. And the dagger plunged into Nathan's chest.

Even as his eyes bulged and his mouth worked to release a scream, the man's body remained rigidly still. The sorcerer slowly moved the knife in a circle, cutting Nathan's chest open.

When the sorcerer reached into the opened chest cavity, Vic squeezed her eyes shut, fighting back both the bile and the scream that threatened to give her away. Her mind chattered denials at what she saw, trying to block the memory as quickly as it tormented her. She choked back a silent sob, the air suddenly too thick to breathe. Her heart pumped painfully fast and, for an instant, she thought she would pass out.

She couldn't watch any more. Couldn't stand to listen to the wet sucking sounds beneath her. When she caught the first scent of burning meat, she gagged. In a near mindless panic, she slipped back across the rafters to the basement stairs. More noises, sounds she was too horrified to identify, muffled the thump she made when she hit the landing. She darted up the stairs, past the comatose guards and ran to the inn's front door.

The lock had long been removed, but when she opened the door, it squeaked. Panic thrummed more adrenaline through her blood. She darted outside, closing the door despite the noise, and shot up the street like an arrow.

Melting into the darkened shadow of a building, she watched the inn long enough to see if anyone followed. A movement just inside the dark gap was the only warning she needed. Vic raced through a labyrinth of streets toward the castle without ever looking back.

She didn't throw up until she reached the castle walls.

Chapter Twelve

Jacob," Vic whispered. She had come in through his balcony door
to find him in front of the fireplace in his sitting room. When he
stood and turned, she raced forward and threw herself into his arms.
She clung to his waist so tightly, the guard of her wrist dagger dug into
her arm. The pain was nothing to her fear.

"Victoria, what happened? Are you hurt?"

He tried to ease her away far enough to look into her face.

She only clung tighter. "Don't let go," she pleaded, squeezing her
eyes shut.

He wrapped his arms around her again, resting his cheek on the top
of her head.

In the warm, encompassing strength of his embrace, her trembling
slowed. For a long time, she wouldn't open her eyes or loosen her grip.
She breathed in his scent and concentrated on the feel of his powerful
body pressed against hers. The image of the white-faced sorcerer and
the basement ceremony began to fade…slowly.

She swallowed the sour taste in her mouth and finally opened her eyes.
Taking a stuttering breath, she whispered, "Thank you," against his chest.

"Are you all right?" he asked, still keeping her securely pressed against him.

"I...I'm not hurt." She took another shaky breath. "The sorcerer at the inn is a blood magician. Nathan Cap is dead."

"Oh, Victoria. Damn, I'm sorry you had to see that."

She realized Jacob had dealt with the horror of a blood magician once before. Had he seen a ceremony, too? Or just the results?

"I should never have let you go."

"Yes, you should have. Now you know for certain and you can stop him. Them. I overheard the sorcerer talking to Malkiney. There are three of them in the city. The one I discovered by accident and the third is a woman. She's being kept somewhere in the northern district."

"Three?"

Vic looked up into his face. Concern shadowed his handsome features. "You can stop them, can't you?"

"We'll stop them, love. Don't worry about that now." He studied her face. "Do you want a drink? You look pale."

She nodded, but didn't want to let go long enough for him to move to the table by his chair. He handed her a goblet of amber liquid. She gulped it down without tasting it, thankful for the pain as it seared her throat and washed away the bile in her mouth. After a moment, when her eyes stopped watering, she handed back the empty goblet.

"More?"

His voice was quiet, so full of concern it made her ache. "No. I'm fine now." She was grateful beyond measure when he set the goblet aside and wrapped her in his arms again. She'd never needed the strength and heat of another human being so much in her life. "Do you think...are you sure you'll be able to stop all three?"

"I won't lie to you, Victoria. I'm concerned about the third. We can take the other two, but without an exact location, the third could slip away."

"As long as she's not in the city, I don't care."

He petted the back of her head. "I have to care. She could be a danger to the realm. I just wish we knew why they're here."

"They had maps of the city and of Karasnia. But that's all I saw. After I saw the… Well, I ran."

"Good. Why did you go in tonight?"

"I saw them bring in Nathan. He was walking weird. Goddess, Jacob, he was helpless but still conscious when…" She stopped and took another slow breath before continuing. "Something else… The guards, the ones guarding the door and the ones in the basement were all…it was like they weren't there. They just stared into the air in front of their faces. All but Malkiney. He watched the ceremony."

"And you still didn't see Tracker?"

"No. But now that I know there are three of those things, it's more than likely he's with one of the others. Probably the woman since I haven't seen him."

Jacob nodded, then he looked back into her eyes. "Are you okay now?"

"Yeah. I've just never seen…I mean, I've seen people die. I've had to kill before, but…" She swallowed hard.

"I know, love. I understand." With a gentle smile, he led her to the seat he'd abandoned when she'd whispered his name. "Sit here for a minute. I have to send word to King John. Do you think you can tell him your story?"

"I think so." She let go of his waist reluctantly, then sat in the oversized chair and watched his every move, afraid that if she looked away, the images from the basement would overwhelm her again.

He stepped just outside his door and talked in hushed tones to someone she couldn't see. Moments later he was back. He picked her up, then sat, cuddling her in his lap. "The king will send word when he's ready to see us."

She tucked her head under his chin and pressed her arms against his chest. "Let's talk about something else for now. What book were you reading?"

"It's called *Dreial the Pirate and Her Hundred Thieves.*"

"Never heard of it. You like pirate stories?"

"Not especially. It was a gift from Tiya. She thought I'd enjoy it."

"Why? I mean, if you don't like pirate stories—"

"Probably because she knows I'm completely silly over this little thief I just met."

"Silly?"

"Insanely silly."

She looked up grinning despite herself. "Sounds bad," she whispered. "You should watch out for those thief types. They'll steal you blind."

"I'm afraid it's too late."

He kissed her gently, and Vic's heart started to hammer again from something other than fear. She lost herself in his kiss, concentrating on the feel of his lips, the taste of his mouth, the scrape of his evening stubble, the gentle caressing of his hands along her back and hips. She allowed no other thought.

When a light tap at the door broke the spell, she came close to whimpering in protest, something she hadn't done since she was a child.

Jacob looked long and hard into her eyes. "Are you sure you can go through with this? I can tell the king."

"No. I'll go. He should hear my account."

After another pause and a second knock, Jacob rose, taking Vic with him. He set her feet on the ground and kissed her one final time before going to the door. He kept his arm firmly circled around her shoulders, and she silently thanked both him and the Goddess because she wasn't sure her knees would hold her weight without his support.

A young squire waited in the hall. Without a word, he led them to the king's chambers. The two guards outside the door nodded to Jacob as he and Vic passed. Inside the large, richly furnished sitting room, both King John and Queen Sara waited.

Vic wasn't sure what she'd expected, but the image before her shattered her preconceived image of the king and queen. Queen Sara stood in a long heavy black robe, her long brown hair tumbling freely down her back. She was in her mid-fifties and still a striking woman. Her green eyes, dark in the dim lighting, held an expression that was at once anxious and caring.

King John looked more like a soldier than a king in his light tunic and leather breeches. His sandy blond hair stuck out in disorganized tufts, his brown eyes were filled with compassion and worry, echoing the look in his wife's gaze.

Without preamble, Queen Sara strode toward them and took Vic's hands in hers. "My dear, I'd hoped we'd meet under more congenial circumstances. Please, come sit." She led Vic to a large, heavily cushioned couch and sat, keeping Vic's hands firmly clasped in her own. Both the king and Jacob followed. "Now, if it's not too difficult, I need you to tell me everything. Leave out no detail."

Vic glanced at Jacob and fleetingly at the king before looking back to Queen Sara. She told her story in painful detail, from her initial observations to her run from the inn. She made sure to provide the location of the second sorcerer as well as a description of both men. When she'd finished, King John and Queen Sara stared at each other for a long, silent moment.

"It's worse than we suspected," Queen Sara said plainly.

"Three?" King John ran a hand through his rumpled hair and let out a heavy exhale.

"They'll not be easy to take, John," the queen said. "They aren't like…" She paused and shook her head. "From Victoria's description, they are, in all likelihood, more powerful than what we've dealt with before. The spell on the guards, selectively cast, is like nothing I've heard of. At least, not something that can be accomplished by a single magician."

She continued to hold Vic's hands as she talked. When the queen squeezed her fingers, she felt remarkably comforted.

"Majesty," Jacob said through a frown, "I can, with some help from the Guild and your queen, capture the two we know of. But, without the location of the third…"

"What use?" King John finished. After another deep breath, he looked back at Queen Sara. "How long will it take to coordinate an attack with the Guild?"

"Two days at most."

"Very well. Jacob, you have two days to locate the last."

Jacob's gaze darted to Vic. She saw his conflict but before she could respond, the king spoke.

"I'd like you to use our internal spy network on this one. Victoria has been successful, but she's risked far more than is necessary. And with only two days, it'll take more than one person to track down the third magician." The king turned to her. "Thank you, Victoria. You've served your king and your country beyond expectations. You have my debt."

"Thank you, Majesty," she mumbled, both relieved and a little upset at being left out. She didn't want to face another blood sorcerer, but she hated having to trust others to find her. Queen Sara squeezed her hand again. When Vic met her gaze, she saw an understanding pass through the queen's eyes and tried not to frown. She'd heard that Queen Sara had a way of looking into the soul of a person. It made her uncomfortable to think that rumor might be true.

"Jacob." King John turned back to his general. "You'll need to organize your men for the raid immediately. Inform General Thack first thing in the morning. The queen will let you know when the Guild is ready, so be prepared to move at a moment's notice. I'll leave the deployment of the spies to you also.

"But, Jacob, if we haven't found the third sorcerer by the time the Guild is ready, we won't be able to wait. I have no idea what they're doing in my city, but whatever it is, it can't be good. We've no time to waste. Even two days seems an intolerably long time. If we haven't located that third magician, we can only hope to catch her as she tries to flee or that she's forced back to wherever she came from after we take the other two."

"Yes, Sire."

Jacob extended a hand to Vic, but before she could rise, Queen Sara said, "When this is all over, Victoria, it would please me very much to talk with you again. I've never met anyone who could cheat Joe Missek's eye."

Her mouth dropped open in surprise. She snapped it shut, forcing enough composure to thank the queen and ensure her she'd await the queen's pleasure. She even managed to leave the room with some semblance of dignity.

In the hall, however, her mouth dropped open again as she looked incredulously at Jacob. "You told the queen about me cheating at cards?"

"She asked how we met," he answered with a shrug.

She shook her head, relaxing into his side when he circled an arm about her shoulders. "It's been a strange night. In fact, everything has been strange since meeting you, Jacob. Why is that?"

"I'm a strange sort of person?" he suggested.

Against her will, she chuckled. After retelling her story, she hadn't expected to be able to laugh. She chose to ignore the slight hint of hysteria in her voice. When they entered Jacob's rooms once more, she turned to look up at him. "Thanks for…earlier."

"Anything for you, love," he whispered.

She smiled, feeling almost bashful. She'd never had someone to go to when she was scared. It was disconcerting to realize how easy it had been to run to Jacob for comfort and safety. Too easy. She averted her gaze and changed the subject. "Do you have a pen and paper?"

Her sudden question made his brow furrow. "Over in the desk. What's it for, little thief?"

"I have to get a message to the Hole. If that sorcerer got Nathan, then he could get to a lot of the younger Hole people. They need to know what to avoid."

Jacob pulled a sheet of paper, an ink well and an intricately shaped, colored glass pen from the desk's top drawer. When she sat, he stood behind her, hands on her shoulders.

"How will you get the letter to them?" he asked.

"We have a way. I'll need to go into the city tomorrow."

His hands tightened. "Do you think that's a good idea? You'd be safer here."

A secretive smile touched her lips as she dipped the pen's point into the black ink. "I have to. I'll be all right."

"I'll go with you."

"Jacob…"

"Don't argue with me, Victoria. I'm going with you." Against her temple, he whispered, "Besides, we still need to buy you that new dress."

She couldn't even pretend to be upset. Though she'd never admit it out loud, she would feel safer with him near when she went into the city. She tilted her head back to kiss him lightly before turning to the paper, ignoring the uneasiness that nagged her for feeling safer with Jacob.

"Who taught you to write?" he asked, leaning against the back of the chair.

"Peggy. She always said that every good con should know how to read and write. That way, nothing can get past you."

"Very logical."

He leaned over her shoulder throwing a slight shadow over the paper as she finished writing.

"'Three Black Melons rotting in the street. Cap over. Eleven great star. Ninety unknown. Under midnight still end. Word? Watch.' What does that mean?" he said.

She glanced sideways to see him scowling at her scratchy writing. "Three blood magicians in town," she translated, running the pen in the air above the sentences as she read. "Nathan's been killed. One is in the eastern section near the gate. The one in the northern section hasn't been found. The magician near Upper Market is still there. Do they have any news? And be careful."

He straightened. "They'll understand that?"

"Of course." She dropped her head back against his stomach to look into his eyes. "And you've just learned one of the Hole's secrets."

"I promise not to tell."

His smile made her pulse race. "I don't suppose you have a yellow ribbon lying about."

"Not that I know of."

She shrugged. "I can get one tomorrow." She blew on the paper until the ink dried, folded the paper in half and left it on the desk.

Rising, she turned and ran her hands up around Jacob's neck, still consciously keeping the memories of the basement out of her mind.

"If all goes well, this should be over by the final night of festival," he said, hugging her tight. "Would you like to go with me to the masquerade that night?"

"In the palace?"

"Um hmm."

"I don't have a mask or clothes…"

"I'll take care of everything."

"Jacob, I don't—"

He silenced her with a lingering kiss. "I'd like you to go, Victoria," he whispered against her mouth. "Please."

"Well…" She felt his triumphant grin against her mouth even as he stopped further comment with another kiss.

"I'm glad you're here tonight, love. I would have slept badly otherwise."

"I'm glad to be here, too." She squeezed closer. "Help me forget, Jacob. Help me to forget…"

She didn't need to ask again.

Vic had fallen into an exhausted and dreamless sleep. When she woke, sunlight shafted thinly through the closed curtains. She stared at the light, listening to Jacob's quiet breathing. His arm circled her waist, keeping her back pressed against his stomach and chest. She hugged his arm, surprised anew by how comfortable and safe she felt with him.

There'd never been a time in her life when she could sleep without a part of her mind alert and wary. Now, at a time when she should be most afraid, she'd found a safe place to sleep. And that scared her more than anything else.

Before she registered the change in his breathing, Jacob's arm tightened at her waist. "Good morning," she said quietly.

"Morning, love. Did you sleep all right?"

"Yeah. Not a single dream."

"Good."

"You do realize you're going to have to drive me to exhaustion every night from now on."

His arm squeezed her tighter still. "That would be my pleasure, Victoria."

She rolled into his waiting kiss. The kiss deepened as she felt the familiar stirrings of heat through her stomach. She couldn't be in this man's presence without wanting him. When he rolled her onto her back, she vaguely wondered if this was like being addicted to a drug or strong drink. She'd known a lot of people addicted to something. Now it seemed she'd found her own.

Not so bad, really. She arched to meet his wandering mouth. In fact, a rather pleasant addiction. Thoughts scattered into sensation as his hands and mouth slipped down her body.

Later, sated and content, she cuddled against his side and sighed. "What a delightful way to wake up in the morning."

"I couldn't agree more, love." He kissed the top of her head then rolled out of bed.

Her gaze drank in the strong lines of his body as he slipped on his breeches.

When he caught her look, he grinned crookedly. "Are you trying to tempt me, little thief?"

"Well, I suppose we'd better not. We both have things to do today. But you can't blame me for admiring the view."

His throaty chuckle preceded a rough kiss. "Hungry?" he asked, pulling back.

"Yes. But I think I'd like some breakfast first."

"Minx." His kiss pressed her back onto the bed.

"Okay," she breathed against his mouth, "breakfast can wait."

Jacob groaned. "What are you doing to me, little thief?"

"I thought I was kissing you."

"You're stealing my willpower."

"I warned you last night about thieves."

He sighed dramatically. "Ah, yes. Well. I didn't really need willpower anyway."

He spoke so seriously, she broke into a fit of giggles. "Okay, General. Go get us something to eat, and I'll take a bath."

"I'm supposed to leave after that?"

He heaved another tragic sigh, before getting out of bed to order food.

Vic sauntered into the washroom. Humming to herself, she pumped first hot then cold water into the marble tub. The room fairly steamed with the heat. The only full baths she'd managed previously were ones paid for at bathhouses and inns. And there, the hot water had been hand carried most of the time. This luxury of a private bath with hot water at hand was almost as intoxicating as Jacob's kiss. Well, not quite.

Submersed to her chin in honeysuckle-scented water, she closed her eyes and tried not to think. The horrors of the night before seemed a distant shadow. An incident from years earlier. A dream.

Her eyes popped open when she realized she was being watched. "How long have you been standing there?"

Jacob leaned against the doorframe, a strange smile touching the corners of his mouth. He hadn't donned a shirt yet and her gaze moved once more across the hard muscles lining his torso. He pulled away from the door and knelt next to the tub.

"A few minutes. Breakfast will be here soon."

"Good. I'm starving now." His expression was so odd and unreadable, she frowned. "What?"

"Nothing. Sorry. I was just thinking."

"Worried about the magicians?"

His gaze shifted so subtly, she wasn't sure she'd seen the change.

"Yes," he said after a moment.

His tone made her doubt that had truly been the topic occupying his thoughts. She decided to let his misdirection go. "You have to talk with your guard and General Thack this morning?"

"Um hmm. I've already sent word to the general to meet me here after he's breakfasted. I'll have to talk to a few people in town, as well." He frowned and his brow wrinkled.

She almost laughed. "Don't worry, General. I have to sneak off on my own for a bit, too. We can arrange to meet later. Then I can finish repaying my gambling debt by letting you buy me a dress."

"You read my mind now, too?"

"No. I understand the necessity of secrets."

"If they were mine to divulge, Victoria, I wouldn't hesitate."

She studied his eyes and almost bit her lip as she realized the meaning behind his declaration. "You trust me?"

"With my life. You find that so hard to believe?"

"Yes." Trust wasn't common on the streets.

A knock from the sitting room stilled his response and announced the arrival of breakfast. Before he rose to answer the door, though, he placed a tender kiss on her lips. Vic watched him leave, swallowing around the lump in her throat.

Chapter Thirteen

❧

They were just finishing breakfast when General Thack knocked. "Ran into the king already this morning, and he's told me most everything," Thack said without preamble. "Queen Sara said the magicians should be ready for an attack tomorrow night."

"Good." Jacob offered the general a seat, but he refused with a nod. "I'll set up spies in the north today."

"This mess with a missing magician makes my shoulder ache," Thack said, rubbing his massive shoulder. "I just hope we track her down before the raid. No telling what one loose in the city could do."

"Agreed. You'll see to the men today?"

"Aye. One last thing. Our patrols haven't spotted any more of those damned goblins in the city. Seems they've all but vanished from the forest as well. None of our patrols have seen a sign of their ugly, green faces."

Jacob's brow furrowed. "Damn, that's strange. But since we have more pressing things to worry about… Thanks for seeing me here, General."

"No problem. Wife had me up at the crack of dawn to feed the baby."

Thack shook his head tragically, and Vic almost laughed aloud at the large man's martyred expression.

In town, after being shown the dress shop where they'd meet later, she left Jacob to deliver her message. She detoured long enough to change into the wine velvet dress, a better daylight disguise than her blacks. Then she worked her way to the Goddess's shrine.

The tall stone pyramid had a single entrance through which only women could pass. The theological school and monastery provided places for men to worship, but the shrine itself was reserved for women. The pyramid was the only shrine to the Goddess in all of Karasnia. Worship was generally a private thing, done without the confines of walls. But this place was special, built centuries earlier by the warrior queen, Breanna, thought to be a favorite of the Goddess.

Against the wall opposite the entrance, a large garden grew with remarkable tenacity. Only rarely did a plant die inside the shrine. Light flooded the garden from a single window set high in the pyramid wall. In the midst of the greenery, a tiny waterfall's quiet tinkling was the only sound. The rest of the shrine remained an empty open space, save for a scattering of mats on the stone floor. The air inside the pyramid remained cool in the summer and warm in the winter. No one quite knew why. Several women sat along the walls or near the garden, lost in silent meditation.

Vic walked on soundless feet to the edge of the garden. There, ribbon-wrapped rocks were piled in small pyramids. Each rock was an offering to the Goddess, a prayer, a giving of thanks, a loving acknowledgment. Near the far left of the garden, the rock pyramids stopped. Vic took her offering to this side. Inside the yellow ribbon neatly tied around a smooth black stone was the message she'd written to the Hole. She set the rock beneath the front leaves of a large fern. A woman from the Hole checked that spot every day for messages. As long as the note was left after the garden had been tended, the Hole received it.

Vic knelt and offered a silent prayer to the Goddess, thanking Her once more for the necklace she still wore. She stood and left just as one of the silent mediators knelt to the right of the garden, the woman's eyes full of relief and contentment. The shrine had that effect, Vic mused as she walked back into the bright light of a cloudless, autumn day. Few walked out of that solitude without feeling refreshed and revived.

By the time she entered the small dress shop a few streets back from Upper Market, Jacob was already waiting. He chatted affably with the head seamstress, a small, round woman in her late fifties. Vic didn't miss the undisguised looks of adoration on the faces of the seamstress's three assistants every time he spoke.

When he noticed her, he flashed his sexy smile and strolled to her, gaze running along the lines of her dress. He kissed her in greeting, much to the audible dismay of the assistants.

"All done?" he asked.

"Yeah. You?"

"A couple more things, but only one is business. First." He took her hand and led her to the head seamstress. "Victoria, this is Nola Letrow, finest seamstress in all of Dareelia. Nola, this is Victoria."

Nola studied her for several minutes, then a smile split her face. "Pleasure to meet you, Victoria. Jacob has left thorough instructions. We should have both dresses suited to you in no time."

"Both?" She looked up at Jacob, her eyebrows raised in question.

"One is for the masquerade. Nola helped me pick the perfect dress to go with the mask."

He looked very pleased with himself. "You've bought me a mask? Already?"

"Um hmm."

She wasn't sure whether to be pleased or annoyed. "What does it look like?"

Nola produced a white silk-covered eye mask. The edges came to points and swept up to meet small plumes of white and black feathers. Silver sequins lined the eyeholes, and black and silver sequins ringed the outer edge of the mask. The long handle was wrapped in black and white ribbon.

"It's beautiful," she breathed, taking the mask from Nola to examine it closer.

"I'm glad you like it. Wait 'til you see the dress." Jacob kissed her cheek then, giving her hand a squeeze, said, "I'll be back soon. Take good care of her, Nola."

"As you say, General."

Vic and the dressmaker's three assistants watched him leave.

"Now, Victoria," Nola said, calling her attention. "Let's get to those dresses before the shoemaker arrives."

As Vic had requested, one dress was purple, a deep violet satin trimmed with lilac lace and an underskirt of deep jade. The second was white samite silk interwoven with silver thread over an ebony underskirt. To the black trim at the neckline and off-the-shoulder sleeves, Nola promised to add silver trim and black feathers. At Vic's scowl, she assured her that the hoop worn under the white gown was necessary for the style of the dress. The shoemaker appeared to take measurements of her feet shortly after Vic had slipped into the white dress. She returned moments before Jacob with a pair of silk slippers to match each gown.

When Jacob walked through the door, Vic was standing on a raised platform for the final hemming of the violet gown. She was trying not to tap her foot, but she couldn't hold back her sighs. His admiring gaze wiped away her impatience in an instant. "You like?" she asked, holding up her arms to reveal the short trains on the sleeves.

"Yeah, I like." His dark eyes smoldered as he looked her over slowly. "You look beautiful."

She grinned. The final adjustments were easier to take. "Did you do what you needed to do?"

"Um hmm."

"What are you grinning about?" she asked, narrowing her eyes.

"I bought you something."

"Something else? What?" She frowned, still suspicious of his cat's grin.

He produced a short, thin sheath and dagger. At the top of the black leather sheath, two thin gold handles looped out and down. The dagger's hilt was gold and encrusted with dark emeralds.

"A breast dagger," Vic exclaimed. "It's beautiful."

"I thought it would go nicely with your new look."

He eyed the dress and pointedly rested his gaze on the curve of her breasts just above the neckline.

She extended a hand for the dagger. Locking gazes with him, she slid the sheath inside the gown's tight bodice until the golden handles hooked on her corset. A quick glance confirmed that the hilt was completely hidden. She met Jacob's heated gaze again with a slight smile, fighting the urge to bit her lip. Nola hummed around the hem of her gown, politely ignoring their exchange.

With the final touches completed on the gown, Nola promised to have the black and white dress delivered before the masquerade. Vic bundled her velvet gown while Jacob collected the mask, then they walked lazily back to the castle arm in arm.

***

"Wait here."

Jacob sat her near the fireplace in his sitting room and disappeared into his bedroom, closing the door behind him. Natural curiosity had her rising the instant the door closed, tempted almost beyond her ability to resist peeking at what he was up to. Before she could talk herself into spying, a knock called her to the door.

She opened it to the face of a large, round table. The table entered, revealing the servant who carried it. Behind came four other servants, one with a large tray of food, one with a bottle of wine and two goblets, one with a set of chairs and one with a cloth for the table and a small candelabra.

They quickly set up the table before the bay windows, served the food, and lit the candles. Outside, the sky had darkened and a mist was settling over the courtyard below. They left with pleasant good evenings to which she could only grunt in reply.

For several minutes after closing the door, she stood with her hand still on the latch. Then she went to inspect the table. The wine was a deep ruby, probably his favorite. The meal was an elegant arrangement of some meat she'd never seen, a portion of potatoes shaped like roses, and an assortment of carrots, green beans and beets. A bowl of bread and a plate of shell-shaped butter chunks completed the table. The plates were china, the utensils gold and the wineglasses crystal with a gold rim.

When had he had time to arrange all this?

She'd grown up on pub food and vendor goods. On occasion after a particularly good hand of cards, she'd even been able to afford really good pub food. But she'd never seen anything like this.

The bedroom door opened while she still gaped at the table. She turned to find Jacob standing in the doorway, smiling. Her mouth almost dropped open.

He wore a pair of snug tan breeches and a short, navy tunic, cut to fit his torso perfectly. His hair was combed smooth and tied with a leather thong into a low tail. She'd never seen him wear anything more elegant than his uniform, and she didn't remember seeing these clothes in his wardrobe. He took her breath away.

"Jacob," she whispered. "You look magnificent." Her heart rate leapt when he chuckled and moved toward her.

"Thank you, Victoria."

He stopped in front of her, forcing her to drop her head back to look into his face.

"Shall we?" he asked, indicating the table.

"You want me to think about food? Now?"

"Yes, love. I have a special evening planned and it begins with dinner." He moved around and pulled her chair out.

Vic sat, but her pulse raced. "The table is lovely," she said, to distract herself.

"I'm glad you like it. Wine?"

She nodded. His smile never left his lips, even when he raised his own glass for a drink. With an effort, she pulled her gaze away from his face to sip the wine. "This is your favorite? The wine we had at the Winnow?"

"Yes. Try the steak. It's marinated in a mushroom sauce."

She put knife and fork to the meat, suddenly all too aware of her lack of table manners. Her shoulders hunched when the knife scraped loudly across the plate. She met his gaze as she put the bite of steak into her mouth. He was still smiling and hadn't seemed to notice her lack of etiquette. She took a relieved breath and let herself taste the food that melted in her mouth.

"I've never tasted anything so wonderful." Suddenly, she was ravenous. With a great deal of effort, she didn't wolf down her food. But only barely.

When the meal finished, Jacob poured her a second glass of wine and stood. "I'll be back in just a minute."

She watched him disappear into the bedroom and return carrying a small red box. He held it at her eye level and opened the lid to reveal a tray full of chocolate truffles. Her grin grew. Unconsciously, she bit her lip as she selected a dark chocolate. "I can't remember the last time I had chocolate," she said, staring at the sweet like it was a precious jewel.

He set down the box, and when she still hadn't taken a bite, he took hold of her hand and brought the sweet gently to her lips.

She closed her eyes, biting the chocolate with a heavy sigh. The rich flavor melted between her tongue and the roof of her mouth. Before she opened her eyes, Jacob's mouth closed over hers. But when she would have deepened the kiss, he pulled back.

"Would you like to dance, Victoria?"

"Now? There's no music."

"We don't need any."

She bit her bottom lip again and looked at her lap. "I don't know how," she whispered.

He raised her chin with one finger. "Then I'll teach you." He pulled her gently to her feet. "Relax," he said, placing one hand at the small of her back and clasping her hand in his other. "Follow my feet."

Slowly, he began moving her around the room in gentle circles. She watched his feet, but after a few moments, he pressed her tighter against him, hiding his feet from view.

"Look into my eyes," he whispered.

Meeting his dark gaze, she forgot to worry about her feet or his. She melted against him, trusting him to guide her, losing herself in the depths of his eyes. He sung quietly, a song she didn't know, but his deep baritone was rich and enchanting.

"You could have been a bard," she murmured.

"If I'd been a bard, we might never have met. And I couldn't have lived with that."

Her heart slammed against her ribs. The lump in her throat prevented any response. Jacob continued to sing softly, spinning her around the room, until she was dizzy from the blood pounding in her veins. When they stopped, she clung to him to keep her feet beneath her.

"Would you like more wine?" he asked, leading her back to the table.

"I don't think I should." At his quizzical look, she said, "I feel quite drunk already."

He arched an eyebrow and gave her another sultry smile. "Perhaps another chocolate?" He plucked a truffle from the box and placed it against her parted lips.

Keeping her gaze locked with his, she ran her tongue along the confection before taking a slow bite. She took the rest of the chocolate into her mouth along with the tips of two of his fingers. She sucked gently, running her tongue around the tips. She released her hold only when she heard him groan.

"Dinner was marvelous," she said through a half smile. "The chocolates were decadent." She ran her hands slowly along his chest, her gaze following their movements. "Thank you for teaching me to dance." When her hands wrapped around his neck, she tipped her head back to look into his dark eyes. "Now, make the night perfect. Make love to me."

His hands slipped to her waist. His mouth dropped to her upturned face. As his lips brushed against hers, he whispered, "Promise me something, love."

"What?"

"Don't take any more unnecessary risks. It would kill me to lose you now."

"You won't lose me, Jacob. No unnecessary risks. I promise."

The time for words over, he lifted her into his arms and carried her to the bedroom, moving unbearably slowly. Setting her on the edge of the bed, he did no more than kiss her for a long time. Vic ran her fingers along his neck to loosen his hair from the thong. She could taste the rich wine on his lips and the scent of leather and musk surrounded her. Her body screamed for him, but her mind savored their slow pace.

When his hands moved up her sides, she pulled her body back and moved his hands to cover her breasts. He kissed his way down her neck to the swell of her bosom just above the neck of her gown. His tongue traced intricate patterns as his hands kneaded her aching skin. Tangling her fingers into his hair, she dropped her head back and moaned softly.

With trembling fingers, he untied the laces on the front of her bodice and pulled it apart. She closed her eyes, feeling the material slip just over her shoulders. She squeezed her eyes tighter and bit her lip when his mouth closed over her nipple. She was only vaguely aware as he pulled her new breast dagger from its perch. All of her thoughts were centered on the skin he sucked and nipped to an almost painful peak.

He moved away from her long enough to set the dagger on his night table. Then, inch by inch, he slid her dress to the floor. He knelt at her feet as she stepped out of the mounds of material, then pushed the garment aside and stood to claim her mouth again. Slow and torturous minutes passed before he finally removed her corset and shift. Her entire body was a quivering, aching need when he finally allowed her to pull off his tunic.

A hand closed over hers as her fingers sought the lacings of his breeches, but she would no longer be denied. Her other hand deftly untied his bonds. She slipped his pants to the floor then ran her hands along his thighs to grasp his pulsing erection.

"No more waiting," she commanded, squeezing until he groaned.

"No more waiting," he agreed in a ragged voice.

She lay across the bed, pulling him on top of her and wrapping her legs around his waist. Her body exploded with his first thrust, forcing a shuddering groan through clenched teeth. She captured his mouth with hers even as her body built to another agonizing climax. Lost in his rhythm, she felt only him, thinking of nothing beyond the moment. He made her feel wild and sexy and more like a woman than she'd ever realized she could be. He gave her a safe place to be free. She clung to his shoulders, panting and helpless before his passion. When she heard him groan her name, a part of her, deep in her soul, knew she would never be the same again.

They collapsed together, sweat-soaked and breathless. After a time, Jacob rolled and pulled her on top of him. He caressed her damp hair and face, kissing the top of her head. Her lips moved over his chest as she nuzzled against him.

When she looked up at his shoulders, she gasped. Fingering the scratch marks, she grimaced. "Sorry."

"Don't be, love." He grinned wolfishly. "For the next few days, those will be a pleasant reminder of this night."

"Mmm. I don't need a reminder. This is a night I'll never forget."

His grin softened. "Good."

He kissed her lightly then rolled to his side. Pulling up the covers, he wrapped them both in a warm cocoon. She nestled close, and very soon, fell into a deep, dreamless sleep.

Jacob remained awake for as long as he could, even after her breathing slowed and steadied. Every moment with Victoria was precious. His own exhausted body wouldn't be denied sleep for long. But as his eyes began to close, he tightened his hold on the little thief.

"Sleep well, my love," he whispered into her hair just as exhaustion overcame him.

Vic woke slowly, her mind climbing lazily to full awareness. She was alone in the bed, but quiet movement let her know Jacob was still there. Pulling the covers up under her chin, she inadvertently touched the onyx charm still at her throat.

"Jacob," she murmured, sitting up.

"Good morning, love. Did you dream?"

"Not a single one, thank you very much."

"You're welcome." He joined her on the bed, dressed in his King's Own uniform.

"The raid is tonight?" she spoke quietly, but held his gaze.

"Yes."

She untied the necklace. "Wear this." When he started to protest, she pushed it toward him. "Please, Jacob. Please."

He gave in with a nod, allowing her to tie the black cord around his neck. Running her fingers over the onyx where it hung at the hollow of his throat, she smiled. "That makes me feel a little better. Though, if you were to let me go with you…"

"No." He took her hand in his and squeezed. "Absolutely not and don't you dare follow. Remember your promise last night."

"Okay," she sighed. "But I'm not happy. You better not get yourself hurt, Jacob Marin."

He smiled, cocky and self-assured. "Worried?"

"No." She set her mouth in a pout, but it dissolved into a lopsided grin.

"You'll stay here today." It wasn't a question.

"No," she said. "I have to go into town to see if the Hole has any news. Don't frown at me. I need to know what's happening. And this isn't an unnecessary risk. I'll be careful. I'll wear my new dress. None of Charlie's men will recognize me in that. Hell, *I* don't recognize me in that."

He laughed, shaking his head. "All right, little thief. But be careful."

"Always." Her smile started him chuckling again.

"You'll come back here tonight?"

"You won't be here." She wanted to stay in his room, to wait for his return, to make sure he did return, but she hadn't wanted to ask. She hadn't even wanted to address the topic. Despite his actions, Vic was still insecure about his true feelings. She couldn't help it. For all she knew, he acted this way with all of his lovers. Which would explain why the women of Karasnia spoke so highly of him.

"I'd like you to be here," he said, running a hand across her cheek and into her hair. "I'll know you're safe if you're here. And I like the idea of coming home to you."

"'Coming home to me?' That sounds very domestic." Her stomach tumbled in giddy pleasure at the thought.

"It does, doesn't it?"

His smile touched her heart.

"Will you be here?"

"Yes," she breathed. "I'll be here when you come home."

CHAPTER FOURTEEN

Vic heard the familiar whistle just before she entered the shrine. The open floor of the pyramid was empty except for a single woman, deep in meditation. Vic knelt before the garden for a full five minutes, offering a prayer of hope that the news she was about to receive wasn't bad. Outside, she slipped around to the backside of the pyramid where few passed.

"Hey, Pfreal." Ren grinned, his eyes wide, his eyebrows hiked up to his hairline. "Never seen you in a dress before. Least not one like that. You look good. What'd you do, win a bet?"

Vic smiled crookedly, dropping the hood of the cloak she'd borrowed from Jacob. "Lost one actually. Hey, speaking of bets, how's the big game going?"

"Brad's doing all right. But Joe's leading the table."

"Figures. Brad never could hold up to Missek." She shot a glance around then leaned against the stone wall close to Ren. "So what's the word? You obviously got my message."

He paled slightly, his expression freezing into serious lines. "Some of the Hole's people are already missing, Pfreal."

"Who?"

"Nick. Thrilaa. Bankt. Wats."

Vic closed her eyes, bit her bottom lip, and breathed in deeply. "Damn."

"There's more. Some of Charlie's men have turned up missing, too. He doesn't believe Gip about the magicians."

"He thinks the Hole is responsible." She wasn't really surprised.

"Yeah."

"Is Charlie responsible for any of our losses?"

"We don't know. But he's declared war."

"Goddess help us." She felt like she'd been slugged in the stomach. She ran a hand over her eyes, then up through her hair. Looking into the too-young face of her friend, she said, "Ren, hide. Go deep. Damn the Hole. Damn Charlie. Keep out of sight until this thing ends."

He dropped his gaze. "I can't, Pfreal," he said just above a whisper. "I have to do my part."

"Damn it, this isn't just about Charlie. You don't know what those magicians can do."

"I've got a pretty good idea."

He met her gaze, his hazel eyes old for his adolescent face.

"They gonna stop the magicians, Pfreal?"

She didn't need to ask who they were. "Yeah, they're taking care of it. But it's not over yet." She heaved a heavy sigh. "All right, little man. You do what you have to. But watch your neck."

His mouth lifted in a half grin. "You got it. You, too. Stay standing."

"Always."

Vic slipped around to the front of the shrine. Her mind tangled over Charlie's lousy timing. Just when the gangs should work together to keep their people alive, Charlie goes and starts a war.

A war that began with her.

She heaved another sigh. She couldn't solve the problem. Not yet. But when the magicians were out of the way, she was going to have a talk with Charlie. Enough was enough. She wouldn't be responsible for the deaths of Hole people. Not when her actions had started the whole thing.

Working a twisted path toward Upper Market, she was almost to the place where she'd hidden her blacks when a hand closed over her mouth and dragged her into an alley. She started to struggle, but her feet twisted in her skirts. Her hand was already reaching for her new breast dagger, when her assailant whispered in her ear.

"No knives, Vic," the raspy, nasal voice commanded. "I just want to talk."

The hands holding her loosened, and she spun to look into the face of her assailant. Her dagger jumped instantly to hand. "Tracker," she growled.

"Shut up, Vic. No one knows I'm in town."

"We couldn't have guessed? Your men are everywhere."

"Put away the knife, Flash. My men are why I want to talk to you."

She studied the smuggler's face. He was dirty, unwashed for at least two weeks by the smell. Tangled dark hair framed his beaten face. Above the crooked lump of his nose, his dark eyes darted almost continuously. He looked like a starving animal trapped in a cage.

"Okay. Make it a good story," she said, sliding her dagger back into its sheath.

Tracker eyed the dagger's place then her attire. "You look good in a dress, Flash."

"Careful. This time I'll break something more than just your nose."

He raised his hands, palms facing her. "No offense intended. Just an observation. Actually, you did me a favor by smashing my nose."

"How'd I do that?"

His eyes darted around the alley again, then he motioned to a door. She followed warily. When he nodded her in, she said, "After you." With a shrug, Tracker entered. She passed through the door behind him, ready to bolt at the first sign of trouble.

They walked into a small, empty, spotless room. The space was used for storage, but its current cargo hadn't come into the city yet. Tracker paced to the opposite side of the room and dropped heavily against the wall. A single torch flickered in a wall sconce to his right, the only illumination in the windowless square.

Vic stood by the door, her hand resting lightly on the latch. She closed it enough to block most of their conversation, but left enough of a gap so she could watch the street. "All right, Tracker. Talk."

"It's a long story. Started on that last run through Georna to Bthak. We were camping half a day from the border, Bthak side, on our way back into Karasnia, when Malkiney goes missing. We waited for a full day. No one knew where he'd gone or what had happened. Next morning, we're getting ready to give up and pull out, and he shows up. He gives me some story about coming across a mountaineer's daughter who was up for a little play. Said he'd have caught up with us eventually."

"And that's strange?" Vic leaned against a wall, her gaze darting between her view of the street and Tracker. She didn't trust him, never had, but the man looked more nervous than she'd ever seen him. His hands jerked with each movement, the skin under his right eye twitched, his mouth worked even when he wasn't talking. It took a lot to make a man like him nervous and that worried her more than being cornered in this room.

"Malkiney's never gone off like that before, Flash, but I've had others who have, so I figured the story was true enough. And Malkiney seemed all right, you know? Nothing different, nothing suspicious.

So we started for the border and just before we get there, we come across this man, all alone, standing in the middle of the road. And I'm thinking it's a trap, but the men I'd sent to scout had come back with nothing.

"The man tells me he has a job for me. Top pay. I ask what. He tells me he's got some people he needs smuggled into Dareelia, quick and quiet. Says they're a few hours ride away. Now I'm real suspicious and I'm about to tell him no deal 'cause we're going to our wintering hole when he tosses this bag at me. Flash, the bag almost knocked me on my ass it was so heavy. Full of gold. Real gold. And this guy tells me there's lots more."

Tracker hacked out a harsh laugh and shook his head. "At the time, I thought, what the hell, yeah. My men are good. Nothing they can't handle. And if things go bad, we could always cut out, take the bag and run. There was enough gold to last us through winter and into next summer."

"What'd this guy look like?"

"Don't remember."

"What?" She straightened from the wall. "What do you mean you don't remember?"

"It's like the image of him ain't in my memory. I wouldn't know him if I tripped over him. All I remember is he seemed…harmless. You know? Like we could take him, no problem."

"What happened after you picked up the magicians?"

His eyes narrowed, but he said, "The one that hired us left instructions that the three were to be brought in from separate directions to specific places in town. The fourth—"

"Fourth?!" Her voice echoed in the small room.

"Quiet if you're gonna leave that door open," Tracker hissed. "Yeah, there're four. The fourth would stay in the Karasnian Forest.

When I asked about guarding the fourth, the man said not to worry about it. Then he disappeared. So we break into three groups to pass into Karasnia. The fourth, he comes along with mine and Malkiney's group."

"Which of the other three did you have?"

"The white one. The one from the inn."

Her suspicions jumped and her fingers twitched for a blade. "Why you telling me this? What do you want from me?"

"I saw you go in the other night, Flash. I saw you go into the inn and get out without being killed. No small feat. I tracked you back to the castle, so I know you've got a connection there. I want to help you stop these twisted spawn of the damned."

"Why?" She took no pains to hide her distrust.

He looked at his feet then met her gaze. His right eye twitched hard enough that it looked like he was winking.

"That's the rest of the story," he said. "We were down near the Karasnian province-Georna border when I saw the goblins keeping pace with us. No one else noticed. When I pointed them out to Malkiney, he said I must be seeing things. These goblins were… different. Quiet, moving in twos or threes, and taller than any goblin I've ever seen. But I never got a good look at them. They never came near us. Not once.

"Then, just after I started seeing the goblins, my men started disappearing. One, two at a time. Every night. And again, no one else noticed. Malkiney says they probably cut for a wintering hole or found themselves a bed to warm. But too many of them were missing.

"One night, I stay awake. I pretended to sleep, but I kept an eye on the fire. That's when I saw him—the white one—throw something into the flames. This purple smoke came up from the fire and spread over the men while they're sleeping. I don't know what it was. But next thing I know, Malkiney and two other guys are standing. The other men, they're moving funny, all stiff and jerky.

"I watched Malkiney, the two others and both sorcerers go into the woods. I tried to follow but, just past the edge of the trees, they were gone. So I tried going back to the camp to wake some of the others. None of 'em budged. Nothing. They weren't dead, just…"

"Not there," Vic provided. "The men in the inn were the same. All but Malkiney."

Tracker shook his head. "It was the powder stuff the white one threw in the fire."

"Why weren't you affected?"

He tapped his nose and smiled. "Only reason I can figure. I haven't been able to smell since you crushed my nose, so all I can guess is that you have to be able to smell the stuff for it to work. So, you see, Flash, you saved my life."

"If all you have to do is smell it, why wasn't I affected when I went in the inn? Why isn't Malkiney affected?"

"Don't know about Malkiney. But the stuff builds the more you're exposed to it. I watched for the next few nights and the white one used less and less each time. I imagine, by now, the men only need a little before they go under. There probably wasn't enough in the air to affect you that night."

The sound of voices in the alley outside the door silenced them both. Vic watched as two men and a woman strolled past, deep in conversation. As they neared the door, she caught a few words on the state of horse prices that year. They passed the door without looking up from their conversation. When the alley fell silent again, she asked, "What happened that first night? When the magicians came back?"

"Only Malkiney came back with them. I can only guess what happened to the other two. That's when I realized we were smuggling blood magicians, not just magical thieves. Next morning, I ask Malkiney where the two men are and I get pretty much the same story. But he starts looking at me kinda strange, suspicious. I stayed for four more nights, watching. Every night the same. On the day after the fourth night, I see him talking real quiet-like to the copper-skinned magician—he's the one not in town. And they're looking in my direction. I didn't wait around. I disappeared that night."

"So why are you here? I mean if Malkiney sees you…"

"I told you, I want the bastards stopped. They took my right-arm man, Flash. Killed a lot of good men. Now I might not be an upstanding citizen of Karasnia, but I don't like blood magicians in my kingdom. After that mess with Prince Erick…well, I figure I owe it to the men who've been killed to make sure these blooded damned are caught."

"I still don't know what you think I can do for you." And she wasn't sure if she should even believe his story. This could easily be a way to lure Jacob and the King's Guard into a trap. But if it was, Tracker was a pawn in the plan and not the one in charge. She'd seen him try to con before. He didn't do it by going without baths and twitching with every move.

"I know you know where the one is." His voice dropped. "I can tell you where the other two are."

"You know? Where?"

"I want to talk to your man inside the castle. I want protection."

"How do I know you're telling the truth? How do I know this isn't some elaborate trap?"

Tracker wiped the back of his hand across his mouth. "I'm scared, Flash. If they find me here, I'm dead. And I know how they kill."

She swallowed hard. She knew how they killed, too. "I know where two of them are. If you confirm the location of the second, I'll take you to the castle."

He pursed his thin lips. "Which magician?"

"The sorceress."

"North. Mid-sector, in the basement of a leather shop. A few blocks from the old tannery."

She bit the inside of her bottom lip. Even if he were lying, she now had the location of the third magician. "Okay, I'll take you to my man. But I'm wanted around town right now—"

"Charlie? Yeah, I heard. Three Devil's High with Joe Missek? I'm impressed."

She snorted. "Yeah, well, it's caused a lot more trouble than I'd anticipated. Should have stuck to two. Anyway, we'll have to play a part up to the castle." She looked him over. "Keep your cowl up and walk a pace behind me. Puff up a little."

"Bodyguard to the lady?"

"Yeah." Vic studied his face. The skin under his eye still jumped, but he no longer looked like he was winking. "If you're lying to me, Tracker…if this is a trap, I'll kill you myself."

"If it's a choice between one of your knives and one of theirs, I'll take yours with a smile."

She gave him a short nod then slid moved out the door, bringing her own hood up around her head. She walked back toward the castle with her head up, her shoulders thrown back, affecting as much noble negligence as she could muster, taking time to stop at an occasional stand or shop window despite her anxiety to get back. Tracker played his part well, a permanent scowl across his features, a forbidding look to any man who glanced at her, a carefully hidden hand beneath his cloak. Even his twitches worked to his advantage. He was the image of a dangerous bodyguard.

As Vic moved away from an apple stand, she heard him grunt. When she turned, he was scowling at a very broad, brown-cloaked figure, hurrying down the street. "What?"

"Guy just plowed into me. Must be drunk. He's already started celebrating new year's night."

"Why do you say that?" She resumed her walk toward the castle.

"He had a mask on already. Really ugly green one, too."

At the castle entrance, Vic approached one of the King's Own who stood guard. He was a tall young man with friendly blue eyes, short, light brown hair, and a classically handsome face. As she walked toward him, he grinned. "Good day, Victoria."

"Hi, Garath."

"You look very nice. New?" He nodded to her dress.

She smiled, just short of being embarrassed. The compliments on how she looked in a dress were coming a little too frequently. "Yeah. Listen, I need to find General Marin." Behind her, Tracker hissed in a sharp breath.

Garath glanced past her at the hooded man then back, the question plain in his blue eyes.

"We may have found the third," she told the guard simply.

"Follow me." Garath nodded at the other two guards, who proceeded to spread out to make up for his absence. "I'll send someone," he said before leading Vic and Tracker into the castle. The first King's Guard they passed was sent back to the entrance.

As Garath told the young woman in King's green what was needed, Tracker whispered in Vic's ear, "You didn't mention your man inside the castle was General Marin."

"You got a problem with Marin?"

"No. Just didn't think I'd be lucky enough to give this to him directly. I mean, he actually knows what he's dealing with, after the Prince and all. I gotta hand it to you, Flash, you couldn't have picked a better connection."

She tried not to smile. Tracker didn't need to know that Jacob had come to her. Garath rejoined them and led them through a series of corridors to a training field. Jacob stood at the edge of the grounds with General Thack, watching his men drill, a slight frown touching his mouth. Vic couldn't hold her smile this time.

"Generals," Garath said as they approached.

Jacob turned, looked at his lieutenant, then noticed Vic and a smile lit his face. A smile that turned to a concerned frown when he noticed the third person.

"What's going on, Victoria?"

"Jacob, this is Tracker. Tracker, General Jacob Marin. General George Thack."

Tracker lowered his hood, and Jacob scowled.

Thack cursed loudly at the sight of the sought-after smuggler.

When Jacob looked back at her, Vic shrugged. "He knows where the third magician is."

***

"Are you sure?"

King John stood in front of his desk, his eyes narrowed, his lips a thin line.

Vic's gaze darted between the king and Jacob. A little lump of fear and anticipation sat in her stomach.

"I've already sent men to check the story, Sire," Jacob said. "They should report back within the hour."

King John looked out his window, gauging the angle of the sun. "Victoria, do you think this is a trap?"

She unconsciously bit her lip before answering. "I don't know, Your Majesty, but I don't think it is. Tracker was scared. Scared enough to come to me and we don't exactly have a friendly past. He didn't know Jacob and I are working together. He only knew I had a connection in

191

the castle. And he saw me go into the inn and come out. No one else in that inn besides Malkiney and the sorcerer were conscious. He could have come in after I was already inside, but…I don't think he's lying."

The king nodded, his brow knitting in thought, a frown deepening the creases around his strong mouth. "This Tracker, he's still in custody?"

"Yes, Majesty," Jacob answered. "We're keeping him under close guard. He won't be getting out before the raid, and no one's mentioned that there will be a raid."

"What he doesn't know won't hurt us," King John said, raising one brow. "Very well, Jacob. If your scouts confirm the location of the third magician, then move ahead with the raid on all three locations. The Guild is prepared for that contingency. I'll have the queen send word that they're to be ready."

"Yes, Majesty."

King John faced her, a smile touching his troubled expression. "Seems we're once more in your debt, Victoria."

"This was more of an accident than any of my doing, Majesty," she said, wanting to fidget under his intense gaze.

"Nevertheless. You have my debt yet again. Thank you."

She bowed her head and mumbled, "You're welcome, Majesty."

In the hall, Jacob circled an arm around her shoulders. "Seems you're destined to get into the middle of this mess no matter what I do, little thief."

She chuckled, wrapping her arm around his waist. "It's not my fault Tracker came to me." Her expression sobered. "Jacob? Are…are you keeping Tracker in the dungeon?"

"No, he's in a room in the guest wing under close guard. Why?"

"I just…let's just say I don't like dungeons. Actually, I hate dungeons. Even for people I can't stand." When Jacob cast her a questioning glance, she didn't bother to elaborate. After a thoughtful pause, she asked, "What about the fourth? The one in the woods?"

He took a slow, deep breath and tightened his hold. "There's nothing we can do before tonight. We'll have to send troops into the forest to hunt him down and send the goblins back north. I'm sure the goblins are working for the magicians, but I can't figure out why or to what purpose. Especially now that they seem to have disappeared."

"No sight of them, huh?"

"Not for a few days. Not even in the forest."

They reached the turn in the corridor where they'd have to separate. Jacob pulled her into a tight hug. "You'll stay in now?"

"Yes." She smiled.

"Good. And Victoria?"

"Yes?"

He leaned in very close. "You were biting your lip in there. It's hard for me to see that and not react. But I don't think King John would have appreciated me kissing you in his presence."

Before she could answer, he covered her mouth, his drugging kiss hard and potent. She melted against him, knowing that, until the raid was over, this would be the last time she'd see him. Her fear for his safety strengthened her kiss to near desperation. She didn't want to let go.

He eased away slowly, ran a finger over her cheek then started to walk away still holding her hand.

"Jacob," she said, tugging him gently. When he looked back, she swallowed the lump forming in her throat and said, "Stay standing, General."

"Be here when I get back."

She nodded, releasing his hand only when her arm wouldn't stretch any further. She watched his retreating back until he disappeared around a corner then slowly worked her way back to his rooms.

CHAPTER FIFTEEN

Heee's still in there, General," Garath whispered.

Jacob stared at the blue door. His spies had been watching the house all day. The sorcerer was still inside. The few smugglers that had left were being tailed. They wouldn't return in the middle of the raid.

"The others are ready," Henry whispered in Jacob's ear.

Jacob glanced at the young sorcerer attached to his group. Black breeches and tunic replaced his usual long black robe. Sharp angles and high cheekbones formed a face that looked too young for the power contained beneath. Only the ice blue of his slanted eyes and the shock of white hair against tawny skin hinted at Henry's strength.

In the palm of his hand, a small emerald pulsed. The jewel was magically linked with the magicians attached to the other two raiding teams. Patterned pulses of green light communicated a code known only to the Guild magicians.

With a hand gesture, Jacob signaled his soldiers forward. Every window was guarded. The sewers had been checked for escape routes. There were none from the house. It was just after midnight and the streets in that part of town were quiet.

The crashing of glass and splintering of wood erupted into the silent night when Jacob's soldiers plowed into the house. The smugglers were quick to respond, but surprise gave the king's soldiers the advantage. Jacob, leading the way through the front door, slashed through scrambling men. Henry followed close behind.

The charcoal sorcerer wasn't hard to find. In the very midst of the battle, he worked, mouth moving silently, hands twisting in a convoluted pattern. From the corner of his eye, Jacob saw one of his men fall as the sorcerer's hand flung outward. Then Henry moved from behind Jacob.

The magical battle was engaged.

Jacob moved with strength and precision, cutting down all who came near the sorcerers. Most of the smugglers fought to the death, a few threw down their weapons and surrendered. The battle didn't last long. Behind them, lights flashed and flickered, but the magical duel was silent. Only the rumbling of the house around them spoke of the thrusts being exchanged.

When Jacob turned to the magicians, he faced the blood sorcerer's back. Henry tossed a bolt of green light, his expression calm and confident, even when the energy sizzled harmlessly around the blood mage's shield. His stance wide, his shoulders straight, Henry looked in complete control, limitless in energy. But sweat beaded his forehead and he flinched under the blood mage's attack. Henry struck again, hard and without hesitation, and the blood mage began to waver, falling slowly backward toward Jacob.

A shout from Henry alerted Jacob in time to see the sorcerer pull a small, smooth cube from the folds of his robe. Blasts of white-blue power slammed against the blood mage's shield but dissipated without breaking through. Henry took a step closer, forcing the blood mage back, continuing to bombard him with a rapid series of varying attacks, striking without pause.

Giving Jacob an opening.

He swung his sword, slashing through the magician's neck. Blood splattered his clothing and face as the sorcerer's body collapsed to the ground. The cube slipped from his fingers, clattering across the wooden floor, stopping when it touched Henry's boot.

Jacob met Henry's blue eyes and nodded once before walking out of the house into the cold night air.

"What do you mean they got away?" Jacob scowled at Henry.

"That's the message I'm receiving, General Marin. The other two gated out."

"How? I thought you'd taken precautions against gating." Jacob kept his voice low, but anger and frustration threatened to burst out. He kept his hands fisted to maintain his control.

"The gates weren't magic gates, General."

"Not magic gates? What then?"

"Mechanical. The cube."

Henry held up the device, flipping it in his hand. The surface was smooth seamless copper.

"I've read of similar devices, General, but they're notoriously unpredictable and impractical. They can't be made to gate for more than a mile at most. No one in memory has been able to extend the limit and repeatedly gating increases the chances of something going wrong, so the use of them was largely abandoned."

"Then why? Why did the magicians use them?"

Henry shrugged. "They can't be stopped with magic, and they don't require a magician to activate them."

"What about the controls?" Jacob nodded to the cube's smooth surface.

"It's an illusion. Any magician of sufficient skill can place an illusion on the cube so only the user can see the controls. If it's stolen or lost, it can't be used."

Henry stared intently at the cube for a heartbeat, his brow crinkling in concentration. As Jacob watched, the illusion slipped away, revealing a flat dial and two metal buttons.

Jacob let out a heavy breath. He wanted to yell at somebody. Instead, he turned to Garath. "Have the prisoners taken back to the castle, Lieutenant. Henry, come with me. We'll have to tell the king about this…mechanical gating. And that two of the magicians escaped."

Worry continued to nag Jacob as he quietly slipped into his room. The sun was just beginning to lighten the sky through the windows. Exhaustion weighed so heavily on him, he wasn't sure if he'd be able to sleep. And something still bothered him.

The loss of the magicians was bad. And, as it turned out, Malkiney had managed to escape also. But that wasn't what disturbed Jacob. There was a problem, a possibility that hung just beyond his tired mind's ability to grasp. Something about the gating. Maybe after a bath and a few hours sleep he'd be able to pinpoint his unease.

The sight of Victoria curled beneath the blankets made him smile. At least she'd been safe. Silently, he closed the door to the washroom and filled the washbasin with warm water. Blood still caked his hands and splattered his clothing, but he couldn't smell the metallic stench anymore. He'd been coated in it for too long.

Turning back to the washstand, basin in hand, he was more than a little surprised to see Victoria standing in the doorway. He hadn't heard her. Her arms crossed over her stomach, bunching the front of the shirt she'd borrowed from his wardrobe. Her hair hung in a tangled mass around her face.

"Is any of that yours?" she asked, nodding at the blood covering him.

"No, love. I wasn't hurt."

Her shoulders slumped visibly with her exhaled breath. Then she smiled.

Despite his exhaustion, he found his heart jumping. He smiled back. "I didn't mean to wake you," he murmured, setting the full basin back on the table.

"You didn't. I wasn't asleep." She went to the tub and began filling it with warm water. "Get out of those." She nodded at his clothes.

He washed the blood from his hands then stripped. The waiting bath was hot and soothing to his tight, tired muscles. He settled into its heat and closed his eyes as Victoria washed the remaining blood from his neck and face with a washcloth. When he opened his eyes, she was staring at him. "What's wrong, love?"

"Something didn't go right," she said, shifting so her chin rested on the edge of the tub. "Did it?"

He reached to cup her cheek. "There was a problem. Two of the magicians got away. The third was killed."

"Which one?"

"The one in the house near the eastern gate."

"That's where you were, wasn't it?"

"Um hmm."

"Did you…?"

"Yes."

She touched the onyx hanging at his throat. "How did the others escape?"

"Gated out. Mechanical gates. The Guild magicians couldn't stop it."

She nodded. After a silent moment, she looked back into his eyes. "I'm glad you're safe."

He smiled and leaned forward, kissing her gently. The warm scent of her skin, the soft touch of her hair, the taste of her lips, stilled his worrying mind and banished the stench of blood still heavy in his nostrils. "I'm glad you're here," he said, running a hand through her curls.

"You must be tired." She stood and plucked a fresh towel from the washstand. "Time for sleep."

At her nod, he stepped out of the tub and she wrapped the towel around his hips. Then, quite suddenly, she melted against him, circling her arms about his waist. Holding her close, he felt the thud of her heartbeat. "Worried?" he whispered to the top of her head.

"No," she answered, but she kept her face pressed to his chest and tightened her grip.

He chuckled. "Come on, little thief. Let's both get some sleep."

***

The maid left the bedroom, giggling into her hand as she closed the door behind her. Vic grinned into the mirror, turning to get a side view. Jacob was going to love this. Her masquerade gown had been delivered that afternoon. Shortly after, when the maid arrived to help her get dressed and fix her hair, she'd forced Jacob from his bedroom.

She studied the finished effect. The top of her hair was pulled back into a loose bun with curls left to hang around her shoulders. Silver thread woven through her hair caught the light with every move. The addition of feathers and silver sequins to the gown had perfected the outfit. Just one last touch. She retrieved her breast dagger and slipped it into place.

At last ready, she continued to delay her entrance, knowing Jacob was pacing the outer room. She couldn't wait to see him, but the anticipation and mild torture inflicted on him was too much fun to hurry. She stood by the door, listening to his restless stalking, trying not to chuckle out loud. When her own excitement got the better of her, she moved the mask to her face and opened the door wide.

He stopped and stared.

He looked too sexy for his own good, she thought, staring back and coming very close to biting her lip. He was also dressed in black and white—tight black leather breeches, a loose white shirt with full sleeves, stiff cuffs and a high collar, and a snug black leather vest. His mask was a red wooden full-face mask with a hooked nose and a mischievous grin lifting its cheeks. It hung precariously from his fingers.

"Victoria, you look…absolutely stunning."

"Thank you." She flashed him a sexy smile and sauntered to him. "I'm glad you like. You look *very* good, too." She shifted her mask away from her face and looked him over with undisguised admiration.

His free hand circled her waist and pulled her roughly against his body. She clutched his leather vest.

"Perhaps we should stay in," he said huskily.

"Not after all the trouble it took to get into this thing," she answered. Her mood sobered when she added, "Besides, you have to be there tonight." She nodded at the sword prominently strapped to his hip.

He gave in with a groan, but didn't loosen his grip. "Do you have your daggers?"

"I've got the breast dagger."

His gaze lowered to the curve of her breasts and a dangerous smile touched his lips. "You know, I could always help you get back into that dress. We aren't expected right away."

"Uh uh, Jacob Marin. You'd muss my hair." She fluttered her lashes and feigned a prim, ladylike pout.

"Very well, you minx." He laughed. "But don't expect that dress to stay on for long after we return tonight."

"Well, I should hope not."

Stepping back, Jacob slipped his mask over his head, tying the ribbons that held it in place, and then took her arm.

As they strolled through the castle, Vic noted the increased number of guards. After losing two of the blood magicians, Jacob and General Thack had tripled the castle guard and sent military troops to patrol the city streets. Both generals were required to attend the masquerade ball, but both would also spend the evening alert and armed. Despite his banter, she knew Jacob was worried.

When they reached the large double doors opening onto the ballroom, music washed over them. The hall was unlike anything Vic had ever seen. The long walls were lined at the base with dark wooden panels. From the panels to the high ceiling, the stones were covered with pale cream silk decorated with abstract designs in gold leaf. The ceiling was carved of dark wood shot with gold accents. Candles circled the thick wooden pillars lining the hall, but the lighting was dim, giving the room an eerie, unreal feel. On the highly polished pale gold wood of the dance floor, couples in both ghoulish and festive masks twirled at maddening speeds to the orchestra's strange, haunting music.

"I've never seen anything like this," she said as Jacob led her into the hall, leaning close so he could hear her above the music. The gold detailing in both the ceiling and the silk wall coverings glittered in the dim lighting, painting strange patterns at the edges of her vision.

"You know, I think this is the first time I've ever seen you *really* impressed."

She smiled wickedly. "Oh, I think you've seen me impressed once or twice before."

His arm tightened around her waist. "We'd better dance, or I'm going to drag you away from all of this early."

Before she could stop him, he pulled her onto the dance floor. The room passed in a rush. Lights and colors swirled together, solid objects became blurred and indistinct, the other couples faded into a mass of noisy specters, making the dance eerily surreal. For just that instant, Jacob was the only solid thing in her world, the focus of all her senses. He took her breath away.

When the song ended, she shook off the strange, dream-like quality of the dance and grinned. "That was fun," she said as they walked toward the side of the room.

"Good," he murmured in her ear. Her entire body began to tingle in reaction to the heat of his breath on her skin.

He led her to where General Thack stood with his wife, a tall, powerfully built woman with fiery red hair almost a match to her husband's. Thack also had a sword strapped to his hip.

"Good evening, George, Rea," Jacob greeted with a nod.

"General Marin," the woman smiled. "It's good to see you again."

"How's the little one?"

"He's fine and strong. Lungs like bellows."

"Aye," Thack groaned. "And he knows when to use 'em too."

"Rea, I'd like you to meet Victoria Flash. Victoria, this is Rea Von Thack."

"Pleasure to meet you," Vic said.

"Aye, so you're the spy George's been telling me about. Well, it's a pleasure to meet you too, Victoria."

Rea's green-eyed gaze danced between her and Jacob, making Vic want to fidget.

"Are you enjoying the ball?" Thack asked.

Grateful for the diversion, she smiled. "It's wonderful. Some of these masks are grotesque." She nodded toward one in particular.

The ugly mask approached their small group, much to her surprise, accompanied by a lady wearing an elegant, very alien mask covered in feathers and tufts of purple and red velvet.

"Good evening, Majesties," Thack greeted.

Vic's stomach dropped.

Queen Sara moved her mask aside, her smile warm and encompassing. "Good evening, George, Rea, Jacob." She turned to Vic. "Victoria, I'm so glad you could attend tonight's little gathering. I'm sure you've made Jacob's night. You look marvelous."

Her cheeks warmed. She couldn't believe it, but she'd sworn she was blushing. "Thank you, Majesty," she managed.

"Victoria was just commenting on your mask, Sire," Jacob told the king.

She glared up at him, sensing the teasing smile behind his mask.

"It's ghastly, isn't it?" King John asked, his chest puffing up. "I think I've managed the ugliest mask here."

"Yes, you did, dear," the queen said, patting his arm.

Vic could hardly believe she was talking to the king and queen of Karasnia like they were normal people. Then Lord and Lady Fordin joined the group. She bit the inside of her lip at the sight of Lady Tiya. The sorceress looked very much like the fairies Vic had heard about in stories, ethereal and perfect in a gown of lavender and gold. Even her mask—a cat's eye mask—covered with white, blue and pale purple velvet and lined with golden sequins, looked like something that might belong to a fairy.

Glancing covertly at Jacob while everyone greeted the newcomers, she couldn't decide if she was glad his mask hid his expression or not.

"Hello, Victoria," Tiya said. "It's wonderful to see you here. Are you enjoying yourself?"

She blinked and faced the sorceress again. "Lady Tiya," she greeted with a nod. Lady Fordin was so friendly, she wanted to snarl. Instead, she said, "I'm enjoying myself very much, thank you," and hoped her smile didn't look too strained.

A sultry, slow song began in the background and Jacob took her arm. "Shall we?" he asked.

Through the eyeholes in his mask, she could see him studying her. She nodded and let him lead her onto the dance floor.

He pulled her close, turning her in slow circles until they were across the room.

"What's wrong, little thief?"

"Nothing. Everything's fine."

Jacob pushed his mask off his face and shook his head. "And I thought you were supposed to be good at lying."

The jibe hit its mark. Her professional pride rose to meet the challenge. "I'm an excellent liar, General."

He chuckled. "Most of the time, little thief, I'd agree with you. But perhaps I know you too well."

She snorted. "I could lie to you if I really wanted."

"Ahh. Then you really want me to know what's bothering you?"

She frowned at being danced into that obvious trap.

He leaned close to her ear and whispered, "I know what you're worrying about, Victoria, but I told you before, you needn't worry about Tiya." Straightening, he looked down into her upturned face. "Everyone else has noticed the change. I'm surprised you haven't."

"They've known you longer," she said, trying to be surly. But her frown dissolved into an embarrassed grimace when Jacob's laughter tumbled over her head.

"Victoria Flash, stop worrying and enjoy the music."

The hand at the small of her back pressed her tighter, and she forgot to be jealous. Soon, she was caught in the sultry beat of the music, enjoying the heat of Jacob's sexy half smile.

During the next song, a man in an orange and yellow bird mask interrupted their dance. "Do you mind if I cut in for a song, General?"

the bird asked before removing his mask to reveal Garath's smiling face.

Jacob scowled at his lieutenant. When he looked back at her, she grinned wickedly. "Stop worrying and enjoy the music," she said, taking Garath's hand.

"All right," Jacob said, "but only one song."

She chuckled as he walked off the floor.

"What was that about?" Garath asked.

"Nothing. Just giving back a little of the grief he gave me earlier."

"Well, I have to admire anyone who can give the general grief. You look quite enchanting this evening, Victoria."

"Thank you, Garath. That's very nice of you to say."

"Not nice, just honest. But I'm afraid I do have an ulterior reason for dragging you away from Jacob. I wanted to privately thank you for not telling him I was the one who let you through that day just before the festival started."

"No need for thanks. That wasn't your fault. I make my living conning people. And I am good at what I do."

"Yes." Garath nodded. "You are. But thank you anyway. He gave the whole company a dressing-down the next day, and I was more than a little relieved when he didn't turn on me directly."

"Tell you what. One day, when all this mess is over, I'll teach you how to spot a con like me. But you have to promise not to tell anyone. Otherwise, I might not be able to sneak in again."

"You've got yourself a deal, Victoria Flash."

As the song ended, a short, broad man in a baby-face mask stepped up. "Would you mind?" the man asked Garath, nodding at Vic.

Garath raised a brow. "I don't mind if the lady doesn't, but I wouldn't expect your time with her to last long."

The guard smiled knowingly before replacing his mask and moving off the floor.

"My lady." The short man pulled her very tightly into his arms.

She grunted and braced a hand on his shoulder to keep some space between their bodies.

"I am Lord Cathius of Dareelia."

"Lord Cathius," Vic repeated. The man's mask made her want to giggle. His attitude made her want to knock him down a rung or two.

"I don't believe I've ever had the pleasure of your acquaintance, my lady. You're not from Dareelia?"

"Why, no, Lord Cathius, I've lived all my life in Dareelia. Strange we haven't met before. Is this the first event you've attended at the royal castle?"

"My lady, I'm often present at royal events."

"Really?" she said mildly, enjoying his bristling indignation. "How very odd. Perhaps it's the mask."

"Perhaps." Lord Cathius visibly worked at restoring his charming persona.

She forced her expression to remain mild, but a chuckle tickled her throat.

"Might I have the pleasure of your name, my lady?"

"But of course, Lord Cathius. You may call me Victoria."

"Lady Victoria. What a lovely name for a lovely lady."

She let loose a coquettish giggle. She'd been practicing that laugh since she'd started wearing dresses to hide from Charlie. It appeared to work because Lord Cathius puffed higher, his hand splaying across her back in a less than formal manner. She smiled, preparing another barrage of ego-damaging chatter when their dance was interrupted.

"Lord Cathius."

Jacob's voice slid over her shoulder.

"Good evening, General Marin."

The man made no attempt to loosen his hold on her, though he did stop moving her in awkward circles.

"If you would excuse us." Jacob extended a hand.

"I do believe that's Lady Victoria's choice, General."

"Well, *Lady* Victoria?"

She grinned at Jacob, then looked at Cathius and fluttered her eyelashes. "I do hope you'll forgive me, my lord, but I promised the general a dance."

Cathius tilted his head, reluctantly taking a step away from her. "As the lady wishes. Perhaps we'll have an opportunity to speak later?"

"Perhaps."

Cathius bowed stiffly to Jacob and left the floor.

"Okay," Jacob said, pulling her close, "that will be enough of that, *Lady* Victoria."

"Enough of what, General?" She widened her eyes in feigned innocence.

"I didn't invite you to this thing to watch you dance with other men."

"Why did you invite me?" She relaxed against him, grinning contentedly.

"To force you into wearing this sexy gown. To keep you to myself all night. To dance with you until you can't think, then to carry you off to ravish you."

"You do realize you could have ravished me without going to all that trouble?"

"Don't tempt me, love. I'm just jealous enough that I might have to carry you off now to prove why you should want to dance with only me."

"Jealous?"

"Yes, little thief. And don't look so pleased with yourself."

"I just think there's something funny about the man who can't walk down the street without every woman in town gawking, being worried about Lord Cathius."

"I'm not worried about Cathius. I'm worried about Garath."

"Garath! Why?"

"I don't like the way he looked at you."

She giggled. "Thank you, Jacob. I know why you're doing this, and I do appreciate it."

"You think I'm pretending to be jealous?"

"I think you're trying to convince me to stop worrying about Lady Tiya."

Jacob stared into her eyes for a long moment. "You don't have any idea what you've done to me, do you?"

"I suppose I don't." She focused on his chest, feeling uncharacteristically shy for the second time that night.

"Victoria." Jacob lifted her chin. "You've stolen—"

A sudden disturbance near the entrance interrupted him. They both turned in time to see the first goblins breaking through the crowd into the hall.

Chapter Sixteen

Before Vic had fully absorbed what she saw, Jacob charged the goblins, drawing his sword. Screams echoed through the hall, followed by the sounds of clashing metal and a rumbling boom that Vic couldn't identify. Taking a quick glance toward the king, she saw Garath, General Thack and Kevin Fordin surrounding him, swords at the ready. Queen Sara had dropped her mask and was working a silent spell. To her right, Lady Tiya was also mouthing a spell, but from Tiya's extended fingers, bolts of blue energy sizzled into the chests of attacking goblins, the magical strikes creating the rumbling sound that beat beneath the chaos of the room. Vic took in the scene in seconds then ran after Jacob, pulling her knife, her mask forgotten on the dance floor.

The first goblin she encountered almost paralyzed her ability to act.

He was huge, a half foot over her head and almost twice as broad as Jacob. Large, dark eyes narrowed to slits beneath heavy brow ridges. Green-tinted skin pulled tightly over bulging muscles and sharp, thick bones. He wore a pair of human leather breeches while the rest of his body remained bare.

But the most frightening feature was also the most unexpected. From his opened, lipless mouth, two huge fangs protruded from his upper jaw.

Vic barely managed to avoid the swing of his curved saber blade, she was so stunned by fangs in a goblin face. She didn't remain inactive for long. Despite her hooped skirt, fear had her moving with the speed of her nickname. She darted beneath the goblin's extended reach, slashing her knife across his exposed chest as she skirted behind him.

He roared, swinging around, his blade moving in an arch aimed at her head.

She dropped to one knee, but the skirt prevented her from rolling away.

Just as he shifted his grip, preparing to bring his blade through her neck, the goblin froze. The saber slipped from his fingers as wide, dark eyes looked from Vic's face to the gold and emerald-encrusted dagger hilt protruding from his heart.

By the time he hit the floor, she'd recovered her knife and turned to meet her next opponent. To her left, Jacob fought two goblins. His sword blocked and shifted, parried and struck, but against two of the warrior creatures, all he could do was hold them off. She sucked in a breath. Time to even the odds.

Moving deftly through the chaos surrounding her, she drew nearer to the fight. A flick of her wrist sent her dagger into the throat of one of Jacob's opponents. The second wasn't distracted by the loss of his comrade, but one-on-one, Jacob was able to drive him back. Vic slipped in to recover her knife. When she looked toward Jacob, he was pulling his sword from the goblin's chest.

He swung back toward her where she crouched, dagger in hand. His eyes blazed.

"Jacob!" she shouted, but it was all she had time to say as she watched the curved blade of a goblin saber descend toward his head.

The clash of steel on steel made her stomach lurch as she watched Jacob's sword take the blow directed at his skull. She exhaled and dropped one knee to the floor to balance her shaking limbs. But her gaze stayed latched to Jacob. He swiveled to face his attacker. The goblin was shorter than him by half a foot but superior in width. Her expression was alien and unreadable even as she slashed with deadly accuracy at Jacob's exposed side.

He countered the blow, swiveled and attacked, so fast she stopped breathing for an instant. Flickering specks of light from the room's candles reflected off the steel of both weapons. Jacob took advantage of the goblin's superior strength, slipping in and out of the warrior's lunges, carefully avoiding her direct blows, always moving. But she didn't tire easily. When her saber slipped just under Jacob's lunge, Vic started to yell. Her shout died in her throat as she watched him avoid the blow while pulling his sword around in an impossible arch across the back of the warrior's thick neck.

The goblin's head rolled across the floor as her thick body collapsed.

Vic, fingers clutched painfully around her dagger hilt, watched the head roll to a stop. Then she looked back at Jacob. He stood breathing heavily, head bowed, sword lowered so the tip just touched the ground. Blood had sprayed a dotted pattern across his white shirt. Her gaze focused on those spots of red, and her throat closed.

Around them, the sounds of the fight were dying. Only a few isolated clashes still echoed in the near-empty chamber. The number of soldiers and castle guards far exceeded the number of attacking goblins. Many of the goblins had died, very few had retreated. But the damage was done. Dead goblins lay scattered across the floor next to the bodies of many soldiers and young nobles of Karasnia.

Jacob caught her gaze. He strode to her and, with his free hand, pulled her to her feet. "Are you all right?"

She nodded, her throat too dry to speak.

"Good."

His sword clattered to the floor as he circled his arms around her, pulling her into a hard kiss. His heart beat rapidly against the palm of her hand.

"Thank you," he whispered against her mouth then kissed her again.

"You're welcome," she muttered when she could speak again. Behind her, the last sounds of battle had dimmed to a quiet murmur of groans, shifting steel, and troubled whispers. "Don't ever scare me like that again."

His cheeks lifted in the barest of smiles before the serious line returned. He looked past her toward the main hall, brow creased. "Come on." He retrieved his sword, then took her hand and led her to a small cluster of people.

Vic exhaled slowly, relieved to see both the king and queen uninjured. They stood with Garath, General Thack, and Lord and Lady Fordin over the bodies of a dead soldier and a dead goblin. The soldier was an obscene shade of purple, his skin bloated to the point of bursting, his face an unrecognizable mask of agony. Vic clenched her teeth against the bile in her throat and looked away.

"I don't believe it." Thack ran a blood-splattered hand over his red beard.

"That's the only explanation for the fangs," Tiya said, nodding to the dead goblin, "and this reaction." She pointed to the soldier. "GeMorin clan."

"I thought the GeMorin were a legend," Kevin said, his handsome face set in grim lines.

"No," King John said, just above a whisper, "they're real." He never took his gaze from the dead soldier.

"Who are the GeMorin?" Vic asked Jacob, keeping her voice low.

Tiya answered. "They're a warrior clan of goblins. The only goblins of notable intelligence. They're cunning, strong, brutal warriors. Their most distinctive feature, though, is the fangs. They're venomous. No other goblin race has fangs like this."

"The GeMorin clan hasn't moved past the upper Georna border in centuries, since before the goblin war," Queen Sara continued the story, gently taking her husband's hand. "There are occasional skirmishes between the GeMorin and the Geornans of the border lands, but, for the most part, the fights remain small. They aren't often spoken of, which is why most Karasnians think the GeMorin a legend from another time."

"But they still exist," Tiya finished. "And they're more dangerous than any other race of goblins ever known."

"Why?" King John demanded, still staring at the fallen soldier. "Why?"

No one had an answer.

Vic looked around at the solemn faces of their small group and noticed an absence. "General Thack, where is Mrs. Von Thack?"

"She's gone to check the baby."

His response snapped Tiya's head up. She looked at Kevin, closed her eyes, and gasped, the color draining from her face. "Arlana!" Before anyone could react, she was running for the door, Kevin close behind.

"General Thack, organize this mess," King John ordered. "Then check with the city guard and, if necessary, send more troops to chase these GeMorin from my city. Jacob, with me."

Jacob followed close behind the king and queen as they hurried toward the guest quarters. Vic, her hand still engulfed in Jacob's, had to jog to keep pace.

Outside the reception hall, beyond the view of the milling courtiers and busy soldiers, Queen Sara started to run. The king stayed with her while Jacob and Vic did their best to keep up. They were just entering the guest wing when the ground beneath their feet began to tremble.

Vic found herself abruptly seated on the floor as the castle walls shook and the ground rolled. Dust from the ceiling fell in a choking powder. A low rumbling echoed, mingling with the distant sounds of screams. Queen Sara, still on her feet, stumbled for the Fordin suite.

When the tumult stopped, Vic stared at Jacob, who'd gone to one knee and was covering most of her body with his own. "What in the name of the Goddess was that?" she breathed, blinking dust from her eyes.

"Earthquake?" Jacob looked at King John, who was braced against the corridor wall.

The king shook his head, frowning slightly, and hurried to the Fordin suite. After Jacob helped Vic to her feet, they followed.

They then trotted into a room dominated by the boiling rage of Kevin Fordin and the near-transformed features of Lady Tiya. Her face was set in stony, furious lines, her anger held in check by the soothing words of Queen Sara, who sat next to her on a window seat. Tiya's eyes burned holes in the air.

"What happened?" the king demanded.

"She's been kidnapped," Kevin said through a clenched jaw. "Arlana's been taken."

"What?" King John and Jacob roared at the same time.

In a corner of the room, Vic caught sight of a young woman cowering against the wall, tears staining her cheeks, her eyes puffy and red. "I'm so sorry, my lady. I'm so sorry," she mumbled, over and over again.

"Apparently," the queen said in a very calm voice, "the nurse was knocked unconscious." She nodded to the cowering woman. "She didn't see anything. When she came to, the baby was gone."

"Seal the castle," King John ordered. "Have the city gates closed. I want…"

"She's no longer in the city," Tiya spoke quietly, her voice a hollow menace.

"Tiya, dear," Queen Sara said, "how can you tell? I can't feel Arlana anymore, which means she's being shielded by a magician."

Tiya looked the queen in the eyes. "They can't shield my daughter from me. She's no longer in the city."

Queen Sara's eyes narrowed, but she didn't argue with the young mother.

"How?" King John demanded. "How could they have been here only moments before and be out of the city now?"

"There's no telling how long the nurse was unconscious," Jacob provided.

"No," the woman squeaked from her corner, "I wasn't out for long. I heard the battle echoing down the hall. I was going to the door to find out what was happening when I blacked out."

"You mean this corresponded with the beginnings of the goblin raid?" King John's anger tinged his carefully modulated tone of voice.

"Yes, Sire." Kevin paced the length of the sitting room like a prowling tiger.

"How?" King John demanded again.

"They gated," both Jacob and a new voice from the door said.

The group turned to see Garath entering the room. He handed Jacob a smooth cube, and Jacob cursed. "One of these was found on each of the dead goblins," Garath said.

"Damn it to hell." Jacob's fist clenched tightly around the cube. "I knew I was missing something." He turned to the king. "Majesty, this confirms that the goblins were working for the blood magicians."

"You mean to say the reason they were in my city was to kidnap my granddaughter?"

"Ransom?" Kevin asked incredulously.

Jacob frowned. "I don't think so. Not with Arlana's power."

Kevin's suntanned skin paled and his eyes widened. "You don't mean they intend to sacrifice my daughter!"

"No," Jacob said, hand raised in an attempt to pacify. "At least, not yet. They went to far too much trouble for one sacrifice. They lost one of their fellow magicians in the process. No, I think they have more in mind than a simple sacrifice."

The ground beneath Vic's feet trembled again. Her gaze snapped to Lady Tiya. Rage glowed from her features like an exploding star. As the trembling increased, Vic heard Queen Sara's calm voice, "Tiya. Tiya, stop. If you destroy the castle around us, we won't be able to help Arlana."

Visibly struggling to control her anger, Tiya closed her eyes for a long moment. The floor stopped its crazy rolling. The walls stilled. When she opened her eyes again, her fists were clenched, her jaw tight, but the castle no longer quaked.

"They move north," she breathed.

"We'll follow," Kevin said, swinging toward the door.

"Wait." King John stopped the young giant with a hand on his chest. "Jacob and the King's Guard will go with you. But you'll be facing the GeMorin, Kevin. You saw what those fangs do. You need to go to Georna first."

"There's no time—" Kevin started, but King John stopped him with a raised hand.

"There's a smith along the northern Georna border. For generations, his family has produced special weapons from a metal found only in the Georna Reaches. It's the only metal strong enough to break GeMorin fangs. Without protection from the venom, you won't be able to rescue Arlana."

Kevin turned away, his face set in stubborn lines. After a moment, though, he nodded his assent.

"Sara," King John turned to his wife. "Baroness Georna's magician, Dreem…is he still in contact with Master Caul through one of those emerald links?"

"Yes."

"Good. Have Caul send a message to Baroness Georna requesting the presence of the smith, Brandon, at Castle Georna. Tell her that a group approaches quickly to purchase some of Brandon's special merchandise."

"Of course."

"What about my daughter?" Tiya asked quietly.

"You can still feel her?" Queen Sara turned back to the young mother.

"Yes."

"Then you can follow her."

"Maybe Tracker would know where they're headed." Vic suggested hesitantly. Every eye in the room turned. She sucked in her bottom lip and shrugged.

"He's still in custody?" the king asked Jacob.

"Yes, Majesty."

"All right. Jacob, arrange for the guard that'll travel with you and begin preparations for the journey. Kevin, come with me. We'll have a talk with the smuggler."

"Sire," Garath spoke before King John could leave the room. "May I be given permission to accompany the party?"

King John paused for a moment, then nodded. He left without further comment, Kevin close at his elbow.

"Garath," Jacob turned to his lieutenant, "stay here with Lady Tiya and Queen Sara until a fresh guard is sent up. If she isn't too frightened, try to get as much information as you can from the nurse. But be gentle." Jacob took Vic's hand and started for the door. He stopped just before leaving the room. "And Garath, glad to have you with us."

Garath nodded, the slightest of smiles touching his mouth.

Vic and Jacob walked back to his chambers in silence. At the door, he turned to face her. "I'll be busy for most of the night now. You should try to sleep."

"When will you leave?"

"Midmorning at the latest. I'll come back before we leave…to say goodbye." He kissed her, quick and hard, before walking away.

"'Say goodbye'?" Vic said to the air. "Like hell you will, Jacob Marin." She hurried back to the Fordin's suite. Garath was just leaving when she approached.

"Victoria?"

"Garath, I need a favor. I need you to have a horse and supplies readied for me. I'll be going with you on this little adventure."

His blue eyes narrowed. "Jacob has agreed to let you go?"

"Jacob doesn't know yet."

"Victoria, I don't know if that's a good idea. I don't think Jacob—"

"Will you help me or do I have to buy a mount and supplies on my own? I'm going. One way or the other."

He let out a long breath. "Okay. I'll have a horse readied. But what should I tell the general when he invariably asks about the extra horse?"

"Tell him it's for me."

***

Vic slipped into the dimly lit office and shut the door.

Deraun's head snapped up at the intrusion. "What the hell are you doing here, Flash? I thought I told you to—"

She held up a hand to silence him. "You hear about the attack on the castle tonight?" She kept her tone perfectly even, but low-pitched so no one passing Gip's office would be able to recognize her voice. She'd snuck into the Hole's headquarters in the confusion that blanketed the city, managing to avoid the other Hole members on her way to Gip's office.

"Of course," his voice dropped to match hers. "Goblins made a mess in the streets, too." Deraun rose and stepped around his desk to face Vic. "You were in the castle?"

"Um hmm. It's a long story, but I'll be leaving town now. For a couple of months."

His eyes narrowed. He looked over her black attire and the bundle slung over her shoulder. "This have to do with the blood magicians? We heard about the raid and the two that escaped."

"Yeah. The magicians and the goblins. Seems they've taken something that didn't belong to them. We're going to get it back."

"We?"

"King's Guard."

"Marin, too?"

"Yeah."

He nodded. His mouth stretched to a taut line. After a silent moment, he said, "This mean the trouble's moving away from the city?"

"Looks that way."

"Well, since I've got enough on my hands with Charlie and now the aftermath of tonight's mess…guess I'll leave the goblins and magicians to people who know what they're doing."

Her mouth tilted up in the barest of smiles. "See ya when I get back, Gip."

She cracked open the door and checked to make sure the hall was empty. As she slipped out into the corridor, she heard him whisper, "Stay standing, Vic Flash."

***

When Jacob stormed into his room shortly before dawn, Vic was sitting at his desk, feet propped up, dressed in her blacks, her small satchel resting next to the chair leg.

"What do you think you're doing, Victoria?"

The effort to keep his voice calm showed in the flexing of his jaw muscles. "I thought I was sitting," she said.

"You know what I mean. Why did you tell Garath to have a horse readied?" He stepped closer.

"Because I'm going with you." She stood slowly, balancing on her toes, ready for a fight.

"No, Victoria. You're not going with us. It's too dangerous."

"Ha! And being here isn't dangerous for me. I've got nothing better to do and nowhere better to go. I'm going with you."

"I won't allow it. You'll stay here. Safe."

"Here where, General? I can't live in the castle. I'll go back to the streets and, sooner or later, Charlie's thugs will find me. I'm going with you." She stood straight, her hands casually at her sides. Though they were skillfully concealed, she wore all seven daggers.

Jacob let out an exasperated breath and moved to stand mere inches from her. "Why, Victoria? Why do you have to go?"

She tried to hold his gaze and failed. She glanced around the room, looking for an excuse. Finally, she looked back into his face, focusing on his mouth when she couldn't meet his gaze. "Because, damn it, I care for you, Jacob Marin, and I won't have you disappear."

Her hard attitude dissolved. She closed the space between them and clung, burying her face against his chest. The smell of his leather vest mingled with the faint metallic stench of blood in her nostrils. "Too many people in my life have disappeared. If something happens to you, I want to be there. I want to know." She felt his body relax as his arms circled her.

"Victoria, I won't disappear on you." He patted her hair and kissed the top of her head. "I don't want you in such a dangerous situation."

"I can take care of myself, Jacob." Her voice turned desperate, pleading. "You won't have to worry about me."

"But I do."

"I can watch your back. We make a good team…last night with the goblins…we work well together."

His arms tightened. She felt the ruffle of his breath against her hair.

"What am I going to do with you, little thief?"

"You're going to let me go," she said, looking into his face with a cocky, hopeful grin, finally able to meet his gaze.

"I'm not happy with this," he said sternly. His frown turned to a crooked smile. "But you go."

Two hours after sunrise, the company gathered in the castle's main courtyard, ready to leave. Fifty of the king's best guards were lined to accompany Jacob, Vic, Tiya, Kevin and Garath. The group was small but able to move faster than an army.

Vic hesitated at the head of the horse Garath held.

"Have you ever been on horseback?" the lieutenant asked.

"Once. When I was eight. But that was sort of an accident."

Garath chuckled. "Victoria, this is Night's Gale," he introduced the horse. "She's one of the Queen's Mares. They're specially trained warhorses. Originally, they were bred and trained to carry the Karasnian queens into battle. That tradition has continued for eight centuries, with or without a warrior queen on the throne. They're extremely gentle with their riders, but are trained to react unguided in battle situations. If something happens, all you need to worry about is staying on her back." Patting the mare's chest, he said, "Now, blow gently into her nostrils."

"What?" Vic looked from Garath to the mare and back again.

"Blow into her nostrils. Let her get your scent. Remember to be gentle. When she blows back in your face, make a show of sniffing. That way she knows you've gotten her scent."

She nibbled her bottom lip, sure this was some weird joke, but followed Garath's instructions. When she blew in the mare's nostrils, Night's Gale threw her head in the air and wrinkled her upper lip until her nostrils were almost closed.

At Vic's gasp, Garath grinned and said, "Don't worry. She's supposed to do that. She's smelling your scent."

In the next moment, the mare lowered her head and snorted softly in Vic's face. She did as instructed, sniffing at the mare's nose. The only scent she received was a standard horse smell, though she had to admit it wasn't unpleasant. The subtle scent of clean hay beneath the natural musk of the horse was actually quite nice. Then, to her surprise, Night's Gale touched her face gently with her velvety soft nose. After that, the mare stood placidly, waiting for her rider.

"Hmm," she muttered as she moved around to the horse's left side.

"Now mount by placing your left foot in the stirrup first," Garath instructed.

Despite her lurching scrabble to get into the saddle, Night's Gale continued to stand quietly. "Thanks, lady," she whispered to the horse, awkwardly patting her neck while Garath handed her the reins.

"You're a natural, Vic Flash. Now, just be gentle on the reins. She needs little guidance. When you want her to stop, simply say 'halt'.

She's trained to obey even when frightened, but then she's also trained not to be frightened by very many things." Garath patted the mare's shoulder again before going to his own horse.

Jacob stood to one side, talking to Kevin, King John and Queen Sara. Lady Tiya was already mounted, looking perfectly comfortable on horseback, Vic noted with a little annoyance. *Bet she can't pull a Devil's High out of thin air.* Except the lady was also an extremely powerful magician so she probably could. Her shoulders slumped.

"Don't let me embarrass myself, okay?" she whispered to the mare. Night's Gale snorted her response.

Jacob was poised to mount his own horse when a newcomer rode in through the open castle gates. His white hair and crystal blue eyes were a strange but attractive contrast to his tawny skin. *Henry?* Vic had only seen the magician a few times before and, then, always with Kritta on his arm. She hardly recognized him now in dark breeches and tunic, wrapped in a short black cloak, sitting atop his mount as if part of the animal.

"Henry." Queen Sara approached the new rider. "What are you doing here?"

He looked first at the queen, then Jacob, and finally settled his gaze on Tiya. "I thought you might need a second magician. There are three of the blooded ones."

Tiya stared at the sorcerer for a long, charged moment then approved his company in a short nod.

"Very well," Jacob said, mounting up. "You go."

Henry fell in with the group as they rode from the castle.

King John and Queen Sara quietly watched them go.

CHAPTER SEVENTEEN

Bserea scowled at the infant in her lap. At least it was quiet now. And sort of smiling. She didn't really want to know why the infant looked happy.

What did she know about caring for something this small? She was as powerful as the other two, if not more. She'd spent her life building that power, developing it. And now she was reduced to the role of nursemaid. How dare they!

A sharp flick of her hand pushed a stray lock of her short hair behind her ear. The infant found the gesture amusing, which only irritated Bserea further. When Ptaun approached, she turned her scowl on him.

"Why must I always care for this thing?" she hissed.

"You are the woman," Ptaun said simply. His white skin shimmered in the dark, glowing like a misshapen moon.

"You fool," she spat, rising from the log she'd been resting on, the infant held precariously in her hands. "You think I'll take this insult happily? I'm not some lackey, Ptaun. And I'm not afraid of your paltry powers."

"Paltry!" Ptaun snarled. "You dare insult me, woman?"

Bserea threw her head back and cackled. "I'll do more than insult you if you don't start helping me with this." She extended her hands, shoving the baby close to his face.

Pseer chose that moment to step into the conversation, and Bserea turned her rancor on him.

"The only reason you are here, woman," the copper-skinned sorcerer said, "is to care for the child." Pseer towered above Bserea's head, smiling at her seductively. The man looked more like a warrior than a sorcerer and enjoyed the effects his physical appearance had on Bserea. At that moment, however, she was too angry to be turned on.

"You, Pseer, should be very careful of your words. I could squash you beneath my little finger without a second thought. Or perhaps," she sneered, "I'll simply make you my slave. You must have some useful qualities."

Ptaun chuckled, a sound like the grinding of rock. Pseer snarled. "You find that funny, old man," he whispered, the threat just at the edge of his voice.

"Mind your manners, boy," Ptaun growled. "Or I'll make you that infant's wet nurse."

Bserea let loose a howl at the insult, her grip on the infant relaxing further.

"The child is becoming upset," a quiet voice that rolled like distant thunder through the glade said into their argument.

Bserea swallowed another biting comment and hitched up the baby, cradling it more securely in her arms. All three magicians fell silent and turned to face the GeMorin clan chief, their eyes downcast. She risked a glance at the goblin, to gauge his mood.

GeRon was taller than the rest of his clan and as broad as two human men, his green-tinted skin lean over a muscular frame. Dark, short hair covered his broad head and heavy brow ridges. The blue tattoo circling his biceps was the only thing that distinguished his rank from the rest of his male warriors. His lipless mouth was set in a grim line. When his dark-eyed gaze swung in her direction, she lowered her lashes.

"She must be treated well," GeRon said.

Bserea risked a brief glance up. The clan chief was staring at the babe, his expression the goblin equivalent of reverence.

"She is to be His daughter," he said. "His wife." GeRon turned his gaze to her. "You will ensure her wellbeing." He then looked to Pseer, and finally rested his gaze on Ptaun. "All of you."

"Yes, my lord," the three magicians said in unison. GeRon looked once more at the baby then strode across the camp.

Bserea snarled up at Ptaun, but her irritation had cooled under the goblin chief's command. "Bring me her milk skin," she ordered the white sorcerer. "And make sure the milk isn't too warm or you'll have to deal with GeRon's displeasure."

Ptaun stared hostilely at her for a heartbeat before turning to fetch the milk.

***

The King's Guard entered Karasnian Forest the day after leaving Dareelia. Vic stared in awe. The oak and elms had turned, their oranges, yellows and reds threading through the backdrop of evergreen. Leaves crunched beneath the horse's hooves and covered the forest floor. Bird calls overhead and the sounds of the group's passage were the only noise. Sunlight from a thankfully clear sky filtered across the ground and set the upturned leaves alight. The warm scent of damp soil and pine needles was sharp and clean in her city-hardened nostrils.

"First time in a forest?" Jacob asked, grinning.

"I've never seen this before," she breathed, afraid speaking too loudly would disturb the forest in some way. "The gardens and parks in the city can't even hint that the rest of the world could look like this."

"Wait until we get to Georna," he teased.

They rode along a narrow forester's trail, staying away from the main road for fear of ambush. Kevin and Tiya lead the group. Just behind them, Jacob rode alongside Vic, smiling at her amazement.

The first day of travel had passed in a blur. They'd ridden hard across the open ground between Dareelia and Karasnian Forest. That night, she'd fallen into an exhausted sleep beside the campfire, her entire body a mass of aching muscles. Before drifting to sleep, she'd mumbled something about never being able to move again. When she woke the next morning, she was positive that she'd been right in her assessment the night before. Though Garath had seen to it that she had her own tent and trail blankets, she woke that morning nestled in Jacob's arms in the middle of his tent completely unaware of how she'd gotten there. She couldn't have been more pleased with the arrangement.

The second day of riding, until they'd reached the forest, had been just as quick. They'd set a pace that was fast enough to cover ground without damaging the animals. Vic found she was more comfortable on Night's Gale's back, but her protesting muscles didn't make the ride enjoyable.

Then they entered the forest. She spent the rest of the day gawking at the trees. In a strange way, the forest reminded her of Upper Market—on a somber day. The myriad hues decorating the dark trees and covering the ground were like the jewels and rich fabrics of Upper Market's noble clients. Rich, sparkling and awe-inspiring.

That night, they camped near a stream in a clearing back away from the trail. Sentries were immediately posted. Guards were set to stand watch throughout the night.

Despite her pleasure in her surroundings, Vic couldn't forget the reason for this trip or ignore the tension in the group. All eyes watched Lady Tiya. Though the sorceress was more sedate now that they were following her daughter, not a single person in the camp doubted that, if frustrated or upset, the lady could shake the very Earth beneath their feet.

Their evening meal was a rough but tasty mix of fresh fowl and travel biscuits. The urgency of their trip prevented them from bringing a supply wagon, so the scouts sent ahead to look for ambush and signs of the GeMorin were also instructed to hunt when the opportunity arose. Vic had never considered herself a particularly choosy eater, but after the leathery jerky of their midday meal, she was grateful to the scouts who'd brought back fresh meat.

As night deepened, filling the spaces between the trees, she suddenly became aware of the absolute darkness in the forest. Their small cooking fire gave some light, but just beyond that pool, she couldn't see a thing. She stared into the dark, her ears straining to hear anything out of the ordinary. Unfortunately, everything in the forest was out of the ordinary for her.

"What was that?" she asked, turning to Jacob.

"An owl." He sat with his back resting against a tree, watching her with an expression somewhere between bemused and amazed.

"Owl? Don't they live in barns where there's mice?" She strained her eyes, still searching the inky blackness just beyond the firelight. Her ears rang with the oppressive silence that was broken only by the sounds of their group and those noises she couldn't identify.

"Barns aren't the owl's natural habitat, little thief. Some do live in the forest."

"Well, they're noisy. What was that?" She turned in a half circle to face a different part of the forest.

"Sounds like a small animal. Probably a raccoon. Or raccoons, since they're usually in groups."

"Raccoons? Are they dangerous?"

He chuckled. "No. Just curious. They're probably more afraid of us. We're a lot bigger than they are."

"Yeah, well, you're a lot bigger than I am, but that doesn't mean I couldn't take you if I wanted to."

He arched an eyebrow. "Sounds interesting. Maybe we should try that."

She scowled, but her gaze continued moving. When a loud screech exploded into the clearing, she jumped and half rose. "What in the name of the Goddess was that?"

"That was the owl again. Sounds like she caught dinner." He studied her a moment before adding, "Would you feel better sitting closer to me?"

"No," she said then crawled over and sat between his legs, leaning against his chest. When she felt the rumble of his laughter against her back, she slapped his knee. "How do you know so much about forests, General?"

"I grew up in the forest."

"You did?"

"Um hmm. Georna Reaches, as a matter of fact. You sound surprised."

"Well, I assumed you'd grown up in Dareelia. You know the city pretty well. For a rich man," she teased. "Not as well as I know it, but..."

"Oh, really?"

"Yes." She scooted closer, wrapping her arms over his where they circled her waist. "Well..."

"Well what?"

"Let's have your story. You know mine—"

"With holes," he interrupted.

She continued as if he hadn't spoken. "Jacob Marin's early years."

"There's not much to my early years."

"Yeah. Sure. Come on, Jacob. Tell me a bedtime story."

"It's not a good story to sleep on."

"Better than mine."

"Hmm. Okay, but remember you asked. Most of my early life was quiet. I lived with my parents in a small, isolated house in Georna. The nearest town is a two-day ride. My father was a hunter. My mother raised mountain goats and grew vegetables."

"Sounds nice," she sighed.

"It was. They were good people. My da taught me to hunt and fish. He taught me about the forest and how to move through it. My mom taught me to fletch arrows and cook."

"You cook?"

"Um hmm. I'll cook you dinner when we get back to Dareelia."

"I'll hold you to that. Where are your parents now?"

"My mom died when I was eleven. We'd had a harsh winter. Avalanches had sealed off the pass to the town, so we were basically snowbound. She caught a cold. My da knew a bit about healing, but he couldn't seem to help her cough. One day, she started coughing up blood. A few days later, she was gone."

"I'm sorry."

"It's okay, Victoria. She had a chance to say goodbye, to tell us she loved us. That's more than a lot of people get to do before they die."

"Yeah," she murmured, "I know."

He hugged her a little tighter.

With a deep breath, he said, "It was probably better that she died then anyway."

"Why?"

"A little over a year later, during the last few weeks of the short mountain summer, four men came to our house. They were a real scruffy lot and smelled worse than our goats. My father was wary, but not an overly suspicious type. There were a lot of mountainmen in Georna. When they asked if we could spare a meal, my da invited them in. They ate our food, drank our coffee, then slit my father's throat before he knew what hit him."

"You saw?" Her question was rhetorical, but he answered anyway.

"Yeah. I'm still not sure why they didn't kill me. I heard something later about getting a good price for me from a slaver, but I never was certain that was their intent. I started screaming when they killed my da, making an awful lot of noise. They beat me, but kept me alive. After looting the house for anything useful, they torched it, tied my hands and headed north.

"I stayed in a numbed daze for the next three days. They had to force food into me. I don't think I had a single thought that whole time. At least none that I can remember. Just sort of shut off. That's probably why they stopped watching me. On the fourth day, three of them went out to hunt, leaving me with a single guard. He proceeded to drink himself unconscious.

"Sometime during his drinking, I came out of my daze and the numbness was replaced by rage. I already knew how to move silently over the forest floor, but he was too drunk to notice me anyway. I pulled his knife, cut my bonds, slit his throat, and he never even grunted.

"I waited for the others in a tree. The first never noticed that his companion was dead. The last two came back shortly after. They noticed the one, flat on the ground with an arrow through his throat, but by that time, I'd already loosed two more."

"Good."

He kissed the top of her head and his fingers caressed her side as he continued with his story. "After that, I existed. I built a shack that was good enough to get me through winter. I hunted and scavenged enough to live. That first winter was hard. I hadn't had time to build a store and the animals I did find were lean. But I survived."

He sounded so calm, so resigned. As if it had been part of another life that no longer affected him. But a hint of melancholy and anger colored his deep voice. Vic could identify with the feeling. "How long did you live like that?" she murmured.

"About three years."

"Three years? Why didn't you go to a town?"

"At that time, I didn't know anything about town living, little thief. I knew the forest."

"Didn't you get lonely?"

"Yes, I did."

"What about your parents' families?"

"I had an aunt, my mother's sister, but no one knew where she was. She wandered the mountains, appearing every once in a while, then she'd disappear again for years. She'd been gone for two years when my mom died, and we never saw her after."

"So, for three years, you lived all alone in the deep forests of Georna? And you thought I had a rough beginning."

"You did. My beginning was easy. It wasn't until later that it got hard."

"What brought you out of the forest?"

"There was a day, late in the spring, when an old woman showed up at my shack. I was outside, roasting the day's catch over an open pit. And this bent and wrinkled woman strolled up to me and said, 'You'll share a bit of that, I think.' Then she sat, smiled and waited for me to finish cooking. At first, I thought she was crazy, so I went ahead and fed her. I'd caught a big bird that morning. But as we talked, I discovered she wasn't crazy. In fact, she had one of the sharpest minds I'd ever come across in my limited experience."

She glanced up and caught him smiling at the memory.

His somber tone lightened. "She was something. She made me laugh. It had been just over three years since the last time I'd talked to another human being, and it felt good to laugh again. I offered her shelter for the night, which she took. Then the next morning she said, 'Get your things, Jacob.' When I asked why, she told me I was going with her to Georna village. To this day, I'm not sure what made me go. Hell, I didn't even question her. I just collected my quiver and bow, my hunting knife and a few clothes and followed her.

"It took us the better part of the summer to get there, walking at her pace. I hunted and she foraged a wide range of edible plants, some of which I'd never seen before. And I thought I knew the forests pretty well."

Vic chuckled. "You thought you knew Dareelia pretty well, too," she said playfully. The fire before them was starting to die. Darkness filled the glade.

"Shall we retire?" Jacob asked in her ear.

His breath sent a shiver of anticipation up her spine. She nodded and stood. "Will you finish your story?"

"There's not much left." He rested an arm across her shoulders as they walked to his tent, stopping once so Jacob could talk to one of the men just coming off watch.

Inside, he finished the last of his tale. "We reached Georna Village at the beginning of autumn," he said, pulling off his tunic. "That was right after Baroness Georna's father died, and she became Baroness. We walked into the village during her ceremonial procession. For reasons I'm completely in the dark about, she stopped her carriage when she reached our place in the crowd. I can't be certain, but I think she recognized the old woman. She motioned us over and asked the woman who I was."

"Didn't the old woman have a name?" Vic slipped her hands into his hair, running her fingers through the thick strands as he plucked her shirt from her breeches and began unbuttoning it.

"She never told me. I never needed to refer to her by name. The Baroness didn't call her by name either." He threw her shirt aside, shifting his fingers to the lacing of her breeches.

"What did she tell the Baroness about you?"

"That I was a forest boy. That I was good with a bow. I was already tall but still a gangly kid. The Baroness was so kind and such a striking woman that I blushed the entire time she talked with the old woman."

"You blushed?" Vic lay down on their trail blankets, pulling Jacob with her. Despite the cold night, her skin tingled with warmth.

"I was young," he said, kissing her cheek.

"What happened then?" She arched her neck as his hot mouth moved across her pulse.

"We went to the castle."

"What?" She lifted his head to look into his eyes.

"I know, it sounds strange now. At the time, it seemed perfectly normal. We got into the carriage with the Baroness, and I was placed in the castle guard the next day."

"What happened to the old woman?"

"She left. I never saw her again. When I was older and braver, I asked the Baroness, but she shrugged and smiled and never explained."

"That is very odd." She playfully nipped his chin.

"Yeah. But that's how I started as a guard."

"How'd you end up in Dareelia?" She closed her eyes with a sigh as his hand moved to her breast.

"Baroness Georna thought I'd make a good King's Own. She was always looking out for me. And I'd managed to get in enough trouble in Georna. I think she decided if she could get me to a bigger city, I might stay away from married women."

"Jacob!" Her eyes popped open. "You didn't! I thought you said the rumors were exaggerated."

"Well, I wasn't always the honorable man I am now," he said a bit ruefully. "I'm afraid I was irresponsible when I was younger. But the ladies were so kind and their husbands so…inattentive."

"Did you have the same effect on women then that you do now?" Her breath caught when his mouth closed over her nipple.

"Similar," he said, moving his mouth back to hers and nibbling at her lower lip. "Ever since meeting the old woman, I've been very fond of women. I like listening to and talking with them. Unfortunately, that kind of attention given to certain women got me into situations my body had a hard time saying no to."

She chuckled, running her hands down his back to his buttocks. "And since coming to Dareelia?"

"Well, let's just say I've grown up."

"Mmm. I'll say." She smiled and ground her hips against his erection.

Jacob growled and covered her mouth with his, kissing her deeply. He pulled away only long enough to say, "Good enough bedtime story?"

"Yes. Now it's time for you to help me sleep." Just to make her point, she bit her bottom lip.

That night, she slept without a single dream.

Chapter Eighteen

They woke the next morning to a heavy fog enveloping everything in gray. The scouts were sent ahead as the rest of the group packed camp and began the day's journey. They rode in relative silence, the heavy fog masking the noises of the forest while at the same time magnifying the sounds of their passage.

As the morning wore on, Vic started to worry over a suspicion twitching at the back of her mind. She moved up next to Jacob and whispered, "Why haven't we seen any sign of the kidnappers yet? They only had a twelve-hour lead, if that."

Henry, who rode just in front of Jacob, answered. "They're gating a few miles every day. To keep that much farther ahead of pursuers."

"Gating? With those cube things?"

"Yes."

"But can't you disrupt gates?" Vic didn't know that much about magic, but no one lived on the streets without picking up a little.

"We can only disrupt magical gates," Tiya answered over her shoulder from where she rode next to Kevin at the head of the group. "Those cubes are mechanical gates."

"Then why didn't they just gate to where they're going?" Vic asked.

"The mechanical gates can only gate a mile at a time," Henry said, "and gating more than three times in a single day is very dangerous. The chances of molecular scrambling increase considerably."

"Molecular scrambling?" Vic had no idea what that meant but it sounded painful.

Henry chuckled, a strangely musical sound. "Essentially, it means you'll come out as a pile of gray mush. If you're lucky. I've heard stories of people coming out of a mechanical gate so deformed, their bodies so twisted and scrambled, they no longer looked human. But they were still alive."

"You're right," Vic said through a grimace. "That would be worse than coming out mush. But if they're gating even three miles a day, how will we catch them?" She asked Jacob this last very quietly, hoping Lady Tiya wouldn't hear. The fog worked against her, carrying her voice despite her effort.

"We'll catch them," Tiya said, "because I can still feel Arlana. They don't realize that."

"And Tracker was able to give us the location of the ruins where they first rendezvoused with the sorcerers," Jacob said, his voice hard. "From what Tiya says, they're heading northeast toward Georna. If they continue as they have been, the most likely heading is the Bthak border and those ruins."

"Time will tell if we've guessed right," Henry added. "But the fact Tiya still feels Arlana gives us an advantage they can't predict."

"What concerns me," Kevin said, entering the conversation, "is they haven't set an ambush. Surely, by now, they know where we are."

Henry coughed, cleared his throat, then said, "They don't know where we are."

"What?" Jacob and Vic said at the same time.

"I've been shielding us," Henry said almost shyly. "I didn't mention it earlier because I wasn't sure how long it would work. The shield is…well, there's an element of illusion worked into the shield spell, and it is possible for magicians to detect an illusion if they know to look for one. We still need to take the usual precautions, but I thought any extra time we could gain would be beneficial."

Tiya looked back over her shoulder. "Thank you, Henry. I wouldn't have thought to try something like that."

Vic frowned quizzically at the sorceress.

She smiled. "I've only been in training for two years, Victoria. I still have a lot to learn."

She returned the lady's smile, both surprised and pleased to hear Lady Tiya wasn't perfect. When she glanced back at Jacob, she wasn't surprised to see his half smile. "What?" she said sourly.

"Nothing." His smile didn't fade when he looked back to the trail.

The scouts met them in a clearing at midday. The trail for the next few miles was clear. The group stopped for a short break before pushing on. They were moving as quickly as a group their size could along a game trail. Along the main roads at a quick pace, the trip would have lasted a mere eight days. Slowed by the narrower trail, they expected to reach Georna castle in eleven.

Only the continued movement of the kidnappers in the same general direction kept Tiya from protesting the necessary stop at Georna castle. Vic, whose street instincts kept her on constant alert in the strange environment, was more concerned with being able to reach Georna before having to face the goblins again. After seeing what those fangs could do, she didn't want to fight the GeMorin again without the help of the Georna smith's special weaponry. But she knew the odds weren't in their favor.

She was thinking quietly about the remaining eight days of their journey, unconsciously gnawing on her bottom lip, when a new question occurred to her. "Henry," she said, riding closer to the young sorcerer. "Why don't we gate?"

"Magically? Because they're too easy to disrupt. If we gated ahead of the blood magicians, they'd feel it—gating makes ripples in the fabric of magic—and they'd disrupt the spell. Whether they realized it was us or not. They wouldn't take a chance that the gate opening onto their path just happened to be formed by some innocent sorcerer."

"But why not gate to Georna castle, instead of ambushing the sorcerers? That would save us a week."

"Gating also takes a lot of power, Vic. Tiya and I couldn't build a gate for a group this size on our own. It would take a large number of the more powerful Guild magicians to gate this group all the way to Georna. And the blood mages would still feel the ripples and could still disrupt the spell. They'd never discount the formation of a gate that big, using that much power, as mere coincidence."

"Damn," Vic said, frowning. "I don't know about you, Henry, but my street sense is telling me we won't be able to reach Georna castle before the blood magicians send those GeMorin to slow us down."

Henry's white eyebrows drew together. "I'm afraid you may be right. But until they find us, they can't ambush us. And the closer we get to Georna, the better. We'll just have to hope my shield can give us the time we need."

She nodded, trying to look optimistic and knowing she failed. Slowing Night's Gale, she fell in beside Jacob again.

"You okay, little thief?" he asked quietly.

"Yeah. Just…" She shrugged.

"I know. Me too."

The fog clung to the ground throughout the day, bringing darkness to the forest early.

On the sixth day of travel, they crossed the main road leading to Bthak's western border. Scouts were sent ahead, but they found no sign of a GeMorin ambush. Henry's shield seemed to be working. But Vic's unease grew each day. The closer they got to Georna, the more her fingers twitched.

The sky was a heavy slate gray, keeping even the brightest parts of the day dim. As the sun ducked behind the mountains, they set up camp in a rock-circled glade. Vic fussed over Night's Gale for a long time after they'd stopped for the night. Once her muscles had finally adapted to being on horseback, she found herself growing quite fond of the mare.

The horses were picketed along the edge of the glade just inside the trees. She was combing out Gale's mane when an unexpected sound floated down from the camp. Quiet laughter.

She looked up to see Tiya sitting by a fire, circled in Kevin's arms, watching Jacob as he told an animated story. And the lady was actually smiling. And laughing. The first genuine laughter Vic had heard from her since the kidnapping.

Just behind Gale, Vic heard another quiet chuckle. "Good to see her laughing again, isn't it?" Garath walked to Gale's head and petted her chest.

"Yeah." She glanced back at Tiya, then looked up at Garath. "You're one of the lady's admirers, too?" she asked, hoping her smile didn't look too much like a smirk.

"What do you mean?"

"I mean, do you carry a secret…affection for Lady Tiya?"

Garath smiled and shook his head. "No. Lady Tiya is very beautiful, but she's not my type."

"I thought she was every man's type." Vic's brow furrowed. She wasn't sure she believed Garath.

"If everyone had the same taste in potential mates, we'd all look alike. There are all kinds of men who like all kinds of women."

"Really?" Vic said, still skeptical. Her gaze wandered back to where Tiya sat, engrossed in the tale Jacob was spinning.

"Of course," Garath said. "Some men like tall blondes, others prefer short brunettes with curly hair and huge brown eyes." He paused for a heartbeat, looking into her eyes, then shifted his gaze to the mare and continued, "Some men prefer redheads, some like fat women, some like skinny women, some like dark skin, some like light skin. And some men prefer other men and their varieties. That's one of the great things about the human species, Vic. The variety."

She smiled crookedly. "I suppose you're right."

"Of course I am."

"Thanks."

"You're welcome." He finally met her gaze again. "I'd better get going. I'm on first watch."

As he stepped away, she said, "Garath…"

He turned a questioning glance back over his shoulder.

"Stay standing."

A brief flicker of surprise crossed through his blue eyes, then he grinned, nodded in understanding and moved off to take his post.

She watched him retreat, a little concerned. She couldn't decide if she'd imagined his brief pause after describing her or if she'd really seen that flash of emotion he'd so far kept hidden. Must have been her imagination, she decided with a slight nod, closing the matter.

The feel of hands on her shoulders made her jump. "Jacob," she scolded, glancing up.

He chuckled. "Sorry, love." His gaze moved to the spot where Garath had disappeared into the forest. "What were you and Garath discussing?"

"Why the human animal comes in such a wide variety," she said.

He studied her upturned face. "And what did you come up with?"

"That humans like variety."

His eyebrows drew together, but he let the answer go with a shrug, his thoughts obviously on something other than the conversation she'd been having with Garath.

She changed the subject. "Lady Tiya sounded entertained by your story."

"She needed to laugh."

"Um hmm."

He kissed her forehead before saying, "Would you prefer she lost her temper again?"

"No," Vic admitted, "that wouldn't be good."

"Exactly." He turned her around to face him. "Are you through with Gale for the night?"

"Yes. Why?"

"I want to talk to you about something."

He ran a finger over her forehead, softening the creases that had collected at his statement. She nodded uncertainly and let him lead her back to his tent.

Inside, he turned to face her, staring into her eyes for a long moment before beginning. "I've been thinking about this since we left…actually no, I've been thinking about this since before we left Dareelia, but…" He inhaled deeply. "Victoria, I want you to quit Thieves' Hole. When we get back to Dareelia, I don't want you to go back to work for them."

"Why?" she said, not a little confused.

"I worry about you all the time. I'm still not happy about you being here, but at least here, I can look out for you."

"Jacob, I've survived in the Hole for fourteen years."

"I know, love. But things are different now. Please, when we get back, quit."

"What else would I do? I have to feed myself. Being part of Thieves' Hole…it's all I know."

"I'll take care of you. We'll come up with something." He pulled her close, wrapping his arms around her. "I don't want you in any more danger."

She dropped her gaze, resting her forehead against his chest. She stared at her fingertips, where they pressed against his stomach, and considered what he was asking her to do. He was asking her to change what she was, who she was. She'd never relied on anyone to take care of her, even when she was very young. Now he was asking her to put herself completely in his keeping.

And she found the idea tempting.

To sleep without being wary. To pass the day without worrying if she'd eat the next day. To live without having to stay on guard. To be warm in the winter and cool in the summer. To be able to take her knives off. To feel safe.

Yes, the idea was very tempting.

But a cynical, street-wise voice shouted in the back of her mind, *What happens when he's through with you, Flash? What happens when he leaves? What happens a year or even ten years from now, when your speed and strength have faded, when you're no long as agile and your skills have become brittle from disuse? What will you do then, Flash? How will you feed yourself then?*

He might not leave, she argued with the cynical voice.

You don't really believe that, do you? He'll leave. They all leave. You've seen it before. You'll be left to fend for yourself and you won't be Flash anymore. You'll just be Victoria. Where do you think that will take you?

I can do other things, she protested.

No, Flash. You won't be good for anything but the whorehouse, and you know it.

She squeezed her eyes tight, not wanting to hear that hard voice, yet knowing it was right. Her only defense was to be able to take care of herself, always. If she started to rely on someone else, she'd lose all the abilities she'd worked so hard to develop. She couldn't allow that to happen. But how could she explain that to Jacob?

With a deep breath, she looked into his worried gaze and decided the best course of action—avoidance. "I don't want to talk about this now," she said resolutely.

"Victoria…"

"No. Not now. If we survive, when we get back to Dareelia, we'll talk more."

He looked hard into her eyes, but after a moment gave in with a slight shake of his head. "Okay, love," he murmured. "But we will discuss this further when we get back to Dareelia."

"Okay."

"In the meantime…" He reached up and unfastened the onyx charm he still wore. "I want you to wear this."

"But…"

"Victoria, please wear it. I'll feel better."

She gave in with a shy nod.

He tied the leather thong around her neck, then ran his fingers over the stone hanging in the hollow of her throat.

"You don't need to worry about me," she said, cupping his cheeks in her hands. "I've survived this long, haven't I? I won't disappear on you." She pulled his face to hers. The kiss she'd intended to be gentle quickly turned urgent and hard. She willed him to forget his fears even as she fought her own dread.

Both their worries quickly turned to passionate need. Roughly, she jerked his shirt loose from his breeches, pulling away only long enough to remove the offending garment. Her own shirt followed in a rush.

His kisses were brutal and desperate. He pulled her down to their blankets, rolling her beneath him. He didn't bother to remove the daggers strapped to her shoulders and wrist, and she didn't notice. She clutched at him, twining her fingers in his hair as his mouth moved to her breasts. He was rough, and she reveled in that heat.

She threw herself into their lovemaking with the same aggressive determination she brought to a fight. Only this fight was with herself. A struggle to silence the hard cynic in the back of her mind. To prove that voice wrong. She forced his mouth back to hers as he pulled open her breeches.

Sitting back on his knees, he removed first her boots and calf daggers, then all but ripped off her breeches. She threw herself upward, taking his mouth roughly with hers as she forced him onto his back. She burned to feel him inside her, to possess him completely even if only for a short time. She disposed of his boots and pants then threw herself on top of him again. With one thrust, she took all of him inside of her.

Mercilessly, she rode him, slamming herself against him until her body splintered into mindless sensation. She arched her back and gave in to the wave of ecstasy.

But the fight wasn't yet won. He rolled her onto her back, taking his turn to silence the doubts. She clung, her nails digging unnoticed gashes in his shoulders and on his back, her mouth sucking and biting his ears and neck. The power she so often saw just beneath his surface slipped his control, enveloping and energizing her even as it burned her skin.

In that thoughtless realm of passion, she found peace from the street voice. For the briefest instant, the voice went quiet, leaving only Victoria and Jacob and their desperate, electric needs.

Their energy spent, their bodies and minds quieted, they collapsed into an exhausted sleep, tangled in each other's arms, defiantly refusing to face their respective fears.

CHAPTER NINETEEN

They reached the lower Georna Reaches on the eighth day. Winter came early to the rugged mountain range that stretched through Georna and up into Bthak. First snow had already whitened the higher peaks. Heavy gray clouds clung to the tops of the mountains, allowing only brief glimpses of blue sky.

The pine-scented breeze rushing across the rocky slopes froze Vic's cheeks and ungloved hands. She pulled her cloak tighter, tucking one hand inside the thick folds and guiding Gale one hand at a time. The lower trees were still swathed in oranges, yellows and reds, but not far above, only evergreen leaves remained against the slate gray rock slopes. To the side of the road they followed, a swift moving river accompanied them, masking all sound but the rush of water.

"So, this is where you grew up," she said, smiling at Jacob.

"What do you think, little thief?"

"I think it's cold." She pulled her cloak tighter and blew out a visible breath. His chuckle sounded faint above the rumble of water.

Just after midday, the road veered away from the river and into a rocky, sparsely vegetated pass. The sound of rushing water followed at their backs. But as they moved farther into the pass, the breeze died, leaving the air eerily still. Even the sounds of the river vanished.

Vic's street sense jumped, and her fingers began to twitch. "Something isn't right," she whispered to Jacob.

He looked as worried as she felt as he scanned the stone walls and rocky outcroppings. The whoosh of passing air was the only warning they had.

"Mimis!" Jacob shouted, dismounting and pulling his sword in a single move. From cracks in the surrounding rocks, impossibly thin creatures emerged in a rush toward their ambushed victims.

Her feet landed on solid ground, her wrist dagger already in hand, but her eyes couldn't keep up with the blurs of movement around them. She caught only a glimpse of thin gray arms, a flash of a long, attenuated body, the hint of a hairless, oblong head, the briefest flicker of sharp teeth.

Her dagger flicked at the passing blurs, yet she never managed to catch anything solid. It was like trying to slice rain. By the time she found a target, the Mimis had already moved away, its body so thin, even her accurate slash missed.

A scream ripped past her lips when the first bite took a chunk of flesh from her hand. She switched tactics, no longer trying to hit the blurs of movement. She simply wanted to keep them as far away as she could. Around her, the soldiers had dismounted, fighting blindly, their screams and shouts of pain evidence of their ineffective efforts.

The horrific image of being eaten alive, chunk by chunk, kept her blade swinging. She pulled a second dagger and windmilled her arms in a protective arch, moving at speeds faster than even she normally moved. She was rewarded with a single hit, cutting easily through the thin gray arm of a reaching Mimis.

But the attack didn't slow. For what seemed an eternity, the creatures came at them, an unrecognizable murmur underlying screams and the sound of metal slicing through air. Vic's gut clenched at that sounds the creatures made, but she kept moving. Her arms grew heavy, her shoulders burned, and still she swung her blades. At the edge of her vision, she saw one soldier fall to the creatures. She didn't look long enough to see the outcome of his fate. His screams were enough.

Panic crept into her consciousness. Her lungs burned with the effort of keeping her defense. She knew she wouldn't be able to hold the creatures off much longer, but the fear of what the Mimis would do kept her moving despite the agonizing fire shooting through her arms and shoulders. Behind her, she could hear Night's Gale attack with hooves and teeth. Yet the Mimis made no attempt to take bites from the horses' flesh. They avoided the animals, even when the war-trained horses struck at them. Vic was too busy keeping the creatures away from her own flesh to wonder about that for long.

Her arms started to slow, despite her mind screaming to keep them moving. She roared, forcing her body to move faster, ignoring the pain seizing her muscles. It didn't work. Her arms felt like lead weights had been tied to them, dragging no matter what she did. In horror, she watched as a gray arm darted under her defenses, clutching her tunic. She screeched and swung, only to feel the grasp of another hungry hand. She threw her heavy arms, blades lurching at the attackers, and knew she'd feel those sharp teeth soon.

Suddenly the Mimis's garbled murmurs stopped. And the still air erupted. A torrential wind bellowed down the narrow pass, whipping Vic's hair into her face and slapping stinging sand against exposed skin. She turned her back to the wind, expending the last of her strength just to remain standing. Her daggers ceased their frantic movements, her arms falling heavily to her sides. She watched through squinted eyes as the long, thin, hairless gray bodies of the Mimis blew away.

Even the arm she'd managed to sever tumbled into the air.

In a matter of minutes, the pass was clear and the wind stopped as abruptly as it had started. Vic took a long, ragged breath, and locked her knees to keep from falling to the ground.

Her heartbeat was just beginning to slow when a fresh wave of panic started her blood surging again. Frantically, she looked around at the weary soldiers. Her knees wobbled when she saw Jacob standing over what remained of the soldier who'd gone down. Except for a rip in his tunic sleeve and a bite on his hand, he didn't look hurt.

She took another deep breath and closed her eyes, leaning heavily against Night's Gale. The mare stood passive, seemingly undisturbed by the recent battle, her sweat-soaked coat the only evidence that she'd just been in a fight. Vic sucked in air, breathing in the sharp musk of Gale's sweat and listened to her heart pounding in her ears.

"Victoria?"

Jacob's soft voice opened her eyes.

"Are you hurt?"

She pulled away from Gale and smiled. "Not bad," she whispered, forcing her leaden arms around his waist. "It only took one bite for me to decide I didn't want to get bit again. You have just the one bite?"

"Yes, love. I didn't much care for the feeling either."

She dropped her head back. "What happened?"

"I'm not sure, but I suspect we'll get answers from our two magicians."

"Was anyone else injured? I saw the one soldier go down."

"A few of the soldiers are chewed badly. We'll have to find a place to hole up so we can tend their wounds."

"Garath?"

"He's all right. Only lost a few chunks."

She nodded, ignoring the flicker of uncertainty in his eyes. She glanced around and saw Kevin, Tiya and Henry were still standing with only a few wounds between them. The soldiers with minor wounds were collecting the horses or helping the seriously wounded. The sound of the river bubbled beneath the groans and mumbled speech of their group. A soft, pine-scented breeze brushed through her hair, cooling her overheated skin.

After a few quiet moments, Kevin, Tiya and Henry joined them.

"We need to find shelter," Kevin said, his voice low.

"There's a cave, not far from here," Jacob said. "It's off the road, but it won't be difficult for the wounded to reach."

Worry still creased Kevin's brow. At Jacob's raised eyebrow, the young giant said, "Henry had to drop the shield to work the wind spell."

"The wind we created," Henry said, nodding toward Tiya, "required a great deal of energy from both of us. I couldn't hold the shield while working the other spell."

"Damn," Jacob whispered. "And now?"

"I'm returning to full strength quickly. Within a quarter of an hour, I'll have the shield back in place, but…"

"The damage has been done," Tiya finished for him and placed a reassuring hand on his arm. "The blood magicians will almost certainly know where we are now. When the shield goes back into place, they won't be able to track us easily, but we've already been forced to reveal our position."

"They'll know which direction we travel," Jacob said flatly. He looked back to his soldiers, silently for several minutes. "We'll take cover in the cave for tonight," he said at last. "Tomorrow, we make for Georna castle as fast as possible."

"Do we stay on the main road?" Kevin asked.

"There's another route, but it's slow and would be difficult for the wounded. I think we stick to the main road, where we can move quickly. It's possible they're too far ahead to send an attack."

Jacob didn't sound convinced, but Vic remained silent. They didn't have many options left. Tomorrow, they'd make a mad dash for Georna castle. She offered a silent prayer to the Goddess, something she found herself doing more often lately than ever before in her life.

The mouth of the cave Jacob led them to was barely large enough to move the horses through one at a time. After only a few feet, though, the interior of the cave opened into a single, massive cavern with more than enough room to accommodate all of the humans and horses.

The wounded were laid out, made as comfortable as possible, and their injuries tended. Of the fifty soldiers, twenty had received serious wounds, only one man, the one she'd seen fall to the Mimis, had died, and the rest had received only minor injuries. Those with the fewest injuries collected wood and soon the cave walls flickered with shadows from several small fires, the scent of wood smoke covering the damp, mossy smell of the cavern.

She and Jacob sat to one side of the cave. After making sure his soldiers were taken care of, Jacob bandaged her hand himself.

"See," she said, when he looked up from her wound, "that wasn't so bad, was it?"

He frowned. "Yes, little thief, that was bad." With a deep breath, he shook his head and let the subject go.

"But why did they attack? I thought Mimis only ate roots."

"On occasion they attack lone human travelers when they happen to come across them. But I've only heard of them attacking large groups like that when they were starving. Thing is, this was a good year. There was no reason for them to be hungry."

"Why didn't they try to eat the horses?"

"Mimis don't like cattle or any other kind of meat except for human flesh."

"Yuck." She grimaced.

"I've never been overly fond of the Mimis myself. Something about being eaten alive…"

His wry grin made her chuckle. "How's your hand?"

"Fine." He held up his bandaged limb for her inspection.

"Did you learn to dress wounds in the guard?"

"My mother taught me."

She squeezed his fingers, a faintly envious sensation clenching her heart. The moment ended when Garath approached.

"General. Vic," he greeted.

"Hey, Garath," Vic said, "good to see you standing."

"Thanks. Good to be standing. Were you hurt badly?"

"No. Just a little chunk out of my hand."

"Glad it wasn't worse." He shifted his gaze to Jacob. "The wounded have all been cared for and a guard set at the mouth of the cave as well as down the path."

"Good. Thanks, Garath."

He glanced at the cave floor, then met Jacob's gaze again. "We'll make a run for Georna castle tomorrow?"

"Yeah. Early."

"Everyone should be ready for the dash by the morning," he said with a firm nod, but uncertainty edged his voice.

"You'd better get some rest." As the young man started to walk away, Jacob called, "Garath, glad you're okay."

"You too, Jacob."

When they were alone again, Vic asked, "How long have you known Garath?"

"About five years now. I've always been able to count on him.

He's a good man."

"Yeah. He is."

Jacob's eyes narrowed. "Should I be worried, little thief?"

"About Garath? No." She slid closer, kissing him lightly. "I've always preferred men with brown eyes," she whispered.

His crooked smile made her heart jump. His warm kiss was interrupted by a hesitant cough.

"Sorry," Henry said, managing to look both embarrassed and distracted at the same time. "But we need to talk."

"Have a seat," Jacob offered with a wave of his hand. Tiya and Kevin joined them just as Henry sat.

"What are we discussing?" Kevin asked, circling his wife in his arms.

"Arlana." Henry paused, his lips pursed. "I was instructed by my master to discuss this only if and when appropriate. I'm afraid that time is now as we can't predict what may meet us tomorrow. There is more to this…situation, than is evident. Several months ago…no, I have to start earlier. There's a prophecy."

Vic sucked in a breath at the mention of the prophecy Kritta had hinted at less than a month earlier. She hadn't expected it to be part of this.

Henry shot her a curious look but continued his story. "The prophecy is over a thousand years old. Its origins, the name of the prophet, all have been lost to time. But the words of the prophecy remain. In essence, it states a child will be born of power so great, she will control all magic and hold the fate of the world in the palm of her hand. She'll control that which cannot be controlled and command that which cannot be commanded."

There was a long, quiet pause. Then Kevin asked, "What are you saying?" His brow set in deep lines over his narrowed green eyes.

"Not my daughter," Tiya whispered.

"Signs were given in the prophecy to predict the coming of this child. A little over two years ago, we saw the first indicators her birth was imminent. Six months ago, we witnessed the final signs. The signs to indicate that the child had been born."

"Henry, there were probably thousands of children…hundreds of thousands born six months ago," Jacob said, his voice even and reasonable. "What makes you think Arlana is the one?"

Vic saw the distress on both Tiya's and Kevin's faces and understood Jacob's reluctance to believe. She'd doubt it, too, if she hadn't looked into Henry's eyes. There was more to the story, things he hadn't told them yet. She could see that as clearly as she could see his conviction in the truth of his belief. She sucked in her bottom lip, thought about their situation. And a fearful certainty crept into her mind.

There were too many coincidences. Too much effort had gone into Arlana's kidnapping. Whether she was the prophesied child or not, someone else besides Henry believed she was the one. That was enough to make their situation much worse than they'd expected.

"The stronger magicians knew the instant she was born," Henry answered Jacob. "There was a wave in the magical energies, an unmistakable wave. It was the final sign. Lord Caul was one who felt this change. Those who knew what to look for knew *when* she was born, as well as *where*. Not the exact place, but the area. Fordin Barony."

"But I'm sure there were many children born in Fordin around that same time, Henry. You can't be certain. You said yourself you didn't know the exact place. The barony is big. You must be wrong. You couldn't *know*." Tiya's voice held a hint of panic, an undercurrent of pleading.

"My lady, her power would be hard to mistake. We have no doubt. Especially…"

"Especially?" Jacob urged.

"Especially now that she's been kidnapped," Vic said, meeting Henry's gaze.

The young magician nodded solemnly. "There's more," he said just above a whisper. "She's an innocent now. As such, she's neutral. She can be corrupted."

Tiya's eyes flared wide. "What do you mean corrupted? Are you telling me my daughter will become evil?"

"No. I'm telling you that she can be influenced now. That she's vulnerable to…"

At his pause, Tiya leaned forward, looking hard into the sorcerer's eyes. "Who?" she demanded. "The magicians who've taken her? Who would hurt my child?"

Vic sat a little straighter, suddenly worried that the young mother's reaction to the news might be a bad thing for the cave walls.

Henry remained quiet for a long moment then shook his head. "I don't know the source, my lady. I only know there's a power to the north, a strong power. One who's also seen the signs, felt the child's birth. One who would control her. And the fate of the world."

"Tracker," Vic whispered.

"What?" Jacob, Tiya and Kevin all said at the same time.

She looked up. All eyes were focused on her. Taking a breath, she said, "When Tracker first told me that he'd been hired to smuggle the blood magicians into Dareelia, he spoke of the man who hired him. He wasn't one of the magicians. He was someone…something else.

"He wasn't able to give me a description. He couldn't remember what the man looked like. He said it was like the image simply wasn't in his memory. He also said that the only impression that had stuck with him was that the man was harmless." She bit her bottom lip and looked at Tiya. "I don't think this man is harmless, my lady. He's the one responsible for Arlana's kidnapping."

The small group fell silent for a long time. Kevin held his wife tighter, the lines on his brow and around his mouth deepened. Tiya looked stunned, her mouth hanging open slightly. Henry never looked up from the cave floor.

At last, Tiya said, very quietly, "You've told us this for a reason, Henry. Besides the fact that, as her mother, I should know these things, why? Why now?"

"We must see that the child isn't allowed to stay with this evil influence. Tomorrow is uncertain. If I shouldn't survive, it's important that you know the risk, the importance behind our mission. We can't, under any circumstances, allow the child to be taken by that power."

Henry fell silent again, but all understood his underlying meaning. *Even if it meant the child must die.* The words echoed in Vic's mind as she studied Kevin and Tiya. Finally, with absolute certainty, she said, "We'll rescue Arlana."

Tiya looked at her for a silent moment. Then the shock began to fade from her bright blue eyes and she nodded.

"We'll rescue Arlana," Jacob echoed. Outside the sun had set, leaving only the fire light inside the cave. It cast the faces of their small group in soft, warm shadows that set a sharp contrast to the seriousness of their discussion. The must and wood smoke scent of the cave now mixed with the smells of roasting meat and boiling stew.

After another long silence, Jacob said, "I think it would be good if we all got some rest. Tomorrow will be a hard ride. With luck, if we push, we should reach Georna village by early morning the day after tomorrow."

"Until tomorrow then," Henry said, standing. "Good night."

The young sorcerer walked to his trail blanket, shoulders slumped. He didn't bother to eat, but collapsed into a restless sleep.

Tiya and Kevin left for one of the small fires after wishing Jacob and Vic quiet good nights. Alone, Jacob turned to her. "Are you hungry? Whatever they've got cooking smells pretty good."

"I am hungry," she agreed. "But, Jacob…"

"What is it, little thief?"

She frowned, unable to put her fears and concerns into words. She wasn't entirely sure what bothered her the most. Obviously, the stranger and what he might represent. The GeMorin that were almost certainly waiting between the cave and Georna castle. The fate of the world, she supposed. Her own life. Jacob's life. But how to explain the gnawing in her gut that had nothing to do with the fate of the world and everything to do with the shock on Tiya's face? She couldn't explain it to herself. With a sigh, she gave up and said, "Nothing. Let's get some food."

That night, she dreamed.

She lay atop a tall stone altar covered with black cloth. Around her, red candles blazed. Beyond the circle of their light, the surrounding darkness was an impenetrable, heavy black. For a heartbeat, she squinted at the candles.

Then she tried to move. And failed. Only her eyes would obey her mind's commands. She tried vainly to lift her arm, to move her foot, to turn her head.

Panic.

She couldn't scream. She couldn't so much as move her lips. Even breathing was difficult. Her chest hurt with the pain of forcing air into her lungs. Her nostrils clogged with a too-sweet scent that made her stomach roll.

Out of the darkness, a shadow emerged. A black robe and cowl hid his features, but she knew who he was. She didn't see the flare of white skin and hair until he stood at the foot of the altar.

He smiled, his colorless lips parting, a baring of teeth more than a sign of humor or amusement. "You have witnessed the ritual," he whispered.

In her mind, she screamed, calling for Jacob, for anyone. For help. She hurled threats, pleas, curses at the white sorcerer. But no sound escaped her motionless lips.

As she watched, he pulled a knife from his sleeve. Unlike the sacrificial dagger, however, this knife had a golden hilt embedded with emeralds. Her heartbeat raced. She looked back at the sorcerer and saw Malkiney now wearing the robe.

He grinned, his eyes glistening with a rapture she knew to be insanity. He stepped forward, twisting the knife in his fingers, giggling in spurts.

"No one survives seeing the ritual, Flash," he said, his voice high and frantic. "No one." He giggled and raised the knife high above his head.

Her mind strained against terror. She tried again, desperate to move, to scream. Her eyes bulged. In the back of her mind, she shouted that this had to be a dream. But her attempts to wake failed, and the knife fell slowly toward her chest. Around her, chanting resonated, rising in volume even as the knife fell. She felt the blade sink into her chest...

And sat up with a strangled cry.

The cave was quiet, dark, but for a small torch flickering in the back. Her pulse raced and cold sweat beaded her forehead. She closed her eyes, breathing deliberately, slowly. *You were dreaming, Flash. Nothing more than a dream.*

She didn't notice Jacob's arms close around her shoulders. Only when he spoke softly in her ear did she realize he was sitting beside her.

"Victoria? Are you all right?"

Her heart still pounded, but the rush of blood and adrenaline began to ease. Her body trembled in the aftershock of terror. She nodded and whispered, "I was dreaming."

His arms tightened, pulling her against his chest. She shuddered and pressed her face against his smooth muscles, absorbing his heat, breathing his familiar, welcome scent. After a time, her heartbeat returned to normal and her breathing eased.

Jacob settled back onto their mat, pulling her with him. Stroking her hair, he coaxed her back to sleep, whispering, "Don't worry about the nightmares, love. I'll keep them away."

Chapter Twenty

By first light, Vic and the rest of the group were awake and ready to travel. The day promised to be bright and cloudless. The morning air was cold and painfully dry. Bird song trilled peacefully overhead.

They rode fast. The wounded rode in the center of the group, with the most seriously wounded riding double with a healthy soldier. They changed horses often to compensate for the extra weight an individual horse had to carry. They stopped twice during that harrowing day, but only briefly.

Vic scanned their surroundings as they passed a forest that grew denser with each mile. The road steadily climbed up into the mountains, taking them into the middle of the range. No hint of ambush.

As night fell and further travel became impossible, they set a hasty camp in a grove. The trees gave protection from the elements, but cold still seeped into her bones despite the thick folds of her cape and tunic. They didn't start even a small cooking fire for fear of giving away their position. Instead, the group huddled together under their travel blankets, using each other to keep warm. Sentries changed frequently, allowing everyone a chance at rest.

But Vic couldn't sleep in the cold with her nerves tensed and ready for any sign of attack. She leaned against Jacob, hugging his arms where they wrapped around her stomach, listened and watched.

When the sky finally began to lighten, she blinked gritty eyes, having dozed no more than a few minutes all night. Jacob looked just as haggard, the loss of sleep evident in his handsome, beard-stubbled face.

The group was up and riding before the sun had fully peaked the eastern slopes. That day, the sky was thick with dark gray clouds. Their heavy mounds added to Vic's agitation, making her feel like she was slowly being pressed into the earth. Around them, the forest had lost its colored plumage, leaving only the deep green of pines. Beneath the canopy of trees, the forest floor was dark and impenetrable.

The faster they rode, the closer they drew to Georna castle, the more her apprehension grew. It was too easy. They were so close, she could feel it. And it was too easy.

Not more than a league from Georna village, things stopped being easy. GeMorin charged out of the forest, surrounding them almost before they noticed their presence. Even the horses hadn't noted the silent passage of the warrior goblins until it was too late.

Vic clung to Gale's mane as the mare skidded to a halt. All around her, the shouts of humans and squeals of horses echoed off the mountains. She pulled her wrist knife, but despite the week on horseback, she couldn't fight and stay on the mare at the same time. For the first few minutes, she clutched Night's Gale's neck while the war-trained mare battled the swarming teams of goblins. And, to her credit, the mare was winning.

But one sideslip too many sent Vic tumbling to the ground. Instinct born of years of climbing buildings and dodging knives allowed her to roll and rise to her feet in a single movement. On the ground, she found her balance in time to face the first GeMorin. The goblin was only a few inches taller than her, but she was as broad as Jacob. If she blocked a blow from the goblin's saber with her dagger, it would shatter her arm. Not a good plan. Instead, she resorted to ducking and avoiding, weaving and dodging the razor-edged blade.

The GeMorin was quick. But Vic's survival instincts worked at a furious pace. Her initial terror fell subservient to tactics. Her vision sharpened, her senses heightened. She felt the saber pass inches above her head, the heat from the goblin's body filling the space between them. Her own breath hit the frigid mountain air in puffs like smoke. She watched, waited, avoiding the deadly goblin blade. And when a minute opening in the goblin's defenses appeared, Vic was ready before her mind consciously registered the warrior's lapse. She slipped behind the GeMorin and buried her knife in the base of the goblin's neck.

Vic spared a glance around the struggling masses, hunting for Jacob. She'd lost sight of him the instant the attack had begun. Fear surged into her blood, clenching her gut, when she couldn't find him. Then another GeMorin closed and she redirected her focus on staying alive.

This goblin was larger than the first, but his overconfidence worked in her favor. He didn't expect the little human to be trouble. She answered his arrogance by sending her dart knife into the GeMorin's throat.

"Vic!"

She swung at the sound of her name, in time to see a third goblin bearing down on her. The warning gave her the seconds she needed. She rolled passed the broad swing of a bloodied saber, surged to her feet, and saw Garath's sword emerge from the goblin's neck. She acknowledged his help with a grateful, brief nod and turned back to the fight.

Around her, GeMorin tumbled from the forest in impossible numbers. As one fell, another appeared to take its place. When one wavered, a second would join. The king's soldiers were losing. There were at least three GeMorin to every soldier still standing.

The bloated, purple body of one guard confirmed that the GeMorin were using their fangs. Vic fought the bile in her throat and tried once more to find Jacob. She slipped into the edge of the forest, moving quietly over the leaf-covered ground. Her natural facility for silent steps let her approach from behind without calling attention to herself. A flick of her wrist planted a knife into the base of a GeMorin skull. When the warrior dropped, she looked into the astounded face of Kevin Fordin. He gave her a sword salute and what was almost a smile before charging back to the road.

She moved to follow, hoping to find Jacob, but she never reached the road. A GeMorin stepped out of the trees and into her path, a tower of menace and rage.

"You killed my mate, cowardly human!" he bellowed.

Before she could take in the unexpected words, the goblin attacked, forcing her to throw herself back in an awkward roll. She didn't have time to reach her feet before the raging warrior was on her, his sword held high, his lipless mouth wide, huge fangs dripping clear liquid down his chin.

She rolled sideways, barely avoiding the downswing of the curved blade. A tree root jolted her to a painful, awkward stop, jamming her arm in the bargain. She looked up to see the goblin hovering, his mouth gaped, his chest rising in rapid, shallow breaths.

"Only cowards attack from behind," he growled. "You will die the hard way, human. No warrior's death for you."

Her gaze snapped to his fangs, and she knew how he wanted her to die. Her wrist knife flew without conscious thought. The GeMorin batted it away with his wrist bracer. A second knife flew before the first hit the ground, but the warrior only gave it a passing grunt as he knocked it away. She scrambled backward, came up hard against the tree.

He bellowed a triumphant call and leaned closer. She pulled one of her calf daggers just as the goblin's face settled in front of hers. Hot, rank breath battered her face. She slashed at his neck, but he clamped her wrist in a vice grip, rendering her arm immobile and useless. He locked gazes with her, and opened his mouth wide.

Her breath stopped at the sight of those fangs moving to the defenseless skin of her arm. She swung her free hand desperately, futilely. The warrior caught that arm and held it motionless without even glancing at the offending limb. She kicked at his groin. She might as well have kicked a rock. She tried sweeping his feet from under him. Pain shot through her leg on contact. She would have been more successful trying to fell a tree with her foot.

Vic stared at the fangs, realizing with a shock of clarity that she was about to die. And she was helpless to prevent it. For the first time in her life, Vic Flash had no escape. A scream of protest died in her throat, terror robbing her of reaction. Her mind reached out to Jacob, calling the image of his rugged face before her mind's eye. A single memory to cling to in the last moments of her life.

Concentrating all the energy she had left on holding that picture, several seconds passed before she realized that the goblin's fangs hadn't reached her arm. When wetness splattered her face, her eyes snapped open to see a sword protruding from the GeMorin's neck.

The goblin fell away, and Vic looked into the face she'd been clinging to. Jacob's eyes shone with rage. And fear. She'd never before seen Jacob afraid.

He glowered for a heartbeat, then jerked her to her feet. Without a word, he dragged her back to the road, slashing through the GeMorin as if they were bits of foliage. He pushed her toward Night's Gale, who'd just finished pulverizing a goblin with her front hooves, and threw her onto the mare's back with amazing ease.

The GeMorin continued to converge on the group in an unending wave. From Gale's back, Vic saw that the numbers of their small band had been slashed. Above the clashes and grunts and screams of battle, Jacob bellowed, "Ride!" He slapped Gale on the rump, and the mare leapt forward, nearly throwing Vic back to the ground. Behind her, she heard Jacob bellowing the same order to the remaining soldiers. "Make for the village! Ride!"

Gale ran too fast for her to do much more than cling to her neck, but Vic did manage to look over her shoulder. Behind her, she saw Jacob mount and follow fast on her flank, the remaining soldiers right behind him. And behind them, the GeMorin pursued, running at a speed nearly matching the horses.

They raced for Georna castle, the GeMorin close behind. Panic raced with them, biting Vic's heels. They weren't going to make it. The horses had been running for two days. If the animals faltered now, they were dead. High mountain slopes rose around them, stark and unforgiving. But no help, no village. No castle. Tears streaked the sides of her face as the wind whipped her raw. The pounding of hooves on the rocky road echoed their death knell. They charged around a bend, into the crook of the mountain's arm.

And before them, the castle rose into view. Along with a charging force of Georna guards. The soldiers parted ranks, allowing the weary king's soldiers to race past, then closed behind them, cutting off the GeMorin's pursuit.

Jacob caught up with Vic and moved past her to lead the way to the castle. Georna castle sat atop a narrow tower of rock, etched from the surrounding mountains to stand alone like a finger pointing toward the sky. The dark red-brown walls of the castle blended with the mountain rock so it was impossible to tell where mountain ended and castle began. Beneath, a small village spread to the north and west, surrounding a swift moving river and filling the flat space between the pinnacle and the mountains at its back.

A path, difficult to find if unaware of its starting point, spiraled up the rock tower. The king's soldiers slowed to a walk for the steep climb. At the top of the long ascent, the open gates of the castle and a small castle guard waited.

The gates sealed shut as the last of the king's soldiers tumbled into the courtyard, and grooms ran forward to take the exhausted horses away. Vic dismounted, legs wobbling beneath her. She hesitated before handing Gale's reins to a young boy, patting the mare on the shoulder. Gale replied with a soft whinny before allowing herself to be led away.

In the safety of the courtyard, Vic scanned the remaining members of their group. Garath, Kevin, Tiya, and Henry were still standing. She blew out a long breath, her relief dampened by the realization that only half of the original fifty King's Guards remained and a number of them were seriously wounded.

She closed her eyes briefly then moved to stand at Jacob's elbow. He didn't glance down at her.

The red-clad figure of Baroness Georna emerged from the castle before she could worry about Jacob's distance. She was stunned by her first close view of Baroness Elizabeth Georna. The woman was as old if not older than Queen Sara, but her porcelain white face showed only the first hint of aging. Her hair was the color of golden thread and her eyes were an amazing violet. She wasn't what Vic would call beautiful—but startling in an attractive, exotic way.

The Baroness, ignoring formalities, walked up to Jacob and took his hand. "I see you've had some trouble returning for a visit," she said calmly.

Her voice reminded Vic of the sound of the river echoing off the mountain walls, soothing and inspiring all at once.

She looked over the haggard remains of their band. "Come. All of you will be given rooms and your injuries tended." Without further comment, she turned and led them up the short curve of stone stairs and into the castle.

Jacob walked a pace behind the Baroness, his expression stony and unreadable. Kevin and Tiya moved to walk alongside Vic, who stayed a step back from Jacob. She glanced up at the young giant beside her. Then looked again. Kevin focused straight ahead, but his gaze kept straying to Baroness Georna, a strained look pinching his eyes and lips. Regret?

Before she could wonder at this new puzzle, the corridor opened into an audience hall. Baroness Georna turned, addressing the group again. "I must apologize for not personally escorting you the rest of the way, but I must see to the reinforcement of our walls and the security of the village. My steward will ensure you are attended." She turned to address Jacob directly. "I'll send Dreem to care for your seriously wounded. When you've settled and your injured tended, send word. The smith, Brandon, arrived yesterday. He's brought sufficient weaponry to outfit your group immediately. I believe you are in a hurry?"

"Yes, my lady," Jacob said, a hint of humor breaking the strain in his voice. "You are as always quite perceptive."

Baroness Georna's cheeks lifted in a small tender smile. "Until this afternoon, then," she said. A tall, lanky man in his early sixties approached the group and led them through the maze of corridors to the guest wing.

Once away from the Baroness, Vic hazarded a second glance at both Jacob and Kevin. Jacob's expression remained unreadable through the blood and grit smeared on his face. But Kevin's still held that hint of something she wanted to call regret. He caught her scrutiny and a slight smile touched his lips.

At her unspoken question, he said softly, "It's a long story, Victoria. Perhaps later, I'll have time to tell you." Tiya took his hand and squeezed, a silent message passing between them.

Vic's room wasn't lavish, but it was a significant improvement over her mat on the floor of the Hole's headquarters. Across from the small four-poster bed draped in Georna red, an open wardrobe displayed a number of evening and day dresses in various sizes. Thoughtful, she mused, as she thumbed through the selection.

To one side of the room sat a wooden bathtub, the inside draped with cloth. Warm water already filled the tub and fresh towels sat atop a nearby table. The fire in the small stone fireplace kept the single room at a comfortable temperature. After the cold journey, the heat warming her cheeks felt as drugging as a jolt of whiskey.

She stripped and climbed into the hot bath, washing away dirt, sweat and blood. Exhaustion hounded her without mercy, but she refused to give in to the overwhelming desire for sleep. There was too much to do. Despite her body-numbed fatigue, her thoughts spun— first to Arlana, then Jacob.

She hadn't had much time to consider the new urgency of their mission. Not really. She knew it was vital to rescue the baby, for her mother's sake as much as anything. But now the full weight of their responsibility crashed on sore muscles. There was so much more at stake now, so much more to lose. Only now, with her body too tired to move, did that reality sink in. She'd had vague fears before, a part of her understanding that the game had changed. But as the warm water swirled around her, the reality of the dangers of this new game laid before her.

The fate of the world depended on them rescuing a baby. She didn't bother to consider any other option. They *would* rescue Arlana because anything short of rescue wasn't acceptable.

She sighed, shifting to a more comfortable position in the tub. Then there was Jacob. His coolness was disturbing and not a little frightening. What if he were hurt and wouldn't admit it? But no. Anger radiated beneath his cool façade. She'd felt his anger as she now felt the warmth of her bath.

She ducked her chin to her chest and pursed her lips. Why in the name of the Goddess was he angry? Was it the loss of so many soldiers? The attack?

Even as her tired mind groped for excuses, she knew Jacob had been expecting an ambush. Something else bothered him. Something he wasn't ready to discuss with her. So she'd have to wait.

Her eyes drifted shut, snapped open, drooped heavily again. Time to get out. Her fingers were wrinkled from her prolonged stay in the water. Wrapping in a warm towel, she went to the wardrobe to inspect the dresses. The thought of putting on a fresh, unsoiled dress made her sigh with pleasure. She didn't want to don her dirty travel clothes now that she was clean. She also didn't want to face the Baroness again in such rough attire.

After minutes of scrutiny, she chose a simple amber silk that looked close to her size. She laid the dress across the foot of her bed, then curled up on the mattress, promising to shut her eyes for only a minute.

The fire had almost died by the time she opened her eyes again.

Outside, the daylight had faded. It was at least mid-afternoon. Groaning, she threw herself out of bed. She dressed in a hurry, finding the dress a remarkably close fit, then ran her fingers through her hair and stepped out into the hall.

She ran, almost literally, into Tiya. The sorceress looked tired but composed in a borrowed gown of blue violet.

"Good afternoon, Victoria," she murmured. "Did you rest well?"

"Yes, my lady."

"Please, call me Tiya. I'm too tired for formality."

"Tiya. I fell asleep." She shook her head, rolling her eyes as if it were a great tragedy.

The gesture brought a rare smile to Tiya's weary face. "Baroness Georna sent for those of us well enough to meet with Brandon. Will you walk with me?"

"Of course." She had to work to keep from frowning. "Will Lord Fordin join us?"

"He and Jacob have been with Baroness Georna for the last hour. He snuck out while I was sleeping."

Tiya scowled, leaving Vic to wonder if the lady was joking or truly upset with her husband.

Tiya led them to the same audience chamber they'd passed through earlier that morning. Kevin, Jacob, Garath and Henry were with the Baroness, the soldiers without serious wounds, and a man who was possibly the largest human Vic had ever seen.

He was almost as tall as Kevin, but closer in breadth to a GeMorin warrior. Great muscles bulged beneath his sleeveless leather tunic and worn leather breeches. Thick golden hair hung to the top of his enormous shoulders, held in place by several small braids. His weathered face was covered in a short, neat blond beard that broadened an already strong jaw. Green eyes peered from behind heavy lids that were at once intimidating and fascinating.

Baroness Georna took the huge man's arm, a slight blush touching her porcelain white cheeks, and led him toward Vic and Tiya. The huge man gently held the Baroness's hand where it rested on his impossibly large biceps. The comfortable way they walked together hinted at a relationship far more intimate than Vic would have suspected. But one she could understand looking at the large smith.

"Lady Tiya," Elizabeth Georna introduced, "Victoria Flash, I'd like you to meet Brandon Kerr, smith of the upper Georna Reaches."

"It's a pleasure, Brandon," Tiya greeted, ducking her head politely.

"Pleasure," Vic mumbled, trying not to feel awkward next to Tiya and the Baroness. She looked into Brandon's gaze. In those green depths, she saw a weapons master, a skilled artisan and the hint of a consummate gambler. She exhaled and smiled.

"The pleasure is mine," Brandon answered.

His voice befitted his profession, sounding like the deep rhythmical beat of a hammer on metal.

"Shall we?" The Baroness nodded back to the waiting soldiers.

Vic automatically sought Jacob. He stood to one side of the group talking in hushed tones with Kevin. When he noticed their approach, he caught her gaze and she faltered. He watched her with a mixture of heated desire and that unnameable anger that had simmered since the GeMorin ambush. Frowning, she questioned him with her gaze, but received no answer, no explanation. She dropped her gaze, sucked in her bottom lip and fell back into step beside Tiya.

As the group gathered around Brandon and Baroness Georna, Jacob moved to stand at Vic's side, taking her arm without speaking. He didn't even meet her upturned and questioning glance.

She paid enough attention to know that they'd soon be selecting the weaponry they'd need for the rest of the journey and, afterward, would retire to the Baroness's private dining hall for dinner. But her gaze kept flicking to Jacob's stormy eyes as the heat of his body pulsed through the thick fabric of her borrowed dress. He gave no clue to his thoughts.

When the weaponry was finally brought into the room and set on a table, she pulled her full attention back to her surroundings. The weapons before them were an amazing blend of artistry and practicality. Intricately carved designs decorated the handles of razor-sharp swords and knives. Bracers of all sizes and styles sat next to small, mirror polished shields. The metal was an odd reddish-gray.

"What type of metal is this?" she asked the hulking smith. "I understand it's the only metal strong enough to break GeMorin teeth. But I've never seen anything that color before."

Brandon smiled, his movement reminding her of an opened fissure during an earthquake.

"The metal comes from a large meteorite buried deep in Davin's Breech," he said, "a mountain peak in Upper Georna. It's the only place, to my knowledge, that such a meteorite has been found."

"Meteorite? As in a rock that fell from the sky?"

"Exactly. It probably fell a billion years ago. Maybe before the Georna range was formed. My ancestors discovered it by accident while mining the mountains and we've been working with it ever since."

"But, if it's a meteor, then your supply is limited?"

"Yes. But we've still not tapped more than a third of the entire rock. I'd say the problem of low supply won't be something my great-great-grandchildren will need to worry about."

Her fingers twitched at the thought of controlling something so valuable. With a heavy sigh, she examined the weapons laid out on the table. Her gaze settled on a splendid short dagger, the broad blade looking like it would fit her neck scabbard.

She ran a finger over the smooth metal and gasped. "It's warm," she announced.

Brandon chuckled. "One of its unique properties. That's a fine knife. Will it be for you or the general here?"

The smith nodded knowingly toward Jacob who still loomed at her elbow.

"For my…" she began.

"She won't be needing any of these."

CHAPTER TWENTY-ONE

Vic frowned at Jacob, as Brandon raised a brow. Jacob's voice was quiet but the anger in his eyes crept through his words.

"Actually," she said, addressing the smith but keeping her gaze locked with Jacob's, "I will be needing some of these." She looked back at the smith. "I lost three good knives in the battle with the GeMorin. I need replacements."

"Ah, a knife fighter, are you? I have some excellent darts." He pulled a small throwing knife from further down the table and presented it.

She weighed the instrument, balancing the hilt in her hand. Then, using her fingertips, she flipped it from grip to point and back to grip several times, testing its balance and feel. "This is a remarkable piece," she said, grinning. "I'll take it. And that thick-bladed dagger. It'll fit nicely into my neck scabbard."

"Neck scabbard? Concealed?"

"Best kind."

"Well, I haven't met anyone who could use one of those effectively in years. And you don't have trouble with clothing or hair interfering with retrieval?"

"I did at first. Had to practice, but I've got the knack of it now." She tried to relax into their discussion of daggers—a well-loved topic—but she couldn't forget Jacob's declaration or ignore his scowl digging into the back of her neck.

After picking a third knife for her boot and a second wrist knife, Brandon presented her with a pair of bracers. The metal circled most of her forearm, parting just enough for her wrist scabbards and knives. Jacob hastily pointed to the sword and bracers he wanted.

"Don't you want a shield?" Vic suggested.

"I won't need one." His answer was clipped and monotone.

She barely had time to thank Brandon when Jacob ushered her away from the table toward Kevin and Tiya, effectively preventing her questions. She wasn't happy with his manipulation, but she held her irritation in check. They'd discuss this later.

Baroness Georna joined them, and Vic couldn't help but notice the way Kevin flinched and dropped his gaze to the floor. He spoke cordially and with obvious respect, but he wouldn't meet her eyes.

The Baroness noted his reaction too.

"Young giant," she said, gently touching his hand. "You still have feelings of remorse? Don't carry this burden, Kevin Fordin. You weren't responsible for her madness. You were responsible for her release. Hreedin would have been pleased with the swift end you gave her."

He took a long breath and raised his head to meet her gaze. She returned his look with a subtle, warm smile. "Come," she said to the entire group, "it's time to dine." She took Brandon's waiting arm and led the way to the dining room.

As they walked to a door at the rear of the audience hall, Vic whispered to Tiya, "Hreedin?"

"Hreedin was a friend of Baroness Georna's," she explained

in tones not meant to carry beyond their small group. "She was a beautiful, gold dragon."

"Dragon? I thought that was a rumor—that the Baroness had a pet dragon."

"Hreedin wasn't a pet," Tiya said. "She was a friend."

"The dragon went mad?"

"She was driven mad," Kevin said softly. "By Prince Erick."

"The Prince," Vic breathed. The late Prince of Karasnia had caused a lot more trouble than was commonly related it seemed. "But…"

"Two years ago, Hreedin attacked the Fordin train on its way to the Baronies Meeting," Jacob said.

She heard the sorrow in his voice overshadowing his earlier anger.

"She wouldn't have attacked but for the twisting of her mind by Erick. Our young friend here was forced to issue the killing blow."

"You killed a dragon?!" Vic wasn't sure which surprised her more—that the Prince had driven a dragon insane or that Kevin had actually killed it.

"With a little magical help," Kevin admitted, smiling at his wife.

"Goddess," Vic exhaled. "I had no idea. And I thought we'd gotten the whole story behind the Prince's treason."

"That particular part was hushed," Tiya said, taking her husband's hand. "Out of respect for Baroness Georna."

"And to prevent needless panic," Jacob added.

They stepped into the dining hall, a small, elegant room with walls bedecked in carved dark wood and a floor carpeted with thick red rugs. A single long oak table took up most of the room. Tiya and Kevin were shown to seats at the Baroness's right. Henry was seated next to Tiya. Brandon sat to the Baroness's left. Vic and Jacob were seated next to the smith.

Vic glanced down the table as the others took their seats. Garath sat midway. He caught her gaze, and they exchanged brief smiles. When she looked away, she found Jacob scowling at her. She raised a brow, her question obvious in the slight gesture, but he didn't respond. Instead, he turned to the Baroness. Vic frowned, but let it go…for the moment.

The meal passed in quiet conversations. Most centering on the GeMorin and the quest of their diminished band. Vic learned that, thanks to Jacob and Brandon's knowledge of the upper Georna Reaches, they'd discovered a quicker route to the Bthak border and the ruins where they hoped to find the kidnappers. Tiya's continued touch with her daughter gave them hope and confirmed that the magicians continued toward the ruins. But they were forced to slow their journey because of the rough terrain.

She also learned that Baroness Georna would be providing thirty soldiers from her own guard to replace those they'd lost that morning. Vic's shoulders sagged when she thought of that loss. Sitting in the well lit hall, with her belly full and her hands and face warm, it was hard to imagine that less than twelve hours ago, she'd almost died.

An involuntary shudder shook her shoulders. Jacob's gaze jerked to her.

"Are you all right?" he asked.

"Yeah," she answered, trying to smile. "I just got a chill."

He nodded, but his eyes narrowed as he stared at her a moment longer.

"Perhaps it's best if we all retire," Baroness Georna suggested. "It's been a long day for everyone. You'll be departing early, Jacob?"

"Yes, my lady. As early as possible."

"The scouts should return within the hour. I'll let you know if they've seen any further signs of the GeMorin."

"Thank you, Baroness. You've been most gracious."

"It's the least I could do."

The concern wrinkling her otherwise smooth brow made it obvious the Baroness had been informed of the seriousness of the matter.

"Until later, then," she said, rising. "Good evening."

The rest of the table stood and began dispersing to their respective rooms. Garath stopped Jacob as he and Vic neared the door. "I'm going to check the horses and gear one last time," he said. "I've a few horses to introduce to their new riders as well."

Fewer horses than soldiers were lost that morning. As there were no better-trained warhorses in all of Karasnia, some of the Georna guards were to be given royal mounts.

"Is there anything else you'd like me to do?"

"No, Garath. Thanks."

Garath smiled hesitantly, then nodded his good nights to both Jacob and Vic.

"See you in the morning," she said as the lieutenant moved away.

"Goodnight, Garath," Jacob added.

As they walked toward the guest quarters, Jacob took her arm. "We have to talk," he whispered.

"Yes, we do."

He led her to his room in silence. The corridors of the stone castle were dim with torchlight, throwing strange shadows at their feet. When they reached his room, Jacob started a fire before speaking. For a long moment, he remained with his back to her, staring at the fire. Then he turned to face her.

"You're not coming, Victoria." His voice left no room for question or protest. "You'll remain here."

She raised a brow and protested anyway. "We've discussed this before, I think," she said calmly. "I'm going."

He reached her in two steps, gripping her shoulders in hard fingers.

"Victoria, you were almost killed! I won't risk that again. Do you know what that did to me? To know that, if I'd arrived a few seconds later, I would have found you dead!" He hissed the last sentence, quiet and intent.

Her mouth dropped open. The anger smoldering behind his gaze flashed to envelope her. Her shoulders hurt where he clung to them, but she barely noticed the pain. "Jacob, we're all at risk…"

"But you don't have to be. You should have been up a damned tree. Safe! Goddess, the fate of the world rests on this mission and—"

"Exactly," she spat, angry herself. "This isn't about you or me anymore, Jacob. This is about the world and Arlana. You need me. You lost a lot of good soldiers…"

"And you were nearly among them. No!"

"Yes!" She pulled out of his grasp and stepped back a pace. "You need as many fighters as you can get. Arlana needs all of us."

"Your presence distracts me."

"And yours doesn't me? I was in the path of that GeMorin because I was looking for you." Her voice rose a notch.

"I can take care of myself."

"Yeah, like at the masquerade when that GeMorin almost took your head."

"If you hadn't put yourself in harm's way in the first place, I wouldn't have had my back to that damned goblin."

"You're blaming me," she all but shouted. "You invited me to the damned ball."

"You should have stayed out of the way," he bellowed.

"No, I shouldn't have." Her voice dropped dangerously. "Jacob Marin, I've been taking care of myself for twenty-one years without your help. I can damned well do it now."

"Victoria, I'll not allow you to continue. You're in my way and I won't risk your life again."

"In your way!" She could hardly believe what she was hearing. "I saved your ass, General. And I've killed a number of goblins along the way. I'm not staying here." She was nearly shouting again. "I'm going with you."

"Victoria, I won't have you hurt. Do you understand? I won't let you risk your life any more. You made me a promise of no more unnecessary risks. You'll stay here."

He ground the words between clenched teeth.

"Listen, General, I'm not one of your soldiers. I don't take orders from you. This isn't an unnecessary risk. This is for the fate of the entire blasted planet." She straightened her shoulders, meeting his blazing gaze with steel resolve, and lowered her voice again. "What do you think I'll do here, Jacob? Wait until you get around to coming back for me? Risk losing Arlana because you were too stubborn to accept the extra help? And what if you don't come back? I'm going."

"If I have to have Baroness Georna throw you in the damn dungeon to keep you here, little thief, I will."

Her breath exploded in an unbelieving gasp. "Jacob," she whispered, "if you even think about having me sent to the dungeon, I'll never speak to you again."

Unblinking, he said very evenly, "I'm thinking it."

She stared for a heartbeat, her mouth set in a grim line. Then, raising her chin, she turned her back and, without another word, left his room.

"Garath, have you seen Victoria?" Jacob scowled at the young lieutenant.

"No, General. If I do, should I tell her you're looking for her?" Garath stood at a rack in front of the stables, combing out his stallion's coat. The cold mountain air turned his breath to fog under the lamplight surrounding the barn.

"If you see her, bring her to me immediately, Lieutenant. Personally."

"Is there a problem?"

"Yes, there's a problem." Jacob stalked off, leaving Garath to stare after him.

When he was finally out of sight, Vic stepped out from inside the barn. She'd changed to her black clothes and carried her travel bag over one shoulder. Just behind her, Night's Gale followed from the barn, saddled and ready to ride.

"Thank you," she said, frowning in the direction where Jacob had disappeared. "But that was risky for you. If he finds out…"

"He won't. I'm pretty good at keeping secrets when my butt's on the line."

She almost laughed. "Still…I appreciate you not turning me over to him. But, why?"

"I owe you."

"After the GeMorin battle, I think we're even."

"And," Garath continued without acknowledging her statement. "I think he's wrong. I think he's let his feelings get in the way. You're good in a fight, and we need all the help we can get. Especially now. One person could make the difference in the battle ahead." He held her gaze. "I wouldn't want to see you hurt either, but I also don't want to see Arlana hurt."

She could tell by his tone that he understood the true urgency of their mission. "Me neither." She took a deep breath. "I'll see you tomorrow morning, and thanks again."

"Will you meet us here?"

"No. I'm not giving him the chance to throw me in the dungeon," she growled. "I'll meet you up the road."

"You're going into the forest tonight? Alone?"

She nodded.

Quietly, he said, "You want me to come with you? There's still GeMorin in that forest."

She studied his steady blue gaze then shook her head. "You'd get into trouble for sure. Thanks, but I can take care of myself. I can be pretty good at hiding."

"Okay." He smiled. "Don't get into too much trouble before tomorrow."

"Me?" she asked through a slanted grin. Garath's chuckle followed her as she disappeared through the castle gates, back down the pillar mountain and into the dark Georna night.

***

Blackness slowly brightened to reveal a single candle at her feet. As slowly, other candles took shape. She stared, trying to see beyond the candlelight, trying to focus her gaze. She tried to move. Failed. Tried again.

He stepped from the shadows and fear clutched her stomach, but she couldn't scream, couldn't move. His white face glowed in the candlelight.

"You have witnessed the ritual," he whispered, baring his teeth.

She tried to scream again, but the sound stopped inside her active mind, never passing her immobile lips. Wide-eyed, she watched him approach, watched him pull the silver dagger, the hilt suddenly becoming gold with a scattering of emerald jewels. And she tried to close her eyes. But they remained open, freezing even as the rest of her body was frozen to the black-covered stone altar.

Before her now-motionless gaze, a new face looked down at her, madness plain in his dark eyes. "No one sees the ritual and survives, Flash." Malkiney raised the dagger and giggled.

Suddenly her gaze was moving, running to the edge of the candlelit

283

circle. He was there, at the edge of the light, watching, his hand resting on the golden hilt of his sword. The green of his formal tunic almost black in the dim light.

She tried to scream once more. Failed. She tried pleading with her eyes. *Don't leave me*, she cried in a voice that couldn't leave her mind. *Jacob!* For a second, she saw recognition. Then he turned away, walking out of the light, disappearing into the unrelenting darkness.

No! Her mind echoed the single word even as she saw the flash of silver from the corner of her eye. Saw the dagger plunge toward her chest, and…

She sat up with a strangled scream, looking wildly around her unfamiliar surroundings, heart pounding brutally against her rib cage, sweat soaking her clothes. Then she remembered.

She was in her tent, a mile north of Georna village. The quiet snuffling of Night's Gale drifted through the canvas with the now-familiar sounds of the forest. Vic took several long, slow breaths. Just a dream, she reminded herself.

The sweat began to cool, chilling her despite the warmth of her trail blanket. She poked her head outside the tent, a knife held ready in her hand. Nothing. Silence. The sky past the trees was already beginning to lighten.

She threw herself back into her blankets and concentrated on slowing her heartbeat. Just a dream, she repeated. But when she tried to close her eyes, she saw the image of Jacob walking out of the circle, leaving her to her fate. She bit back anger and pain, grinding her teeth together.

With a defiant grunt, she threw off her blanket and gave up on sleep. "Just a dream," she whispered aloud in a rough snarl, and began to get ready for the new day.

CHAPTER TWENTY-TWO

When the small, combined army of King's Guard and Georna soldiers approached the lone rider that morning, Kevin hid his smile. He rode ahead of the group to greet Vic.

She gave him a half salute. "Permission to join the train, Lord Fordin?"

"Glad to see you again, Victoria," he said, nodding for her to fall in line. As she passed, he warned, "Jacob is in a foul mood."

She acknowledged him with a short nod. Riding past Jacob without glancing in his direction, she fell in beside Garath. With no little effort, she ignored Jacob's dark glower for the rest of the day, throwing herself into conversation with Garath and some of the other soldiers.

That night, Tiya joined her by the fire. "Good evening, Victoria," she said, taking a seat next to her.

She nodded at the woman, then turned her gaze back to the stick she held in the fire, a lump of meat stuffed onto its end. The fire spit and hissed as grease dripped from the crunchy skin.

"I'm glad you've continued with us. We need your help. And you've been involved from the beginning. I thought Jacob a bit... impulsive in his decision."

"Impulsive, my right eye."

"He acts that way because he cares, Victoria."

"He was going to have me thrown in the dungeon. Did he tell you that?" Her voice emerged in a low growl she barely recognized. "Cares for me? If he cared, he wouldn't consider putting me in a dungeon."

She felt the sorceress's gaze on the side of her face for a long moment, but she didn't look away from her roasting dinner.

Finally, Tiya said, "You've been in a dungeon before?"

Vic shook her head. "I had a friend. A long time ago. When I first started with Thieves' Hole, she looked out for me. But she didn't like to stay in one place for very long, so she was always hooking up with traders and merchants…to see the world. I heard, while in Creo Barony, she was caught pulling a purse and thrown into the dungeon. I never found out exactly what happened, but she died there."

"Does Jacob know about this?"

"He knows I don't like dungeons. We never talked about why."

"If you'd told him, he would never have done it. Jacob isn't like that."

"He shouldn't have threatened in the first place." She refused to meet Tiya's gaze. "You don't do that to someone you care about," she whispered to the fire. "People disappear in dungeons."

Tiya dropped her head, shaking it slightly before rising.

"Victoria, I know Jacob. I know how he feels about you. Don't let words said in an angry moment be the last words you say to each other."

When Vic continued to stare wordlessly at the fire, Tiya left.

They were crossing a wide gorge when the hallucinations started. From behind her, Vic heard the initial scream, saw a flurry of movement. By the time she turned, the soldier was already writhing on the ground, screaming of snakes and beating himself with the flat of his sword. It took three soldiers to restrain him.

But he didn't stop screaming.

Kevin and Jacob had just turned when a second soldier charged off, running his horse up the gorge, whooping wildly. Garath charged after him. He stopped the warhorse easily, but the soldier continued to whoop as if charging into battle.

Henry dismounted and looked closely at both men. Then he closed his eyes and began reciting a soundless spell. A few moments later, the two men stopped shouting and blinked at their surroundings like sleepers rising from a dream.

"Henry?" Kevin asked, nodding toward the two men.

"Hallucinations," Henry replied simply.

"The blood magicians," Jacob added.

"No."

Henry's answer brought a deafening silence down on the group.

"What do you mean?" Tiya asked.

"They don't know we're here," Henry said, meeting her gaze. "They lost us when we left Georna castle. We're still shielded and I've been altering the shield to keep them from pinpointing it."

"Then who?" Garath asked.

Vic's breath caught. She met Henry's gaze. He nodded shortly, confirming her fears, then turned his gaze back to Tiya and Kevin.

"The one who began this I suspect," he told them. "And I don't know how he's doing it. He shouldn't be able to see us through the shield. He shouldn't be able to send a spell through the shield..." Henry whispered. "If it is a spell."

Jacob's eyes narrowed.

Kevin growled low in his throat.

"What can we do?" Tiya asked for all of them.

"I don't know, my lady," Henry said, with a shrug. "I don't know how to keep him out."

"Can you stop the hallucinations once they start?" Jacob asked.

Henry nodded.

"Then we go on. But we keep a close watch on each other. At the first signs of hallucination, restrain the affected individual until Henry can help. The last thing we need is to start killing each other."

The delusions came sporadically after that. No pattern, no particular individual. Only that the same person was never hit twice. After the first incident, Henry taught Tiya the spell to end the hallucinations. Between the two of them, the random outbursts were calmed before damage could be done.

But the effects showed on the group. For the next four days, everyone remained on edge, watching each other, being watched. Rest came fitfully.

And Vic continued to have nightmares.

Her dreams grew worse each night. Every time, she'd wake with a strangled scream, calling Jacob's name. Only to find herself alone in a cold tent in the dark. His absence hurt worse than she could admit to anyone. Even herself.

During the day, she ignored him as best she could, throwing herself into conversations with anyone nearby. Using every ounce of skill she'd developed as a gambler, she hid her pain and loss behind a veil of anger. Anger was easier.

The jaded street voice at the back of her mind gloated, stabbing, telling her the obvious. That this would have happened sooner or later. *They all leave, Flash.* She hid behind that as well. Fell into the cocky attitude that had kept her alive. But the part of her that Jacob had touched, the part that had hidden behind boy's clothes and a set of fast knives, the person called Victoria cried, quietly and alone where no one could see, not even Vic.

On the fifth day, the group entered the thick pine forests a day's ride from the Bthak border. Snow had fallen recently, dusting the ground and trees with a thin layer of white. Above, the sky shone bright and blue, raising sparkles and glimmers along the ice crystals blanketing the ground. Beneath the trees, the forest was dark, despite the bright daylight.

They camped in a pine-circled clearing that night. There hadn't been a hallucination for many hours, and the strain was palpable. Every eye watched closely for the beginnings of magical madness.

Vic spent extra time grooming Gale, avoiding the others. Wary tension mixed with her individual pain made for a sour taste—too many of the wrong ingredients. Staying with Gale helped a little. The monotonous brushing, the quiet snuffling of the mare, the smell of leather and dirt and campfires at a distance, helped her blank her mind and lulled her into a blissfully thoughtless state.

When the white-faced sorcerer stepped out of the woods, she blinked once. Then she lurched back, pulling two knives from their hidden spots.

The sorcerer smiled, pushed aside his robe and revealed a small bundle. The child began to wail.

Vic started forward, circling the sorcerer, keeping her gaze on his face.

He merely smiled and turned back into the woods, dismissing any threat she might be.

Without thinking, she charged after him, her street-trained footing nearly silent along the patchy, snow-dusted underbrush. She could see the form of the sorcerer just ahead, but the faster she moved, the wider the gap became.

Then he stopped, turned, and smiled, opening a crater in the moon that was his face.

With a feral cry, she charged, knives raised. She came to a skidding halt when a second shape stepped into her path. She barely recognized Malkiney's face before slashing.

Malkiney blocked her two quick jabs with red-gray metal bracers, and then her arms were pinned to her side. She struggled against her unseen attacker, but strong arms lifted her off the ground. She looked back as Malkiney approached, smiling with that mad glimmer she saw in her nightmares. From beside him, a new figure stepped out to face Vic, one she didn't recognize. But she knew who it was. There had been a blood sorceress in Dareelia, the third magician, the one she'd never seen.

The woman stepped closer, her blonde-white hair alight under the dark canopy, her blue eyes glowing with the same evil Vic had seen in the white sorcerer's eyes.

She tried to scream, to warn those still in the camp, but the sound froze in her throat just as it had in her nightmares. She struggled harder against the steel arms holding her in place. When the sorceress placed her hands on Vic's cheeks, she went limp.

The sorceress crooked her mouth, then stepped back and began a soundless chant. Flashes of a sacrificial altar, red candles inside a triangle inside a circle, the glimmer of light off a silver blade.

Vic closed her eyes, unwilling to see her nightmares come true, and softly she breathed Jacob's name. After what felt like hours, the steel around her relaxed, her feet touched the ground, and a recognizable voice broke through her fear. "Victoria?"

She opened her eyes and looked into the soft, compassionate blue eyes of Tiya. She blinked. Then blinked again. Beside Tiya, Jacob was also staring intently, concern obliterating the hostility that had hardened his features since they'd left Georna castle.

Kevin stepped around from behind her. He smiled gently at her confusion. "I didn't hurt you, did I?" he asked.

She shook her head, distracted, then looked to the place where she'd seen the white-faced sorcerer. "I saw him," she muttered. "The white sorcerer. He had Arlana." She looked back at Tiya. "What happened?"

The lines creasing Tiya's brow fell away with her smile. "Hallucination. You were too far away for us to intervene quickly. Lucky for you these two know their way through a forest." She nodded fondly at the two men.

"You were moving like an old forester yourself," Kevin said, his grin widening. "Didn't know you could cut through the trees like that."

"Talent," she said, waving her hand absently. She still couldn't resolve what she'd just experienced with what she was now facing. Kevin's chuckle startled her.

As did the crunching of booted feet nearby. She turned to see Henry, Garath and a number of the other soldiers hurrying to join them.

Henry reached them first. "Are you all right?"

"Yeah. Thanks to these three." She shook her head. "It was so real. Knowing about the hallucinations didn't make a difference. I can't believe I didn't realize, but…"

Garath patted her shoulder and smiled. "My little encounter with a mountain lion this morning seemed pretty real, too."

She allowed a smile despite the lingering disorientation.

"I'm glad you're okay," Henry said. "And since they don't seem to hit the same person twice, you can relax now."

"I'll relax when we get back to Dareelia," she said.

A chortle of agreement rustled through the soldiers and the group split, heading back toward camp.

Vic stood for a long moment, still staring at the place where she'd seen the white sorcerer. She didn't notice that Kevin and Tiya had walked away until Jacob cleared his throat, bringing her attention back to her immediate surroundings. Her gaze fell on the bracers covering his forearms.

"I almost cut you," she whispered. Her guard dropped in that instant, concern slipping into her voice. When she realized the slip, she forced her gambler's expression back into place. "Sorry," she said in as offhanded a manner as she could muster.

The side of his mouth crooked, almost a smile. "Well, I'm glad I had on the bracers." The smile dropped away. "So you're talking to me again?"

She couldn't meet his gaze. "No."

When she turned back toward camp, he caught her arm. She swung around to face him, pulling her arm roughly from his grasp.

"Victoria, we need to talk. You can't just walk out of my life like this."

"The last time we talked, Marin, you threatened to throw me in a dungeon," she spoke just above a whisper, letting anger fill her voice to cover the pain.

"Tiya told me about your friend. If I'd known…"

"She wasn't the only one, Jacob," she shouted, then lowered her voice. "She was only the first. People disappear in dungeons."

"I wouldn't have allowed that. How can you think so little of me? Of my feelings for you?"

She dropped her gaze, not wanting to see the hurt in his eyes, the accusations, choosing instead to steel herself with her anger. "I don't know how you feel about me, Jacob. All I know is that none of the people I've seen thrown into a dungeon were put there by someone who cared." She didn't wait for a reply. She turned her back and walked stiffly toward camp, ignoring his calls.

Jacob watched the little thief walk away, a familiar ache clenching his chest. He didn't hear Tiya approach until she placed a gentle hand on his shoulder.

"It didn't go well," she said.

"No." His jaw clenched and unclenched. "She won't even talk to me. She still thinks I would have abandoned her. After all we've… She doesn't believe I have any feelings for her. Goddess, Tiya, she's ripping out my heart and she thinks I don't feel anything."

He clenched his fists, fighting the fear that had clawed him since their argument. He'd never been so afraid of losing someone. After all the years and all the women, he'd finally found the woman he wanted to spend his life with and she thought him capable of tossing her aside. It hurt to know she thought so little of him. It hurt worse to think he might have given her reason.

"Jacob!"

Tiya's voice sounded distant. Several heartbeats passed before he heard her.

"Jacob, when was the last time you told her how much you love her?"

He looked into her gentle eyes and blinked. His mind couldn't grasp what she'd just asked.

After a silent moment, she said, "You have told her you love her, haven't you?"

"Of course, I…" he started harshly, then paused. The truth hit him like a metal gauntlet. "No," he whispered, letting his gaze fall to the forest floor. "Never in words. Never *the* words. I started to once, but the GeMorin…" He closed his eyes.

"That might explain why she doesn't know. Until she hears the words, it's easy for her to wonder."

A smile nudged at his mouth. "Do you remember once, a few years back, I told you that young men do stupid things in the name of pride?"

She smiled at the memory and nodded.

"Well, *all* men do stupid things in the name of love."

"I think it's time to correct that," she said, patting his shoulder and ushering him in the direction the thief had disappeared.

Before he moved away, though, he bent and brushed her cheek with a kiss. "Thank you, my friend."

He moved into the trees, a lifetime of practice keeping his footsteps light and nearly silent. He didn't catch sight of Victoria until he was almost at camp.

Her back was to him. She walked slower than she had when stomping away. Her movements were limp and heavy, her arms dragging at her sides.

The difference shocked him for a moment, and he couldn't follow. He'd never seen his little thief look so beaten. His heart tore further to realize what he'd done. But in her solemn gate, he finally saw the pain that had, until that moment, remained safely hidden behind anger. And in a strange way, it gave him hope.

He covered the remaining distance in a quick trot. "Victoria," he called, as he drew closer. "Victoria, please."

She stopped at the tree line before entering the clearing, but she didn't turn to face him.

He stared at the back of her head, his jaw and throat too tight to speak. Had he been fooling himself, thinking that she could be hurting just as he was? Or did she really feel only anger now? Was she lost forever?

He couldn't accept that option.

Taking a shallow breath, he whispered, "I was being selfish. At the castle. Trying to protect you so I could protect myself. When you get hurt, it hurts me. If you were to get killed, it would kill me. But I never thought anything could hurt this much. To see you every day. To see anger in your eyes where there was once affection. To know that this… I'd rather be dead than lose you this way."

She remained motionless, her back stiff, her head tilted to one side, listening, but not acknowledging. He closed his eyes, forcing back the fear that threatened to close his throat for good.

Then he looked once more at the soft brown curls falling around her shoulders, the small, athletic frame covered in black, the stubborn stance. And the words came tumbling out. "I love you, Victoria. I love you so much…it's like a knife in my gut. Except a knife would hurt less. I've never loved anyone like this before. Love has always been pleasant and, on occasion, dangerous or sad, but it's never been the wrenching pain I'm feeling now." He swallowed hard, straining past the lump in his throat to get the last few words out. "Please, Victoria. I can't lose you. Don't walk away from me."

He watched her shoulders shake, the first movement since she'd stopped. Then they rose, straightening, and she held her head high. She moved a step forward, away from him.

And turned around.

A single tear slid over her cheek, the first tear he'd ever seen her shed. But her jaw was rigid, her mouth a hard line.

"Don't *ever* do anything like that to me again," she said and threw herself into his arms.

Chapter Twenty-Three

They crossed the border into Bthak just before sunset the next day. Their journey had been slowed by an increase in the number of hallucinations, plaguing their every step until they passed the border. Then the hallucinations suddenly stopped.

They camped on a rocky outcropping circled by thick stands of trees and posted a larger number of sentries. There was no sign of civilization in this part of Bthak, but this was GeMorin territory. No campfires were lit.

By Tracker's account, they were a short ride from the ruins. Tiya could still feel Arlana, closer than she had since the night of the kidnapping. They'd moved ahead of the magicians, but not far. It would be a race to the ruins—if nothing went wrong.

No scouts were sent out for fear of detection. Henry could hold the shield, but only if they stayed together. So far, their secret was safe.

The need for rest pressed all of them, but knowing sleep was necessary and actually being able to sleep were two different things. Vic tried to doze, feeling warm and protected in Jacob's arms once more. But even his comforting strength couldn't banish the anticipation and anxiety.

They'd reach the ruins tomorrow. Only then would they know if the kidnappers traveled to these ruins or were actually intent on some unknown destination. Either they'd fight tomorrow or be forced once more into the chase.

In the predawn darkness, they broke camp. Even before the sun had poked above the mountains, they rode. The air was sharp and cold, so dry it choked Vic's throat.

Around them, the ground was dusted with a light fall of snow, painting, without covering, the rocks and brush along the trail and beneath the trees. Ice clung to the leafless limbs and the brown grass along the roadside. In the light of the sun as it rose to meet a cloudless sky, the ice crystals became glittering strings of gold upon a bed of white down.

The trail they followed turned east into the rising sun. They rode fast and hard to the ruins. By midmorning, they reached their destination.

Thick forest opened just before the deteriorating walls of what had once been a monastery. A standing archway, cut from the red stone wall, opened to a large front courtyard, its stone floor now covered with moss and weeds. A single tree grew to one side of the yard, black and leafless for winter. The walls surrounding the courtyard, though crumbling and weed-choked, still stood five feet at their lowest points.

Opposite the arch were the remains of what had once been a large building, its outline and interior structure still evident in the weatherworn stone walls. Behind this building, another courtyard. The rear wall still stood almost twelve feet high. Embrasures gave glimpses of the snow-covered valley beyond.

To the left of the central building stood the lower third of what had been a round tower. Sun slanted through the open top and arched frame of the doorway into the front courtyard. A second intact round tower stood along the right wall of the rear courtyard, climbing four stories to a low battlement. There was one visible window, near the tower's top level, and one doorway. A green wooden door kept the tower sealed.

Everything was covered by a thin film of snow like dust in an unused room. The silence of a place long abandoned was disturbed only by the sounds of the soldiers and their mounts.

Jacob motioned his soldiers around the ruins, checking for traps. Curiosity took Vic to the intact tower. She dismounted at the foot, dropping Gale's reins to the ground. A series of stones extended from the tower wall in a spiral, the remains of what had once been an external stairway circling up to the battlement. Now only the upper third of the stones remained, ending just below the window, which looked into the courtyard.

Vic turned her attention to the large door, approaching it with a knife in hand. She pushed, but it held firm. She tried twisting the latch, but it wouldn't move.

She was inspecting the lock, considering picking it, when Jacob came up behind her.

"Anything?" he said, nodding at the door.

"Locked. Want me to open it?"

He stared for a moment then shook his head. "Better if we don't give them a potential hiding place or a place to defend from."

"What do you think?" she said, sweeping the ruins with her gaze.

"I think we're too exposed. There's not enough cover for our entire group, and the GeMorin will know we're here before they're close enough to attack."

"Not good."

"No. Henry might as well have not bothered with the shield." He took a deep breath and looked at the soldiers still combing the area.

"Are they coming from the same direction we did?"

"Yeah. Tiya says they're approaching fast."

She frowned, studying the courtyard. Then she nodded to the rear wall. "What's behind that?"

"The ground slopes to the valley. No tree cover, just snow-covered fields."

She walked to the wall and looked out one of the embrasures, pressing her hands against the stone sill and standing on her toes to see down to the wall's base. "It's not steep, Jacob. What if we hide most of the soldiers behind here, place a group back in the woods..."

"And trap the kidnappers inside the ruins?" he finished. His brow wrinkled as he stared at the rear wall. After a moment, he turned and motioned Kevin, Tiya and Henry over. "Victoria has an idea." He sketched her plan.

"Can you hold the shield if we spread that far?" Kevin asked.

Henry looked dubious. "I don't think so. But, if Tiya could shield the group in the woods, I can shield the group behind the wall."

"It's worth a try," Tiya said. "We need every advantage we can get. But do you think it'll work?"

No one looked convinced.

"If we stand and wait," Jacob said, "they'll most likely avoid the ruins altogether. If they think we're here, they won't fall into the trap. And there's always the chance that they'll discover us despite the shield and turn the trap around on us."

"But it's the only chance we have," Kevin said.

Jacob nodded. "Kevin, you stay with Tiya and twenty of the soldiers in the woods. Henry, you'll come with me and the rest of the guard. We'll wait until all of the GeMorin are inside the ruins. Assume they'll post a guard at the entrance. They may send some to check the perimeter. As soon as most are inside, Kevin, you signal and follow them in. We'll sweep the perimeter and meet you inside."

"Jacob?" Vic caught his attention. She nodded over her shoulder at the tower. "I'd be willing to bet the view from the top of that thing is pretty good."

His eyes narrowed. She saw his initial protest, but he paused. He looked up at the tower, then back at her. "I don't suppose I could talk you into staying there once the fighting starts?"

She smiled and shook her head.

"I didn't think so."

"One whistle when they're all inside. Followed by three if there's a problem."

She met his gaze, letting him see her confidence.

"How much time do we have?" Henry asked.

"They're no more than an hour away," Tiya answered.

"Then we'd better hurry."

"Halt," Bserea called back. Her gaze swept the trees before them. They were less than a mile from the ruins.

"What are you doing?" Pseer demanded, moving his horse beside her. "We don't have time for this."

"Something's wrong." She didn't bother to look at him. Her horse shifted beneath her. She stilled it with a sharp pull on the reins.

"What's going on?" Ptaun asked, concern edging his voice.

"You two are jumping at shadows," Pseer puffed. "I feel nothing."

Bserea checked the insult that leapt to her tongue and said instead, "It's obvious they've shielded from mage sight again, you fool. You're not supposed to feel them. But they're here. Near."

"You're imagining things, woman," Pseer snarled. "If we aren't there when he arrives…"

"We will be," Bserea hissed. The infant she was still forced to carry started to whimper. She held the blanket-swathed child in one arm, controlling her mount with the other. Absently, she bounced the child, but her eyes and senses still focused on the woods. "Would you run into a trap first, Pseer?"

"I'd prefer a battle to this running and hiding," the young magician mumbled.

When GeRon stepped forward, all three magicians fell silent. "You have felt them," he asked Bserea, glancing up. The GeMorin didn't ride horses. They didn't need to.

"No, my lord. It's only a suspicion." The infant chose that time to whimper again, a sound just short of a cry, forcing Bserea to turn her attention to it.

"My lord," Pseer said, "she imagines things again. Would not your scouts have discovered them if they were near?"

GeRon stared at the copper-skinned sorcerer until the man was forced to drop his gaze. Bserea hid a smile behind the cooing sounds she directed toward the child.

"My scouts have not yet returned."

Bserea's head shot up at GeRon's statement. She dropped her gaze an instant later when the goblin clan leader turned his unblinking stare back on her.

"Perhaps she does not imagine," GeRon said. "But the master bids us arrive by noon. We must be there."

"What do you suggest, my lord?" Ptaun asked, stepping into the conversation.

"We continue. Bserea and the child will stay behind until the battle is begun." He faced her again. "Then you will gate in and take the child to the meeting place."

"You anticipate battle then, my lord?" Pseer made no effort to hide his excitement.

"There will be a battle. It was inevitable." He looked back at the young sorcerer. "And of no consequence. All that matters is that she," he nodded to the baby, "be brought to the master safely."

Pseer smiled, battle fury already glimmering in his ice blue eyes. Ptaun maintain his stoic expression, keeping his thoughts concealed. Bserea shifted the fussy child and scanned the woods again. The sun was nearing its apex. It was time.

From her vantage atop the tower, Vic could see all of the ruins, the King's Guard hiding behind the rear wall, and the forest where it opened onto the ruins. She hid behind a merlon and scanned for the first signs of movement.

Somehow she managed to miss the signs before the forward guard of GeMorin warriors stepped from the forest. They marched straight into the center of the front courtyard. In the midst of close to a hundred goblin warriors, rode two of the blood magicians.

Her breath caught at the sight of the white-faced magician. He looked very much the same as the night she'd first seen him. Long black robe, split in the front and back for riding, heavy cloak pulled over his colorless face. The same terrifying knowledge behind his blue eyes. She absently fingered the onyx at her throat and concentrated on breathing slowly.

Beside the white sorcerer rode a young man with the white hair and blazing blue eyes of their kind, but with the build of a warrior. His copper skin was stretched tight across the sharply chiseled bones of his face. Tight black breeches and tunic displayed his muscular build to good effect. He was handsome in a frightening way but the sight of him left her cold. And wary. His eyes glimmered with an inner fire she'd seen before. Battle fury.

She watched as most of the group entered the ruins. Five goblins remained outside the archway, five more were sent to check the outer perimeter. The rest clustered into the front courtyard. The sorceress was missing. And so was Arlana.

Vic warbled out a single note.

And followed with three sharp whistles.

King's soldiers erupted from the forest, pouring into the archway, overwhelming the five guards. Tiya and Kevin led the charge. From the rear, Vic heard the clash of swords as the remaining soldiers dispatched the goblins checking the outer wall. She looked down in time to see the guard racing around the sides of the monastery. Their horses leapt the lower remains of the wall, taking them into the center of the battle. Henry was the first over the wall. Jacob was a single step behind him.

Vic started to move from her perch to join in the fight when the movements of the four magicians caught her attention. She watched as all four abandoned their horses. The two blood mages stood in the center of the courtyard. Henry and Tiya approached from opposite sides. GeMorin and king's soldiers parted before them, opening the center of the yard to the strange quartet.

All four wore the black of their profession. All had the snow-white hair, the ice blue eyes, and the casual determination in their stance. And all four carried a frightening amount of power. Silence fell across the ruins. Everyone froze and watched as a charge built in the air.

The copper-skinned sorcerer smiled at Tiya, boldly looking over her curves. "I will take the pretty woman," he said in Karasnian to the white sorcerer, loud enough for all to hear.

Tiya's expression didn't change as she faced him. But Kevin's anger wasn't as well controlled. He charged the young sorcerer, screaming a war cry, sword raised high above his head.

The sorcerer didn't even look in Kevin's direction. A flick of his wrist stilled the young giant's movements. "Does he belong to you?" he asked Tiya.

Without breaking eye contact with the warrior mage, Tiya raised her arm, palm facing the ground. As her palm snapped shut, the spell holding Kevin in place collapsed. "That is your best?" she said without emotions.

"So," he said, still leering, "the pretty woman has power." He snapped his hand, sending a ball of white energy toward her.

She raised one hand and effortlessly caught it. When her hand opened, the ball had disappeared, her hand remained unmarked. "The pretty woman," she said, "is the baby's mother." Tilting her head to one side, she threw out her other hand and released a bolt of blue energy that sizzled along the sorcerer's shield, knocking him back a step.

The young blood magician's eyes narrowed, and the fight was engaged.

Henry and the white-faced sorcerer had locked gazes during Tiya and the other sorcerer's show. Now they too began to slowly test each other's strengths and weaknesses, gauging the other's endurance. Jolts of power, fire, wind and ice flew back and forth, a swirl of elements gone crazy.

The ground shuddered beneath them, but the enchantment that had held the rest of the soldiers in place broke. Soon the sounds of clashing metal filled the old monastery. Vic, released from her own trance, scaled down the tower walls.

The fight had spread across the entire area by the time her feet hit the ground. Goblins and humans competed in a chaotic melee of individual battles. Vic scanned the area for Jacob and was confronted with a GeMorin warrior instead. She smiled at the green-faced goblin and dove away from his attack.

Two knives jumped into her hands, both made of the meteor metal. She circled the GeMorin, watching for an opening. He leapt, swinging his saber high and wide toward her head. She ducked his swing and moved in close. She slashed at him with her left hand, forcing him to sway away from her knife. Before he could recover his balance, Vic swept her right arm around, but instead of striking with her knife, she slammed the metal bracer on her forearm into the goblin's face.

He screamed, dropping his saber to the ground, and clenched at his mouth. Vic had seen the fangs break. Before her eyes, the goblin fell to the ground, writhing in pain, his body beginning to turn purple. She didn't wait to see the outcome.

The ground continued to roll, stealing some of her balance, but she charged across the compound, toward the next GeMorin warrior. She fought with a single-minded determination that cleared away all other thoughts.

When she bumped into Kevin, she almost didn't recognize him.

"Vic, Arlana?" Kevin said, not wasting time with words as, back to back, they fought two more GeMorin.

"She must be with the sorceress," Vic responded, flinging a hidden dart into the chest of her assailant. "Break their teeth," she shouted, as she ducked under a goblin saber. "Has the same reaction on them as their bite has on us."

The battle currents pulled them apart before Kevin could answer. Around her, the ring of metal on metal now mixed with the sounds of shouts and screams, the low rumbling of the ground, and the hissing clap of explosions.

Vic was pulling one of her knives from a dead goblin when a violent quake knocked her to the ground. She looked up in time to see Henry fall under the white magician's onslaught.

She raced to his side. The young sorcerer lay on the ground, his chest a blackened mess. His breathing was shallow and harsh. She knelt beside him, futilely looking for some way to help him when she heard the gravelly chuckle of the white-faced sorcerer.

Her head snapped around to face the same smile she'd first seen from a roof in Dareelia.

"I know you, girl," he said quietly. "You were the spy atop the building." His eyes widened slightly, and he glanced at the onyx at her throat. "Ah, it was you in the building that night during the ceremony. Wasn't it?"

She didn't bother to answer. The flash of silver was the only indication that she had thrown her boot knife. The knife stopped in midair and clattered harmlessly to the ground. Her heart lodged in her throat as she met the sorcerer's amused gaze.

"You do realize, don't you?" he whispered. "Anyone who sees the ceremony must die."

She threw up her arm to cover her face as his fingertips began to glow red. When nothing happened, she lowered her arm. And saw the bloody stump that had once been the sorcerer's hand.

Jacob was already bringing his sword around for a killing blow when his movements froze. She watched in a moment of horror as her boot knife slowly rose from the ground and pointed toward Jacob's throat. The sorcerer spared her a single glowering gaze before letting the knife fly.

She was on her feet and moving in that same instant, ignoring everything else around her, blocking out the sight of Jacob as he fell. Her full attention was focused on the exposed neck of the sorcerer. Inches from him, she felt a sudden shift in the air, but she didn't stop to consider it. She lurched forward and plunged her breast dagger into the soft side of his throat.

Blood sprayed her hand and face, painting her feral snarl.

The sorcerer turned slowly, his eyes wide, astonished. A bloody gurgle bubbled from his lips before his ice blue eyes clouded, and he collapsed to the ground. "You must have witnessed the ceremony," Vic growled. Then quietly, "Jacob!"

He lay against the ruins of a wall, one hand clamped tightly against his right side, his eyes closed. "Jacob," she said, crouching down beside him. "Jacob Marin, don't you dare leave me now."

"I'm not that easy to get rid of," he whispered.

His eyes opened. A half smile touched his lips, and she took a stuttering breath.

"Worried, little thief?"

"No," she said before kissing him gently. "What happened?" The relief that came from knowing his throat hadn't been slit vanished when she saw the blood covering his side and hand.

"I'm not sure, but I'd guess Henry managed to knock the blade off course." His face pinched and he hissed in a sharp breath.

"Jacob?" Panic raised her voice.

"Still here, love." He glanced at the fallen blood magician. "Don't forget to get that blade back."

The sudden cry of a baby snapped their attention to the standing tower near the rear wall. The green door hung open. A shock of white against black disappeared through the archway leading to the interior of the circular tower. A second pitiful wail echoed back through the ancient stones.

She looked back into Jacob's eyes. He nodded in understanding. "I love you, Jacob," she whispered against his mouth before kissing him one last time.

When she started to rise, he clamped down on her arm. "Victoria…" He swallowed hard. "Stay standing, Victoria Flash."

"Aye, General." She nodded shortly. Pausing at the fallen sorcerer long enough to retrieve her breast dagger, she sprinted to the building where Arlana and the sorceress had disappeared.

Chapter Twenty-Four

At the top of the tower stairs, a single massive oak door hung partially open onto the only room in the building. Vic edged to the door and peeked inside.

The room looked larger than she would have guessed from the outside. Pillars as thick as redwood trunks supported the planking of the roof, a roof she'd so recently walked. The floor, also of wood planking, was oddly free of dust. Three large windows, big enough to stand in, fed light into the room. One faced north, one east, the other west into the compound below.

Across from the door, between the north and east windows, was what looked to be a second plain wooden door. She frowned. A door opening into the air? Just in front of the door, with her back to Vic, the blood sorceress stood immobile, her head bowed, the bottom of her black robe swirling in the breeze. Two red candles burned on the ground at each side of the strange door. Their flames never wavered in the air that moved the sorceress's robe.

In the center of the room, lying inside a stone cradle carved to look like a basket, Arlana cried.

Vic studied the sorceress for several minutes, keeping her breath even with the movements of the breeze, her muscles loose and ready for action. The magician didn't move or take any notice of the baby's cries.

Silently creeping into the room, she kept her gaze on the sorceress as she tested each step, ready to duck behind a pillar at the slightest movement. The low chanting of the magician filled the open room and the air blew warmly when it should have been cold. Each careful inch brought her farther into the heat and chanting until her toe touched stone.

She dropped her gaze. The baby's face was red from crying, her little fingers kneaded the air above her. When she looked into her clear blue eyes, Arlana stopped crying. And smiled. Vic looked back at the sorceress. She didn't seem to notice the baby's sudden silence.

Smiling back at Arlana, she put her fingers to her lips in a gesture for quiet and knelt. *Okay, little one*, she thought, *we're gonna get you back to your mom now. But I need you to stay very quiet.* To her surprise, the child didn't so much as gurgle. In fact, when she looked again at the baby, she fancied seeing understanding.

Pushing aside the idea as silly, she lifted Arlana from the cradle and shifted her gaze back to the sorceress. Every fiber of her being scanned for the tiniest movement as she edged toward the door. She was still several yards from escape, at a point near the west-facing window, when the sorceress raised her head and began to turn.

Damn! She ducked behind a pillar. The open door was in front of her. If she sprinted, maybe…

The door slammed shut, cutting off her only escape route.

"All right, whoever you are," the sorceress's voice coiled through the room, a seductive whisper. "You may as well reveal yourself. You won't be leaving through that door and the only other way out is a rather long drop."

Vic heard the shifting of material along the floor as she scanned her surroundings for another escape route.

"Place the baby in the cradle and perhaps I'll let you live," the sorceress purred. "Perhaps I'll even reward you."

A slight smile tugged Vic's mouth as she looked into Arlana's eyes. *She can't feel me*, she explained silently to the baby for no real reason other than that she found the idea amusing. *I'd bet a winter's worth of kern that she thinks I'm a man.*

"You think you're hidden from me?"

An edge crept into the sorceress's voice. *Doesn't like to be ignored, does she, Arlana?* Her moving gaze fell on the western window. And she remembered the remains of the external stairway.

"Your charm can't shield the child. I know where you are. You can't escape. Cooperate. I'm sure we can come to some sort of arrangement."

She obviously doesn't want you hurt, Arlana, so maybe we can come to some arrangement. Wonder if she's a gambling woman? With a cocky grin, Vic stepped from behind the pillar, placing herself closer to the window.

The sorceress snarled. "A woman? How disappointing."

Vic chuckled. "Oh, I think we can still come to an arrangement."

"Really?"

The white-haired woman took a step closer, and Vic shook her head. "Uh huh. I know you need the child alive." She took two steps backward. "I even suspect why she's been brought here. And I know that, if she's harmed, it'll be very bad for you."

The sorceress froze, her eyes narrowing to mere slits. "You won't harm the child," she said.

But Vic's trained eye detected her uncertainty. "Oh, I'm prepared to kill her if I have to." She moved backward a few more steps, never taking her gaze from the woman.

"The babe's mother is in the courtyard. She would not have come this far to let her daughter be killed."

"I'm not the child's mother." Vic stopped. She felt the cold air from the window just behind her, felt the first touch of sunshine on her back.

The sorceress paused, studying her.

"An arrangement then," she agreed after several silent minutes.

Vic nodded.

"And what would you like, girl? You want power? Wealth?"

She shrugged. "You're offering power? Wealth? Until I set the child down. Then you'll offer me death. Yes?"

The sorceress smiled. "I like you, girl. You have a quick mind. Too bad. This would have been easier if you were a man."

At that instant, both doors came to life. The one leading back to the stairs began to shudder as something large pounded against it. The other, leading to nowhere, began to glow with a subtle brownish light.

The sorceress's gaze flicked to both doors. Vic took advantage of her momentary distraction to step onto the window's low sill. She could still stand at her full height inside the frame. When the sorceress turned back, she said, "Looks like mom wants her daughter back."

Arlana began to whimper again.

"We're still at a standoff," Vic said as casually as she could manage, but her heart pounded loudly against her rib cage. She shifted the baby into a more comfortable, one-armed hold, freeing one hand. "Mine are at one door. Yours are on their way," she nodded to the glowing door. "And I still hold the child." Her wrist knife dropped into her hand. She set it lightly just beneath Arlana's neck.

"Standoff?" The sorceress tilted her head to the side and pursed her red lips. "I don't think so."

Vic sent her knife flying before the sorceress finished her sentence. She swished her hand absently at the air. The knife skittered harmlessly to the floor. But it was all the distraction Vic needed.

She was out the window and up the first several stones when she heard the sorceress's bellow of rage. Without looking behind her, she negotiated the perilous steps to the top of the tower. Her only hope was to keep out of the sorceress's way until the king's soldiers could break into the tower's upper room. She didn't want to consider what would happen if the sorceress's allies arrived through the other door first.

She crawled over a crenel, Arlana still held firmly in one arm, and onto the wooden roof of the tower just as a flash of light exploded in the air over her head. She ducked instinctively, then raced to the opposite side of the roof where she could look into the courtyard and down to the tower's western window. She couldn't see any movement from within the window, but a glimpse of black material revealed that the sorceress was already heading up the exterior stairs.

Damn! Gauging the distance back to the window, she frowned. She wouldn't be able to climb that far and still hold onto the baby. She glanced back over her shoulder to the point where the stairs reached the roof and jerked her black sash from around her waist with her free hand. She looked over the roof, hoping for signs of a secret hatch, the type that would open back into the room below and have a ladder extension. But the wood planking was unbroken.

Her focus returned to her only other option. She fumbled, working to form an improvised sling for Arlana when the sorceress crested the battlement. Slipping effortlessly between the merlons, she gained the roof. Her face was set in lines of controlled fury. Vic watched her closely, warily, even as she continued tying a sling with her sash.

"Now what, girl?" the woman snarled, her voice harsh. Sweat

beaded her forehead, dripping down her jaw. Her eyes were sunken in her pretty, oval face.

Vic's eyes narrowed. The climb couldn't have been that hard.

When Vic didn't answer, the sorceress took a step toward her and bellowed, "Set the child down. Now!" Her voice dropped to a hiss. "Or you'll die a slow, painful death. I promise you that."

"I don't think so," Vic said evenly, trying to get the sash around one shoulder without taking her attention from the raging magician. She nodded at the woman's sweat-soaked features and smiled. "Bit out of shape? Or is it the altitude?"

The sorceress screamed in a language Vic didn't know and flung her hand outward. The gesture gave her just enough warning to duck to one side as the merlon behind her exploded in a shower of stone. But her movements were clumsy and off balance because of the extra weight of the child. In her haste to dodge the blow, she dropped her sash.

Before she could snatch it back, a second merlon erupted just to her left, forcing her into another clumsy dive. Arlana shrieked once, then fell eerily silent. Vic didn't have time to worry about the baby's silence as another flash of power blackened the wood in front of her.

The sorceress's features, creased with strain and concentration, suddenly relaxed. She smiled. And Vic's stomach dropped. She took a step back toward the shattered battlement, away from the grinning woman.

"I should have guessed," the sorceress said, her voice ragged and raspy. "That onyx only works on my mage sight."

She laughed, not the maniacal laughter Vic expected, but a rueful, self-mocking chuckle. Vic's gaze darted to the discarded sash, then down at Arlana before meeting the sorceress's blue-eyed gaze again. She took another step toward the edge of the roof. And froze.

She tried to move, tried to lift her feet, to turn her body. And couldn't. Just like in her nightmare, her body refused to respond to mental commands. Panic flared, chilling her skin and paralyzing her mind. She watched helplessly as the sorceress approached and took Arlana from her motionless arms.

"So much energy wasted on you, girl," the woman breathed. "Energy I do not have to spare. I should have done this sooner. Ah well."

A bead of sweat dripped down the sorceress's pale cheek and dropped onto Arlana's forehead. Arlana never uttered a sound. Vic wondered absently if the baby was under the same spell as she, but the thought vanished quickly beneath her fear.

The sorceress shook her head, sighed and turned, walking back toward the external stairway. Vic had a split second to wonder if she'd simply be left there when her body lifted from the ground.

Just before stepping through the crenel and onto the stairs, the sorceress turned to look at her. "Seems a shame to kill you, girl. You'd have made an excellent sacrifice. Such strong will. Such arrogance. But…"

The last thing Vic saw was the back of the woman's head before her world spun and her paralyzed body went tumbling over the edge of the tower.

Chapter Twenty-Five

Jacob grunted with the effort to stand. Pain shot through him, blacking his vision and stealing his labored breathing. He settled against the wall, sweat pouring over his face, and ground his teeth together, trying to remain conscious against the draining flow of blood.

He closed his eyes. The sounds of nearby battle swirled with the ringing in his own ears, building a discordant but lulling music. The heavy scent of blood, sweat and fear enveloped him like a blanket. Where his right hand pressed into the packed earth, he felt the cool edge of steel.

Blinking open his eyes, Jacob glanced at the tower where Victoria had disappeared, then he looked down. The dagger the white magician had used to try and kill him rested between his hand and his thigh, dark with his own blood.

Victoria's dagger.

He closed his fingers over the hilt, cradling it fiercely. Victoria had to live. She had to!

The bright crisp winter day suddenly dimmed. He looked up, the dagger still firmly held in his palm, to see a huge GeMorin staring down at him. This goblin was bigger than any he'd seen. A blue tattoo circled his biceps, but his dress and saber were of the same caliber as the rest of the GeMorin.

For a long, calm moment, they stared at each other, gazes locked. The GeMorin nodded his head, a strange, unreadable expression in his dark, heavy-lidded eyes. "You are General Marin."

Since it wasn't a question, Jacob didn't bother to answer.

"I am GeRon, clan chief of the GeMorin tribe."

The goblin never moved, but Jacob sensed a slight shifting of muscles, a settling of his stance, a tightening of his hold on the saber's grip.

"You should not die by the efforts of a magician, warrior."

Jacob felt GeRon's deep, quiet voice in his bones, like the beginnings of an earthquake.

He stared into the goblin's face, seeing what could almost be called respect. Respect mingled with unreserved determination and cool calculation. There was no regret, only resignation. The expression of a warrior, Jacob acknowledged with a deep breath. He nodded to the goblin clan chief as the saber swung into the air.

He'd experienced this before, the detachment, the lack of fear, the rapid, clear movement of thought, the crystal sharpness of reality. But he'd never felt the edge of sadness as keenly as he did facing death this time.

GeRon might not regret what was about to happen, Jacob thought as his fingers circled the hilt of Victoria's dagger for the last time, but he would.

Vic struck the step with a crunch, pain exploding along her side, ripping her breath from her lungs. Several heartbeats passed as she sucked in air, before she realized her fall to the ground had been intercepted by the stepping stones along the tower wall. She looked along the steps, expecting at any moment to see the sorceress. Then she realized she could move again.

The fall had left her just below the western window, one of the last stones still intact before the wall sheered away. A few feet to the right and she would have tumbled all the way to the ground below. She swallowed hard but pushed aside the rolling fear of what could have happened. She couldn't spare the time to think about it now. Instead, she scrambled painfully to her feet, her breath exploding again at the shock of pain from her side. Teeth gritted, she climbed the remaining two steps to the western window and tumbled inside.

The door leading nowhere was glowing brighter. The sickly brown color of its light had deepened to an almost black. The door leading to the main stairway inside the tower still shook under the onslaught of the king's soldiers trying desperately to break in. From the window, she heard the first wailing cries of the baby.

And those cries grew closer.

Biting her lip against the ache throughout one side of her body, she ducked behind one of the wooden pillars across the room from the west window. She unsheathed her second calf dagger and the dart that rested near the small of her back, swallowing a groan at the movement. The sorceress entered moments later. Arlana's wailing voice echoed in the open room, mingling with the thudding from the stairwell door and a new, low rumbling Vic felt more than heard.

Dust shook loose from the wooden ceiling. She blinked it away, wiping her eyes and face with the back of one hand as she listened to the sorceress move through the room. When those movements stilled, she held her breath. Silence. She spared a quick glance around the pillar.

The sorceress stood with her back to the thief, her head bowed, her shoulders rising and falling with heavy breaths. Arlana was once again in the stone cradle.

Knowing that her daggers could be stopped if the magicians saw them coming, she flipped the dart so she held the point in her fingertips. And aimed for the middle of the sorceress's neck. She'd only get one shot. It had to count.

She took a deep breath and let the dart fly though her injury screamed in protest. Pain seared her body, disrupting her aim and nearly doubling her over. She clamped one hand to her side and gulped a few quick, shallow breaths. The sound of an outraged scream snapped her gaze back to the sorceress.

The dart protruded from the back of the woman's right shoulder. A painful, but not fatal, wound.

Instinct sent Vic plunging forward, despite her pain, her calf dagger raised. She had to kill the sorceress before the woman acted. Or Vic would be the one to die.

But the sorceress was quicker to recover than she'd hoped. The woman spun, blue eyes glistening with pain and anger, and flung her left hand out. Vic froze, once again paralyzed by the sorceress's magic. Inside, she started to tremble.

"You should be dead," the woman hissed.

Her attractive features were now drawn, making her skin look too small to span the bones of her face. Sweat beaded her forehead, dampening the edges of her short white hair. As Vic watched helplessly, she pulled the dagger from her shoulder and snarled at the bloodied dart. Then she chuckled, a low, evil sound.

"You're really quite amazing, girl." Her voice was quiet, but not as ragged as it had been on the roof. "You thought to deal with a magician? With no more than a set of daggers and that trinket at your neck?" She tsked, shaking her head. "Amazing," she murmured, "but not very smart."

Frantically, Vic tried again to move, knowing it was futile but unable to stop herself. She looked at the baby, her little face pinched and red as she continued to wail. *I'm sorry, Arlana.* In the next instant, panic supplanted rational thought as her feet left the ground.

Air whipped past her face as she flew toward the tower wall. Helpless to bring her arms up to block the impact, she slammed hard against the stones and dropped to the floor like a bird shot with an arrow. Air exploded from her lungs. Fresh pain coursed through her body.

And she still couldn't move.

Before she could draw more than a single breath, she was rising from the floor again, flying toward another wall. This one she hit shoulder first. She felt a bone crack and would have screamed, but her mouth wouldn't open. Blackness edged her vision, pulling her toward unconsciousness.

The scream she couldn't push past her lips echoed in her mind through the fog of pain, joining the deafening chorus of pounding and shouting from behind the door, the cries of Arlana, the hysterical laugh of the sorceress, and the strange rumbling sound she felt more than heard. Too much noise. Bile rose in her throat, choking her. She tried to cough and failed. Breaths came in shallow gasps, but not enough. She could move her eyes, but the pain and noise were too much. When she felt her body come off the ground again, she clenched her eyes shut, not wanting to see the wall coming toward her.

Then a silence, sudden and complete, filled the tower room, and she knew she'd died. She had enough time to be relieved that death had come so quickly. An instant later, she dropped with a grunt to the wooden floor. Beneath her, the entire tower trembled. Her eyes flew open in time to see the sorceress staring down at Arlana, eyes wide with astonishment and horror. Then the room exploded into sharp shards of light, cutting the air like broken glass. Vic shut her eyes again, covering her face with her uninjured arm.

Her eyelids glowed red for two heartbeats and then the light faded. Spots of blue and red danced against her lids. She blinked, slowly opening her eyes. She looked at her arm for a long moment before realizing she had control of her body again. Lowering her arm, she looked around the room.

Arlana lay atop the stone cradle, cooing to her fingers as if nothing had happened. The door leading nowhere had vanished. In its place, only a stone wall and the red stains of what had once been candles. The sorceress had vanished as well. The air was heavy with the smell of something burnt.

From across the room, the remaining door burst open. Kevin charged in and stopped. He stared blankly at the scene for a moment. Then he dropped to his knees beside the stone cradle and lifted his daughter into his arms. Tiya pushed through the soldiers blocking the doorway and ran to her husband's side. Tears streamed as she laughed in relief. Kevin handed the baby to her and wrapped both wife and daughter in his arms.

Vic made an effort to sit but collapsed back to the floor, blackness once again threatening the edges of her vision. She released a slow breath, thinking that maybe passing out wouldn't be such a bad thing.

Kevin was at her side by the time her vision cleared. "Victoria, are you hurt?"

She smiled wanly. "I think I've broken some things."

He helped her to a sitting position, an effort that stole her breath and brought tears to her eyes, then he looked around the room.

"What happened?"

She watched the now happy baby cooing at her crying mother. "Arlana must have decided it was time to see her mom again."

Kevin's forehead creased, his mouth hitched up in disbelief. She just shrugged with her uninjured arm. She scanned the soldiers filing into the room. Garath limped in, his sword still unsheathed. She smiled weakly at him when he started toward her and Kevin.

But she didn't see the one person she hoped to see and fear once again grabbed her. "Jacob?" she whispered to Kevin, not meeting his gaze.

"He's with Henry."

She let out a slow breath and closed her eyes. "He's okay?"

"He's hurt, but he'll heal."

Something in his voice caught her attention. "Henry?"

The young giant exchanged glances with Garath, then looked down at the floor and shook his head.

He whispered, "He's alive, but he won't survive the day."

Her shoulders slumped on an exhale. She bit her bottom lip and looked at Garath. His expression mirrored the sad resignation in Kevin's.

"Help me up," she said, her voice low with both physical and emotional pain. They helped her to her feet as gently as possible. "Kevin, go see your daughter. I'm sure she's missed you."

"Thank you, Victoria. Thank you for saving her life."

She chuckled then grimaced with the pain. "All I did was get tossed over the edge of a tower and slammed into a few walls. Go on."

He touched her cheek then turned to his wife and daughter.

"Garath, will you help me down the stairs? I'd like to go see Henry."

"Of course."

He wrapped one strong arm delicately around her waist to give her balance. His limp forced them to move slowly, but the pace suited her battered body. She cradled her broken arm against her side and tried not to wince with every step.

The bright light of the cold afternoon was a brutal contrast to the carnage scattered through the ruins. She didn't look closely at the bodies, figuring she could find out later who had survived. She didn't want to see all the dead right now.

A large tent had been hastily erected in the front courtyard. Inside, the wounded lay on thick furs and travel blankets. Near the back, Jacob sat with Henry who lay motionless on a pile of furs. His wounded torso was covered by a blanket, but she could see the slow rise and fall of his chest.

When Jacob saw them entering, a relieved smile lifted the sadness from his face. She smiled back, unable to control her own relief. Jacob murmured something to Henry then stood and walked toward them.

"You're okay?" she asked.

"Worried?"

"No," she lied pitifully, as she shifted from Garath's arm to Jacob's. "You okay?"

He looked her over, concern creasing the lines around his eyes. She tried on a smile. "Broken up a bit, but I should be all right in a few weeks." She grimaced as a jolt of pain raced up her arm. "Maybe a few months."

He frowned, touched her chin and turned her face gently to one side. "Looks like you're going to have a fat lip tomorrow. Probably a black eye, too."

She fingered her lip and felt the sting. She licked the blood. "I didn't even notice that," she said. "I don't think I want to see a mirror any time soon."

"You look beautiful," Jacob said, seriously.

He ran a gentle hand across her uninjured cheek. For several heartbeats, she could only stare into his dark, loving eyes. After a silent moment, he glanced back over his shoulder at the young sorcerer.

"Henry's…"

"I know," she whispered. "Can I talk to him?"

"Sure." Jacob looked at Garath. "Thanks for helping her. Now you'd better go get that leg tended."

"Aye, General." Garath's smile faltered as his gaze fell back to Henry. He nodded to Vic and Jacob then walked back to the tent's entrance.

With Jacob's help and despite her protesting ribs, she knelt down beside the young sorcerer. His eyes were closed. She could hear the hitch of his labored breathing. His tawny skin was a sickly pale yellow and sweat-soaked despite the cool air. Then his eyes fluttered open.

"Victoria Flash," he whispered, a hoarse shadow of his once melodious voice.

"Hey, Henry," she murmured, smiling weakly.

His lips shifted into a slight smile, and his eyes closed. When he opened them again, he said, "Give Kritta a message for me?"

She sucked in a sharp breath, unable to hide her surprise. "How'd you know I knew Kritta?"

He breathed what was almost a chuckle. "I've always known. That she was part of Thieves' Hole." He swallowed and choked back a cough. "Tell her, would you? Tell her I knew. Tell her what happened to me. Tell her I loved her."

A single tear fell down her cheek as his eyes closed. "I'll tell her," she whispered through the ache in her chest that had nothing to do with her broken ribs.

Chapter Twenty-Six

Moving slowly to accommodate the wounded, they crossed back into Georna at nightfall the next day. A troop of soldiers awaited them. Supply wagons and transport carriages made the journey to Georna castle easier on the wounded and weary soldiers. Baroness Georna once again provided rooms within the castle and a safe place to heal.

After two days of rest and several sessions of healing under Dreem's special touch, most of the survivors recovered quickly. In celebration of Arlana's rescue, Baroness Georna arranged a small private feast that night for Tiya, Kevin, Jacob, Vic, and any of the King's Guard well enough to get out of bed.

Vic twirled in front of Jacob, showing off the gown that was a present from the Baroness. Deep red silk clung to her torso and fell in thick folds around her feet. The low neckline and skirt's hem were embroidered with gold thread. The sleeves were fitted to her arms then flared to long trains also edged with golden thread. "You like?" she asked, cocking her head to one side and smiling.

"Yeah, I like."

Her flirty smile dissolved into a grin. She lifted the brace on her arm and said, "The cast doesn't add much, but…"

"You look stunning, love, cast and all. What does Dreem say about your arm?"

"He said I should be back to my usual perfection by the time we leave." Her bruises and minor cuts had already healed on the return journey to Georna castle. At the least, her face no longer looked like a swollen mess. "How about you?"

He smiled his sultry smile and stalked her. Her gaze was drawn to the strong line of his body beneath the cream breeches and tunic he wore. The gold embroidery on the tunic brought out golden flecks in his eyes that she'd never noticed before. He wrapped one arm gently around her waist, careful not to put pressure on her still tender rib cage or disturb the brace on her left arm.

"I'll have another interesting scar," he whispered, running a hand over her cheek, "but, other than that, I'll heal without complication."

"Good." She tilted her face to meet his lips, drinking in the taste of his mouth, warming beneath the tender caresses of his hand at her waist. "I wish I could heal sooner," she murmured against his mouth.

He pulled back to look into her eyes, a low chuckle vibrating through his body. "You'll heal soon enough, love. And then, I promise, we'll make up for lost time."

"I intend to hold you to that promise, Marin," she said so seriously he laughed again.

"We'd better get going, little thief. The Baroness awaits."

The feast was held in the private dining hall. Vic felt an odd sense of repetition walking through those doors and into the dark paneled, red-carpeted room. The last time she'd been here, they'd just come from a devastating battle with the GeMorin and were preparing to run into another. That same loss, the reminder that so many hadn't returned, from either battle, followed her into the room.

But this dinner wasn't to discuss future battles or difficulties. It was a celebration. She glanced at Jacob and smiled. She had a lot to celebrate now, too.

They were shown to the same seats they'd occupied during the last dinner. Brandon, who hadn't returned to his village yet, sat, as before, to the Baroness's left. Tiya and Kevin were seated to her right. Dreem sat in the place Henry had occupied.

The absence of Henry closed Vic's throat. She swallowed hard and blinked back the unbidden tears. They all mourned his loss, but tonight was a time for enjoying life.

She met Dreem's gaze and smiled. Dreem, a sorcerer of some years according to the servants, looked younger than the Baroness. His blue eyes were dimmer than the blood magicians', dimmer even than Tiya's. But she suspected he did this on purpose. Those soft blue-gray eyes were comforting, soothing, healing.

His particular talent was magic healing. Very, very few magicians were capable of this specialty. He'd used his power to heal the bodies of those who'd returned. The more seriously injured would take longer to heal. Magic could only rush nature so far. But, with Dreem's help, everyone would be ready to ride back to Dareelia in only two weeks.

As the meal began and the wine flowed, the obvious questions came up in conversation.

"Yes," Vic said in answer to Dreem's question. "The sorceress was staring at Arlana when the explosion happened."

He nodded thoughtfully, pursing his lips.

"I agree with Victoria," the Baroness said. "The child did cause the disruption in the gate. Though how a babe could manage it, I cannot even guess."

"The sorceress must have been acting as a focus for the gate,"

Dreem said. "That's the only explanation for why she would have been affected by its destruction."

"Focus?" Kevin asked.

"It's possible to tie two people to the gate as foci, one at each end. This not only helps stabilize a gate over long distances, it also makes magical tampering more difficult." He paused, frowning at his plate.

"What Dreem hesitates to mention," Baroness Georna added, "is that a gate held between focus is virtually impossible to disrupt. The spell is difficult, the foci must be prepared months in advance, and the danger to the people acting as focus is, as you've seen, very great. But the benefits are, for some, worth the risk."

"So you're saying," Tiya said, "that my daughter might have done something that's supposed to be almost impossible."

The Baroness's small smile was full of compassion. "Yes."

Tiya and Kevin exchanged a long look. Any doubt as to Arlana's potential disappeared in that moment.

"Don't worry," Dreem said. "Merig will know how to train her and keep her safe."

Some of the worry eased from both Tiya's and Kevin's expressions. An unspoken agreement circled the table, a look passing from one person to the next. The news of the prophecy and Arlana's potential would remain a secret.

By silent mutual consent, the conversation changed direction. Vic learned of the messages that had been sent to Fordin and Dareelia, briefly relaying the events of their journey and the successful rescue of the baby. She also learned that King John and Queen Sara were preparing a celebration to mark the return of the king's soldiers.

After some debate, Tiya and Kevin decided to return directly to Fordin once a garrison of Fordin soldiers arrived to escort them home. Winter was descending quickly on the northern mountain slopes. It would soon spread across the rest of Karasnia and make travel difficult. With luck, the two groups would just make it back to their respective cities before the worst of the winter storms began.

As the meal wore on and the wine settled into Vic's blood, sleep edged her thoughts. She'd had peaceful, dreamless nights since the battle. She was looking forward to another when she suddenly realized that someone had been missing from the battle at the ruins.

"I wonder what happened to him?" she mumbled aloud.

"Who, love?" Jacob said, leaning on his armrest to be closer.

"Malkiney. He wasn't at the monastery. I wonder what happened?"

"He's probably dead. I doubt the blood magicians were happy with the smuggler after we raided their hideouts."

"Yeah," she nodded, "you're probably right." Uncertainty nagged her as Malkiney hadn't been seen since the raid, but she pushed away her unease. Jacob probably *was* right.

She took another deep gulp of wine and settled back in her seat, determined to stop thinking about anything serious for the rest of the night.

Two weeks later, the king's soldiers prepared to return to Dareelia. The group gathered in the castle's courtyard to say their goodbyes before making their way through the snow-covered Georna mountains.

Tiya, Kevin and Arlana rose with the sun to say farewell. They were due to leave in the next few days as the Fordin garrison was to arrive that afternoon.

"Well, boy," Jacob patted Kevin on the back, "guess we'll be seeing you at the Baronies Meeting."

"Yeah, old man. We'll be there. Don't get into too much trouble."

Kevin winked at Vic. "Thank you, Victoria. Again. We'll never be able to repay you for your help."

"You don't have to," she said, smiling at the baby in Tiya's arms. "I'm just glad she's okay." She stuck her finger into Arlana's tiny palm and said, "You take care of your parents, little one. And don't cause too much trouble." Then she leaned in close and whispered, "A little trouble is all right, but just a little."

Waving their final goodbyes from horseback, Vic, Jacob and the king's soldiers left Georna castle to return home.

Winter had arrived in full force when the soldiers returned home. The outlying fields were covered in thick blankets of snow. Inside the city, white covered the rooftops and gray slush piled alongside roads.

The city Vic had left over two months earlier looked and felt different now. The haunting shadow was gone, replaced with the bright reflections of snow. But the air wasn't the same. A strange sadness crept into her heart when she realized that the city would never be the same again. That she was the one who'd changed.

The streets were lined with people to welcome them home. She pulled her hood over her head and grimaced at the attention. When she was younger, she'd thought being in a procession of victorious heroes would be fun. Now, with the streets so different and the outcome of the war between the gangs unknown, she felt exposed.

Some things never changed.

Just outside the castle gates, townspeople gathered in thick masses to cheer their arrival. Inside the castle courtyard, they were greeted by an honor guard of Karasnian soldiers, a pack of preening nobility and the king and queen. A few of the townspeople had even managed to work their way past the castle gates so the yard was bursting with humanity. They crowded into the large parade ground, shouting and waving at the triumphant returning group.

Vic dismounted, giving Gale an affectionate pat on the chest before turning her over to a groom. She shook her head at the noise and fuss. Any excuse for a celebration, she thought, cocking an eyebrow. She looked at the colorful mass of people and chuckled.

"What's so funny, little thief?" Jacob whispered in her ear. He wrapped an arm around her, absently running his fingers over her shoulder.

His closeness tingled her nerves. She took a deep breath, loving the feel and smell of him so near. "I never thought that nobles," she nodded to an approaching groups, "would welcome me back to town. I can see at least a dozen that I've either picked their pockets or swindled in some other creative fashion." Jacob chuckled, low and husky. The sound warmed her to her core.

During their journey, she'd kept waiting for him to raise the subject of her quitting Thieves' Hole. She dreaded the conversation. She couldn't doubt anymore that he loved her. And she had to admit she loved him, too. She was pretty sure he wouldn't leave her soon, that she would be able to depend on him. Goddess, she hoped she could. She couldn't imagine life without him now. But could she put her life entirely in his hands?

Until that moment, she hadn't known if she could give up everything she'd once been, give up the security of knowing she was reliant only on herself, to place her life and her heart in his care. She nestled closer, avoiding his gaze, as they walked toward the king and queen.

Jacob removed his arm and stood at attention before King John. The rest of the soldiers collected behind them. She glanced back to see them all standing straight and proud, saluting their king.

"We're glad you have returned safely to us, General Marin," King John intoned for the crowd. "We and our queen wish to thank you and these brave soldiers for rescuing our granddaughter. Tonight, in honor of our loyal and brave warriors, we'll give a feast in the great hall."

A cheer rose through the crowd.

Beneath the noise, King John muttered, "Welcome home, Jacob, Victoria." He winked before turning his attention back to the crowd. "Now, we will give our warriors the rest they so richly deserve."

The crowd roared and all formality fell away. The soldiers were instantly surrounded by people, all talking at once, hoping for a firsthand account of the events that had been rumored back to the city. King John and Queen Sara clasped hands with each of the soldiers, personally thanking them and congratulating them on their safe return home.

When Queen Sara returned to where Vic and Jacob stood, she scooped Vic into a tight hug. The gesture caught Vic by surprise and it took several heartbeats before she was able to return the hug with an awkward pat on the queen's back.

"Thank you for helping to save my granddaughter," Queen Sara said. "If there's ever anything I can do for you, Victoria, you have my debt."

"Thank you, Majesty," she muttered, at a loss for anything else.

"And when we're alone," the queen whispered through a conspiratorial grin, "call me Sara."

She could only nod and grin. When Queen Sara moved away, she saw Jacob grinning. Her brow snapped down. "What?" she demanded.

"Nothing. Looks like we'll be having that nice friendly lunch with the royal family after all."

Vic glowered, to hide her embarrassment. He continued to smile.

She turned to scan the crowd, ignoring his chuckle. And a familiar face in the crowd caught her attention. "I'll be back in a minute," she said, moving away before he could protest.

"Well, well, Vic Flash." Deraun Gip leaned against the castle wall, arms crossed over his chest. "Never thought I'd see one of our people riding up Main Street in a parade."

She grinned and bowed. "What can I say?"

He took in her attire in a single scan. She glanced down, seeing her clothing—tan breeches, a white shirt, light brown boots, white half cloak—through his eyes.

"You look different, Flash. Thought you had to be forced to wear colors like that."

"They blend with the snow." She grimaced despite her best efforts when she admitted, "They were a gift."

Gip glanced at Jacob and raised a brow.

"No. Baroness Georna, actually."

"Looks like our best gambler's moving up in the world."

"Yeah." She frowned and stared at the ground. "What brings you out, Gip?"

"Thought you might like to know you're off Charlie's list. War's over."

"Ren?"

"Back to picking pockets."

She let out a breath and raised her gaze. "What happened?"

"Well, seems Joe Missek got wind of the whole situation and, among other things, claimed it was messing the games. After the goblin attack, no one doubted the news of the blood magicians. So Joe told Charlie to leave off or he'd have to deal with Joe's boys."

"And that made Charlie back off? I didn't think Joe had *that* many guys working for him."

Gip studied her before answering. "Charlie knows what only a few of us know. I can trust you with it, right?"

"Sure, but…."

"Joe's the head of Silence."

"The assassin group?" Her stomach dropped.

He chuckled and shifted his hands to his pockets. "Keep that quiet, Flash. He's real private about that part of his life. But that's why a threat was enough to make Charlie back off."

She stared at Gip for a long time. Then with an exhale of amazement, she said, "But won't Charlie just come after me again? Instead of all-out war."

"No. Joe took care of it."

"Why?"

"He called it professional courtesy. Says you owe him a game, though. Another crack at catching your quick hands."

Gip laughed loud, and she was sure her expression showed her shock and fear.

"Don't worry. If he were mad at you because of that hand, you wouldn't be here right now. He's got a healthy respect for talented people. He says you're one of the best. He's right."

"Thanks, Gip." She smiled crookedly, though her pulse still beat a little too fast. "Tell Joe I'll let him know when I'm good for a game." She swallowed to loosen the knot in her chest. "Speaking of games… what happened with the big game?"

"Joe won. Goblins and blood magicians caused a delay, had to push back the final night for a week. But then Joe cleaned the table."

"Brad?"

"He's turned up missing. Sort of vanished right before the goblin attack."

"Charlie?"

Gip shrugged. "Maybe. Maybe the blood magicians. Maybe Joe. Maybe he just ran. Better not to know."

For once in her life, she had to agree.

"Did you ever find Malkiney? We heard he escaped with the two magicians."

She frowned. "Never saw him again, Gip. He wasn't with the

kidnappers when we caught them. It's been bothering me, but…"

"No ideas?"

She could only shrug and shake her head.

"He's probably dead. No bother to me if he's gone. Just curious."

The Thieves' Hole boss looked into her eyes, his lips pursed. His gaze wandered to Jacob where he hovered at the edge of the crowd of nobility, close enough to keep an eye on her but far enough away to give them privacy.

"So what now, Vic Flash?"

She meet his penetrating black-eyed gaze. "Think I'm gonna have to find a new profession," she said evenly.

"Yeah. I sort of suspected. You sure?"

She looked over her shoulder at Jacob. He was talking to one of the noblewomen, a lady in her late sixties, who from her size had led a highly pampered life. The woman was completely awed by Jacob's storytelling, her small mouth a perfect O. Vic grinned and looked back at Gip. "Yeah. I'm sure."

"You know, I always thought you'd take over Thieves' Hole one of these days. Guess I'll have to find another protégé."

"How 'bout Ren? Got a good head on his shoulders, that kid. Little bit of training…"

Gip raised his brows. "Hmm. Might not be a bad idea, Flash. Got a message for him?"

"Yeah. Tell him to watch his butt and stay standing. I'll catch him soon, to make sure he's staying in trouble." She winked. Then more seriously added, "I need to talk to Kritta, too. I've got a message."

Gip frowned, then looked back to the surviving soldiers, and she saw understanding spread across his sharp features.

"Henry?"

"Yeah."

"You want me to deliver it?"

"No. I'll tell her myself. I promised. Henry saved Jacob's life right before… Since I couldn't stop him from dying, I can at least relay the message in person."

"Okay, I'll let her know you're looking for her."

"Thanks, Gip. And thanks for bringing me all the news."

He dipped his head. "Take care of yourself, Flash. If you're ever in need, Thieves' Hole is at your service." He smiled one last time and disappeared into the crowd outside the gate.

She watched the milling throng of people for a long minute, saying goodbye to her old life, when she felt Jacob step in behind her.

"You all right, little thief?"

Dropping her head back, she looked up into his eyes and grinned. "Yeah. I'm all right."

"Come on. Let's go get cleaned up for the feast."

He took her hand and led the way back through the mass of admirers and into the castle.

As they strolled along the bright corridors, toward his rooms, she said, "Do you suppose the king might have a job for me?"

"What?"

"Well, it looks like I'm gonna have to find a new career."

He stopped. "You…you quit Thieves' Hole?"

"Yup."

His face lit with a smile that warmed her like the sun.

"You know," he said casually, wrapping his arm around her shoulders and continuing toward his rooms, "I've been giving some thought to your future lately."

"Really? And what have you come up with?"

"Well, I think you should get married."

It was her turn to stop. Her stomach danced, her heartbeat pounding out the rhythm. "You do?"

"Um hmm. Problem is finding the right man for you. Now, I've been thinking long and hard about that part, but I'm having some trouble… Well, what do you think? Anyone in particular you might want to marry?"

She grinned and started walking again. He fell in beside her. "Hmm…" she mused. She gripped her hands behind her back to control their trembling. "Well, Garath is awfully handsome and a nice man. But…he's got those blue eyes."

"Ah, yes. You prefer brown eyes, don't you?"

"Yeah."

"That does limit your options, doesn't it?"

"Yeah, it does."

"Anyone else?"

She looked sideways. "Can't think of anyone else."

"Well, there's nothing for it then. I guess you'll just have to marry me."

Stopping, she dropped her head back to meet his dancing gaze. "You, huh?"

He nodded.

"Well…" she drawled. "Okay." He hoisted her off the ground, hugging her tight, and she laughed. She wrapped her arms around his neck. "I love you, Jacob Marin," she said, kissing him soundly.

"I love you, too, Victoria Von Marin."

She raised a brow. "Victoria Von Marin? I like the way that sounds."

"Good." He kissed her again then put her down.

"You realize there'll be a lot of angry women all across Karasnia after this?"

"Oh?" He cocked an eyebrow.

"And the flower merchants will hate me."

"Actually…" He took her hand and started walking again. "I thought I'd keep sending the flowers. If you don't mind, that is."

"Really? Why?"

"They go to special people, love. People who should have a flower on their birthdays."

She stared at him then looked back down the corridor. "Well, I suppose as long as I get a flower, too. Not like it's my money."

"Anything that's mine is yours now, little thief," he whispered at her ear. "But I wasn't planning on getting you flowers on your birthday."

"You weren't? Why not?"

"I thought you might prefer something…with a sharper edge."

She started to giggle. "Okay. But hide it in some flowers."

"Anything you want, little thief."

They reached his door and, to her surprise, Jacob scooped her off the ground, cradling her in his arms as he stepped into the sitting room. "I hope you don't expect me to give up everything," she said, as she cuddled closer into his embrace.

"What do you mean?" He carried her toward the bedroom.

"Well, I'm off Charlie's kill list now…"

"Good."

"But it means I owe Joe Missek a game."

"Joe? Why?"

"He's the one who got Charlie off my back."

"Why?" He kicked open the bedroom door.

"Professional courtesy," she said through a grin.

He sat on the edge of the bed, holding her in his lap. "Gambling is what got you in trouble in the first place, little thief."

"Hey, if you can keep sending flowers, I can keep gambling." To her amusement, Jacob bit his lip and frowned.

"Okay. But I'm going with you."

"Now how am I gonna play with you hovering like a bodyguard? No respectable gambler is gonna want to sit at a table with me."

"They'll have to get used to it."

She ran her hand along his broad shoulder, tracing a pattern with her fingertips. "If you insist, then I guess I can get used to it. Maybe we can dirty you up enough to blend in." Her fingers moved along his neck and cradled his cheek. "You're just lucky I love you."

"Yes," he said very seriously, "I am. You've stolen my heart, little thief. Right out from under my nose."

"Don't worry." She tilted her mouth to meet his. "I'll take good care of it."

EPILOGUE

He looked at what was left of Bserea and sighed. A hand gesture brought a skittering servant to clean away the pile of gray ash. Then his gaze darted to the cowering, whimpering shape of Malkiney, huddled against the far wall of his throne room.

All the time invested in the man, and now he's a useless imbecile. But he'd been a good focus while it lasted. And an acceptable servant. He sighed again and sat. The black stone of his throne warmed beneath him, subtly soothing in contrast to his frustration.

It had almost worked. They'd been so close. He still wasn't sure what had gone wrong. But this would make things more difficult.

He'd thought those louts could handle this job. Even without him influencing the Mimis and sending the hallucinations to slow the King's Guard, the magicians should have been able to deal with them. And the GeMorin…

The hesitant clearing of a throat brought his head up. "Yes?"

"Master, GeNol has just arrived," a servant announced.

"Send him in."

He stared at the door until the GeMorin warrior entered. He

continued to stare until the goblin dropped his gaze and knelt before the throne. His anger lay just beneath the surface, waiting for an outlet. But anger wasn't productive.

"GeNol. Your father failed."

GeNol didn't look up. His head bowed farther. Shame.

"You'll be made clan chief now?"

"Yes, master."

He stood, taking a single step toward the kneeling goblin. "For the disgrace of your father's failure, I have the right to take your life and that of your immediate family. Your son. It's GeMorin law."

"It is your right, master."

A smile tugged his mouth. He enjoyed the reverence in the goblin's voice. "Yes. It is my right." He paused, milking the tension. "However, the GeMorin have served me faithfully for almost two centuries. And I still have need of you. I'll spare your life and the life of your son in exchange for the continuation of the blood oath. She's not yet in my care. I must have her."

"Yes, master."

"It is agreed then?"

"I pledge my loyalty, that of my son, and that of my clan, master. I give you my personal GeMorin blood oath. We are yours to command."

GeNol raised his gaze at last. Pride in being able to atone for his father's failure replacing the heavy yoke of shame.

With a gracious nod, he stepped back to his throne and sat. "This… failure is most upsetting to me, GeNol. I'll expect better from you."

"Of course, master. We will attempt to take the child again?"

He'd been considering this very question since the gate had exploded. To try again? They would know by now. Know of the child's potential. At the least, they'd suspect. But no one really knew. Even he had underestimated her.

That wouldn't happen again.

"No, GeNol," he said, tapping the black stone armrest of his throne. A slow smile stretched his mouth. The goblin warrior shuddered and dropped his gaze. "We won't attempt a second kidnapping. It's time for a more subtle approach, I think. Something more…personal."

❧

Don't miss the exciting sequel to Thief's Desire
Destiny's Seduction
Out Now!

About the Author

Isabo Kelly is the award-winning author of numerous science fiction, fantasy, and paranormal romances. She also writes best-selling paranormal romance under the name Kat Simons. Her life has taken her from Las Vegas to Hawaii, where she got her BA in Zoology, back to Vegas where she looked after sharks, then on to Germany and Ireland where she got her Ph.D. in Animal Behavior. Now Isabo focuses on writing. She lives in New York with her Irish husband and two beautiful boys, working as a full time writer and stay-at-home mom.

Don't miss out on new releases from Isabo! Sign up for her Newsletter here: http://eepurl.com/caxHa9

For more on Isabo and her books:

Website: http://www.isabokelly.com
Facebook: http://www.facebook.com/IsaboKelly
Twitter: https://www.twitter.com/IsaboKelly